GUNSMOKE AND THE SHOOTIN' SHERIFF

A WESTERN DOUBLE

NELSON C. NYE

WOLFPACK
PUBLISHING
— EST 2013 —

Gunsmoke and The Shootin' Sheriff
Paperback Edition
© Copyright 2022 (As Revised) Nelson C. Nye

Wolfpack Publishing
5130 S. Fort Apache Rd. 215-380
Las Vegas, NV 89148

wolfpackpublishing.com

Paperback ISBN 978-1-63977-943-7

GUNSMOKE AND THE SHOOTIN' SHERIFF

GUNSMOKE

GUNSMOKE

"I'M NO LIKE FOR DIE!"

"GEORGE! *GEORGE!*"

He who stood outside a door and shouted was a tall young man; a big-framed husky giant, massive of shoulder, lean of hip and long of leg. His forearms, as disclosed by shirt sleeves rolled to the elbows, were deep bronze in color and thick with sinewy muscles. He had big hands of which he often built massive fists. He had a temper, too— though as a rule he held it under stern control.

He was clad in faded Levi's, the bottoms of which were stuffed into soft-topped range boots. In hot weather and in cold his leather vest hung always open, as did the collar of his black-and-white-checked woolen shirt. About his lean-hipped waist a dark gun belt, whose loops were filled with gleaming brass-shelled cartridges, supported the scarred holster hanging low on his right thigh, snug against his leg. From its open top the smooth naked butt of a Colt's .45 protruded within ready reach of his hand.

His strong, aquiline face was clean-shaven. Red hair

peeped from beneath his shoved-back, curly-brim Stetson, and there was humor ordinarily apparent in his jade-green eyes with the little laugh-wrinkles crowfooting from their corners. Yet his was a tight-lipped face, and square of chin.

The door before which he stood led off the dingy ground-floor corridor of the gaunt red-brick building known locally as "The Courthouse." This particular courthouse stood at one end of the long main street of Pecos, in the heart of the West Texas cattle country. Pecos, that sleepy little cowtown sprawled in slumbrous lethargy near the banks of a mud-brown river.

Upon the paint-scarred surface of the door itself, in small black caps was the legend:

SHERIFF'S OFFICE

"George! *Geo-r-rge!*"

From beyond the door the series of grunts, groans and salty ejaculations attesting to the fact that one Pony George Kasta was about to give birth to another of those four-line atrocities which he pridefully labeled "poetry," abruptly ceased.

"That you, Red?"

"Yeah—that's me," Red Lawler, the youngest sheriff Reeves County had ever elected, flung open the door and went striding into his office. "For Gawd's sake, George, leave off that everlastin' caterwaulin'! Have a little consideration for the other gents that occupy this buildin'."

"Shucks," Pony George reluctantly removed his spurred boots from the sheriff's desk and regarded its proprietor with something of disgust. "Shucks," he repeated, "I'm a heap afraid, Red Lawler, you ain't got a mite o' music in yore soul. It's becomin' plainer to me every minute I associate with yuh that you got but mighty little true discernment in yore make-up. Listen:

> "A yarn I'll spin that's full of sin,
> It's a tale both old an' new
> A saga of times when men was bad
> An' women was bold as brew!"

Lawler looked down his nose and snorted.

"Ain't that a pistol?" demanded Pony George.

"It's a cannon!" the sheriff retorted. "See that you don't turn it loose round here no more. You'll be gettin' us thrown out of the place!"

Pony George shook his grizzled head. An expression of haughty contempt stamped his dried-apple countenance. Tugging at his drooping, straw-colored moustache he said, "The trouble with you young squirts is yuh spend too much time hellin' around, an' not a dang bit in the cultivation of the higher arts."

"'The folks in this county didn't elect me sheriff so's I could spend my time cultivatin' art. I was put in this office to weed out a few of the undesirables that have been driftin' into this county in the last few months. Fellows like that Doak hombre that got himself rubbed out last week. You found out who shot him yet?"

"Wal, no—not yet. Yuh see, Red, I been right busy workin' on that new poem of mine the last coupla days—"

"Poem be damned!" Red Lawler's eyes blazed truculently. "Now you listen, George; I'm in earnest. You get busy on sheriff work an' keep busy on it from here on out, or you'll find yourself huntin' another job. We been friends for a right smart spell, but friendship an' consideration have no place when it comes, to carryin' on the business of this office."

Pony George eyed his chief reproachfully. Several times he opened his mouth as though to speak, but seemed to have trouble locating the words he sought.

"Gosh, Red," he mumbled at last, "I expect some careless jasper stepped on yore pet corn, didn't they? 'Pears like yuh're sorta on the peck."

Lawler's straight-line lips compressed at the corners. Thrusting a hand into his pocket he brought out a crumpled bit of paper which he slapped down on the desk in front of his eccentric deputy.

"Read that!" he growled.

Slowly Pony George smoothed the paper out. Scrawled in pencil across its wrinkled surface were the words:

This ain't no helth resort for the old fishermen of Toyah Lake.
    JUSTICE.

Pony George scratched his shaggy head and gave the sheriff an owlish stare.

"What the Sam Hill does that mean? Looks sorta crazy-like to me. Where'd yuh get it, anyhow?"

"The coroner took it from one of Doak's pockets last week an' has been holdin' onto it ever since."

"He has?" growled Pony George. "Some nerve! That fella's got more brass than a military band!"

"Yeah," said Lawler drily. "It's kinda strange you didn't find this note when you went through Doak's pockets. Did you *go* through 'em or was you sidetracked, wrastlin' with that damnfool poetry?"

"'Course I went through 'em!" snapped Pony George indignantly. "Let no man ever say that Paw Kasta's youngest son was a gent tuh shirk his duty!"

Lawler snorted. "I'd give somethin' to know the reason all these strange hombres been driftin' into Reeves County all of a sudden. Reg'lar tough eggs' reunion—an' not one of 'em seems to know the others! Cussed queer! I'd give somethin' to know which one of 'em put the spot on Doak, an' why."

"Put the spot!" the chunky deputy's dried-apple countenance was wreathed in an expression of puzzlement. "What spot yuh talkin' about?"

Lawler waved an airy hand. "That's a new expression some of these city crooks been usin'. F'rinstance, if I should say 'You're the guy that put the spot on Doak,' I'd be meanin' you're the gent that killed him."

"If you sh'd say that," corrected the indignant Pony George, "you'd be a slat-bellied liar! I wasn't within miles of that fella when he got his mark rubbed out."

"Seems like all your brains runs towards poetry, George.

I expect you can't help bein' a little off. Who would you say *did* kill Doak?"

"Some durn gun fighter, I guess likely," Pony George showed a definite lack of interest in the late deceased.

"Gun fighter, heck! Looked more to me like some killer's work."

"What," asked Pony George, filling an evil-looking old cob pipe with tobacco, "is the diff'rence between a gun fighter an' a killer, I'd admire tuh know? They both draws their pay for the same result."

"A gun fighter," Lawler explained patiently, "is a plain cold-blooded shootin' machine—a gent that rubs you out with neither remorse nor hesitation. A killer is a man who takes pleasure in the job."

"Can't figger what makes yuh think Doak's assassin took any pleasure out of his performance."

"There were five bullets in Doak's body. Any one of 'em would have proved fatal. Besides, there was this note the coroner found in his pocket."

"Some misguided son mighta stuck that note in his pants for a joke, knowin' I'd just got done searchin' him," Pony George objected. "Anyhow, Captain Dan an' the coroner was standin' right alongside of me whilst I was searchin' the stiff. So there ain't no sense in you're tryin' tuh make out like I neglected m' duty."

"All right. But here's another thing I don't quite savvy," Lawler pointed out. "I don't sabe the meanin' of that note's reference to the fishermen of Toyah Lake. What could the killer have meant by that?"

"Still harpin' on the killer plantin' that note, are you?"

Pony George made a grimace. "I can't see why yuh're tryin' to make a mystery outa the business. I don't cotton to mysteries, nohow! I got a..."

He broke off in mid-sentence. The match, with which he had been about to light his pipe, fell unheeded from his fingers.

"Say!" he exclaimed, as though struck by inspiration. "Don't yuh remember there used tuh be a outfit of stage an' bank robbers round here what was 'knowed as the Toyah Lake Gang? Sure yuh do!"

"You hintin' that the gent that wrote this note—?"

"Sure!" Pony George said eagerly.

"What happened to the gang? I 'member they got busted up, but I can't recall the circumstances. Most of their didoes was cut before I was big enough to pack man-sized boots. Did they disband, get caught, or what?"

"There was a rumor floatin' round at the time that their leader sold 'em down the river. Raine, his name was—a slick, black-haired devil called 'Rowdy Joe.' He was a real card —'cordin' tuh what I've been told. He could pop a gun with either hand, or even shoot with both hands at the same time. 'Course, he didn't alius make a target, but from what I've heard he sure come close enough tuh make the devil squirm!"

"About the bust-up," Lawler prompted. "What made folks think Rowdy Joe'd caused that?"

"Wal, it was like this," Pony George said reminiscently. "Just before the gang quit operatin', seems like they'd pulled a coupla bank jobs which had netted 'em somewheres close tuh seventy thousand bucks. 'Fore a body could say *scat!* that pile of dinero up an' got itse'f a pair o' wings an' flew plumb away with Rowdy Joe! I expect the gang was some peeved. Things was gettin' pretty hot fer 'em about that time though, so they had tuh split up an' hunt cover."

"Rowdy Joe ever caught?"

"Not that anybody knows of. I reckon he just pocketed that money an' hopped a boat for South America. That's what I'd a done, by cripes."

"Did the sheriff's office ever get out a picture of him?"

"Hell, no! How could they? He alius wore a mask.

All anybody knew about him was that he dressed sorta dudish an' had slick, heavy black hair. Big-boned, he was. Folks thought he musta been a stranger to these parts, but, shucks! any fool can guess. Rowdy Joe mighta been well-knowed around here under some other name. He might even of been a clerk in one of the banks. That gang sure knew just when tuh stop a stage."

"Doak mighta been one of the former members of the gang," Lawler mused.

"Hell! ain't that what I been tryin' tuh tell yuh?" scowled Pony George, lighting up his pipe.

Lawler's face held a thoughtful expression. His eyes had of a sudden a faraway look. "It's just barely possible," he began, when Pony George thrust up a cautioning hand.

"*Shh!* That dang' Manuel Toreva's comin' up the path. Looks like he's comin' straight fer this office," he muttered, staring out the window. "Now what in the devil does he wanta bother us fer?'

"Stick around," Lawler grinned, "an' mebbe you'll find out."

"Humph! I never did hold with Mexicans! Can't see what they wanta come to the U-nited States fer when they got a country of their own right across the border. Heck, we ain't hardly got work enough around here now haff the time for the folks what belongs here!"

"I expect Manuel considers his right here as good as yours," Lawler ventured. "Seems like he's been livin' in Pecos goin' on thirty years."

"An' been in hot water more'n haff the time!"

They relapsed into silence as they heard the clump of booted feet coming down the corridor, and the rattle of dragging spurs.

A shadow momentarily darkened the doorway, then a thin wizened man with a dark leathery face adorned by a tiny black moustache stepped inside.

"*Buenas dias, señors,*" he offered with Mexican languor.

"It ain't a bad day for a fact," Lawler admitted. He gave the visitor a closer look. "Got somethin' special on your mind? Seems like you're lookin' a bit pale about the gills."

"It ees this weather, *señors*. She ees w'at you call 'thirsty,' no?"

"Give Don Manuel a glass of water, George."

Pony George, rising reluctantly, grabbed a glass and, going to the water-cooler, gave its spigot a savage jerk. He did *not*, he told himself, like Mexicans! And he was even less fond of doing chores for them. He glared reproachfully at Lawler when Toreva was not looking.

The Mexican accepted the cool water gratefully. It had a distinct alkaline taste, but he was used to such things, as are all inhabitants of the south-western desert country. When the glass was empty he set it down and, pulling a gay bandanna from his pocket, mopped his perspiring forehead. The smile he turned upon the sheriff was obviously forced.

"What's on your mind, Don Manuel?" Lawler asked again. "I don't guess you came here for a drink?"

"But no," Toreva's faint smile fled and a hunted look came into his close-set eyes. "Meester Lawler," he swept his dry lips with a pink tongue, "I am es-cared."

"Scared!" Lawler stared at the Mexican in amazement. There was certainly the look of fear on the man's swarthy features; he seemed to have taken on age while speaking. A muscle jerked in one damp cheek, a vein throbbed on his forehead.

"*Si*, as the *Señor Dios* is my witness, I am es-cared!"

Pony George scowled. Manuel Toreva had a reputation in this country of being impervious to fear. Indeed the man had always given the appearance of enjoying the hard repute with which his fellow-townsmen had saddled him.

"What's botherin' you?" Lawler asked. "What is it that you're scared of?"

Silently Toreva produced a crumpled bit of paper and passed it to the sheriff. Smoothing it out, Lawler felt his pulses quicken as his glance passed over the scrawled writing.

Idling unnoticed outside the open window a man watched the scene with an unholy mirth in his glinting eyes and a sardonic smile on his heavy lips.

Again Lawler stared at the scrawled words penciled on the scrap of wrinkled paper:

Eight thousand bucks, left to-night by the flat rock out back of yore stable, will mebbe keep yore sinful past a secret some months longer.
JUSTICE.

Eyes upon the sheriff, Toreva sat scowling. Pony George, too, was watching his boss. Handing him the paper, Lawler turned to the Mexican.

"Goin' to dig up the money?"

"*Sangre de Dios,* no!" Toreva snarled. "So much dinero as that I have not!"

Lawler nodded thoughtfully.

"Cripes!" muttered Pony George, passing the note

back to Toreva. "Another one of them crazy 'Justice' notes! That fella's sure puttin' in some overtime. He ain't lettin' no grass grow under his feet! What's he got on you, Toreva?"

"Yes," said Lawler coldly. "What is your sinful past?"

The Mexican gave him a hard stare. Yet Lawler read a furtive, secretive gleam in his shifty eyes.

Toreva grinned abruptly. "Eef I had the dark pas' would I come to you weeth this paper?"

"That depends," said Lawler. "You're admittedly scared, *Why*? If you got nothing to hide, why worry? Just sit tight an' wait for developments."

Toreva blew his breath out in a loud *whssshh!* "Mother of God," he growled. "You do not understan', *senor*. Pairhaps this hombre has the hope I weel not pay, eh? What then? He keels me for furnish w'at you call 'example' for future veectims—like maybe that Doak hombre. W'at you theenk— I'm no like for die!"

"What you better do," Lawler advised, "is to go home, lock your doors an' sit tight. So's you won't have no cause for worry, I'll have George watch your place tonight."

It came to Lawler that the sender of these 'Justice' notes very likely had a grudge against the man who received the messages. Aiming to rub them out, the fellow might take pleasure in making them sweat a little first. But why, he wondered, would anyone want to kill the little Mexican? Was Pony George right in hinting that this business might have some connection with the old Toyah Lake gang?

"Look here, Toreva," he said abruptly. "If you expect any help from the sheriff's office you'll have to come clean. Who is this gent that's signin' himself 'Justice'? I expect you've got some idea, ain't you?"

"*Carramba, no!* Eef I had any idea who this *jibaro* was, I would get hees scalp *muy pronto*. I would like for have the *Senor Caballo* keep the watch on my casa tonight."

"All right, I'll have George do his loafin' in your neighborhood," Lawler promised. "If anyone suspicious-lookin' shows up, George'll grab 'em."

"Mebbe he weel fall es-sleep," Toreva suggested, dubiously.

"Cripes!" growled Pony George indignantly. "Some people have got more crust than a Vienna bun! If yuh're feelin' so dang' critical, fella, s'pose yuh sit up an' do the watchin' yore own self! Gosh, such gall!"

TWO
UNPLEASANT INTERLUDE

AS RED LAWLER, mounted on his big roan gelding, rode slowly out of Pecos along the trail to the Box Bar T, his thoughts were in a whirl. Who was this mysterious person, he wondered, who signed himself Justice? He was filled with foreboding and could not keep his mind from the puzzle for more than a few moments at a time. It was as engrossing to him as was the meaning of the sudden influx of strangers to Reeves County.

The night was cool and among the drifting shadows that hemmed him as he rode, a host of night insects made themselves manifest with steady drone, shrill squeaks, chirps and buzzings. Across his right shoulder Lawler could see a great lop-sided moon climbing the eastern sky and above his head the purple dome of heaven was alive with winking, low-hung stars that looked for all the world like tiny lanterns.

Gradually his somber mood fell away from him and his thoughts became more natural to a youth of his years and temperament. Instead of dwelling longer on sudden death and mystery, they switched to the girl he was to see when the gelding brought him to his destination; the girl every young gent in West Texas had his eye on—the girl Red Lawler had become engaged to just three short days ago.

He touched the gelding with his spurs and the big roan quickened its pace.

For some time only the soft plopping of the pony's hoofs in the sandy trail rivaled the insects' chorus.

Presently Lawler reached a low ridge, looking down from which into a little valley he beheld the weather-whipped adobes of Captain Dan Tranton's Box Bar T. From the windows of the ranch house came the twinkle of lamplight, making cheery contrast to the long cobalt shadows thrown by the argent moon.

Nearing the ranch Lawler could hear the creaking of the windmill that reared its gaunt blades above the yard. It made an eerie, disturbing sound in the vast stillness of the desert night, and was abetted by the soughing wind among the cottonwoods.

Stepping from the saddle beside the wide veranda fronting the house, Lawler wrapped the gelding's reins about one of the hand-hewn posts supporting the veranda roof. As he stepped beneath its shelter he cast a glance toward the dark outline of the bunkhouse. Evidently, he thought irrelevantly, the boys were out on the range.

His face grew sober as he recalled that this was the night Sara had set to acquaint her father with the fact of their engagement. Wondering how the Captain was going to take it, Lawler could not restrain a momentary twinge of fear. The old seadog's love and pride in the daughter whose birth had cost his wife's life was a well-known and respected thing. Every eligible cowpoke in the county was aware that in the jealousy of his love, the old boy hoped that Sara would stay single.

But he shrugged such sober thoughts away and a grin parted his lips as his big hand thumped the door. He could almost picture the joyous smile that would light up Sara's face when she saw him. She, at least, had seemed to hold—

He broke off his thoughts as he heard the sound of her approaching steps. His grin grew wide in expectancy. In a moment now she would be in his arms, he thought.

The door opened and she stood before him in the lamplight streaming from the hall. Her lithe young body was erect as a lodgepole pine and graceful as a doe's; her head, with its wavy mass of spun-gold hair, was held high. There was spirit in the curve of her chin.

But she did not smile, nor did she come to his outstretched arms.

When she saw who it was she stood quite still, one hand upflung to her breast. Her red lips parted slightly, but their parting could not be interpreted as a mark of pleasure. Her grave brown eyes held an odd, indefinable light that brought a frown to the sheriff's face.

He dropped his arms. "Why, Sara—what's wrong, hon? Ain't you glad to see me?"

If she was, she did not show it. She did nothing save continue her silent stare while one hand twisted nervously to a fold in her skirt.

The sheriff's voice grew suddenly husky. "Sara! Why don't you answer?"

"I—I feel so strange, Red; strange and—and frightened. I can't collect my thoughts. Red—someone tried to murder Dad!"

"What!" There was startled incredulity in the roughness of Lawler's voice. Then, "Gosh, Sara, you better quit goin' to them crazy picture shows," he chuckled. "You sure had me fightin' my hat there for a second."

"But I'm serious, Red!" Impatiently she brushed a rebellious curl from before her eyes. "Less than half an hour ago, someone lying on the hill out back fired two shots at Dad as he moved past the office window!"

"Huh?" Lawler's jaw dropped open in surprise. "You—you ain't funnin' me, are you?"

"Don't talk foolish. Of course I'm not."

The news appeared to stun him. And no wonder; no trouble worthy of the name had visited Reeves County for over fifteen years. Aside, that is, from the recent killing of the stranger, Doak.

Lawler pulled himself together. He was Reeves County's youngest sheriff—that meant something to Red Lawler. "Did the Captain call my office?"

"I don't know," Sara's dark eyes clouded and she looked away, seeming to be scanning something in her mind. "I've been too bewildered and frightened to think of anything except that attempt on Dad's life. "Why," she asked piteously, "would anyone want to kill him, Red?"

"I dunno," said Lawler. "Where is he now?"

"He's in his office, I guess. He just came in from poking around out there on the hill. He was trying to find a—a 'clue' I believe he called it."

Lawler nodded. "That's a chore for the sheriff's office," he said sternly. "I'd better talk with him right away."

He swung past her down the hall.

"Red!" she caught him by the arm; stopped him.

He turned impatiently. Looking down at her he thought he detected some sort of hurt in the expression with which she eyed him. "What is it, Sara?" he asked. "You don't want to let this thing worry you too much. He wasn't hit, was he?"

"A scratch," she said, and then—

"Red—I guess—I guess you'd better take this back." She pulled a ring slowly from the third finger of her left hand; a ring that sparkled in the yellow light—the ring he had given her three nights ago to bind their plight. "I have no right to it," she said.

Lawler's big frame stiffened as he stared at her astounded.

"I'm serious. Please take it, Red."

"But—but good gosh, Sara." Lawler looked at her bewilderedly. "What's come over you, honey? Is it Captain Dan? Don't he want you to get engaged to me? Is that it? Or is it this shootin' that's got you so upset?"

She returned his look silently, miserably.

"Say!" Lawler suddenly blurted. "You sure don't think it was *me* that was layin' out there on that hill with a rifle do you?"

"Of course not," she denied indignantly. "But— Oh, I can't explain, Red! We've got to break off this crazy engagement. You're too young to know what you're doing. I'm— we're—we've got to stop being silly. This can't go on."

Mechanically Lawler took the ring she was holding out to him. "Sara," he began, but—

"It's no use," she cut in. "Please don't argue, Red—" her voice broke on a sobbing note and a poignant hush fell between them. When next she spoke her tone was controlled, emotionless:

"There must be nothing further between us. You are not making enough money to support a wife as I desire to be supported. I'm serious, Red. Don't scowl at me like that." She paused, then finished, "Don't call to see me any more."

Jilted! the word raced through Lawler's brain in letters of fire. *Jilted!* She was throwing him down— kicking him aside like a discarded hat!

For a breathless moment he stood quite still, accusing eyes fixed hotly on the pale oval of her face as she stood with her back to the light. Then the ring he held seemed to scorch his fingers. He swore, seemed about to hurl the bauble from him—then abruptly changed his mind.

With a grim nod, his lips twisted in a bitter line, he slipped it in his pocket and strode past her down the hall toward Tranton's office.

THREE
A POINTED HINT

CAPTAIN DAN TRANTON—RETIRED SEADOG AN'
proud of it, as he was wont to boast—though close to
sixty was a man of great vitality. Though not as tall, he
was every inch as broad as Lawler across the shoulders
and his back was every bit as straight. He seemed a
kindly man, portly, florid and jovial. His head—save for
the tiny bald spot at the back—was white as snow; a
bristling mane of hair that looked never to have known
the feel of a brush or comb.

He had a red, clean-shaven face whose expression
was habitually pleasant. If he found the world of horses
and cattle little to his liking, one would never have
guessed as much by searching his large blue eyes.

His talk like himself was salty and well-sprinkled
with sea-goingese. He had, so he said, retired from the
sea about fifteen years ago and, after wallowing in
derelict fashion about the country for some five years,
had finally brought himself and daughter to port in
Pecos, where he had purchased the old Box Bar T and
taken to raising cattle.

When Lawler flung open his door and came striding into the room used by him for an office, Captain Dan, clad in a pair of dark blue trousers and a blue cotton shirt whose collar was eternally open, was seated behind his massive desk staring into space. He brought his eyes to sharp focus on the intruder's face and grunted.

A big lamp, bracketed to the wall above the Captain's desk, gave light; the curtains at the room's two windows were drawn to the sills, Lawler saw as Sara followed him into the office and, closing the door, leaned her willowy figure against it, watching both him and her father with nervous glance.

Lawler lost no time in coming to the point. "Sara tells me you've been shot at, Captain."

"Shot? . . . Eh? . . . Oh—ah—well, yeah. Leastways a gun went off an' broke a mite o' glass. Some playful hand with a load o' rum aboard, I make no doubt."

"Playful!" Lawler frowned. "Sara says you were hit. Hurt bad?"

"No."

"Where'd the bullets strike?"

Almost reluctantly, it seemed, the Captain shifted a stack of papers on his desk. Where they had formerly rested Lawler saw that the wood's polished surface was marred by a splintered hole. "That 'un grazed me amidships after crackin' the port lens."

Lawler, more or less familiar with his salt-water vocabulary, crossed to the left window and raised the shade. The glass had been shattered by a bullet, the bottom half, that is. On the floor beneath it lay fragments of the broken pane and one or two stains that looked like blood. There was also a darkish smear on the sill.

"You say that bullet grazed your ribs? Let's take a look."

"Belay there. It ain't nothin' to get worked up about. I'm plenty seaworthy yet. Just scratched the paint a little, that's all that salvo did."

"Just the same," said Lawler, "I want to take a look." The Captain with a shrug unbuttoned his shirt. Lawler removed a bandage and made a brief examination; an ugly flesh wound, he found, but plainly nothing serious. He re-bandaged it and asked Tranton to step over by the window and stand as when hit.

With a curious stare the Captain obeyed. The bandaged portion of his anatomy was squarely in line with the shattered glass and the hole in the desk.

Lawler motioned him back to his seat. "What were you doin' when the shots were fired? Seems a kind of odd place for you to be standin'."

"I'd been lookin' up a date on the calendar. The only one I got aboard is that one tacked on the bulk-head. I was standin' there givin' 'er the once over when the first gun came through the riggin' an' took me amidships. I dropped to the deck soon's I was hit. A little late," he grinned sheepishly.

"Where'd the second shot strike?" asked Lawler.

Tranton shook his head. "You got me there. I ain't been able to cross its course."

"Mean to say you don't know where it struck? Didn't you hear it?" And, as the Captain shook his head again, "Uncommon odd," Lawler muttered. "Find anything outside?"

"Well, I found a couple shells."

"Did you hear the fella leave?"

"I heard some horse hoofs a-thuddin'."

Crossing to the window Lawler stared up at the moonlit ridge. "Let's see the shells."

" 'Fraid they won't be much help. Forty-fives. I expect nearly everyone uses that caliber. I do myself," he added, patting the pistol-butt protruding from the waistband of his trousers.

"They're common, all right," Lawler admitted, but looked them over closely. No distinguishing pin marks were discernible. "Did you call my office?" he asked, dropping the shells in his pocket.

"Well—no-o. I didn't cal'late there was any sense in botherin' you boys with my troubles. I figured you probably had plenty of your own."

Lawler stood beside the desk, hands deep-thrust in his pockets. "Next time you're shot at, call my office without delay."

A cloud sailed across the Captain's glance. "Knock off, young fellow. I've been captaining my own ships too long to start in takin' orders now."

Lawler scowled. His scowl grew darker when the Captain changed the subject by asking: "How d'ye like the job of bein' sheriff? Pretty soft berth, ain't it?"

Why was the Captain anxious to get off the subject of the shooting? He was, Lawler reflected grimly, acting mighty reticent about the whole affair. "You haven't given me any reason for not calling up my office yet," he reminded.

"Eh? ... Oh! Wal," the Captain reefed his sails and came to anchor, "I'll tell you, Red. I—er—I thought you'd likely be sailin' this way to-night an' cal'lated I might's well wait an' tell, you when you got here. I can't 'bide telephones. A pesky nuisance, I call 'em. I recall one time..."

"Yeah, I reckon," Lawler cut in drily. "But- let's stick to this mysterious shootin'. You haven't got any enemies around here, have you?"

"Lord, no!" the Captain was emphatic. "I ain't had an enemy anyplace since the time I knocked that mutinous first mate across the head with a belayin' pin. 'Twas aboard the *Sally Schuyler,* as I recollect it, just after we'd rounded the Horn. I says to him, steppin' close, 'Mister'."

"You told me about that mate before, Captain," Lawler's voice was cold. Lawler hated mysteries and this, he told himself, bade fair to be a night of them! First, the mystery of his broken engagement; second, the mystery of why anyone should want to kill Captain Dan; and now, the mystery of why Dan Tranton should apparently be trying to shield the sniper who had just come so close to killing him. For the captain, he sensed, either knew or guessed the would-be assassin's identity, and was plainly determined to keep it to himself.

With scowl growing steadily blacker, Lawler turned to the Captain's daughter.

"Sara, where were you when you heard the shots? You heard them, didn't you?"

"I heard them, yes. I was in the sitting-room reading. The shots seemed to come from a long way off. Probably my being on the far side of the house made it seem that way."

Lawler studied her white face, and did not like what he saw. She looked tired, haggard. He felt a wave of sympathy flow through him for her—until he recalled the matter of his spurned ring. His grim jaw hardened. "Did you hear anything else?"

"A sound as might have been made by running feet," she admitted, hesitantly.

He wondered what value to attach to that statement. Her look said she was not sure what she had heard. "Can you describe it more close?"

"A sort of fast *clump-clump* such as pounding boots might make on hard-packed earth. I got the impression that the one who fired the shots might be trying to get away—only," she said, and stopped.

"Only what?" demanded Lawler impatiently.

"Only it seemed to me as though the running sound was approaching the house..."

"An' about that time," Captain Dan interrupted with a chuckle, "Sara got the notion that some fellow might have been shooting at her ol' Dad. She came running down the hall and pounded on my door." He smiled affectionately at Sara. "You ought to go to bed, ol' girl—you look like someone had dragged you through a knothole."

Lawler's glance beat hard against the Captain's as Sara said with a wan smile, "I'm all right. Just a little worried, I guess."

"Was the Captain's door locked?" Lawler asked.

"Of course," said the Captain gruffly. "I locked it quicker'n scat when I heard that runnin' bronc. I figured it was likely that careless-shooter headin' a dust cloud for distant parts. But I couldn't be sure. An' I didn't want take no chances on havin' Sara open the door an' mebbe getting hit."

Lawler said nothing. He was trying to get Sara's eye, but without success. With a muttered something under his breath, he turned his glance on the Captain. The seadog scowled. "He better do his sailin' in other waters in the future."

"An' you better keep your weather eye peeled," Lawler told him. "There's some funny things been goin' on in this county lately."

"Funny?"

"I mean uncommon queer. I don't rightly understand all I know about 'em, but I aim to before I'm through. Hard-lookin' characters have been showin' up around here lately, an' the bulk of 'em better take to walkin' easy or I'll—"

He broke off suddenly. His intent stare was fixed squarely on the Captain's face. "Have you received any notes, either through the mail or otherwise?"

"Er . . . notes? What kind of notes?"

"Blackmail notes."

The Captain laughed and slapped his thigh. "Lord, no! They wouldn't get far tryin' that kind of game on me. What put that notion in your head, boy?"

"I was just wonderin'," Lawler evaded. "Reckon I'll be siftin' on. I got a heap of chores that sure need wranglin'."

There was a peculiar expression in the Captain's bright blue eyes. Abruptly he smiled. "No need to be puttin' off," he said, with the first real display of friendliness he had shown this evening. "Might as well sit down a—"

"Now, Dad," said Sara swiftly, "if Mr. Lawler's duties need his attention, we shouldn't try to keep him. After all, you know, he's the sheriff. I suppose he does have to work— occasionally."

Lawler stared and, staring, scowled. It had been in

his mind to talk again with Sara, if he saw a chance of speaking with her alone. But after a hint like that!

He picked up his hat and strode grimly toward the door. "I'll be sayin' good night," he gruffed as he reached it. "If you locate the place where that second bullet struck, I'll be obliged if you'll let me know."

Captain Dan looked at Sara, and from her to the sheriff. Scratching his snowy mane he said, "Sho' I'll do that, Red. G'night."

FOUR
"HE WAS KNIFED!"

A STRONG WIND was springing up, a wind that sent dark masses of heavy cloud scurrying angrily across the star-flecked heavens. A surly wind that snapped and lashed and screamed. A truculent wind that drove the timid moon to cover and with guttural snarl whipped great balls of tumble-weed before it like senseless flocks of frightened sheep.

Astride the big roan gelding Sheriff Red Lawler struck out for town. Beneath the pony's hoofs the shadow-dappled plain spread vast and rolling. The trail was a dim-seen ribbon.

Riding through the wind-harried night the sheriff, like Odysseus of old, entertained many and divers thoughts— mostly bitter. The world seemed to have soured and he could see no way of sweetening it, the future lay dark as the Devil's smile across the horizon of his mind.

Who, he wondered, was the unknown sniper who had lain out on that ridge back of the Tranton ranch house and hurled rifle lead at the portly Captain? Who, indeed? And why was the Captain so determined not to divulge the fellow's identity, or his suspicions concerning that identity? Was the would-be assassin a one-time friend of his seadog days? Possibly a relative of the black sheep variety who hated to see his kin in better circumstances than he was himself? Or was the Captain's reticence simply that of a strong man treading on unfamiliar ground?

With a mind full of questions, none of which he was able to supply with an adequate answer, Red Lawler rode with a saturnine scowl on his young, bronzed face.

From time to time he glanced upward. He observed with bitter humor that the storm was sweeping nearer with alarming speed. A thick veil of scudding cloud had snuffed the moon's pale light completely. Swiftly the low-hung stars were blotted from the bowl of night. Sheet lightning showed in lurid patches.

Before the sheriff's mental vision recurringly flashed the face of Sara Tranton, pale and haggard. Almost impossible to believe the change that had come over her, he thought. But she had changed. She had discarded him three nights after acceptance—almost, it seemed, without remorse. If she had felt a wave of pity or regret it must have been but passing, for he could not ignore her pointed hint when her father had asked him to stay longer and had appeared about to insist. With the thought he jabbed the gelding savagely with his spurred heels.

The night became inky black and only the sound of the snarling wind died with the thunder and the constant roll of the pony's drumming hoofs.

Lawler pulled his slicker from behind the cantle

and struggled into it without slowing pace as the first raindrops came slanting downward, stinging like bits of hail. A lightning bolt hissed down a ridge, revealing to Lawler a tree-clad rise several hundred yards to the west.

He rode with down-bent head, trying to shield his face from the blast of wind-driven rain. Icy water flowed torrent-like from his hat-brim, spilled from his slicker-clad shoulders.

Another lightning flash illumined momentarily the streaming plain. From the rise, now but a scant hundred yards away, Lawler saw a sudden jet of flame. It lanced from the dripping junipers. The report of the firearm was lost in a smashing, jarring crash of thunder.

The bullet had whined past Lawler's head so close he had heard its whisper—"cousin!" Under the urgent drive of spurs the gelding tore up the slope toward the ambusher's covert as Lawler's big hands dragged loose the rifle from the scabbard beneath his leg.

The junipers' dark bulk loomed empty when he reached them. Stubbornly he drove the gelding backward and forward through the slapping branches. But to no avail. The unknown sniper was gone.

Lawler pulled the pony in and sat there swearing softly. With grimly narrowed glance he probed the surrounding country as again the lightning lit it palely blue.

"Uncommon odd where—"

The sentence was never finished for, warned by that sixth sense of danger possessed by all who ride the owl-hoot trails, Lawler suddenly flung himself out flat across the gelding's neck as lead sheared past, clipping twigs from its path with vicious spite. Even as he ducked, Lawler sank his spurs and the roan lunged forward with hip-jolting violence, crashed headlong through the fringe of trees and out upon its farther side and down the slippery pitch at breakneck speed.

A single glance he'd sent back and that had been enough. Four riders had been disclosed storming up the trail behind; four frantic horsemen whose rocketing mounts were slinging slime hat-high beneath the bite of quirt and spur!

Down the streaming slope went Lawler on his gelding. One stumble, one faltering step or unlucky stride and all would be forever over. But he was forced to take that chance for only Death leered grim behind.

Slime spurted like flying spray from the gelding's hammering hoofs as they left the slope and struck off across the level, swinging diagonally to regain the Pecos trail. More than once Lawler was tempted to turn and fight, but in each instance sager counsel urged him on.

Through rain-drenched murk the chase went doggedly on and on and on. The very persistence of the pursuit told the sheriff the sort of thing that would be his lot if the pursuers caught him. They were plainly bent either on his capture or his complete extermination. The wild night rang to their shouts and cursings. Lawler needed none to tell him who was that burly figure in the lead. He knew that rocky horseman well for the thief he was; tight-lipped, bottle-nosed Link Holladay—gent of easy conscience and rider of the hungry loop. Hardly two weeks past he had very nearly caught the rustler and his men with a herd of stolen cattle. But the wily Holladay had seen him coming and, abandoning his four-footed loot, had called off his men and fled. Link Holladay now was out to even up that score!

That Holladay, should he catch up with the odds in his favor thus, would kill him with neither compunction nor remorse was certain. There was not a spark of mercy in the rustler's make-up. Holladay's hate was said to be of the Indian variety and just as long-enduring. In no possible sense could Holladay be considered a sportsman. He was a man who built his own elastic code and when it proved not sufficient for his purposes he had a habit of ignoring it entirely and resorting to the long-known potency of old Judge Colt.

Again the rip and the whine of lead was singing through the night with whistling fury; dangerously close it came to Lawler lying flattened out on the running roan. With an abrupt snarl Lawler pulled the gelding in and, dropping from the saddle with bitter purpose, whipped his rifle up.

Down on the knee in the squashy slick he crouched, the long gun at his shoulder. His finger dragged its trigger back three times in swift succession. He grinned with malicious pleasure when Holladay's horse went heels over head, down is an outsprawled spill. A horse to its right abruptly faltered in mid-stride, staggered and piled up in a thrashing heap as its rider vaulted clear.

Then Lawler was up in the saddle again, driving his gelding on at a hard run, grinning back at the mud-covered figure of Link Holladay. The rustler was gingerly parting himself from the spiney embrace of a prickly-pear clump where his falling horse had thrown him. As the lightning revealed him, a malignant fury was plainly discernible on his twisted features.

Lawler chuckled in better spirits. "Mebbe that'll

teach them thievin' sidewinders to pull in their horns a mite," he grunted.

Glancing presently upward with his pony travelling at an easier pace he saw that the storm was passing. Blue patches of sky were beginning to show through rifts in the screen of cloud. Yet the wind blew cold with a penetrating chill that whipped his Levi's to his shivering legs in sodden wrinkles. With chattering teeth he pulled the slicker closer about his hunched shoulders.

As the moon peered timidly down through a crack in the scudding clouds Lawler dismissed the burly Holladay from his mind and turned his thoughts once more to Captain Dan. Was the unknown man who had tonight tried to kill the Captain the same who had levered those shots at himself from atop that tree-clad rise? If so, was it one of Holladay's bunch? Perhaps the mean-eyed Link himself?

The sheriff was forced to admit he did not know.

He thought of the hard-faced strangers who had been turning up in the vicinity of Pecos these last three months. Doak had been one, and now Doak was dead. Another called himself Buck Tawson; a third, Max Smith. Still another was known as Reede, a sallow-faced lunger whose clothes clung to his bony frame like the cast-off garments of a scarecrow. And there was still one more of these uncatalogued, loose-footed gentry; Big Ear Lester who had thrown himself up a shack near Barstow and who spent most of his time, so Lawler had heard, in shooting holes through tomato cans.

Tawson and Reede had each bought a small spread and had, apparently, settled down to the business of putting weight on scrubby herds of beef. But in the case of Tawson, anyway, Lawler knew the ranch was but a blind.

Was it one of these strangers who had settled Doak's account with five well-placed bullets through the back? If so, why? To Lawler this appeared a question that would take a deal of finding out!

Who, he wondered grimly, was the mysterious person signing himself "Justice?" Was he the unknown rifleman who tonight had lain upon that ridge behind Tranton's office?

Glancing across the gelding's ears Lawler saw the lights of Pecos twinkling in the distance. The rain had ceased, leaving a range refreshed and a night that was damp and chill.

Arriving in town he put up his mount at Toreva's livery stable, telling the man in charge to see that the gelding was rubbed down carefully and given a measure of oats and water. Then he turned up the street toward his office in the gaunt old red brick courthouse.

Nearing the building he saw the coroner emerge and pass down the far side of the street in the direction of a saloon known as The Merry Widow, into which he vanished as the sheriff stared.

"Now what was he doin' up here at this time of night?" Lawler muttered. He half turned to follow the man, then changed his mind and strode on toward the sheriff's office in the building from which the coroner had emerged. Though the shades of the office's two windows were drawn to the sills, he discerned that the place held a light.

Entering the courthouse, Lawler almost got himself run down by Pony George who was emerging hurriedly and swearing under his breath.

Lawler grabbed his deputy by the collar. "What's up?" he demanded gruffly.

"Up? Hell Crick is up an' about tuh leave its banks!" snapped Pony George. "Leggo my collar, dammit! I'm in a hurry!"

"I should think so. Well, you ain't goin' anyplace until I find out what's going on."

"My Gawd! Ain't you heard?" Pony George looked astounded at the sheriff's ignorance. "Hell, I s'posed 'twas all over town by now!"

"Mebbe so," said Lawler curtly, "but I been outa town. Spill it now; what's happened?"

"Been another blasted murder—that's what!"

"Another . . ." the sheriff's voice trailed off as a grim suspicion rose to mind. "Who's dead?" Lawler controlled his voice with a visible effort. "Not—"

"Yeah—that damn Toreva! An' he had tuh git himself killed while I was settin' on his porch with a double-barreled shotgun!"

"When did it happen?' Lawler snapped.

"Not more'n ten minutes ago—"

"Did you catch a glimpse of the killer?" Lawler broke in, cold chills running up his back.

"No, I—"

"Where was he shot?"

"He wasn't—he was knifed!"

FIVE
THE FAST WORKER

IN THE SUDDEN silence following the deputy's words, Lawler stood motionless. No least twitching muscle or change in shade of expression betrayed the turmoil of his thoughts. Motionless and stiff he stood by the open doorway, his hands deep-thrust in his pockets, staring at Pony George.

Slowly his deep-bronzed, aquiline countenance took on a harshness from inner wrath, an ominous light flared up in his jade-green eyes. "What the hell were you doin' while Toreva was gettin' killed?" A bitter quirk twisted the sheriff's lips. "Wrestlin' with that damnfool poetry, I expect."

"That ain't true," Pony George muttered sullenly. "I was sittin' on that greaser's front porch with my eyes skinned all directions an' a loaded shotgun in m' lap. What more could I do? By cripes, Lawler, I'm gettin' fed up with yore insinuations. If yuh don't like my style, there ain't nothin' tuh keep yuh from gittin' another man!"

"Pin that badge back on an' quit talkin' like a fool."

Reluctantly it seemed Pony George pinned the badge back on his greasy vest. "Wal?"

"Let's go in the office," Lawler said. "We got to talk this over," he added as he followed George down the hall. When they stepped into the sheriff's office, Lawler closed the door, walked over to his desk and dropped wearily into the chair behind it. Then he looked up. "Go on. I'm listenin'. Spill the yarn."

Biting off a generous chew of Brown's Mule, Pony George returned the remnant of the plug to his pocket, masticated a moment in silence, then said:

"It was like this. You told me tuh watch Toreva's place tonight. Not knowing what time if any, the fireworks was due tuh pop, I got over there round eight-thirty an' plunked m'self down in his best porch rocker. He set out there talkin' with me fer quite a spell. Then he knocked out his pipe an' said as how he guessed he'd be goin' inside. That was at ten o'clock.

"'Bout fifteen minutes later I seen that big-eared jasper from over to Barstow come ridin' down the street. I kep' my eye on him till he got off his nag in front of Miguel Garcia's place an' went inside. That was the last time I seen of him. F'r all *I* know, he may be in there yet."

"Well, get on with it," Lawler growled. "Wal, another ten minutes slips by an' then along comes that lunger, Joe Reede—the fella what bought the ol' Lazy R. Like always, he reminds me of a undertaker on a picnic. Cheerful-lookin' as a quarantine fer scarlet fever. Wal, I eyed him till *he* got outa sight.

"No more passers then fer about a hour or so, I guess. Then all of a sudden like, I hears a sorta bump from inside the house. Thinks I, 'what's Manuel up tuh?' Before that I'd heard him movin' around an' rustlin' papers an' what not. But after that bump I didn't hear a damn thing inside the house. After a spell I got sorta restless an' a bit uneasy like. So I got up an' went inside; figgered tuh swap bull awhile with the Mex.

"But the minute I hit the main room I got a shock; I knew somethin' had gone haywire right away. Yuh see, Manuel an' me had agreed tuh leave the livin' room lamp burnin'. When I got there it was out.

"I felt around till I found the lamp—then I got another shock. It was still hot! I waited a bit, then whispered Manuel's same. No answer. Then I called him—kinda loud, like yuh'd call a hawg. Only answer I got was from the echoes. That place gives me the creeps an' I ain't kiddin' yuh. Every-time yuh speak a dang echo plops yore talk right back at yuh. It ain't the sorta thing which makes a nervous gent like me feel comfortable. When I says 'Manuel!' back comes that blasted echo —'Man-u-el-1-1!' "

Pony George paused to wipe his forehead.

"Wal, I finally got a match scratched somehow an' lit the lamp. When I turned round tuh get a good look at the place the shotgun dang nigh dropped from m' hands! There was that cussed greaser settin' right behind me all the time an' he'd never let out a peep. If he'd a laughed then, I'd a brained him. But right now," Pony George sighed, "I wish he had. He never batted a eye an' pretty soon I noticed as how he was hunched forward kinda odd. I moved closer an' right then yuh coulda sold ol' man Kasta's little son George fer less than a nickel. There was a knife stuck in Toreva's throat hilt-deep an' blood all over 'im!"

There was a hard glint to Lawler's eyes. "I reckon

you put that knife where it won't get lost. Handle it careful, did you, so's not to obliterate fingerprints?"

Pony George looked reproachful. "Could yuh ask me such a question? Naturally I took good care o' that blade. I jest got done lockin' it up in yore desk when yuh stopped me in the corridor. Here's yore key," he tossed it on the desk.

Toying with it absently, Lawler asked: "Any sign of the killer? Any clues other than the knife?"

"Just this," Pony George grunted, and dropped a crumpled bit of paper in the sheriff's outstretched hand. "It was tied around the haft of the knife with a hunk of string."

Spreading the crumpled paper out with some trepidation, Lawler read:

Tally two for Justice!

"So he's at it again!" Lawler's voice was harsh with anger. "I've had about enough of this. Somebody will wish they'd never heard of Reeves County time I get through with 'em!"

There was stillness for a space then. Lawler's brooding eyes were fixed unseeingly on the killer's note. His face was like a mask in its absence of mobility. After a bit he sighed, then looking up he asked, "What time's Kringle aimin' to have the inquest?"

"Nine o'clock. Tomorrow mornin', he said."

Nodding, the sheriff picked up the key. "Which drawer?"

"Top left."

Starting to insert the key in the drawer mentioned, Lawler abruptly tensed. With his left hand he reached abruptly out and yanked the drawer open without use of the key in his right. "This lock is broken, George. Was it all right when you put the knife in here?"

"How could I have locked it if it wasn't?" countered Pony George, eyeing Lawler curiously. "Broken, eh? Wal, if it is, whoever broke it must have been a dang fast worker, 'cause he'd of had tuh do it while me an' you was talkin' in the corridor"

Lawler's cold drawl cut in upon George's rambling. "He's a fast worker, all right—too damned fast by far! He's got his knife back. This drawer's empty as last year's sunflowers. We might's well go home an' get to bed."

SIX
"HE'S MEANER'N GAR SOUP!"

HAVING JUST FINISHED AN EARLY BREAKFAST, Red Lawler sauntered up the street to the courthouse, threw away his toothpick and entered the long ground-floor corridor. The first, loudest and *only* thing he heard for several moments was the voice of Pony George. Never a thing to brag about, at this instant it was raised on high in a most dismal yammer—a sound strangely reminiscent of the noise coyotes make when baying at the moon. Lawler paused to listen:

> "—a breeze about Kyote Cal,
> A low-down son of Hell—
> A story about a gal named Lou,
> Who laffed when Kyote fell!"

Lawler's suspicions had been verified; this was more of his deputy's damnfool ballading. With a grimace he reached out to open the door. Pony George sang dolefully on:

> *"This ornery Cal was the sneakin' pal*
> *What stole his pard's best dame;*
> *She was a busy, hystlin' skirt*
> *Thet sang in the Golden Flame."*

Flinging open the door Lawler stood regarding his deputy with a dark scowl. Pony George was sprawled contortionistically in the sheriff's swivel chair with his spurred heels resting on the sheriff's desk. It was the deputy's favorite posture— when Lawler was not around.

Gripped firmly in one hand the poetic Pony George held a pad of paper, balancing it on his knee. In the other hand, gripped with equal firmness, was a stub of pencil. Hearing the opening of the door, George said without looking up:

"This here ballad of mine is gonna be a sure-enough world beater. Listen at this, Gracie—"

> *"Now the snappiest gal in the Golden*
>   *Flame*
> *Was the dame thet was knowed as Lou—*
> *A creation of times when guns was law,*
> *An' women was fast an' few!"*

He looked up in grinning expectancy of "Gracie's" approval. The grin went lop-sided when he saw the scowling Lawler. His face fell like a sponge-cake in a winter gale.

Arms akimbo the sheriff stared. He looked mad, yet was hard put to restrain a chuckle at sight of the comic expression stamping Pony George's dried-apple countenance.

"Wall" said Pony George defiantly. "Go ahead —say it!"

"Who's Gracie?"

"None of yore dang never-mind," snapped Pony George, and took his spurred heels from the sheriff's desk. Then, realizing that no fireworks had exploded, he ventured hesitantly:

"How'd it sound?"

"Terrible," said Lawler with brutal frankness. "You aren't much better poet than you are a deputy sheriff. 'F I was you, I'd find some other way to occupy my time."

Pony George sniffed. "The rewards o' labour," he said loftily, "are notoriously meager." Putting away his pad and pencil stub he began a conscientious searching of his pockets, each and every, with great show of growing wonder.

"Here," Lawler grunted, and tossed his sack of Durham into the deputy's lap.

With a sigh Pony George got out his corncob pipe and filled it generously with the sheriff's tobacco.

"Never mind puttin' the rest in your pocket, George. I got a pipe, too," Lawler reminded.

"Durham," said Pony George musingly. "Not so bad," he added with the air of a connoisseur, "but tobacco as a whole ain't up tuh what it used to be. An' they're chargin' more'n ever. I can't figger what this country's comin' to, what with the high cost o' livin', the disgraceful size o' wages an' the suddenness of death. I—"

"Yeah, deputies don't get a whale of a big salary," remarked Lawler drily. "Still, I expect I could get another one all right, if you're thinkin' of handin' in your star."

"What happened out tuh Tranton's las' night?" Pony George abruptly changed the subject. "See Sara? What'd the ol' man say when yuh popped the question?"

Lawler scowled. "I didn't pop it. Somebody took a coupla shots at the Captain from the ridge out back of his office."

"Miss him?"

"One of 'em did. The other took a little skin off his ribs."

"This country is headin' for hell. Gettin' so a fella ain't safe nowheres!"

Briefly Lawler went over the incidents of the previous evening, up until the time he'd left the Box Bar T.

"You called the turn, Red," Pony George admitted. "We got three mysteries tuh solve. First, the mystery of why any gent would wanta shoot Dan Tranton; second, the question o' why Sara went an' busted yore engagement; an' third, the mystery of why the Captain's tryin' tuh shield the skunk that nearly potted him."

"But from the standpoint of this office," added Lawler slowly, "the most important question we've got to answer is, who is this unknown killer who's signin' himself 'Justice'?"

Pony George nodded. "Far as yore busted engagement is concerned—wal, tuh my way o' thinkin', it's jest a case o' the well-knowed female temperament. Yuh can't never tell what a male of a woman's gonna do next. Downright unreliable—both of 'em!"

Lawler was not paying much attention to his deputy's chatter. He was finding that thinking came hard this morning. Sara Tranton's oval face and golden hair kept so scattering his thoughts as soon as formulated. No plausible reason could he think of to account for that broken engagement. The Captain, he reflected, must have kicked. That hurt a bit, too. For he and the Captain had always gotten along well.

If Sara had been merely exercising a woman's prerogative —the right to change her mind—he told himself she was not worth another thought. But he continued thinking about her, nevertheless, and his thoughts were both confused and painful.

He swore beneath his breath. This would never do —he had his job to think about, and just now that job was big enough to take up all his time. The inquest on Toreva was scheduled for nine o'clock. It was eight-twenty now.

"Somebody sure seems hell-bent on c'ralin' himself some notches," Pony George was saying. "It's gettin' so I count ten ever' time I step outside this office. If 'twas anyone but you that was sheriffin' this county, I'd quit in a minute.

"I don't expect you need to worry, George. You're too small fry."

Pony George was not offended. "Lightnin's been knowed tuh strike in some mighty strange places," he said seriously. "Figger it was Justice tried tuh get old Tranton?"

"Couldn't say. I tell you, George, this is the most tangled-up damn' mess I ever been in. Why should all these strangers pile up around this country?"

"Ah," sighed Pony George, "if we knew that, we'd know somethin' sure enough."

"Humph! If one of these strangers is doin' the killin's he must be settlin' some old grudge, way I look at it. But why here an' now?" demanded Lawler as, with hands deep-thrust in pockets, he paced the floor. "Few people nurse a grudge over a period of years. Doak was a stranger, but Manuel Toreva lived in Pecos dang near all his life. I tell you, this business has got me fightin' my hat, got my nerves to janglin' so I can't keep still."

"I seen where they're advertisin' some kinda stuff in the papers what they claim's good for raw nerves. Believe it's called 'Merkel's Oxidine Bitters'—"

The sudden shrilling of the telephone drowned the rest of the deputy's words. Scooping the receiver to his ear, Pony George said "Hah?" and handed the instrument to Lawler. "Fer you, Red. Sounds like Captain Dan."

"Hello," said Lawler gruffly. "That you, Captain? . . . Yeah. . . . Oh! . . . Where'd you get that notion? . . . Uh-huh. Well, all right. I'll look into it. Much obliged." There was a puzzled expression on his youthful face as he hung up.

"What'd he want?"

"Claimed that after thinkin' things over last night, he's come to the conclusion it was Tawson who took them shots at him."

"Tawson!" Pony George looked startled. Then abruptly he laughed. "Can't yuh jest picture ol' Buck Tawson, U.S. Marshal, layin' belly-down on that ridge a-workin' the lever of a rifle? We oughta tell Tawson— by cripes, that's the best one I ever heard on him!"

Lawler's answer was thoughtful. "But the Captain doesn't know that Tawson's a Federal officer. Like the rest of the folks around here, Tranton likely figures Tawson for a reg'lar

small-spread cowman"

"Comes tuh that," Pony George broke in, "*we* don't *know* that Tawson is a Federal officer. We're jest takin' his word fer it on the strength of his pryin' an' snoopin' an' that badge he's totin' round. Which, when yuh come tuh boil 'er down, don't mean no more'n a hill o' beans." Pony George held no high regard for Federal Agents, and took no shame in saying so.

"I reckon he's a marshal," Lawler said. "He's a newcomer, though, an' likely the Captain—"

"Speakin' o' newcomers," Pony George broke in, "Buck Tawson ain't the only pilgrim tuh like the Pecos climate. There's that walkin' corpse—Joe Reede, what owns the Lazy R. An' that big-eared jasper, Lester, which has bedded down over near Barstow. An' Link Holladay, the damn' rustler— they're all fairly recent importations."

"You're right," Lawler admitted. "It's a wonder the Captain didn't happen to pick on one of them if he's tryin' to throw us off the track. Somehow I got a hunch he knows who the fella is. An' I don't think it was Buck Tawson—do you?"

Pony George sniffed, took the other side of the argument:

"Yuh can't never tell, Red, what them dang Federal agents is apt tuh do. I've knowed some mighty ornery marshals in my time. Worse'n a skittish woman, they are. If Tawson's taken a dislike tuh Captain Dan, I wouldn't put it past the black-faced polecat tuh take a rifle an' lay for him!"

"Black-faced?"

"Wal, mebbe Mexicans is darker—but dang little. He's a sight too dark for me. He's got a pan like a chunk of ol' mahogany. Yeah, an' a mean eye, too."

"I expect his feelin's might be aggravated if he heard you say that, George."

"Hell! A marshal ain't got no feelin's—he'd eat off the same plate with a snake! I wouldn't trust one of 'em farther'n I c'ld sling a hoss by the tail!"

Lawler grinned. He did not attach a great deal of weight to Pony George's opinions— particularly his opinions concerning government officers. Such an officer had once had occasion to hale the deputy into court for running an illicit whisky plant and Pony George's views had become a little warped by the experience.

Tawson, as the Reeves County Sheriff's Office had good cause to know, was a U.S. Marshal detailed to Pecos to investigate an anonymous tip suggesting that members of the old Toyah Lake gang might there be located.

This much, and this much only, had the reticent Tawson confided. Using the tumbledown old Bar 2 for a smoke screen, he was posing as a small-spread rancher.

Both Lawler and his deputy, having been born and raised in the vicinity, had heard plenty of colorful yarns about the former Toyah Lake gang. Their specialty had been the robbing of stages, with an occasional bank robbery and killing thrown in to make the business interesting. Their fame was almost legendary—an ill-starred repute highly unsavory to the honest folk who had been rearing families in the vicinity of the gang's former outrages.

"Any of that bunch ever caught?" Lawler asked abruptly.

"One," said Pony George. "I 'member thinkin' 'twas kinda tough on him, bein' as the others got off scot-free."

"Convicted?"

"I'll say he was! Folks was so glad tuh git their hands on one of that gang they insisted on makin' a example outa him." Pony George knocked the ashes from his pipe. "He was sent up in '20 an' s' far as I know, he's still up! Give his name as Tim Rein-though some folks figgered at the time he mighta been Rowdy Joe himself."

"You told me yesterday," Lawler objected, "that Rowdy Joe skipped off with the swag taken in by the gang on their last two jobs."

"That's so. But this here fella was caught an' sentenced before the gang broke up. That other rumor hadn't got started then. I tell yuh, hellin' around jest don't pay no more— not less'n yuh're king-pin of the gang."

Beside the desk Lawler stood, hands deep-thrust in his pockets, his green eyes brooding on the drawer's broken lock.

"I wonder," he said slowly, musingly, as though speaking his thoughts aloud, "if Captain Dan could ever have been mixed up with that gang?"

Pony George eyed him in surprise. "Don't see how. Shucks, he was out on the boundin' waves when that bunch was hellin' round this country. He never even showed here till five years after the gang broke up."

"I reckon it mebbe was this Justice gent which took them shots at him last night."

"Wal, it don't look like tuh me that that would connect Tranton with the gang."

"You remember," said Lawler, "that in one of his

notes, the killer mentions the unhealthy state of this climate for the 'old fishermen of Toyah Lake.' I'm bettin' large you were right about that meaning Rowdy Joe's gang."

"Wal, speakin' personal-like, the whole thing's a crazy jumble anyhow. Gosh, I jest thought up a new verse for m' Ballad of Kyote Cal—the mos' dangerous man since Billy the Kid. Listen at it:

"She was born in the night: by the night she lived,
But thet's aside o' the point
She lured the crowd of drink-crazed lads
Thet flocked tuh the Golden joint."

The dried-apple countenance of Pony George expanded in grinning pride. "Ain't that a honey!"

"It's an atrocity," said Lawler, and changed the subject "The gent that stole the fatal weapon out of this drawer is nobody's fool. An' he was long on guts. Remember, we were standin' right outside the door practically when he must have slipped in through one of these open windows.

"Then he broke open the desk drawer, closed it an' slid outa the office without us even suspectin' anyone had been in it. That's pretty slick. How long you figure you were outside the office before we went back in?"

"Not more than three minutes at the outside."

"That fellow's not only nervy, he's clever an' fast"

"Fast!" Pony George snorted. "That gent's tobacco juice an' lightnin'!

"And what in heck is that?"

"That's a expression what them waddies in the Florida cow-camps uses."

"Humph—first time I ever heard you'd been to Florida."

"I ain't. I got that outa a book," Pony George admitted. "There's nothin' like readin' tuh edjucate a fella's mind."

Lawler grinned faintly. "Link an' some of his cronies gave me a chase last night," he mentioned. "They quit after I dropped a couple of their broncs. Link got throwed into some prickly-pear. I expect he's feelin' a little wicked this mornin'."

"What brought that up?"

"I just seen him ridin' into town."

"Wal," grinned Pony George, "I'd sure admired tuh have seen him settin' on that cactus. Yuh wanta watch out fer that pelican—he's meaner'n gar soup! I've sorta got a notion his folks, on the mother's side, wore moccasins, if yuh git what I mean. Yuh wanta keep yore eye peeled sharp."

"I'm gonna grab Link with the goods, one of these days," Lawler muttered, "an' we'll take him out of circulation. What time's it gettin' to be, George? I expect we ought to be siftin' along towards the hall. When Obe Kringle holds a inquest he sure don't hanker to have gents droppin' in late."

With a disgusted snort, Pony George glared at his watch. "The damn' thing's stopped plumb complete—an' only last week I paid that dang Jesse James jeweler five good dollars tuh make it go! Cripes, if I'd known he wasn't gonna make it go longer'n a week, I'd of saved m'five bucks an' give him the watch!"

SEVEN
THE INQUEST

MUCH TOO NEAR the turbulent border marked by the Rio Grande was the sleepy cow town of Pecos for the death of a Mexican to be of any great public interest. Therefore, it was with something of surprise that Lawler and Pony George elbowed their way through the throng that overflowed the corridor outside the room set aside for the inquest on Toreva.

Seldom indeed did Obediah Kringle, the coroner, have opportunity to bask in the limelight of the public gaze. To Lawler and Pony George, as they squeezed into the tight-packed room, came the thought that Obe was determined to make the most of this occasion.

A large American flag had been tautly stretched across the dingy back wall. Before this emblem of sovereignty was placed a long bare table behind which, in solemn dignity, reposed the coroner's black-clad figure. An expression of stern righteousness, such as is sometimes worn by a new judge, sat heavily upon his unprepossessing countenance.

It seemed he was intent on surrounding the inquiry

with all the pomp his vanity could suggest. As Pony George told Lawler in a loud stage whisper, "If any fool had told him he could likely use a band, he'd 'a' had all the local talent right on hand, tuh furnish noise between the witnesses remarks!"

It was rumored that Obe *had* hinted strongly that his jury might later be treated to drinks at his expense. Anyhow, he seemed to have had scant trouble in securing the services of twelve good men and true.

Nor could he find reason, Lawler thought, to complain at the size of his prospective audience. The courtroom was jammed to the door and the corridor outside held a muttering throng.

At last Kringle arose to his awkward six-foot-four and rapped loudly on the table for attention. A secretary sat alert beside his elbow.

With the formalities finally disposed of the jury was charged that it was their bounden duty to determine, from the facts presented, whether Toreva's death was a felony, an accident, a suicide, or from natural causes. In the event that they found said death to be a felony they were to determine, if possible the identity of the guilty party.

"Your findings, gentlemen," intoned Kringle with ponderous austerity, "will be presented to the Circuit Court, together with such material evidence as may be in possession of the Sheriff's Office."

The tight-packed throng of lanky, wrinkled-faced men, belted and booted, hatted and unsmiling, overflowing the courtroom leaned forward in eager attention as Kringle handed Pony George a list of names. Expectant silence closed tight upon the perspiring assemblage.

The deputy cleared his throat. "Pony George Kasta!" he shouted, and grinned foolishly as he mounted the improvised platform of soap boxes and took the witness chair. The oath was administered in hushed solemnity.

The crowd about the doorway stirred and muttered as a burly man with tight-lipped mouth and bottle nose shoved his way inside. Lawler, seated at the coroner's table, could not suppress a start at sight of the newcomer here, although he had known the fellow was in town.

The crowd's astonishment rapidly changed to indignation.

"Link Holladay!" someone growled. "He's got a helluva nerve comin' in here!"

Holladay must have heard for his thin lips curled in a saturnine grin as he shoved a place for himself on one of the crowded benches.

Kringle rapped for silence. When the babble lulled he addressed Pony George, asking a few preliminary questions as to how long the witness had known the deceased. Having answered, the deputy was next requested to relate exactly, and in detail, the circumstances under which he had found the body.

"Wal," he drawled, having cleared his throat to insure attention, "it was like this, Obe—"

'That'll do!" snapped the coroner, red-faced. "When you've got occasion to address me, have the kindness to refer to me as 'Your Honor.'"

Pony George grinned. "All right. It was like this, Obe—ah, yore honor." He paused to let the crowd snicker their appreciation. "The sheriff told me tuh keep a eye on Toreva's house las' night—"

"What for?"

"Wal, yuh see, some gent had sent him a note demandin' several thousand bucks hush money, an' Toreva wasn't aimin' tuh pay it."

"Where is this note?" demanded Kringle. "I think this is a matter of public interest. We shall have it read."

Frowning, Lawler produced the note and handed it to the coroner who, adjusting his horn-rimmed spectacles, read aloud:

"Eight thousand bucks, left to-night by the flat rock out back of yore stable, will mebbe keep yore sinful past a secret for some months longer ... Justice."

Interest was breathless as Kringle's voice trailed off. Wiping his flushed face with a large moist handkerchief, he glared accusingly at Lawler. "Who's this Justice fella?"

"If I knew that," Lawler said, "I wouldn't be wastin' my time in here."

"Where'd the note come from?" Kringle demanded, ignoring the sheriff's sarcasm.

Pony George shrugged. "Toreva did not say."

"Then get on with your story, Kasta."

"Wal, like I was sayin' when yuh interrupted me, the sheriff gave me orders to keep m' eye out fer any suspicious gents I caught loiterin' around Toreva's house. I figgered the best way tuh do that was tuh make sure—"

"This court is not interested in what you figured. What did you *do?*"

"Huh? Wal, I set down on Toreva's front porch. With a double-barreled shotgun in m' lap."

Pony George scowled, scratched his head, put his hat back on and resumed: "Manuel sat out there with me fer a spell. But after a while he got tired talkin' to himself an' got up. Said he was goin' inside an' I told him no one was standin' on his shirt-tail. After he went in I sat there for a right smart spell. Presently, as the fella said in the book, comin' down the street I sees that long-eared gent from over near Barstow. The fella what gives out his name is Lester. Wal, I watched him until he got off his nag an' sashayed into Miguel Garcia's cantina."

"What happened after that?" Kringle impatiently prompted.

"Nothin' happened after that. I set some more. Finally down the street comes that lunger, Joe Reede. I kep' my eye on him till he got outa sight. Then I resumed m' settin'. No one else come by. Seems like everyone in town, pretty near, had gone to that carnival what's pitched its tents along the river.

"I set there chewin' fer about another hour. Then, all of a sudden-like, I hears a sorta *bump* from inside the house. Thinks I, what's that dang fool up to? Before that, yuh see, I'd heard 'im rattlin' papers an' walkin' around. But after the bumpin' sound I didn't hear nothin'. The place was quiet as the grave of Twotank-Amen. I tell yuh, it shore made me feel oneasy."

Intense interest stamped the faces of the audience. In a sort of breathless anticipation they awaited Pony George's next words.

"After a time I begun to get kind of suspicious. Anyone would not hearin' no sound. So I got up an' went inside tuh see what was up. I had told Manuel tuh leave the main room lights on, but when I got inside I found the place black as the inside of yore hat!

"I gotta admit it give me a kinda creepy feelin' in m'

stomach as I felt around for that lamp. It was still hot when I found it, provin' that it hadn't been out more'n a coupla minutes. Strikin' a match I lit it. Then I looked round. The shotgun damn near dropped from m'hand!"

Pausing impressively, Pony George glanced round at the bulging eyes that watched him tensely.

"What did you see? Quit wastin' time, George," growled Kringle testily. "You ain't the only witness on this program. Hurry up an' tell this jury what you seen."

"When I looked round I seen Toreva. He was settin' over in a corner, facin' kinda away from me an' sorta hunched-up, if yuh get what I mean. Thinks I, the darned fool's fallen—

"That is not the way in which to refer to the late lamented," snarled Kringle.

"Wal, yuh wanted me tuh tell 'em how I found the body, didn't yuh? Suff'rin' snakes! How can I if yuh keep buttin'in? I swore tuh tell the truth, the whole truth—"

"Go on!"

"Wal," Pony George returned the coroner's murderous glare, "mebbe yuh'd rather tell this yoreself," he growled. "Gosh knows yuh've heard it often enough tuh know 'er by heart!"

Coroner Obe Kringle almost choked, so wroth was he. 'Tell your story or get off that stand!"

"Wal, I forget where—oh! I seen Toreva. He was settin' over in a corner. Thinks I, Manuel's fell asleep. 'Manuel!' I yells, fit tuh wake the dead. But never a peep did he make. Jest kep' a-settin' there like a bump on a log.

"Wal, I tip-toes over tuh get a better look at 'im. An'

right there's where yuh coulda knocked me over with a zephyr. Gentlemen, don't talk! There was Toreva with a knife through his throat an' blood all over!"

The effect of the deputy's testimony upon the jury and the courtroom was electrical. Here, surely, said each man to his neighbor, was a sensation worthy of headlines in anybody's paper! Murder was murder—even in Pecos!

"Describe the fatal weapon, which we shall later mark 'People's exhibit A'."

"I dunno's I can," said Pony George uncomfortably. "It was jest plain everyday bone-handled skinnin' knife. But tied around its haft," he added brightly, "was a little chunk of paper."

"Indeed!" said Kringle as the crowd leaned forward expectantly. "Describe this piece of paper—better still, let me see it."

Lawler handed the smeared note to the coroner. Kringle examined it closely, passed it round among the jury, then read aloud: "Tally two for Justice."

Bewilderment stamped the faces of his listeners. He turned to Pony George. "Just what does this mean?"

"Wal, I'll tell you, Obe—last week, after that fella Doak was killed, it seems like you found a note in his pocket what said somethin' about the climate here not bein' over-healthy for the fishermen of Toyah Lake. That note, like this 'un, yuh remember, was signed by that fella 'Justice.' It's the opinion of the Sheriff's office that this fella killed both Doak an' Toreva."

Excitement claimed the courtroom. Kringle rapped for order. "You may step down from the stand, George. Call the next witness."

"What's the use? Yuh got yore—"

"Call the next witness!"

"Doctor Obediah Kringle, sawbones an' coroner, will now be right pleased tuh take the stand," grunted Pony George and, grinning, slid his chunky form into a chair beside the sheriff.

"Cut out the funny stuff, George," growled Lawler in an undertone. "This ain't the place or occasion for such antics."

With great solemnity Kringle mounted the soap box platform, administered and took the oath, perched himself gingerly upon the extreme edge of the witness chair and surveyed the jury gravely.

"What's he figgerin' tuh do?" asked the irrepressible deputy. "Gonna give 'em a blessin' or bawl 'em out?"

A snicker ran through the nearby spectators. Kringle flushed. "Silence, there, or I'll clear this room!" Then in a graveyard voice he announced:

"Having performed an autopsy on the body of the late deceased, I found him to have a fractured parietal bone and a penetrating stab wound in the neck. The latter was undoubtedly the cause of death."

Lawler, interested, put a question. "Was the fracture sustained recently?"

"Yes. Within one minute of his death."

"You mean some gent struck him before he was stabbed?"

"It is my theory that someone struck him, yes. With a blunt and, evidently, pliable instrument."

"No sign of the skin havin' been broken?"

"Certainly not. There was a bruise—nothing more."

"Would you say the bruise an' fracture could have been caused by a blackjack?"

"Not only could have been, but was. I," Kringle's

voice ill-suppressed the sense of triumph which he felt, "have the weapon in my possession."

* * *

TO SAY that Lawler was startled would be to understate the truth. He was amazed. He looked accusingly at Pony George. George licked his lips and focused his incredulous glance upon the coroner who was relinquishing the witness chair.

"Say that again!" growled Pony George.

"I said that the blackjack's in my possession."

"Where'd yuh get it?"

"Well," Kringle paused, "I was not satisfied with what you had originally told me about finding Toreva. I thought," he said mockingly, "that it was quite possible you might have overlooked some pertinent bit of evidence in searching Toreva's house after finding the body. I was confirmed in my suspicions—"

Pony George jumped to his feet. "Yore *what!*" he snarled.

"Well, perhaps I should have said 'my convictions,'" amended Kringle. "I was confirmed in my convictions when I found, during the autopsy, that Toreva had recently sustained a fracture of the parietal bone. So I went over the house thoroughly, after persuading the old woman who took care of the place that I was not going to steal anything."

"When was this?" asked Lawler.

"Early this morning. I," his chest expanded pridefully, "went over the room carefully. I found the blackjack by a rear window where it had evidently fallen from the killer's pocket as he made his getaway."

"I'd like to have it produced in evidence." Lawler's tone was grim.

"We will mark it 'Exhibit B,'" smiled Kringle broadly. Thrusting a hand inside his coat he produced the blackjack and passed it around among the jurors. The faces of those who examined it seemed to freeze.

"Mr. Foreman of the Jury," spoke Kringle suavely, "will you be so kind as to read the words burned into the leather of exhibit B?"

The foreman rose. Clearing his throat several times as though nervous, he announced, "The name on this thing is 'Link Holladay.'"

The sudden hush that gripped the room was broken by a curse as Holladay surged to his feet. "So that's why yuh sent for me to be here, is it? You damn sidewinder! That's a lie! I never owned a blackjack in my life!"

"The foreman licked his lips uneasily. He shrank back among his fellows.

"A lie?" mocked Kringle. "Well, I only know that your name is burned on it. Seems odd anyone else would put your name on their property. Here, you can look for yourself—"

"Oh, no, he can't," snapped Lawler quickly. "I'll take charge of that blackjack, Kringle. Hand it here."

As the coroner passed it over Holladay snarled:

"By Gawd, it's a dirty frame-up! You can't hang this murder on me, Lawler! You know damn well I wasn't in town! You saw me—"

"Yeah. I saw you, all right. But there was nothin' to keep you from ridin' to town an' murderin' Toreva after I left you."

"You know I didn't have no hoss"

"Some of your friends had horses," Lawler pointed

out. "I'm afraid, my friend, I shall be compelled to place you under lock an' key—"

"Like hell you will!" Holladay's hand dived for his hip where swung the butt of a holstered .45—though it was a violation of the law to carry arms inside town limits. But Holladay's hand never reached his gun. Men grabbed at him from all sides, pinioned his arms and legs and held him fast. His face was a twisted snarl as he cursed them with lurid fury.

* * *

AFTER HOLLADAY HAD BEEN ESCORTED to the jail, disarmed and placed in a cell (charged, for convenience, with unlawfully carrying weapons), the inquest upon the violent death of Manuel Toreva was continued.

Lester, the man who had drifted into the country and had built a shack near Barstow and who had a strange habit of spending most of his time in Pecos, was the last witness called to the stand.

Lester, big-eared, tall and powerfully-built, with smoldering dark eyes in a high-boned face, was sworn in swiftly. After the preliminary questions, Kringle asked:

"Mr. Lester, will you kindly explain to the gentlemen of this jury what you saw last night as you were about to leave this town for home?"

"Sure," grinned Lester. "I had jest left Garcia's cantina an' was forkin' my bronc down the street back of Toreva's place, sorta figgerin' mebbe I'd oughta head for home, when I seen a fella slip through Toreva's back gate an' climb aboard a hoss that was standin' on grounded reins."

"Mr. Lester, I'd like to have you tell us what in your estimation, that man was."

"Wal, it was pretty dark, yuh understand. It had been tolerable cloudy all evenin'—probably rained someplace, I guess. Anyhow, it was considerable dark an' so I ain't right sure, not gettin' a look at the fella's pan. But I think the gent what came through Toreva's back gate was that Holladay jasper which yuh jest lugged off to jail."

After the buzz of excitement had somewhat abated, Kringle asked: "How do you make that out. I mean, if it was dark and you couldn't see his face what makes you think it was Holladay?"

"I could see he was a big hombre, heavy-set an' all. I dunno, but I sorta got the impression that it was Holladay somehow. When he seen me, he climbed aboard his bronc an' made dust. I got sorta suspicious then. Instead of goin' home, I got myself a room at the Orient an' stayed over."

"Did you know that murder had been committed?"

"Nope. I didn't know as anythin' had been com— well, whatever yuh called it. I expect I was jest curious. That fella lit out in such a hurry .. ."

"All right, you may leave the stand." Kringle shot a glance at the jury. "Do any of you gents want to ask questions of any of the witnesses?"

The jury shook their heads.

"Very well, then, gentlemen," Kringle removed his spectacles, carefully wiped their lenses and returned them to his nose. "We've heard a number of interesting things this morning and, ah—by the way, Sheriff. I think the jury had better be shown the fatal weapon. I am referring to the knife with which Manuel Toreva was murdered."

Lawler frowned. "I'm sorry, Kringle, but I can't oblige. Pony George locked the knife in my desk last night. But someone broke the lock and well, the thing has vanished."

"What is this you're trying to tell me?"

"The knife," said Lawler grimly, "is gone."

It was several noisy moments before the coroner could make himself heard. "Silence!" he hammered furiously on the table. "Shut up, damn it!"

And when the crowd had quieted—

"That's criminal negligence—"

But Lawler stopped him. "I've heard all I care to on the subject. I'm accountable for the knife—not you. Get on with your talk."

Ironing out his scowl, Kringle again faced the jury. "We have heard some interesting things this morning, gentlemen. Some *very* interesting things," he added nastily. "There is no use in dragging this inquest along further. Every important bit of information in our possession has been divulged. You may withdraw to determine your verdict—"

"Not necessary," muttered the foreman, and cleared his throat. With a glance at his fellow jurymen, he said nervously:

"We bring in a verdict of murder at the hands of some person, or persons, unknown—but we think it was committed by the fella what signs himself 'Justice.'"

EIGHT
"MURDER'S NEVER OUTLAWED!"

LAWLER and his deputy left the courtroom with the stream of shoving, pushing, grunting men flowing from its opened door at the close of Kringle's inquest. Being close to the noon hour, at which time Pony George had become accustomed to "feeding his face," the chunky deputy could not restrain a number of longing glances from straying in the direction of a sign which read: Lone Star Grub Emporium. Glances, it might be added, which Lawler pointedly ignored.

"Kringle run a fast one on us," the sheriff said coldly, "when he produced that blackjack in evidence."

"Cripes! These amateurs!" Pony George growled. "I don't know anything which gives me a bigger pain."

"When amateurs discover more than a paid professional, it's high time prof grabbed a hold on himself." Lawler's tones grew colder with every sentence uttered.

Pony George shot him a covert glance. In the sheriff's eye he detected a glint that was hinting large toward imminent trouble. He tugged his drooping yellow moustache nervously.

"Suff'rin' snakes!" he grumbled. "All yuh tol' me tuh do was tuh keep a eye on Toreva's house. I done 'er. Then findin' him dead with a knife in his crop it never struck me that I'd ort tuh gone over the carpet with a magnifyin' glass an' a fine-tooth comb! Nor I didn't figger I was supposed tuh pore plaster all over the place takin' casts of imaginary footprints like them Hollywood jaspers do in all their cock-eyed pitchers! Hell's bells—I ain't no Spurlock Holmes!"

"You sure told the truth that time," Lawler retorted drily.

"Wal, good sakes! How'd I know the fool Mex went an' got his prital bone cracked? Hell, I never knowed a Mex had that kinduva bone! What kinda thing is it, anyway?"

"It's a bone in the side of most people's heads. But that ain't what I'm referrin' to. You oughta been able to spot that blackjack."

"That's right—rub it in, rub it in! By cripes, I got a notion tuh kick that dang coroner halfway tuh El Paso! Why can't he mind his own business? It sure is boomin' these days!"

Hands thrust deep within his pockets, Red Lawler was standing inattentive by his desk, his brooding eyes fixed unseeingly upon the broken lock of the pilfered drawer.

"Funny about Holladay showin' up. Wonder if Kringle *did* send for him? Can't see how he'd get hold of him. Link's strong on driftin' . . ." Musingly Lawler added. " 'Death by person, or persons, unknown . . .'"

Pony George growled, "Yeah—the bunch of ol' women! They was scared plumb stiff of Link. Any fool could see it. They'd no more thought of accusin' him of that murder than of slashin' their own throats!"

"I expect they did right. I ain't at all sure Link's our man. No doubt about him twirlin' a wide loop, though. I'll be gettin' him for that, one of these days. But murder—"

"Wal," Pony George chipped in, "he shore gave you one murderous look when yuh told him yuh was goin' to slap 'im in jail!"

"But if Link was innocent, you can't hardly blame him for bein' a bit proddy."

"Yeah," said Pony George with fine sarcasm. "*If* he's innocent!"

"Well, let's take a look at him."

When Lawler and his deputy were seen by Link Holladay to be standing outside the door to his cell, the rustler's thin lips twisted into an ugly sneer.

"You fellas got yore cinches crossed," he jeered "This ain't visitin' day at the zoo. I'll thank yuh to get the hell outa here an' leave me a little privacy."

"Why, Link!" Pony George said reprovingly. "We was figgerin' tuh bring yuh some posies an' a book of psalms— rest an' meditation bein' good fer the soul."

When Pony George had gone the sheriff sat listlessly watching a large horse-fly washing its face in the sweat beading the water-cooler's exterior.

"You ain't funny," snarled Holladay, scowling. "An' I'll take pleasure in wipin' that grin off yore homely mug soon's I get outa here."

"I don't know's yuh're goin' to get out, Link. It all depends—"

"Yes," said Lawler. "Suppose you open up an' treat us to a heart-to-heart talk."

"I got nothin' tuh say," Holladay growled. "You know as well as I do, Red Lawler, that I didn't stab that greaser. You an' me was exchangin' rifle shots out on the range last night."

"That's so. But it is barely possible that you beat me to town. An' if you did, I reckon you had time enough to murder poor Manuel an' make your getaway by that back gate ..."

"What the hell you talkin' about? I don't know nothin' about no back gate, an' you can't make out I do."

"We don't have tuh make it out," chuckled Pony George. "That big-eared gent from Barstow done that after we dragged you off tuh jail. Lester said he saw you comin' out Toreva's back gate. An' the time checks up slick as a whistle."

"It's a damn frame-up!" bellowed Holladay. "I never done it!" His ugly chin shot forward belligerently, "When I get outa here I'm shore gonna make somebody hard tuh catch!"

"Then I reckon we'll keep you right where you are, for a spell," said Lawler, softly. "I don't see no sense in takin' unnecessary chances with gents of your antecedents. You're a tough egg, Link, an' this rest will do you good."

Back in the Sheriff's office, Pony George said:

"That fella's bad medicine, Red. If we let him loose another murder would foller sure as summer follers spring!"

"There's one thing sure," he muttered morosely. "If I let Holladay loose a couple gents are goin' to find themselves up against a Texas cyclone—an' I don't mean me an' Pony George!"

Presently his thoughts turned as ever to Sara Tranton. What lay behind her incomprehensible action in breaking off their engagement? The whole business seemed alien to her nature as he knew it. At first he had been too hurt and angry to think clearly on the subject. But now that his red-headed nature had had time to cool, he found himself unable to believe she no longer cared for him.

"I'll be jiggered if *I* can figure it out!" he exclaimed. "It's sure got me fightin' my hat!"

The most logical explanation he could think of was that Sara had told her father of their engagement and he, disapproving, had bidden her break it off. But why? He and the Captain had always got along handsomely.

Yet, good as he knew Dan Tranton to be to his only daughter, it did not seem like her to throw down the man she loved simply to please his idle whim of selfish desire to keep her to himself.

In the language of the West Texas cow country, Sara Tranton was a girl of backbone. She had, as Red well knew, qualities of grit and loyalty far beyond the ordinary. Too, she had a bulldog tenacity—if she loved a man, he thought, she'd stick to him come hell or high-water.

The least she could have done would have been to tell him fairly that her father disapproved and to have suggested that they wait until somehow they should win him to their side.

But no! She had termed their engagement "Silly!"

With a baffled snort Red Lawler temporarily gave up trying to solve the problem of her strange behavior. He could discern neither head nor tail to the puzzle, and felt that if he wrestled longer with it in his present mood he would surely do something downright desperate.

A clump of boots and the jingle of dragging spur chains announced the return of Pony George. Entering the office, the chunky deputy tossed his hat on the Sheriff's desk. Drawing up a chair beside the water-cooler, he terminated the fastidious ablutions of the large horse-fly bathing languorously upon its sweat-beaded surface.

"Hotter'n election day in a hornet's nest," he growled, mopping his face with his neckerchief. "Red, this here's the thirstiest country I ever seen."

"I expect you ain't never been to Gila Bend," said Lawler, grinning. "Nor Yuma. Nor yet Needles. Ah, Needles—there's a hot place for you. It's got hell backed off the map. Averages round about a hundred an' thirty-six in the daytime an' at night she sweats you down like a tallow candle. Folks livin' there does all their cookin' out in the sand of their front door-yards. An' has to feed their chickens cracked ice to keep 'em from layin' hard-boiled eggs!"

Pony George sniffed. "Yeah? Wal, Pecos has got all the heat I ever wanta see. An' I don't like aiggs nohow. Speakin' of aiggs, Red, reminds me of a new verse I've writ—

> "*The rest o' the gals thet danced in the*
> *Flame,*
> *Was ornery, too, I opine—*
> *But the boys from the range that haunted*
> *the town,*
> *Came mostly with Lou fer to jine.*

"An' gosh, thet gives me a idee for another! Listen at this, fella:

> "Now Cal was right jealous—By Gawd,
>   but he was!
> An' he wanted young Lou fer his own;
> So he warned off the boys thet came in
>   from the range,
> An' he put ev'ry meddler 'neath stone!

"Gosh—ain't that a pistol!"

"Couldn't say. I'm not an authority on firearms."

"Wal, for the love of Mike! Who's talkin' about firearms? I ast yuh ain't that highferlootin' poetry."

"Oh—the poetry. Is that what it was?" Lawler, about to duck the paperweight Pony George was reaching for, suddenly tensed. "Shh!"

The corridor outside rang to the clump of spurred boots. Lawler shot a hurried glance through the window. "Strange horse outside. Reckon we're gettin' company."

There was one stranger in the county whom neither the sheriff or his deputy had yet seen. There was good reason for the fact; this stranger was something of a recluse, was admittedly shy of strange faces and did most of his travelling by night. Furthermore, so far he had been steering a careful course that avoided the county seat.

He was a little man with sharp eyes that glanced uneasily from face to face. His bat-wing chaps had seen much wear, his cotton shirt was dusty and patched in many places. His hat was a thing too disreputable to attract more than a passing glance from a range tramp.

He entered the office with a sidling motion and when he paused before Lawler's desk, stood shuffling his feet nervously.

"Restless as a wet hen," Pony George commented *sotto voce.*

"This the sheriff's office?" the stranger's voice was a husky squeak.

"Nope," Pony George spoke promptly. "This here's the headquarters for the Knights of Rest. Light down, comrade, an' rest yore saddle. Gotcha dues paid up?"

The dusty stranger blinked, looked suspiciously from Pony George to the sheriff, whose star was plain to be seen. "I—I thought," he began hesitantly, when Pony George interrupted with—

"'Tain't noways necessary in this lodge, pardner. The Supreme Sea-Gull takes care o' that."

"What's on your mind, stranger?" Lawler cut short his deputy's fun.

"Why—er—nothin' much, I reckon," the man essayed a nervous smile. "Uh—I wonder could you gents tell a driftin' pilgrim how to get to Dan Tranton's place? I—I'm kinda strange to this part of the country."

"An' how!" agreed Pony George. "I never seen anythin' like yuh in all my horned days! Where'd yuh hail from?"

"Why, er—ah—I jest sort of drifted over from east of here."

"That's coverin' a heap of territory, pilgrim," Pony George eyed the little stranger suspiciously. "I reckon yuh better keep on driftin'. They tell me the climate's somethin' elegant over in Mexico. Ever been there? . . . Wal, I suggest yuh try 'er out."

"But—uh—you see, I'd sort of like to visit a spell

with Tranton. Him an' me's ol' buddies. We've et from the same tin plate. Ain't his spread called the Box Bar T?"

Lawler, looking the stranger over, had a feeling that the peculiar pale blue of his eyes might be common to great strategists and notorious killers. "Yes," he answered, "Tranton runs the Box Bar T. You say you know the Captain?"

"Uh—I believe I used to know him," the stranger cautiously replied.

Lawler exchanged swift glances with Pony George. There was something about this self-confessed drifter.

"S'pose yuh describe this here Tranton fer us," Pony George suggested.

The stranger shifted his pale eyes uneasily. "Why, he's a sort of tall, rangy, black-haired gent—"

"I expect," drawled Lawler, cutting in, "you've got the wrong Tranton. Captain Dan's a white-headed gent an' averages some considerable round the waist."

"It might be him. I ain't seen him in fourteen-fifteen years. I been figurin' mebbe he'd give me some kind of a ridin' job. How do I get out there?"

"Not so fast, fella," Lawler said. "There's been a powerful lot too many strangers floatin' round this county durin' the last coupla months. From now on I'm aimin' to look up their pedigrees before I put out the welcome mat. What did you say your name was?"

"I didn't say," grinned the man ingratiatingly. "But it's Smith."

"Smith what?"

"Smith's the last name. First name's Max."

"Max Smith, eh? Do you know anyone else round this neck of the timber?"

"Friend of mine named Doak drifted over this way a spell back ..."

"Well you can cross him off your callin' list. His mark's been taken off the board."

"Yuh mean to say he's—he's dead?"

"That's right. He was rubbed out a couple weeks ago. Know anyone else?"

The stranger swallowed in what seemed to be a painful manner, ran a dirty finger round the inside of his dirty collar. "I know a fella what runs a place known as the Raego spread —gent named Joe Reede. Calls his place the Lazy R, I heard."

"You heard right," Lawler said, and thrust out his hand. "Your connection's sound, Smith. I'm glad to meet up with you. My name's Lawler—I'm sheriff. This here's my deputy, Pony George Kasta."

"Glad tuh make you gents' acquaintance," said Smith shaking hands.

Lawler did not like the nervous grin on this stranger's face, but he kept the fact to himself. "You get to the Box Bar T," he directed, "by followin' that trail down there—see? The one goin' over that ridge yonder," Lawler pointed out the window and the stranger bobbed his head.

A moment later, with hurried thanks, the man calling himself Max Smith took his departure.

Soon as he was out of the door Pony George jumped from his chair, spun the combination of the sheriff's safe and swung open its thick steel door. Reaching in he dragged forth a great pile of miscellaneous papers, yellow, tattered with age— reward notices.

Lawler grinned knowingly as Pony George pawed

through the dusty pile. "I expect you noticed Smith's left hand. Unusual to see a gent with the index finger missin'. Probably don't mean anything, though."

'The heck it don't," growled Pony George with fine disregard for grammar. "Three fingers an' a thumb on the left hand—I seen a notice in this bunch a while back that read almost word for word like that."

"So you been lookin' through those flyers, have you? Gettin' uncommon industrious. How far back they go?"

"Far enough. There's references to the Toyah Lake bunch, But no pitchers. I reckon them birds wasn't what yuh'd call 'partial' tuh havin' their mugs plastered round the country. Stage an' bank robbin's *one* perfession what can't see any advantage in advertisin'."

Lawler nodded. "When you find that stuff, put it where we can get our hands on it real quick. No tellin' when we may be needin' it."

Pony George gave him a curious look. "Where you goin'?"

"Right now I'm goin' to grab a bite to eat—if there's anything left. If I ain't back here in a reasonable amount of time, you can figure I've gone out to Box Bar T. I'm admittin' to a little curiosity about that Smith jigger. If Captain Dan knows him that'll mean one thing, mebbe. If he don't, it'll mebbe mean somethin' else again."

"Can't yuh talk American?" Pony George complained.

Lawler grinned. "It's just possible," he said, "that this Smith hombre is the gent that took those shots at Dan last night."

"You puttin' on?"

Lawler's grin grew broader. But he did not answer his deputy's question. Instead he said, "My stomach's tellin' me to get a move on. Crimes like stage an' bank robbery make interestin' study for earnest deputies. George, so you keep right on lookin' up them things. Not that they're apt to do us any great amount of good. Such crimes are forgiven after a period of years—'outlawed' is the term."

"Yeah?" grunted Pony George. "Well, murder's never outlawed! An' the paper I'm lookin' for is headed 'Murder!'"

NINE
CONCERNING SMITH

WHEN LAWLER LEFT the office the deputy dropped his stack of musty papers and clumped to the door. For some while he stood there peering out. He watched the sheriff stride down the street and enter the stable where he kept his horse. A few moments later he saw Lawler emerge atop his big roan gelding.

Lawler was a good horseman and sat the saddle with an easy grace. His big shoulders seemed to slouch a little forward and there was, the deputy thought, an unaccustomed bleakness to face.

For some moments after Lawler had swung his mount into the trail leading to the Box Bar T, Pony George stood watching by the doorway. Shoving back his hat to scratch his head, he muttered, "Plumb forgot tuh eat his dinner first. Must be right anxious tuh get out there,"

Finally he returned to his task, but the lackadaisical manner in which he thumbed through the faded notices proved that his mind was not on the work. When, eventually, he found the flyers for which he had been searching, he hardly glanced at them. Thrusting them carelessly into his shirt pocket, he got out his pad of paper, his stub of pencil and prepared to engage in the serious and competitive business of manufacturing poetry.

But preparation and actual achievement, he had often found, were two decidedly different things. There had been occasions, he recalled, when he had sat for hours, pencil in hand and pad on knee, without the production of a single word. The present bade fair to be such an occasion.

He wet the pencil on his tongue, screwed his dried-apple countenance into one vast array of deep-etched wrinkles, and wet the pencil-point again. But all to no avail. The pad's top sheet remained a virgin white.

Suddenly, then, with neither preliminary tremor nor other warning, the pencil raced across the pad, leaving in its wake a series of ungainly scrawls resembling hen tracks which— when deciphered—would have formed a string of words in this rotation:

> *"One night at the Flame, Cal an'*
> *his dame*
> *Was havin' a damn mean row—"*

It was many minutes before Pony George, licking his pencil frequently, was able to add:

> *"When in through the door stepped a tall*
> *slim gent,*
> *With his hat pulled low on his brow."*

The large horsefly was again at its ablutions on the

water-cooler. Cocking an eye in its direction, Pony George said in a voice that was tremulous:

"Gosh! Ain't that a corker!"

But the horsefly only buzzed away.

* * *

IT WAS five o'clock that afternoon when, going to the door at the sound of approaching hoofbeats, the manufacturing poet saw Lawler riding up the street leading an extra horse. Stuffing pencil and pad hurriedly into his hip pocket, Pony George ran a gnarled hand over his drooping straw-colored moustache and muttered:

"Sure looks like Red wa'n't ast tuh stay an' eat."

As his young boss drew closer the puckered eyes in George's dried-apple face drew wide with startled interest. When Lawler swung from the big roan gelding and tethered both horses to the rack before the courthouse the chunky deputy remained, still staring, in the doorway.

Mounting the steps Lawler pushed him protesting down the corridor and into the office. Outside the sun still shone bright and the air was hot and dust-filled, yet Lawler insisted on closing the door.

"Did you locate them notices, George?"

"Sure— 'course I did," Pony George pulled the papers from his shirt and thrust them out. There were three, and Lawler read them with a scowl. They were all alike:

WANTED FOR MURDER

$3,000—Dead or alive

Max Smith, alias Four-Finger Durr. Five feet two.
Weighs about 120 pounds. Brown hair and small blue
eyes. Smooth-shaven usually. Eyes shifty. Has old bullet
wound in right shoulder, another in left thigh.
Occupation, cowhand. Uses one gun—*fast*. Carries
.30-.30 rifle in saddle scabbard. Has shy, nervous
manner but will fight if cornered. Known to be a
member of Toyah Lake gang. Officers warned to be
careful. Durr has missing index finger on left hand.

"That's the fella," he said, as he finished reading.

"Where'd yuh get his hoss, Red?"

"You know the trail that goes out past the Box Bar
T? You remember that little tree-clad hill with the
junipers 'bout four miles from Captain Dan's—the
place where Link an' me exchanged shots last night? . . .
Well, right along this side the hill I found Durr's horse
standin' tied to a cactus."

"Didn't get tuh go tuh Tranton's then? Did yuh find
Durr's body?"

"What give you the idea it was there to be
found?"

"Wal, I jest sort of opined it was by the look on yore
face. Did yuh find it?"

"Yeah—beside the horse. He was sprawled on the
trail, face down."

"Dead, eh?"

"Yeah. Dead. There was a bullet hole between his
eyes an' powder marks on his face. He must been in the
saddle talkin' with the killer, not thinkin' to be bumped
off. No sign of a struggle. Killer must have drew an'

fired while Durr was palaverin'. I seen the tracks of the killer's horse."

"Foller 'em?"

"Naturally. Followed 'em far's I could—which wasn't far. Lost 'em in a maze of other tracks 'bout a mile from town. Unless he's done some tall an' handsome circlin', that killer's in Pecos right this minute. Prob'ly laughin' up his sleeve."

Pony George, well aware of Lawler's repute as a trailer of no mean skill, looked the astonishment he felt. More than once it had been said that Lawler was one gent who could follow a trail to hell, and back. He had often been likened to a wolfhound; keen, tireless, unshakable as Death itself.

Yet George had just listened to him admit that this mysterious killer had eluded him, had gotten clean away. Small wonder Pony George pursed his lips in a soundless whistle. "Where's the body?"

"I packed it back to town an' left it with Kringle."

"Must be gettin' plumb absent-minded," growled the deputy. "Yuh forgettin' thet blackjack episode? Hell! that fella's apt tuh perduce Durr's pedigree by starin' at his fingernails, an' haul his paw outa Durr's hat with a fistful of loot from the Toyah Lake days!"

"Not hardly. I've been through Durr's clothes pretty careful. This here," said Lawler softly, flicking a scrap of yellow paper across the desk, "was buttoned on his shirt. We won't tell Kringle."

Gingerly Pony George picked up the paper and spread it out. "Three down—some more to go!" This note, like the ones preceding it, was signed "Justice."

"Reckon he figgered 'twould be a good idee tuh keep Durr away from Cap'n Dan. But I can't see why less'n he thought Durr might have somethin' tuh spill an' be aimin' tuh do so."

"I got no idea what he thought," Lawler admitted. "Far as I'm concerned, the whole affair's a complete muddle. Fact is, George, I ain't even sure Durr was goin' to the Box Bar T."

"Wal, cripes! He was on his way, wa'n't he?"

Lawler's voice was grim. "That don't signify."

"But sufferin' snakes—all that talk! He *said* he was goin' out there. Said him an' the Cap'n was ol' bunkies, or some-thin' tuh that effect."

"Smoke screen," Lawler opined, succinctly. "Cam-ouflage —hot air."

"Wal then, he sure went to a powerful lot o' trouble, that's all I gotta say."

"Of course," Lawler admitted, "Durr *may* actually have been headin' for Tranton's."

"But yuh jest said—"

"Skip it! I ain't in no mood to argue, George. My head aches like a trip-hammer."

"Wal, if he *was* goin' out there tuh see the Cap'n, do yuh reckon mebbe he was thinkin' of blackmail?"

"It's possible. If Durr really knew the bunch he claimed he knew, it might be said to indicate that all of 'em had once belonged to the Toyah Lake outfit. I think, however, it might mean a lot of other things. Durr may have been lyin'. Durr may have known one of those gents. If so, does it seem logical he would let it be known he was aimin' to visit him?"

"Wal, good gosh! After all that gassin' I'm damned if I know what we was palaverin' about in the first place!" Pony George growled disgustedly. "Let's change the subject— wanta hear my latest verse?"

"What are you talkin' about?"

"My ballad of Kyote Cal. M' latest verse is a honey. Wanta hear it?"

"No—I got too many other things to think about right now. By the way, where'd you borrow the tune?"

"Borry? Why, hell! I made it up. Do yuh like it?"

" 'Bout as well as I like the words, I guess."

Pony George sniffed. "Trouble is with you, yuh ain't got no ear for music."

"I can hear *music*, all right," Lawler said, and switched the subject. "Look who's comin' up the walk. That Reede gent Now let me do the talkin', George. I think this bird's smelled trouble."

TEN
"HE'S GONNA KILL US ALL!"

BOTH LAWMEN TURNED toward the door as booted feet came clumping down the corridor. Abruptly the door flung open.

"My, my, my!" clucked Pony George. "Ain't yuh never learned tuh knock?"

A tall gangling man in wrinkled black clothes that hung to his bony frame like the cast-off garments of a scarecrow stood in the open doorway. He turned a wrinkled face to Pony George—a face that was chalky white in a land where men were bronzed.

"Howdy, Deputy. How you feelin'?"

"Finer'n a hummin-bird's pin-feathers! How's yoreself?"

"I have been better," Reede admitted. He turned to Lawler. "That right what I heard about some stranger gettin' rubbed out?"

"What did you hear?"

"I heard some fella got snuffed out over near Tranton's. That right?" And at the sheriff's nod, "Looks kinda bad for Tranton, I'd say."

"Does it?" Lawler eyed the consumptive coldly. "I don't expect I'd go so far as to say that. To my mind it looks much worse for a couple other gents I could name. Guess you been talkin' to them bar-room loafers that saw me packin' the stranger in. By the way, Reede," he added as an apparent afterthought, "gent gave his name as Smith—Max Smith. Stopped in here a while this noon. Said he was a friend of yours."

Reede shrugged and took the seat by the water-cooler. "Lotsa gents claim they're friends of mine. I can't think of any Smith. What sort of a lookin' jasper was he?"

Lawler's eyes were inscrutable as he leaned forward on his desk and stared at Reede. Then casually he took some papers from his pocket, glanced at them and said,

"Well, Max Smith was five feet two, weighed one-twenty, he had light brown hair an' pale, shifty blue eyes. He was togged out in things so run down a range tramp woulda blushed to be seen dead in." Looking up, Lawler's jade-green glance beat hard against Reede's face.

Reede said, "I don't recognize that description. Is it official?"

"Had any experience with such things?"

Reede's lips twisted in a cold smile. "Hell, a man don't need experience to know a reward notice when he sees it! So Smith was a bad 'un, eh?"

"I'm thinkin' you knew him better'n me. What did you think of him?"

But Reede only smiled. "I never met the gent. By the way," he broke off with a hacking cough that shook his bony form from heels to head. When the paroxysm passed he wiped his colorless lips. "I hear ol' Cap'n Dan was shot at in his office las' night."

"For a man who don't get around much, you certainly hear a lot. Where'd you get that information?"

Reede grinned and a cold glitter came into his eyes like sun on windswept ice. "A little bird whispered it in my ear."

"By G—" Lawler broke off as the telephone rang. Scooping up the receiver he growled, "Sheriff Lawler speaking . . .Oh! Long Distance, eh? All right, put 'em on! . . . Huh? Who? . . . Lester? . . . When? . . . Okay, Ed. Keep your eyes skinned."

"What's up?" demanded Pony George when Lawler faced them. "Quit lookin' like yo' in a trance an'—" he paused as Lawler grabbed a sheet of paper and hastily began scribbling.

Looking up, Lawler made a visible effort to pull himself together. "Hustle this down to the telegraph office," he said, handing the paper to Pony George, "an' see that it gets off right away. Tell the operator to bring the answer here. If I ain't here, tell him to leave it on my desk. Now step on it! I'll tell you about that phone call soon's you get back."

Lawler's face was nearly pale as that of Reede! About his mouth were new, pinched lines. In his eyes was a strangely troubled light. Moisture glistened on his upper lip and forehead.

Pony George, for once, did not stop to argue. As he left there was a tiny sharp burst of sound outside the open window —such a sound as might be made by a snapping twig beneath a booted foot.

Lawler sprang to the window, startled. But though he thrust his head and shoulders out he saw nothing unusual. No man was in sight nor did hear any sound that resembled a hurried retreat.

"Reckon I'm developin' a case of nerves," he grunted, pulling in his head.

Reede did not smile. He stared at Lawler straightly; appraisingly, one might have said. Eyes jade-green and eyes of faded blue locked and neither pair wavered. It was like a duel.

On a shelf a battered clock ticked off the dragging minutes. Presently Pony George returned, dropped perspiring into the chair behind the desk; the chair Lawler had vacated. "Wal," he puffed, "let's hear about that long-distance phone call. I been fair a-quiver with curiosity."

"From Ed Lamb, at Barstow," Lawler said. "Big-Ear Lester was just found dead outside his shack—been dead for several hours, Ed says. He'd been stabbed in the back an' had one of them 'Justice' notes in his chaps pocket."

"Big—Ear—Lester!" the whispered words crept through the twisted lips of Reede's livid face. Abruptly, then, an hysterical laugh spread wide his mouth and showed his pointed teeth. "Lester!" he echoed. "Doak—Tranton—Durr—Lester! Why the crazy coot's gone batty! He's tryin' to kill us all!" and, with a final snarling oath, he lunged from the office, broke into a headlong run when he hit the street.

Lawler stared at Pony George. Pony George stared back.

ELEVEN
KRINGLE SHOWS HIS TEETH

"DAFFY AS A GOPHER!" said Pony George with conviction.

"I ain't so sure about that. There's somethin'—"

Leaving the sentence unfinished, Lawler began to pace the office with hands deep-thrust in his pockets, shoulders hunched a little forward and a fierce look of determined concentration in his brooding eyes.

"If he ain't plumb batty," sniffed Pony George, getting out his pipe, "then he's sure doin' one powerful lot of puttin' on." He tinkered with his pipe for a number of moments in the hope that Lawler would toss over his sack of Durham. But Lawler was too enwrapped in his thoughts. With a grunt the deputy pulled out his own.

Then Lawler spoke. "I've been thinkin' that mebbe Big-Ear Lester was this 'Justice' fella. Now Reede's gone and smashed that theory plumb to splinters. 'He's tryin' to kill us all!' Them's the words he used. An' Lester's killed already so that leaves him out of our future calculations."

"So what?" growled Pony George. "Jest bein' dead don't prove he ain't the Pecos Killer. One of his perspective victims —providin' there's any left—mighta got wise an' beat him to the bump. Don't that sound?"

"It sounds," admitted Lawler, "but it's off-key, George. Reede's words rule it out as a possibility. He said: 'The crazy coot's gone batty! He's trying to kill us all!'"

"Talk—an' talk's cheaper'n flies at brandin' time."

"Ah!" said Lawler softly.

"What yuh mean by that?"

"Well, look here. This killer's nobody's fool. He's slick, cunning, ruthless. He's a man who knows what he's after an' is aimin' to get it. He's not figurin' to let anyone stand in his way. He's got some reason, I'd say, to do away with Doak, Toreva, Durr an' Big-Ear Lester. There's a connection between them fellas someplace. We know he tried to polish off Captain Dan. It's my opinion he'll try again."

"Can't see why he'd be so dang anxious tuh plant these gents," Pony George objected. "What's he got on 'em, or them on him?"

"Must be somethin' behind it."

"Then he's keepin' it dang well hidden."

"That's open to doubt. The men who are being killed must represent a very real danger or the killer wouldn't be riskin' his neck to get 'em out of the way."

He resumed his pacing, a thoughtful expression in his vacant glance. "At least we know that Smith was once the Durr of the Toyah Lake bunch. Seems to me each of the killers other victims might likewise once have been a member of that gang."

"Don't look at me," grunted Pony George. "I can't make head nor tail—"

"It's possible," Lawler broke in, "that the killer was once a victim of some outrage of the gang, and has at last tracked the surviving members down with the idea of exacting vengeance."

"Don't sound a heap likely tuh me," Pony George growled, puffing on his pipe. "Like I said before, I ain't no Spurlock Holmes, but it don't look like tuh me no fella would be apt tuh nurse such burnin' hate for a period of fifteen years. Bird like Link Holladay might. Still, I wouldn't bet on it."

"Holladay? Guess you're barkin' up the wrong tree, there. Link's been under lock an' key too long to have been the killer of Lester. An' it's my notion these murders are all the work of the same dry-gulchin' pole-cat. Tain't sensible to think we got more'n one killer slappin' leather here in Pecos."

"Humph! 'Tain't sensible to figger we got any, if it comes tuh that."

Lawler paused beside his desk. "Here's another angle. Why should this hombre sign his murder notes 'Justice'? That sounds like a vengeance motive."

"Gosh, don't ask me no more questions," grumbled Pony George. "M' head's hummin' like a hive full of bees!"

"If the killer was a member of the Toyah Lake gang an' these victims were members likewise, that vengeance motive sounds pretty strong."

"But if that murderin' hound knew the identity of his enemies," Pony George pointed out, "why should he wait fifteen year tuh knock 'em off?"

"Oh, hell," growled Lawler, disgusted. "All my figurin' travels in circles."

He resumed his restless pacing of the room, his brooding eyes passing unseeingly over its scant and roughly-made furnishings. Throwing his hat abruptly into a corner, he rumpled his sweaty, thick red hair. "This damn business is enough to tie knots in a iron bar. I reckon I oughta confess it's got me licked—but I won't. I ain't never laid down yet George, do some thinkin' for a change!"

"*No?* Cripes, don't start pickin' on me—I don't savvy nothin' about this wave o' crime! I wa'n't cut out tuh be no Philo Vance!"

Despite the seriousness of the situation, Lawler chuckled. "I expect you spoke the truth."

Fervently he hoped the last of these murders had been committed. Up and down the room he strode, trying to find some path out of this maze of leads—some path which would bring him to the murderer and bring the murderer to the hempen noose he so richly deserved. Pony George, smoking, watched him uneasily.

Then suddenly Lawler stopped his pacing in midstride. "Lord!" he exclaimed. "What a fool I've been!"

"Wal," Pony George commented sagely, "men was borned tuh be fools, I expect. An' women was borned tuh fool 'em."

"Listen!" Lawler's glance, as it jumped to the deputy's face, was hard as polished agate. "You've got to get right out on Reede's trail! Quick! *Wake up!* It may be too late already. God! we've blundered terrible, George!"

"Mebbe so, but yuh know I ain't much of a trailer"

"You ain't much good sittin' round twiddlin' your thumbs or writin' poetry, either! Fork your horse pronto an' get on his trail!"

Pony George heaved a doleful sigh. "That Reede's got a awful mean pair o' eyes—"

"If you're afraid of the job, turn in your star!"

There was reproach in the chunky deputy's eyes. "It ain't that, only—"

"It looks that way to me."

"Oh! . . . Wal, if that's the way yuh feel—" Pony George shrugged, pulled his hat down aslant his eyes and with wooden face rose from his chair. "What yuh wantin' me tuh do?"

"Trail Reede. Find out where he goes an', if possible, why. See he don't get wise you're followin' him. If he looks like he's fixin' to pull his freight, clap on the bracelets an' bring him in. I think we're gonna get this thing wound up."

"Reede might not like the idee of them bracelets—"

"You got a gun. Don't be scared to use it. Whatever you do, don't let him get away!"

"All right, Red. So long."

Thrusting his cob pipe in his pocket, Pony George stepped out of the courthouse into the red gush of the dying sun's last rays and went bow-legging down the street.

* * *

LEFT ALONE, Lawler sat in gloomy silence. Pony George had said, "If thet murderin' hound knew the identity of his enemies, why should he wait fifteen years to knock 'em off?" Only one of the gang's members had ever been apprehended. That man, according to Pony George, had gone to jail, and from all the deputy knew to the contrary was still there.

"But he ain't," growled Lawler viciously. "It's damn' evident he's been let out!"

Presently the sheriff's churning thoughts reverted as they always did of late, to Sara Tranton. Despite all attempts to concentrate on the ugly business in hand, he could not put the girl from his mind, could not banish her image from his mental vision. It was there— it would not go.

Why had she turned him down? What reason could she have? What had he unwittingly done to offend her? He sighed amid the maze of questions. Answers seemed at a premium of late.

He reached for the phone; he'd call the Box Bar T.

It might be, he thought, that he'd find Sara in a better frame of mind than that in which he'd left her the night before. Perhaps she would tell him that she had not really meant to end their engagement permanently.

But when Sara come to the phone, she told him no such thing.

"Father isn't here right now," she said. "But I'm expecting him any minute. Could you leave a message for him? ... Oh! you want to talk with me! But I *can't* talk right now; I'm getting supper. . . . But, if I stand here gabbing, the supper'll burn up! By the way, Red— Dad said to tell you if you called, that he spent all morning hunting for that second bullet, but did not have any luck . . . Two more killed?" he heard her gasp, then: "Yes, I'll tell him to be careful. Now I really *must* hang up—something's burning. 'Bye!"

Lawler alternately sat in glowering silence and paced in impotent anger, The world was certainly going haywire fast! Nothing came out right! He recalled a random phrase of Pony George's—"A life o' mis'ry from the cradle to the grave!" He nevertheless snorted at such foolishness. If there was something wrong between Sara and himself, he felt, the rub must be in something he had done or left undone. But thinking so gave him precious little consolation.

He put on his hat and left the office. He headed for the "Lone Star Grub Emporium." He told himself he might feel better with a little nourishment under his belt.

Being close to the border, some few of Pecos' houses housed Mexican families. Several doorways he passed as he strode along the street were filled, he saw, by sleepy-eyed *mestizo* women, resting before the necessity of cleaning up their supper dishes. Against adobe walls lolled the women's *saraped* menfolk. These roused themselves sufficiently to reveal a lazy interest in the sheriff's movements. One or two murmured respectful greetings, which Lawler returned. One fellow grinned sardonically. The sheriff paid him no attention.

There were no customers in the restaurant when he entered. The regular patrons had evidently eaten their meals and gone off about their various businesses. Along one side of the place stretched a rough board counter, oilcloth-covered; at the other were a number of littered tables. Lawler took a stool at the counter.

At the rear of the restaurant the doors leading to the kitchen swung abruptly open and a girl emerged. She was not bad looking. She had dark wavy hair and a complexion innocent of make-up. She had hazel eyes that smiled when they met the sheriff's.

"Hello, Red," she leaned across the counter. "Long time no see."

Lawler smiled. "I was here this noon—no, I wasn't either. Out—"

"You bet you weren't. If you'd been here I'd have waited on you. How goes the sheriff business? From things I've heard I'd say it was on the up-an'-up."

Lawler scowled. "I'll have" he began. But a burst of silvery laughter that showed white even teeth between her vivid lips interrupted him.

Her eyes twinkled. "You want," she prophesied, "a pair of hen-fruit an' a double order of ham."

"You're a mind-reader," Lawler grinned. "What else am I wantin'?"

"A cup of java—black. An' the whole works in a hurry."

"Marv'lous." Lawler picked up a soiled copy of last Friday's paper.

As he was finishing his supper, Obe Kringle came in. The black-frocked coroner smirked at sight of the sheriff. "Well, well," he said. "Quite an inquest we had this mornin', eh?"

Lawler nodded briefly and downed the last of his coffee. "Hope you're intendin' to put a extra guard on the jail to-night," Kringle said.

Lawler set down his empty cup. "What for?"

"I understand you put Link Holladay in jail."

"What's that got to do with it?"

"Link's a tough customer. Seems tuh me if I was you—"

"You ain't," was Lawler's curt interruption. "You

better be careful. Link Holladay's got friends. They might try to spring him."

"Are you aimin' to tell me how to run my office?"

"It's time somebody did," the coroner snapped. "Three men murdered inside of two weeks an'—"

"Listen, Kringle," Lawler's drawl was soft and cold. "It may be time I was showin' some results. I'll admit that much, in fact. But I got no call to take any back-talk outa you. What's more I ain't figurin' to. *Savvy?*"

Obe Kringle's chest expanded with importance. "See here, young fella. You can't talk to me that way. For two bits I'd have you thrown out of office!"

Lawler's extended hand showed two bits at the coroner. "You aimin' to do the throwin'?"

"By Gawd, I'm big enough!" fist drawn back and tightly balled, Kringle stepped forward threateningly. "The way you let the killer get that knife outa your office is a disgrace to Reeves County. I've got a damned good notion—"

"Then be kind to it," Lawler drawled, "because it's in one hell of a strange place!"

Slapping the two bits down on the counter to pay for his meal, he strode from the restaurant without a backward glance.

TWELVE
THE CAPTAIN'S PHONE RINGS
TWICE

RETURNING to the office Lawler flung his hat into a corner, lit the lamp above his desk and dropped disgustedly into his chair. This situation, he told himself grimly, bade fair to lick him and get him turned out of office unless he swiftly made some progress. "Sure as a Chinaman's eyes is slanted!"

He well realized that Kringle's words were but a slice of what he soon would hear on every side unless he swiftly succeeded in unmasking and capturing the man who was taking ironic pleasure in signing himself "Justice."

But how to do it? This was a tough layout, and no mistake!

Reede might be the angle by which he could crack the whole business—but, Reede had got away from town before Lawler had thought to put someone on his trail. It was very possible that Pony George would be unable to trail the man any great distance before losing "sign" completely.

If Reede was as clever as Lawler was beginning to think him—

His thought turned to Tawson. Like Reede, Tawson employed no hands on his spread. Like Reede, too, Tawson tended such stock as he had himself and only bothered with his cattle when they seemed in danger of wandering off. More than once Lawler had thought it strange Link Holladay's long-loopers had not gobbled up these two small herds. Perhaps their mediocrity alone protected them.

What Tawson and Reede did with the bulk of their time few persons in the vicinity had any notion. Tawson, Lawler supposed, spent most of his leisure on looking into the thing he had been sent out here to investigate. But if he were being more successful at it than Lawler, the sheriff felt the man deserved a danged sight more than he was getting for the work.

What Reede did with *his* spare time, Lawler had no idea— up to the present, that is to say. Right now he had a mighty dark suspicion.

Reede had appeared in the country about three months previously, mounted on a flea-bitten horse and appearing much the same as he now looked. His marked pallor would have been cause for interested speculation on the part of his neighbors, had it not been self-evident that he was slowly dying from consumption.

Reede claimed to have hailed from Colorado, but his speech and manner belied the claim. His was the soft drawl of the Texan and his ungainly, slouching walk would have branded him Texan in any Colorado gathering. Lawler was wondering if the past fifteen years of

Reede's life might not account for the man's lie, when the telephone on his desk awoke with a hoarse, insistent jangle. Picking up the instrument, Lawler scooped the receiver to his ear and into the mouthpiece growled:

"Red Lawler speakin'."

It was Pony George. "Listen, Red. I got on to Reede's trail all right. But I lost him headin' fer the Bar 2."

Lawler scowled. "Lost him, eh? Where you at now?"

"Tawson's."

"'Tawson there?"

"No—nor Reede, neither. No hosses in the corral an' only one in the stable. Tawson's got two so I reckon he must be out prowlin' someplace. Listen: what do yuh want I should do now? Want me tuh wait here an' see if Reede comes?"

"No. He won't show up at Tawson's. Use your head f'r a change! Get over to the Lazy R an' if Reede ain't there, wait until he comes. See that you get your bronc put outa sight so's he won't know you're around. An' listen to me, George; once you pick Reede up, you be damn well sure he doesn't give you the slip a second time."

"Hey—hold on a sec, Red! Where yuh gunna be, case I wanta call yuh?"

"I'll be out to Tranton's. You can get me there in about an hour."

Lawler hung up and strode across the room to retrieve his hat, little guessing that crouched in the black shadows outside the open windows a man stood tensely listening. The eyes behind his sleepy lids were concealed by the down-turned brim of a black Stetson.

There was a grin upon his parted lips—but not a pretty thing to see.

Picking up his hat, Lawler closed the office door behind him and went striding down the corridor, spur-chains jingling musically.

Outside the courthouse beneath the star-filled heavens, he lost no time stepping into the saddle atop his big roan gelding. Picking up the reins he kneed the willing animal forward, swinging him into a lope a short time later on the trail that led past the Box Bar T.

Save for the pounding of the gelding's hoofs the night's vast silence seemed absolute.

* * *

RED AND FAT, the moon crept above the distant eastern skyline with the slow solemnity of a royal progression. The stars blinked balefully as the glowing disc ascended; showed the sandy trail twisting between intermittent borders of desert growth. Occasionally a gnarled juniper reared its bleached and splintery form in lonely solitude beside the way. Rabbit brush and mesquite stretched away on either side.

As he neared the Box Bar T, Red Lawler was recalling the eager expectancy which had flooded through him last night as he approached this place. Before the veranda he stepped from the saddle and left the gelding with trailing reins. Sara stood watching him from the doorway. Never, he felt, would he be able to understand the strange moods that swayed her mind and governed her inexplicable actions.

Yet he could not but admire her lithe and graceful

form as she stood there outlined against the lamplight streaming from the hall.

"What is it, Red?"

The lack of emotion in her low voice struck against the denied yearning of young Lawler with definite impact. It was almost a minute before he replied. Then he said, "Too cold out here for you without no coat. Let's get inside."

Sara listlessly led the way into the big sitting room. It was across the hall from the Captain's office. She took a chair that placed her back to the light, thus discounting at the start the revealing mobility of her piquant features. Lawler stood, hat in hand, beside the door.

"I asked you not to call again, Red."

Lawler fidgeted with his hat. "Well, er, it's 'fficial business, Sara..."

"What do you mean, 'official?'"

"I come over," Red lied, "to talk with your Dad about that second bullet."

There might have been read in her glance at that moment a strange look of mingled pity and longing, a wistful combination that did not harmonize with her words—a look Red Lawler could not see because of the light that was behind her on the table.

Her gaze rested long upon his clean-shaven, aquiline features beneath the tousled red hair. It seemed as though she might be studying his face and striving to impress it on her memory that she might recall its detail later. If so, she could not have failed to note that the usual glint of humor was totally absent from his eyes: that there were new, grim lines about his tight-lipped mouth. Indeed she must have seen and steeled her heart against him, for her voice was cold:

"I told you last night it would be foolish to keep this up. I'm not in love with you, nor you with me. That infatuation that we felt for one another now is dead. It won't be rekindled. There can be nothing more between us, Red. I—I think you'd better go."

For long moments he stared, then a cold oath dropped from his lips. "So you're throwin' me down! That's final, eh?"

In the light of the lamp behind her he saw her head nod once. A grim, dogged stubbornness crept into the forward throw of his jaw as the poignant silence threatened to become insupportable.

A chill wind was rising off the desert; it soughed eerily through the dust-coated branches of the cottonwoods and pig-locusts and rattled loose panes in the windows. The creak and clatter of the windmill was plainly audible. In her lap Sara's hands nervously twisted a fold in her skirt. Her glance appeared to study the pattern of the worn carpet on the floor.

"Well, I ain't figurin' to take it as final," Lawler growled. "You ain't given me no reason for breaking things off like this. You—"

"I don't intend to say any more on the subject!" Sara's chin could show stubbornness, too.

"Like that, eh?"

"Yes."

"Seems like you're gettin' kinda persnickety when the sheriff of Reeves County ain't good enough for you."

"It isn't the sheriff so much as it is the pay he draws."

"What's the matter with it?"

"It's too meager to support a wife as I wish to be supported."

Lawler stared. Certainly this was a side of the Captain's daughter he had not been privileged to see before. "It's a heap better'n cowpuncher pay."

"But we're not discussing cowpunchers and I'm not expecting to marry one."

"We ain't discussin' much of anythin', if you're askin' me!"

"Well, there's nothing left to discuss. I told you not to come out here again."

"I don't get this, Sara. I don't get it a-tall! It ain't like you to act this way. If your ol' man don't want me for a son-in-law, quit beatin' round the bush an' say so."

"The Captain hasn't anything to do with this matter."

Lawler thought he detected a flush of color in her cheeks but could not be sure because of that cussed light behind her. To him her face was hardly more than a vague oval with radiant golden hair. "Really," she was saying, "I don't care to talk about it longer."

"All right." There was a new, cold bleakness in the sheriff's voice—it was like the crunch of wagon wheels on frozen snow. "Last night you said you'd heard the sound of running feet after them gunshots. You seemed to think they was movin' towards the house. Don't you reckon mebbe the angle from which you caught the sound made it seem like that, while actually the sound was movin' *away?*"

"I suppose so. The wind was blowing. It was almost impossible to tell anything definite about it. I was merely giving an impression when I told you that. My father—"

"Captain's explanation," he cut in, "described the sound as that of a runnin' horse. *He* seemed to think it was the sniper forkin' his bronc away."

"Well? Probably that is the way it was."

"What?"

"A horseman moving off."

"Oh." He bent a bleak look upon her. But he had little success in making out her expression with that light before his eyes. Thrusting his hands deep-down in his pockets he took a turn or two about the room.

"Did you hear a galloping horse?"

"I don't know what I heard!" she exclaimed defiantly. "It was on the other side of the house, whatever it was. I wasn't expecting to hear anything and didn't pay much attention to it when I did hear it. What difference does it make? The main thing now, it seems to me, is to see to it no one tries to shoot Dad a second time."

Lawler's eyes were a jade-like, fathomless green; baffling, mocking.

She lashed out at him, "If you want to help us, why don't

you send Pony George out here to see that no further attempts

are—"

"Does the Captain want Pony George out here?"

"Of course he doesn't. He's got men of his own, if he wants to bring them in off the range. But he makes light of the whole business—tries to make me think it was hardly worth mentioning. Just a crazy drunken cowboy antic. But I know better." Her voice rose fierce with passionate protest. "Half an inch to the left and that shot would have killed him!"

"I don't reckon you'd have been so upset if it had

been me," he said sardonically. "Where's the Captain now?"

"I think you'd better be going," she said.

"I expect there ain't any great hurry. I'm waitin' for a call from Pony George."

"Where is he?"

"Bein' that George's whereabouts ain't got nothin' to do with your precious father," growled Lawler bitterly, "I don't guess you'd be a heap interested."

She flared up like tow. "My father has been mighty good to me—a sight better than you could *ever* be! I've never wanted a thing he hasn't gotten me. There is nothing he would not do for me—"

"That's what's the matter with you," Lawler cut in drily. "You been spoiled. What you need's a damn' good spankin'!"

Her breath was drawn in sharply. She surged from her chair and crossed the room to stand rigid beside the window, staring stormily out at the windy night.

"Get away from that window!" Lawler snapped.

She half turned her head and Lawler saw that her eyes were bright with anger, "This happens to be my house and your jurisdiction does not extend inside it. I'll do as I please. And if it doesn't suit you, Red Lawler, you can take yourself off any time you see fit!"

Lawler's red hair got the best of him, then. "You little fool!" In three strides he was across the room. His big hands caught her by the shoulders, jerked her back from the window. "Ain't you got no sense a-tall?" He shook her roughly so that her teeth chattered and her golden hair came down about her face and shoulders. "Don't you know better'n to stand in front of a lighted window? You figurin' to get yourself killed?"

Color blazed against the paleness of her cheeks. Lawler saw that her lower lip was trembling. But whether these were signs of anger, shame, or fear, he could not tell. All he knew was that her beauty caused a dull pounding in his breast, a constriction of his throat.

He stepped closer till her eyes came up and stopped him. Deep brown they were, and just now bright and sparkly.

"Sara," he said, and paused, confused by the searching scrutiny of her glance.

"Well?" she seemed throbbing with emotion. "Make your apology and go."

"I've no apology to make," he said, and squared his shoulders stubbornly. "If there's an apology due, I expect it's comin' to me. Anyway, I'm not pullin' out till I hear from George."

"I can't see why he should call you here. Or any other place, for that matter."

"I expect there's a lot of things you don't see," he told her flatly.

"Where is Pony George? Why does he have to call you?"

"Where's the Captain?" Lawler countered.

"The movements of Pony George are mighty secret. " she sneered.

"The movements of Pony George are the business of the Sheriff's office, an' I'm not aimin' to broadcast 'em to the general public. This county's had four murders now since I took oath of office, an' I ain't figurin' to have a fifth."

"Four!"

"So that gives you a jolt, does it? Well it jolted me

too. The next jolt's comin' to that killer when he finds me starin' at him down the barrel of a gun!"

But she was not listening, he saw. There was an added brightness in her eyes, an added pallor to her cheeks.

"Doak and Toreva" her voice grew breathless. "Who are the others?"

"A gent called Max Smith an' that big-eared fella over at Barstow."

"Smith and Lester." She was staring at him fixedly. "Who's Smith?"

"A driftin' pilgrim that's dropped his picket pin permanent."

"Where was—"

"No use your askin' me any more questions," Lawler cut in gruffly. "The Sheriff of Reeves County ain't no information bureau. I'm goin' to get that killer an get him quick. He won't get another chance at Captain Dan, so quit lookin' at me so funny-like."

"Was I?" she crossed to the table, stood looking down at the lamp. "You'd put duty to your office above every other consideration—above personal danger, for instance?"

"Of course—what kind of an officer would I be if I didn't? Naturally, I put my duty first. I swore to do that when I took my oath of office."

She nodded as though to something in her mind. She gave no sign of hearing him, but said, "Duty and loyalty are fine things, I guess. Dad's like that, too. Unswervable as granite."

"Sure," Lawler agreed. "He learned that captaining his ships. What kind of a skipper would he have been if he'd spent all his time worrying about his own neck an' the awful chances he'd be takin' in every storm an' fog? It's a mighty poor specimen of a man who ain't willin' to lay down his life in the performance of what he conceives to be his duty."

"Then you'd put loyalty to your office—what you conceive to be your duty," Sara asked listlessly, "before every other consideration?"

He nodded emphatically.

"And in the case of Dad captaining a ship . . . you'd expect him to stay with a ship he knew was sinking— even though it cost him his life—purely out of respect and loyalty to his owners?"

"If that would be his duty—sure. I'd certainly expect that from a man like Captain Dan."

She nodded slowly, reluctantly, it seemed. Her shoulders seemed to droop a little. When she spoke, so softly were the words sent forth that he could hardly catch them: "Duty and loyalty must be very dear to a man, I think."

"I'll say this," remarked Lawler grimly. "When you broke off our engagement I was powerfully astonished. I sure hadn't expected anythin' like that from you. I thought you had a lot of loyalty in *your* make-up. Shows how a fella—"

"I don't guess we need bring that up again," she cut in smoothly, and turned to rearrange her disheveled hair. "You've worn that subject pretty thin."

For a second Lawler glared, and then: "Where's Captain Dan?" he demanded gruffly.

"He went to town right after supper."

"What for?"

"I didn't ask him."

A hard, brittle silence fell between them. Sara sat

by the table, busy with her hair, ignoring Lawler completely. He stood against the wall near the window, his hands in his pockets, a look of resentment in his brooding eyes.

Presently, from the Captain's office, came the jangle of the telephone.

Sara started for the door with quickened stride, but Lawler got there first. "I'll take it," he said shortly, and passed out into the hall. Sara pressed close behind.

Entering the Captain's office, Lawler grabbed up the phone. He held the receiver against his ear. Yet Sara, standing close, could hear nearly as well as he. It was Pony George, and the deputy's voice was loud with excitement.

"I got here a bit too late, Red"

"Where are you?" Lawler growled with a scowl at the listening Sara.

"Lazy R, of course. But I didn't get here quick enough— Reede's cashed his chips! Killer sifted him s' full of holes yuh couldn't float him in a bucket of brine! I found one of them notes on him—one of them 'Justice' things."

"Read it!"

"It says: 'Only the wise an' the dead keep motionless tongues.' What yuh s'pose he means by that? Yuh don't reckon he coulda learned what Reede let slip as he left our office, do yuh? Say—want I should bring the body back tuh town?"

"Never mind the body," growled Lawler grimly. "Get busy an' search his clothes. Search the whole place while you're about it! Grab everything you can find relatin' to the Toyah Lake gang. Call me back when you're finished searchin'. I'll wait here till I hear from you."

Sara saw that his hand was shaking as he returned the receiver to its hook. And small wonder, she thought. The strain, together with the unsolvable aspect of these murders, was enough to wrench anyone's nerves. More than enough if the man were the sheriff. This business was taking toll of Lawler. Each passing hour new lines of strain and worry etched deeper into the bronze of his face. She would have felt sorry for him had it not been for the viewpoint he had so forcibly expressed.

She saw a strange, intent, startled light abruptly flare in the depths of his deep green glance. She watched him lower his weight heavily to the Captain's desk, watched his lips grow tight and grim.

Several moments he sat there rigid as Sara stared at him. Slowly he seemed to grow aware of her glance. A dark wave of color crept up behind the bronze of his cheeks. And then the phone beside him jangled loudly.

THIRTEEN
PONY GEORGE MAKES A DISCOVERY

IN THE SINGLE room of the shack at Bar 2, an unpretentious structure intended originally for a line camp but promoted by its present owner to the dignity of being styled a ranch house, Pony George put down the phone with a sigh of genuine relief. The expected fireworks had not materialized. For Red Lawler, the sheriff, had been quite mild, his deputy reflected, merely ordering him to proceed to the Lazy R and await the coming of Reede.

Pony George felt no call to hurry. "Rome wa'n't built in no day!" he muttered and proceeded to look around.

The furnishings with which Tawson had equipped the Bar 2 shack were simple. A disheveled pile of blankets covered the single bunk against the far wall. Above this rustic pallet was a bracket lamp with a tin reflector and, tacked to the hand-hewn logs beside it, the picture of a nude dancer clipped from some lewd magazine. Suspended from the opposite wall by a thick wooden peg hung a silver-mounted saddle, its black leather bright and shiny in the light from the kerosene lamp. A pail of water with a dipper stood beside the door. Across from the bunk was a chair on which reposed a battered clock and a tiny pad of yellow paper.

A burly man with smoldering eyes in a high-boned face the color of mahogany stepped suddenly into the room, softly closing the door behind him. A pair of black-butted six-shooters swung at his hips.

Pony George looked up with a start from the engrossing task of examining more closely the pad of yellow paper. "Gosh!" he spluttered. "Whyn't yuh scare a man tuh death an' be done with it?"

The smoldering eyes of Buck Tawson raked the shack's interior with a sweeping, comprehensive glance. "Did I scare yuh? Must have a guilty conscience."

"Guilty, hell! For a fella of yore weight yuh sure can move uncommon silent!"

"That's the Indian in me croppin' out. 'D you put that pad of yeller paper on that chair, George?"

"Huh? . . . No—course I didn't. D'yuh think I'm Santy Claus?"

"Funny how it got there, then."

"Why? Ain't it yores?"

"It certainly ain't," said Tawson grimly. "Never saw it before. Looks like you might not be the only visitor I've had tonight. Let's see . . ." he stepped across to the chair and gingerly picked up the object under discussion. Holding it at various angles, his smoldering eyes suddenly became intent and he stepped closer to the lamp. One more swift look he gave the pad then, fumbling in his pockets, he produced a pencil.

"Someone wrote somethin' on a sheet of this then tore it off," he said, and there was about him the air of a person having made a discovery. "There's a faint impression of the writin' on this top sheet."

"Bravo!" cried Pony George. "Spurlock Holmes in person! What's it say?"

Tawson's smoldering eyes gave the chunky deputy an enigmatic glance. "I can't make it out—yet. I'll try an' bring it out by rubbin' this pencil across it."

Suiting his actions to the words the marshal began lightly rubbing his pencil point across the paper's indentations. Gradually the pencil's strokes grew heavier and heavier.

A scowl creased the dried-apple countenance of Pony George. "Hell! Yuh've lost 'er now, complete!"

"You ain't tellin' me a thing," growled Tawson, and thrust the pad and pencil into a vest pocket. "Did you come out here to see me?"

"Do yuh think I'd travel this far on a chilly night jest fer a squint at yore homely mug?" demanded George. "I'm here on official business. I'm trailin' a gent."

"Yeah? I guess you ain't scuffin' up his heels any, are yuh?"

Pony George ignored this thrust. "My horse needs rest"

"This ain't no halfway station." Tawson picked up his clock, shook it, listened and proceeded to give it a belated winding. "Got any notion what time it is?"

Pony George glared.' "I wish tuh hell yuh could shut up fer about five seconds. Yuh got more damn lip than a muley cow! I had a swell verse right on the edge of m' tongue, an' yuh went an' scairt 'er plumb away!"

"Verse?"

Pony George glared. "Yeah—v-e-r-s-e: VERSE! I'm

writin' a poem called 'The Ballad of Kyote Cal— 'It's a pistol —yuh wanta hear it?"

Tawson shook his head. "I ain't strong on poetry. Didn't you say you was supposed to be trailin' a gent?"

"I don't see how yuh ever got tuh be a marshal! Y'ain't got a lick o' sense! I can trail gents any day in the week, fella; but bursts of inspiration is powerful rare events!" Scowling, the chunky deputy rose to his feet. "Yuh've scairt the muse plumb tuh Halifax now. I might's well be joggin' on Napoleon as settin' here gassin' with the likes of you."

"Napoleon!" Tawson guffawed. "Bone Rack would be a dang sight more fittin' name for the crowbait you're forkin'!"

"I've been told Napoleon had some bony parts," snapped George, and with a tug at his hat went striding outside. As he was swinging into the saddle Tawson came out, still chuckling. "I might's well ride along with you, I reckon. Where you goin'?"

"Lazy R," growled Pony George, and kicked Napoleon urgently in the ribs.

For some while they rode in silence, only the soft thudding of their horses' hoofs in the sandy soil disturbing the vast silence that cloaked the land. Even the noises of the night creatures seemed strangely hushed, as though before the majesty of the Law. Above their heads millions of stars twinkled like guttering candles in the purple bowl of night, and almost directly over them the moon, filled to yellow roundness, drifted lazily along.

"Fine night for a murder," offered Tawson, conversationally.

Pony George sniffed. "Fer company," he said,

"yuh're about as cheerful as a graveyard. Don't yuh never think of nothin' but murder, gunfights an' brawls?"

"Sure—once in a while I think of jails an' scaffolds an' hangmen's ropes."

Conversation lapsed.

A short distance to the north they could see the dark smear of trees marking the length of Toyah Lake. To the southwest, behind them, the dark bulk of Newman Peak blotted out a section of stars along the skyline. The down-slanting moonlight picked out the gear metal of their mounts' trappings and was reflected from the badge on the vest of Pony George, and from the shoulder-plates of the rifles that were sheathed in their saddle scabbards.

A wind seemed to have abruptly risen, cold and penetrating. It created an eerie swishing in the chaparral and soughed unpleasantly in the deputy's ears.

"Mebbe we better move a bit faster," he muttered presently. "Red's expectin' me tuh call him, come tuh think of it. Le's lope awhile."

From time to time he threw a sidelong glance at Tawson as they rode with heads bent against the wind. But he could not read the man's expression; his face, though turned to Pony George, was but a vague oval in the half-light.

Eight miles it was from Tawson's Bar 2 to Reede's Lazy R —a mere stone's throw as distances are measured in the West. In the daytime one ranch could easily be seen by a person at the other; that is, the clump of trees shading its buildings could be seen. Even now they could see the trees at the Lazy R, but only as a dark blur against the lighter color of the sand.

A half hour passed to the steady beating of the horses' hoofs and the pounding of the animals' hearts against their riders' knees.

"Colder'n a well-chain in February, ain't it?"

"A little chilly," Tawson admitted briefly.

Odd about that pad of paper, Pony George was thinking. If it was not Tawson's how had it come to be in Tawson's shack? That it had been generously left there by someone else sounded rather thin to the chunky deputy. If it *was* Tawson's, why had he sought to establish it as the property of someone else?

A coyote's dismal yammer came wailing across the wind.

"Bad omen, that," growled Tawson grimly.

"Yuh're sure one happy jasper!" George grunted. "Reg'lar li'l ray of sunshine, ain't yuh?"

From the south came mournfully the deep answering howl of a lobo.

"All we need now," spluttered Pony George, "is a corpse tuh make the evenin' a huge success!"

The night was shimmering with tiny silver gleams where the moon-glare lay upon the lake when the two lawmen arrived at the Lazy R. Pulling his horse in behind the stable where lay thick shadows, the marshal asked, "What you figgerin' to do now?"

"Dunno," admitted Pony George, glancing round apprehensively. "I expect we better leave the nags here an' go on up to the house. What's yore idee?"

Tawson shrugged. "Mebbe we better squint inside this stable first. See if the blue roan's here."

"Why the—Say! How'd yuh know he was ridin' the roan tonight?"

"Saw 'im leavin' town this afternoon 'fore supper."

"Was yuh in town?"

"How else?"

"Wal, unless yuh was there round supper time as well, I don't sabe how yuh could see Reede pullin' out. S'far as *I* know, Reede didn't leave till nearly dark."

"Expect you don't know everything," Tawson's tone was curt. Ground-hitching his horse, he strode round to the stable door and went inside. Grumbling, Pony George followed.

Inside Tawson struck a match. It burst purple and yellow against the hovering shadows. Reede's blue roan was in a stall munching oats contentedly.

"Reckon Reede's home," Tawson said, and led the way from the stable. "Funny he ain't got a light on."

"Mebbe he's gone to bed," suggested Pony George dubiously. "He might have, yuh know. I suppose the fella sleeps sometimes."

"Sure—daytimes."

"Yuh seem to know a powerful lot about Reede's business."

"Ought to. I been keepin' my eye on 'im," Tawson said. "He's one of the ol' Toyah Lake gang—the only one that ever got sent up. Took the rap under the handle of Tim Rein. He got released six months ago f' good behavior an' because he'd developed consumption an' woulda passed out if they'd kep' him in much longer."

An exclamation of astonishment escaped the chunky deputy. "Didn't he ever squeal on the rest of the gang?"

"Nope. You got to give him credit f' that. He kep' his mouth shut tight."

Approaching the ranch house they stepped into the murky shadows obscuring the porch. Their spurs rang loudly as they crossed it to knock upon the door. They might have saved themselves the bother, for no answer came. The creaking of the windmill and the rattling of the windows made the only sound.

This place of Reede's was a small adobe, one story high, with a flat adobe roof—its mud plastered over cedar logs whose ends projected a foot or so over the front and rear walls. There might be three rooms within, George thought; a large front room with a kitchen and bedroom at the rear.

Tawson knocked again and called Reede's name. Still no answer came. And no faintest sound of inside movement betrayed a person's presence. Tawson opened the door. Pony George crowded in behind him. Through an uncurtained window came sufficient radiance from the moon to disclose a lamp upon a table. Tawson lifted its chimney and struck a match. When he replaced the chimney he and Pony George glanced round. They were in the main room of the ex-convict's establishment and saw that, though scantily furnished, the place was neat and clean.

In the room's rear wall were two closed doors bearing out Pony George's surmise. "Bring the light," he growled, approaching them. "He's prob'ly sleepin' back here."

"He's probably," said Tawson, picking up the lamp, "saddled another bronc an' gone for a ride."

The first door tried led to the kitchen. A hasty glance sufficed to show that no one sat in the chair drawn up beside the stove.

Returning to the main room, Tawson held the lamp above his head while Pony George grasped the knob of the second door with the intention of continuing the search. But it was not to be that easy. This door, he found, was locked. He bent down and put his eye to the keyhole, but the only thing he discovered was that the key had been removed.

"Reckon yuh was right," he said, straightening. "The door's locked an' the key ain't in it so it looks like he mighta took a ride, like yuh said. Can't figger why he'd wanta lock the door though. Must have somethin' valu'ble in there."

Tawson scowled. "I doubt it. Here—hold the lamp."

Pony George had the lamp in his hands before he realized that Tawson had usurped his place as boss. Resentfully he watched the marshal hurl his burly shoulder against the door. His first onslaught split a panel in its upper half. "Some brawn!" thought George, and was glad it had not been *his* shoulder which had dealt the splintering blow. Another lunge and the battered door cracked open. Tawson kicked the hanging wood aside and entered. Pony George followed with the lamp.

He nearly dropped the lamp when his startled eyes took in the contents of the room. A muttered prayer slipped past his lips. For a bed occupied the room's center and face-down across it lay a moveless form—a man's! Dusty black clothes hung limply to his bony frame. The back of his head was smashed and blood was on the bed-sheets.

"Is—is he dead?" gasped Pony George.

"If he ain't," Tawson's humor was grim, "the undertaker'll be playin' him a dirty trick!"

George shivered. "Who done it?"

"I wouldn't know. Better call the coroner."

"I better call Red Lawler first..."

Setting the lamp on the floor Pony George clumped back to the front room. After a brief search he found the telephone box, and just as he did Tawson called:

"There's a note on him, George. Says 'Only the wise an' the dead keep motionless tongues.' It's signed 'Justice,' like them others."

When Pony George put down the phone, with Lawler's instructions still ringing in his ears, Tawson came slowly from the bedroom carrying the lamp. He set it down on the table and buttoned up his coat.

"Reckon I'll be moseyin' along, George. See yuh later, mebbe."

"What's yore hurry, fella? I got no special hankerin' tuh be stayin' here alone with Reede's corpse."

"Tough. But I got other fish to fry," said Tawson, grinning. "S'long."

And while Pony George watched him resentfully, Buck Tawson—who had introduced himself to the Sheriff's office as a U.S. Marshal—jingled his spurs across the room and out the door. Some moments later diminishing hoofbeats announced the departure of a horse.

Pony George swore with feeling. "He sure was in some lather tuh get away from here! Fella with his gloomy dis-posishun oughta feel right tuh home in such surroundin's. Dang 'im, anyway!" He stared apprehensively about. "I never did pretend tuh be no Spurlock Holmes," he muttered. "Nor did I ever have any leanin' towards the undertakin' business. Cripes, I gotta notion tuh pull outa here myself!"

He threw a narrowed glance around him, searching out the shadows. But he saw nothing to alarm him. Despite this fact he pulled the heavy six-shooter from his holster and examined its chamber carefully. Having done so, he retained the weapon in his hand.

Lawler had told him definitely to search this place for clues. Well, he would—so long as such a search did not involve returning to the bedroom. So, one eye peeled for likely hiding places, one eye keening the hovering shadows, Pony George began his probing.

He kept to the open places as much as he could. He preferred to search where the lamplight shone the brightest. Thus it was that upon the wall above the telephone box he became aware of a large calendar. And seeing it, his attention became suddenly gripped.

Yet because of his rising interest in the calendar, he failed to see or hear the burly form of a crouching man who moved across the porch with catlike steps to pause in the open door.

The calendar that held Pony George's attention was a large ornate affair, decorated with the picture of a chorus girl in colors. Still it was not her buxom charms so flashily displayed that held George's wondering gaze.

It was the four tacks, one at each of the calendar's corners, holding the thing to the wall that drew his interest.

"No need of *four* tacks tuh hold that thing up," he muttered thoughtfully. "One tack driven through the eye at the top would do the trick." Out of curiosity he ripped the calendar from the two tacks that held its lower edge against the wall. An envelope dropped to the floor. Picking it up George thrust his gun in the waistband of his trousers. Though having been through the mails, the envelope was no longer sealed so George felt no compunction in removing from it a twice-folded sheet of yellow paper. He unfolded it with trembling fingers, so great was his mounting interest upon noting its color.

One swift glance he gave the pencilled lines. With an oath he grabbed the phone-box crank and twirled it wildly. Those pencilled lines had read:

"I'll see that you get your share of the loot if you sit tight and keep yore lip buttoned."

A single initial was used for signature; though blurred, Pony George guessed the letter instantly.

FOURTEEN
"THE CARDS IS DEALT"

AS LAWLER SWUNG round on the Captain's desk, reaching for the phone, it seemed that all sound throughout the house had abruptly become suspended; all sound save the solitary ticking of a clock.

Feeling Sara's eyes upon him Lawler clapped the receiver to his ear. "Well," he growled, "spit it out, George."

The receiver made metallic noises; Lawler said "Oh!" real odd, added a hurried "Thanks" and hung up. He looked at Sara. "Wasn't George—it was the jailer at Pecos. Link Holladay's slipped his picket pin."

Sara stared at him strangely, he thought. "You mean he's got away?" A dry little sob escaped her lips as he nodded.

"Lord, Sara" Lawler was off the desk and by her side.

But she waved him back.

"I'm all right, Red. Just a little unstrung, I guess. What," she cleared her throat, "did you mean about him getting away? Away from what? He wasn't in jail, was he?"

"He sure was. I put him there yesterday durin' the inquest on Toreva. There was some evidence against him in connection with the fella's killin'."

"When did he get out?"

"Jailer didn't seem to know. He'd been off to visit his sick wife. When he got back he recalled he had a prisoner and got some supper for him at the restaurant. But when he went to the cell, Holladay was gone."

"How could—"

But his raised hand stopped her question. "You're gonna say 'How could he be guilty of killin' Toreva—he hardly knew the Mexican.' But—a blackjack with Link's name burned on the handle was found under one of the windows in the room where we found Toreva's body. Toreva had been struck across the head with some blunt instrument The blow caused a fracture of the parietal bone."

"But Link Holladay didn't kill Toreva—surely he didn't You can't hold him for it; he's innocent!"

"Yeah. Seems like that was the opinion of the coroner's jury, too. They," he added drily, "turned in a verdict of murder by parties unknown."

"But can't you see, Red? Someone is trying to frame him— trying to shift their own guilt on to his shoulders." Deep feeling came into her tones:

"He's not guilty, Red. He can't be."

"You ain't heard all the evidence. Big-Ear Lester claims he saw a man sneakin' out Toreva's back gate last night. Time's about right, near as we can tell. Lester claims the man was Holladay; he doesn't swear to it, but he seems pretty sure." In a moment he added softly, "Lester describes him as a big fellow—heavy-set."

"But can't you see? " she pleaded desperately. "That almost proves they're trying to frame him. I tell you, Link Holladay is no more guilty of killing Toreva than I am."

Lawler eyed her grimly. "Kinda interested in Link, ain't yuh?"

"Don't be silly! I don't want to see a man accused of something he didn't do! And if that jury did not bring in a verdict against him you've no right to hold him!"

"I ain't," he drawled. "He's departed."

"Then let him go. Forget about him."

"Mmm-m-m. How 'bout that blackjack? You want I should forget that, too?"

"Who found it?"

"Obe Kringle."

Her lip curled with disdain. "I wouldn't trust Mr. Kringle any farther than I could see him."

"Don't know's I would, either," Lawler answered. "But I don't reckon I'd go so far's to say Obe planted that evidence deliberate."

"Somebody did."

"Did what?"

Her brown eyes flashed. "It isn't fair to hound a man like that!"

For several minutes they eyed one another steadily, appraisingly; green glance probing into brown glance. Brown eyes staring back unwavering.

Sara asked, "How did he get away?"

"Jailer didn't know. Said Kringle visited right after I left the office, but that Kringle left before he did."

"Was Link there when Kringle visited—" Sara stopped abruptly, but Lawler caught her meaning.

"You mean did the jailer get a look at Link while Kringle was visiting? Hmm. I dunno. I didn't think to ask. But it's a damn good point!"

"But Kringle wouldn't have let him out after all the work he went to put him in there," Sara protested. "Maybe the jailer—"

"I think not, though of course it's possible. In my opinion the coroner fixed Link's getaway." "Why?"

"Obe an' me passed a few words at the Lone Star Grub to-night. He told me like he was bossin' the job I better put a extra guard round the jail. I couldn't see it. Kringle said some of Link's friends would be makin' a try to spring him." Lawler paused, as though scanning something in his mind, then added:

"Obe's the sort of gent who'd do anything that might be expected to put me in bad with the voters. I wouldn't put it past him to have helped Link out, even though he is the one who put Link in. I'll admit, however, that I have no definite knowledge that Link was still in jail when Obe came over. I thought he was. But he might have gotten loose while I was still in town."

"But wouldn't you have known it?"

"I haven't visited the cells since noon. Link's the only prisoner I had. I expected the jailer to feed him—"

"Red," Sara broke in, "why don't you resign?"

"What?" Lawler laughed shortly. 'Throw up the job just when I'm about to put the rope round the killer's neck? Humph! I guess not, Sara. Seems like I ain't in a real good givin'-up mood, this evenin'."

For several seconds the room was silent. Then, drawling, Lawler asked:

"Who was here tonight to see the Captain?"

"Who was here?" she echoed.

"Yeah—who?"

"Mister Tawson came over from the Bar 2 for a short time after supper. He and Dad left together." She eyed him anxiously. "What makes you ask? Do you think Link Holladay had been here?"

"No, I didn't expect Link had been here. I don't expect him to come within miles of here tonight. I—"

"What are you going to do about him?"

"Do about him?" Lawler looked blank.

"You know what I mean. What are you going to do about him breaking jail?"

"Why are you so anxious about him?"

Her lips quivered. She was facing the light and her eyes held an odd, sort of anxious expression. He thought it was the expression of a woman, sorely troubled, striving to remain courageous despite the crushing force of some black thing aligned against her.

She finally shrugged and turned away without speaking.

Lawler watched her, his hands deep-thrust in his Levi's pockets, big shoulders hunched a little forward, his eyes brooding.

He took a turn about the room, paused before the windows and drew their shades down level with the sills.

"What's that for?"

"I got no hankerin' to get shot," he answered bluntly. "Did the Cap'n find where that second bullet struck?"

One hand went to her lips; her eyes went wide with some unreadable emotion.

And abruptly Lawler, watching her, laughed. A short and bitter laugh it was, and rang jarringly across the sullen stillness.

Sara sprang forward. "Red—"

But he held her off. "Never mind," he growled. "That second shot struck there!" he jabbed a finger at the splintered hole in the polished surface of Dan Tranton's desk. "Yeah—right there!"

"But—but that's where the first bullet hit . . ."

"Oh, no it ain't! The second bullet drilled that hole. An' I believe you know it!"

"No, no, *no!*" Sara retreated before the light in Lawler's eyes. Retreated until her back was against the farther wall. "'The first shot—"

"Quit lyin' to me, Sara! I know where the first slug struck. That hole in the desk was made by the second."

She huddled against the wall, silent, trembling, stark misery in her glance.

"By Gawd," Lawler snarled, "I believe I know who this blasted killer is!"

"Red!" Sara's broken cry seemed wrung from her very soul. "Give up this awful job—Turn in your star tonight and I'll go with you anywhere! I'll marry you—"

While she was speaking it seemed for a moment that Red Lawler was going to yield. It was the squaring of his jaw in stubborn grimness that stopped her voice.

He shook his head. "No use. The cards is dealt, Sara. We got to play our hands."

At that moment the phone on the desk rang loudly.

Picking up the receiver Lawler pressed it to his ear. The voice coming over the wire was that of Pony

George and its timbre was surcharged with a wild excitement.

"That you, Red? Wal, listen—I found a note here in a envelope. It was tucked behind a calendar. Envelope's been through the mail the twenty-third of las' month. Reede's the bird that went tuh the Big House under the name of Tim Rein. The note in this envelope's on yeller paper like them 'Justice' notes was writ on—"

"What name's signed to it?" Lawler barked.

"Note says Reede'll get his cut if"

"Whose name is signed to it?" Lawler snarled, exasperated.

"No name's signed to it. The signature is a T."

Pony George's voice was abruptly drowned in the sound of a shot. A second, third and fourth concussion smashed out in swift succession from that room at the line's far end. Tingling from the metallic vibrations, Lawler's ears scarcely heard the thud of a falling body. But he caught the mocking laugh that followed before the line went dead and its sound closed icy fingers about his heart.

Sara sank against him as he relinquished the phone. "Wh— what happened?"

She was shaking as though with cold when Lawler looked down into her white face.

There was a smothered feeling in Lawler's throat, in his mouth was the taste of brass. Staring down into her pitiful upturned face Lawler's eyes went bleak. No longer was there any kindliness or humor in his glance. His was now the bronzed and emotionless countenance of the sworn man-hunter, tight of lip and square of chin.

Sara's form went tense against him. She stared with eyes dilated.

"Red!"

His glance went past her unseeing. Turning, he strode toward the door.

"Red! *Red!*" she cried wildly, clutching at his arm. "Where are you going?"

"Going?" he shook her off with a bleak laugh. "'*I'sa* goin' to get the black-hearted skunk that's makin' a buzzard's paradise of this country. That's where I'm goin'.'"

"Red—*Wait!*"

But he was gone.

FIFTEEN
TURKEY TALK

HOT ANGER RAGED in the sheriff's heart as he left the house. Anger at this scurvy trick played him by a fickle Fate. No longer was he pulled between two courses; no longer could he disregard his duty. He had sworn to uphold the Law and to punish evil-doers. If hard, his path lay no less plain.

And it *was* hard, damnably, bitterly hard. But no alternative was left him. As Reede only this afternoon had said "The crazy coot's gone batty! He's tryin' to kill us all!"

But now the killing spree was over if he—Red Lawler— had anything to say about it!

Whipping the gelding's reins from the veranda post, he flung himself into the saddle. At a fast run they pounded from the yard, dust rising balloon-like in their wake.

But hardly a mile had they travelled when Lawler beheld a vague horseman riding toward them. The unknown was riding leisurely, sitting straight up in the saddle, elbows flapping at either side.

Lawler pulled up and waited as a hail came down the wind. When the oncoming horseman drew close the sheriff recognized him with a snort of disgust. It was the coroner, Obe Kringle.

"Now what in seven devils does *he* want?" Lawler muttered impatiently.

He was not long in finding out.

Pulling in his horse beside that of the sheriff, Kringle halted. By the moonlight Lawler saw that there was a sly smile on the coroner's unprepossessing countenance.

"Well, well! Takin' a ride, Mr. Lawler?"

"I got no time for foolish questions," Lawler scowled. "If you got somethin' to say. then say it. If you ain't, then get outa my way. I'm in a hurry. There's been another killin'— mebbe two."

The news seemed to please the coroner for he grinned. "That's awful, Lawler—awful. I don't know what this county's comin' to. I guess you've heard Link Holladay busted loose? Remember, I warned you to put on a extra guard. If there's been two more murders you're responsible for 'em. I told you Link's friends would spring him."

"How'd he get out?"

"No one seems to know," Kringle grinned maliciously. "Quite a mystery, 'cordin' to what I've heard—"

"I guess you know as much about it as the next!" snapped Lawler, angrily.

"Are you aimin' to insinuate—?'"

"If the boot fits—pull it on!"

Obe Kringle stared. But he made no move to fetch his gun. He knew better than to try a thing like that with Lawler. The sheriff was reputed to be "some fast."

"You're ridin' for a fall!" Kringle snarled vindictively.

"Don't try to act tough, Obe. You ain't big enough to cut the mustard."

"Ain't, eh? Well," sneered Kringle, "you won't be singin' so high yoreself in about two minutes. Trouble is with you, Lawler, you're all lather an' no action. You do a heap of talkin' but that's far as it ever gets. I'm bettin' you ain't got a notion now who's pullin' these killin's—"

"You're bettin' wrong then," Lawler cut in, holding his temper with an effort. "I'm on my way to nab that killer now."

Obe Kringle's jaw dropped. "Who is he?"

"I'm not sayin'. You'll find out quick enough when I bring 'im in."

A jeering laugh left the coroner's mouth. "Wind! I'm the only one round here who's got a notion who this murderin' polecat really is—an' it ain't Link Holladay!"

"Well?"

"It's that secretive, bushy-browed, bed-slat Tawson —the skunk that's been posin' as a U.S. Marshal!"

Lawler leaned forward in his saddle. "You interest me strangely. Thought you'd picked Link Holladay for the killer?"

"Not me! I was just usin' Link for a smoke screen so's I could lull Tawson into gettin' careless. Cripes, if you had half the brains I've got you'd have known all along it wasn't that cow-stealin' Holladay. I knew right from the start it was Tawson."

Lawler eyed the coroner silently. Kringle added "But knowin' it won't do you any good now."

Lawler stiffened as from far away the wind brought a vague sound of drumming hoofs. He scanned the moonlit terrain but saw no sign of the horseman. He turned to the coroner grimly.

"Just what was the meanin' of that last remark?"

"This—fella! The worthy citizens of Pecos have elected me a committee of one to ask for your resignation. You can hand over that star right now."

"Like hell!"

Lawler's right hand lashed out with unexpected suddenness. The fingers of that hand were balled into a rock-hard fist that caught Obe Kringle behind the left ear and shook him from his saddle with a wicked force. The coroner struck the sand all spraddled out.

Glaring down at him Lawler growled:

"When the Board of County Supervisors ask me for my star they can have it. Until that time it stays right here on my vest. Tell that to Pecos' worthy citizens when you get back to town!"

And, without further dallying, the sheriff slapped in his spurs and rode away.

SIXTEEN
THE MAN IN THE DOORWAY

AS RED LAWLER rode through the starry night, the rush and slap of the gusty wind beat incessantly against his face and chest, plastering the clothes to his body and slowing the gelding's speed in no uncertain manner.

He found himself not only recalling but actually thinking of those vague-pounding hoofbeats he had heard while palavering with Kringle. What did they mean? Who was the unseen rider? Or were there two?

Soon however the futility of such speculations caused him to swerve his thoughts to the man who had escaped from the Pecos jail.

When had he gotten free? Lawler recognized that this was an important question.

Link Holladay, as he well knew, was no man's fool. Thus far he had carried on his cattle-stealing operations without having once been apprehended. The closest call the rustler had had, was the time when Lawler himself had come upon the scene just as Holladay's helpers had been about to make off with a small herd. At sight of the sheriff, the miscreants had cut loose of the stolen critters and made their getaway in safety.

Lawler did not, however, think that a man as slick as Holladay had shown himself would linger long in this vicinity when it was so palpably evident that someone was doing his best to frame him for the series of murders that were being perpetrated. To the young sheriff of Reeves County, it seemed a pretty safe bet that by this time Link Holladay would be pounding a streak of dust in the shortest cut to the Mexican border.

So thinking, he dismissed the rustler from his mind, content to let the fellow go.

He grinned faintly to himself as he recalled how he had sent the sneering coroner sprawling headlong in the sand. Perhaps the spill would teach the fellow to keep his long nose out of other folk's business. Lawler hoped so.

With an abruptness that set his nerves a-quivering the sound of a shot tore a hole through the night as Lawler crested a ridge. It came from somewhere to the left and slightly up-wind. At the same instant the big roan gelding staggered, shivered through every fiber and reared as though to take a mighty forward leap. But the leap was never taken. Instead the gelding crumpled in mid-air. Lawler felt the gallant animal that had carried him successfully through many a tight scrape go to pieces under his saddle.

With a single, smooth, lightning-quick movement the sheriff kicked his feet free of the stirrups and slid from the saddle as his horse crashed down and lay kicking spasmodically beside the trail. Dropping swiftly behind the dying animal Lawler put a period to its agony with a well-directed shot.

Red-haired anger mounted to the sheriff's brain. Some— bushwhacking son had killed his favorite mount! All thought of caution was momentarily blotted from his mind as up he sprang, pistol in hand, and ran zig-zagging forward, his spur-rowels clacking out a warning whir.

A streak of flame blazed against the blue-black mark of a mesquite clump. Lawler ducked but kept up his zig-zag charge. The unseen's lead bit past him with the sound of angry wasps. A bullet slapped the brim of his hat; a second tugged at his sleeve as he stormed across the moonlit open.

From off to the right a second gun hurled flame-wreathed lead; a third from dead ahead. Realization of his danger took the sheriff by the throat. He dropped flat against the earth.

Momentarily a running figure appeared sky-lighted acrest the ridge. Lawler's heavy Colt kicked back. The figure reeled and fell from view.

A rocking, roaring world of sound filled Lawler's ears; his pulses raced to the thrill of open combat. A bullet spattered sand beside him. Another ripped the heel from his right boot. Gunpowder's acrid stench tore at his nostrils. For fast red moments all was turmoil and confusion. Snarls and curses resounded from the brush. Wild yells and choking screams. And over all the whine and smack of flying lead.

Then suddenly the roaring chaos of sound fell away, melting in the swift diminishing beat of fleeing hoofs and the sheriff found himself alone. Alone and horseless, a good three miles from Tranton's.

Getting himself afoot Lawler crossed to his dead gelding and removed his rifle from the scabbard thrust beneath the saddle skirts. For the moment the saddle must be left where it was. He was in a hurry and felt no desire for a three-mile walk cumbered by such a weight.

Breaking the heel from his left boot that his gait might be more even, Lawler struck out for the Box Bar T, knowing it to be the nearest place at which he could procure another mount. Seemed like everything was breaking wrong for him! Plainly this was to be a night he would long remember.

Who could have been responsible for that ornery ambush he had ridden into? Kringle? It did not seem likely for he had left the coroner spreadeagled in the sand not half an hour ago. It hardly seemed plausible that Kringle could have rounded up any partisans in such brief time and cut in ahead of the sheriff swiftly enough to have laid that ambush.

Nor did it seem to Lawler that the man responsible for that ambuscade could be the killer who signed an ironic "Justice" to his notes. For, as Lawler looked at it, the killer always worked alone.

That left but a single good alternative in the sheriff's mind. Link Holladay!

The more he thought about the rustler, the more firmly Lawler became convinced that it was indeed Link and his men who had laid that unsuccessful trap. It had, he told himself, all the earmarks of the rustler's methods. Swift attack and flight had ever been Holladay's way. He seemed to be a firm believer in the old adage that "He who fights and runs away will live to fight another day."

Evidently Holladay was too anxious to pay off his grudges to leave the country yet awhile. Likely enough, Lawler reasoned, his next step would be directed against Obe Kringle. Still one could never be certain where a man like Link was concerned. Cunning he undoubtedly was, but his vindictive nature made his probable course of action a difficult thing to gauge.

The sheriff found it no pleasure to tramp the rough miles back to the Box Bar T, and by the time he came again in sight of Tranton's ranch Lawler's hair-trigger temper was fast coming to a boil.

Recalling that Sara had said that she would likely go to bed as soon "as he left, he was not surprised upon returning to see no lights in evidence.

No sense disturbing her, he reflected. He would go to the corral and rope him out a bronc and soon be on his way once more. Seemed likely he might find an extra saddle in the stable. With this thought in mind, he bent his weary steps in that direction.

Inside the building it was black as pitch and in the atmosphere there was a smell of hay. There was another smell, too—the rank smell of damp horsehide, and the lesser odors of dust and leather.

Lawler got a match from his hatband and struck it. Crimson it burst against the hovering blackness that filled the stable. It showed a drooping horse on spraddled legs, its sides slashed cruelly from the many bites of driven spurs. Still as rock the animal stood save for its heaving flanks, its head hung listless between its legs. Blood and sweat trickled from its sides.

The match in Lawler's hand went out, but not before he had seen a saddle hanging from a peg driven deep in a nearby post. Lifting it down he left the stable at an awkward run.

Dropping the saddle to the ground outside the pole corral, he removed its coil of rope and shook out a loop.

Carefully he slipped inside the enclosure, closing the gate behind him. It shut with a grating squeak that put his caution to naught. The horses circled, milled at the corral's far side.

"Lost so much time now, I might's well stop an' see Sara again before I leave," he thought as softly he stalked the horses.

The twirling loop abruptly left his hand, but the horse it was aimed at ducked and the rope slid harmlessly past. The horses circled, milled again and stood watching the sheriff warily as he edged toward them building another loop.

Again the rope snaked forward. This time the long-legged bay the sheriff was after ducked too slow and Lawler hauled him in. He led the captured horse from the pen and shut the gate.

The borrowed saddle loudly smacked the back of the borrowed bay. Another ten seconds and the sheriff's Levi's smacked the saddle. In no time he was dismounting before the ranch house veranda. Tethering the bay to a post he strode to the door, his spurs rasping loudly across the squeaking floorboards.

Having knocked, he stood back and built himself a cigarette while waiting for Sara's coming.

She did not come at once, so after lighting his quirly he knocked again. Inhaling deeply he felt his raw nerves soothing to the fragrant draught. "What's keepin' her?" he wondered. He could hear no kind of movement inside the house.

Slowly he grew aware, of something menacing, something sinister about this stillness. A vague uneasiness gripped him. He thought suddenly of the ruined horse inside the stable. The horse recalled to his mind the drumming beat of hoofs he had heard while talking with Obe Kringle. Was that the answer to this uncanny silence?

"Lord!" he muttered, and knocked again, louder. Only echoes replied. A tingling thrill swept up the sheriff's spine. With sudden decision he grasped the knob. He pushed the door abruptly open. ...

Gasping and groaning, Pony George's squinty eyes came blinking open. He stared in astonishment at what he saw. Twelve feet before him was a broad, flat expanse of glaring white.

"Suff'rin' snakes!" he gasped, "where be I? That there's the dangest lookin' sky ever I see in all m' borned days!"

He struggled hazily to an elbow; more hazily and with far greater alacrity he slumped back to his former position, which some time later he realized was flat on his back. It was not a comfortable position, but it did have the advantage of being stationary. And that was something!

His head ached as though some monstrous giant were beating it with the world's largest hammer. He could not understand it. What had he ever done to deserve such treatment? Where in hell was he, anyway?

He could see no flames; there was no smell of sulphur or brimstone in the air. Thus he judged he had not as yet entered the Devil's jurisdiction. That, he thought vaguely, was at least something to feel thankful for.

He glanced about him out of the corners of his eyes. He dared not move his aching head again for fear the world would spin around as crazily as it had when he'd struggled to his elbow. A wall rose up beside him on the right—a wall with a queer box-like contraption protruding from it from which dangled a funny-looking black thing on a cord.

Suddenly he realized that he was on his back and that the glaring white expanse before him was a white-washed ceiling. Realization of his surroundings came flooding back. "My Gawd!" he exclaimed in startled conviction. "Reede's Lazy R! Who the hell brung me out here?"

Somehow he got himself afoot. He leaned groggily against the wall until his dizziness lessened to some extent. He put a hand to his aching head and it came away covered with blood. His eyes grew horror-stricken as he goggled at the crimson smearing his hand.

"I'm shot!" he howled, and likely would have swooned if he had not been so scared. His rolling eyes took in the queer box-like thing against the wall. Telephone! His glance lit on the dangling receiver that was banging against his leg and remembrance of the dire happenings presaging his present plight came swarming back. Grabbing the cord he scooped the receiver to his ear, dropping it disgustedly when he found the line was dead.

"Gosh!" as a new thought struck him, "what if that killin' fool's still lurkin' around here someplace? Cripes! George Kasta," he upbraided himself solemnly, "what the hell yuh waitin' on? If yuh got haff the sense yuh was borned. with, yuh'll drag yore picket pin an' drift! An' what I mean is *now!*"

He peered about the floor seeking the envelope and letter he had dropped when the sound of that first shot had rung through the house and something hot had stung his head above the ear and shown him countless constellations he had never guessed existed. He found the papers presently and snatched them eagerly up. Red Lawler would want these! He looked again at the blurred signature initial.

"Well, mebbe it ain't a T," he muttered, holding the paper nearer to his squinted eyes. "It *might* be a J." He scowled but presently shrugged. "Anyhow I'm bettin' it's a T an' stands for Tawson. The dirty polecat! An' here I'd thought he hit fer home! The ornery, two-faced hound!"

Pony George decided that the double-dealing marshal must have been standing on the porch when he'd fired that murderous salvo. Certainly Pony George had neither sensed nor expected the other's reappearance until sound of that first treacherous shot. From then on he'd been in no position to do anything about it.

He went over himself slowly, inch by cautious inch, endeavoring to ascertain the extent of his injuries. A nasty gash along his left side below the armpit and a painful crease across the scalp, seemed to be the total extent of his damages.

"Gosh," he growled, astonished. "He sure is one careless jasper! 'Magine anyone aimin' tuh murder a gent goin' off without makin' sure his lead had done the trick!" George had, of course, no knowledge of the bloody, battered spectacle he presented or he would not have wondered at the killer's seeming negligence.

His pistol was still stuffed in the waistband of his trousers, he found with satisfaction. Making sure it still was loaded, he thrust it into his open-topped holster and proceeded to bind the wound in his side with strips torn from his shirt-tail. This done to his satisfaction, he wound his neckerchief about his head and gingerly donned his shabby Stetson.

"Next thing in order, before I clear outa this dang dump fer good," he announced loudly, "is tuh take a final squint around so's tuh be sure that dang' double-crossin' polecat's gone!" Of course he did not actually doubt the killer *had* cleared out or nothing would have induced him to remain a second longer on these premises. But he liked to make himself, and any possible spectators think he had been unimpressed by the danger he had undergone during the killer's visit.

So it was with a fine air of cautious nonchalance that Pony George went tip-toeing into the kitchen with the lamp in one hand and his pistol in the other. He saw no one in the kitchen.

"An' dang lucky that hellion is thet he sloped afore I come to!"

Somewhat reassured by the barrenness of the culinary department Pony George next hazarded a peep into the room where rested Reede's mortal remains. It was a most unfortunate peep. For, sticking his head around the door, he received a nasty shock.

Across the room he beheld another door and in it a crouching man who held a lamp in one hand and a ready pistol in me other. And a more villainous-looking hombre Pony George had never seen.

A dirty Stetson was pulled low across the stranger's glaring eyes which, in the flickering light, gleamed like bits of polished jet. One side of his face was a ghastly smear of blood. Sighting Pony George his twisted lips jerked open in a fearful snarl and the straggly moustache above them appeared to bristle like a lion's mane!

"Throw up them hands or I'll blast yore m-mortal

tintype!" howled the quavering notes of Pony George. But the fellow's gun came up instead. "Stop, dammit! *Stop!*" he shrilled, and his gun kicked back against his palm. The loud report chased deafening echoes smashing back and forth between the walls, through which came faintly the tinkle of shattered glass.

A great hole gaped in the stranger's chest. But he neither fell nor even staggered. Great radiating lines ran out in all directions from the place of the bullet's entrance. Yet still the hombre stood there eyeing George in shocked surprise.

And then abruptly the gun sagged in the deputy's hand.

"Gawd! A blasted mirror!" Pony George sagged, weakly against the wall.

With a doleful sigh the mortified deputy roused himself at last. "If the folks in Pecos ever hears about this they'll laff me plumb outa the state o' Texas. Cripes! What a fright that fella give me! *Whew!*"

Putting the lamp down on the table in the main room, Pony George blew it out and hastily tiptoed from the house. Like a flitting shadow he moved to the rear of the stable and got his horse. Finding the animal still standing where he'd left it gave him a gorgeous feeling —gorgeous!

"This ain't no place for Ol' Man Kasta's son," he muttered nervously. "The quicker I gets back tuh town the better I'm gonna like it. Some folks might mebbe think I ort tuh go gallivantin' over to the Bar 2 an' line my sights on that Polecat Tawson—but me, I think diff'rent!"

He nodded his head emphatically as he scrambled up into the saddle. "What you need, George Kasta," he firmly told himself, "is a dang good rest! The atmosphere round this here spread is enough tuh make a bull-moose shiver! The sooner yuh gets back tuh Pecos an' barricaded in the sheriff's office, the quicker yore blasted knees is gonna stop shakin'. Hoss—giddap!"

SEVENTEEN
WHEN THE KILLER LAUGHED

FOR A SECOND LAWLER paused after pushing open the front door of Tranton's ranch house. Swiftly, then, he stepped inside the darkened hall and crouched against the wall, ready to go into action at the first warning note. Among the drifting shadows the rambling old house lay silent, lay stilled with a breathless hush that sent cold chills along the sheriff's spine.

Slowly, inch by cautious inch, he made his way along the wall. He guided himself by touch alone, for the hall was black with the Stygian murk found at the bottom of a well.

Then suddenly one reaching, feeling, outstretched hand encountered the cold frame of the sitting-room door. Again Lawler stiffened against the wall, listening. Yet only the soughing of the wind among the broad-leafed foliage of the cottonwoods drifted to his ears.

With one swift bound he placed himself inside the room with his back to a solid wall. Once more he grew stiff with listening. But naught happened and, assured, he made his way to the table, guided by the moonlight streaming in through a window. There he struck a match and lit the lamp.

Other than himself there appeared to be no one in the room. But the place was full of shadows and the sense of danger which he felt did not in any degree lessen. If anything, it grew constantly stronger as though some malignant, unseen presence watched him from a hidden place with mocking eyes.

The sheriff thrust both big hands deep within his Levi's pockets. He eyed the room with narrowed glance. He could think of nothing which seemed to have been disturbed; all within his range of vision seemed as he had left it earlier in the evening.

Picking up the lamp he made his way about the room, probing its shadowed corners. There was something wrong. Of this he was certain, for a sense of deep foreboding lay heavy in this house.

Lamp in hand he left the sitting-room on a tour of inspection. Despite his muscular weight he moved almost silently down the hall, his alert eyes wary.

He looked into the kitchen but found nothing out of order. No sign of an alien presence was apparent. All seemed as it should be. and wrapped in a slumbrous quiet.

He looked in the captain's bedroom, but there too everything appeared shipshape. The room was half timber, half adobe, having been added to the house ten years or so ago when the Captain had taken possession. It was cool and plainly furnished. Thick Navajo rugs were on the floor, there were two Remington lithographs on the walls and curtains at the deep-embrasured windows. A locked desk stood in one corner.

Lawler sent a final glance around and returned to

the hall. His lamp cast reflections on the polished Mexican cedar of its walls and its reflections kept pace with him as he strode along. Before the door to Sara's room he hesitated. It seemed almost sacrilege to profane such hallowed spot with his uninvited presence.

What if he had guessed wrong? Supposing this' crazy conviction that filled his mind were—

"Hell!" was his bitter oath. "I've got to make sure!"

Turning the knob he flung the door wide. The light of his lamp streamed in across the threshold in a yellow flood.

On that threshold he paused; stood stock-still while a tide of fear gripped up. His eyes bulged; beneath its heavy bronze his face went pale. With an effort he placed his lamp upon a dresser.

God knew his suspicions had been only too correct! No need now to see the answer to that telegram he'd sent by Pony George! No need for further guessing, worrying, or hopes.

In that endless moment that he stood there by the door he seemed weighed down by countless centuries of despair. His last vain hope was gone, his worries and suspicions proved well founded.

Now he held the answer to the question of why Captain Dan had been shot at; why Sara had broken their engagement; why the second bullet fired at Captain Dan had not been found. He saw now why the bushwhacking killer signed his taunting notes with the word "Justice" and why the murders themselves had been committed; saw, too, why certain of the girl's explanations of the circumstances surrounding that shooting last night had not agreed precisely with the explanation given by Captain Dan.

He was satisfied beyond the possibility of a doubt he knew the killer's identity, and his soul was filled with dread.

Inside Sara's room a small table by the bed was overturned, one leg broken off with every evidence of violence. The fragments of a shattered lamp lay near the door and there was a reek of coal-oil in the air. On the farther wall a picture hung lop-sided, its glass a mass of splinters. On the floor the worn rug was rumpled as though by scuffling feet. The girl herself was gone.

The murderer had been back!

There was a red neckerchief on the scuffled rug. It was Tranton's and it held the appearance of having been jerked forcibly from his neck. There were bullet holes in it and the searing mark of powder showed about the rents. And something sparkled on the floor nearby.

Lawler recognized it for what it was; a bit of braid— gold braid from the fancy vest of Tawson. Buck Tawson, the U.S. Marshal.

Lawler swayed in the doorway—swayed like a punch-drunk pugilist.

What a fool he'd been! He should have investigated his suspicions sooner! Should have waited in his office for the answer to the telegram he'd given Pony George to send! He'd been acting like a knot-head! And all because he'd been afraid to believe his astounding suspicions correct—because he had not wanted them to prove correct!

But they had been all along. He knew it now.

He bent above the lamp and blew it out. Straightening he turned and went lurching from the room and groped his way down the murky stone-flagged hall, where his spurs rang loudly, and out across the dark veranda. The moonlight struck across his face and showed it harsh with anger as he jerked the bay's reins from about the post.

It was late, damned late—but not too late to do his duty: not yet too late to vindicate the oath he'd sworn when taking office. He would go to Tawson's pronto! He would see that the Pecos Killer paid!

The long-legged bay was travelling at a dead run when Lawler settled in the saddle, his face a grim-lipped mask.

The bay's blurred hoofs beat like a drum through the moonlight night. Twisting, treacherous trails lay between its rolling muscles and the Bar 2 ranch, yet its rider drove a breakneck pace in an effort to outdistance his own black thoughts. Again and again in that nightmare ride a three-word phrase rang through Lawler's brain in letters of brass: *"Killers must pay!"*

He raked the bay's flanks with his bloody spurs but the hated phrase rang like a trumpet through the madness of his mind and would not hush. Speed could not retard it; not even the rush of his pony's hoofs could drown those bitter words.

On they raced, while beneath them the blurry miles slid by in a smeary haze of light and shadow.

They must reach the Bar 2 ere the killer fled, for it seemed plain to Lawler that the sender of these "Justice" notes was planning to leave the country just as fast as a horse could take him. And only a horse could hope to carry him beyond reach of the Law's long arm. He must reach the badlands, must lose himself and the girl in the maze of canyons, draws, ravines and gulches that cut the country to the south and west, for that way lay Mexico—Mexico and safety.

The big bay's smooth-rolling muscles between Lawler's legs made a comfortable feeling; brought to the sheriff a sense of conviction that the end of this ride would see the end of the trail.

The moon slid lower above his head, yet continued to dim the twinkling stars with its radiant splendor. Lawler rode now with loose-held rein, giving the bay a chance to choose its gait and opportunity to pick its footing. A coyote's wail came yammering across the wind that beat at his face with gusty fury and plastered his clothes tight against him in front and billowed them out behind.

The bay turned down a shallow gulch that loomed in the moonlight a natural corridor. The pony crossed its length, and up and out on the open range with never a faltering stride.

Lawler's thoughts turned to the bushwhacking killer he hoped to catch ere morning came. Long since he had figured the man for Rowdy Joe Raine, one-time leader of the notorious Toyah Lake gang. Evidently, Lawler thought, the fellow's men had at last tracked their absconding leader to his lair. They had trailed him for a split or vengeance. Yet all they'd got was death.

And those "Justice" notes! Red Lawler laughed. How slick it had been of the wily Raine to make it seem that he, *the killer,* was the sufferer; that *he* was the man on vengeance bent! *Justice!* What grim mockery that signature was!

But Rowdy Joe's race was nearly run. Distasteful as the task might be, Red Lawler was fully determined to make the killer pay the price of murder.

Around a curve went the hard-running bay, and down a long straight slope. Ahead lay a bit of desert country—sand and sage and greasewood, prickly-pear and cholla. A dun, dreary expanse that glowed and shimmered in the light of the argent moon.

The sheriff crossed a casual arroyo, the bay's fast pace never faltering. Trees with twisted branches and scrubby trunks thickened along a ridgeside that soon was left in their dusty wake. The stillness of the night held awe, solemnity, and only the bay's drumming hoofs made sound.

Hard's Pass Draw lay ahead.

Before them now the trail dropped dizzily to a deep ravine. Down there in the darkness grew blighted, stunted trees. Beneath their murky shadows flowed the gurgling yellow waters of Toyah Creek.

Straight down the precipitous slope Lawler drove the plunging bay. Down into the hollow and across the gurgling creek and on into the murky shadows beneath the grotesque trees where the night lay black.

A streak of crimson slashed the murk. A sharp report beat the wind apart and sent its crashing echoes back against the slope. The bay went down in a headlong fall.

When the echoes faded the thunder of hoofs was stilled. For a time the gurgling waters of the Creek made all the sound in the deathly hush. Then, sheering through the splash of unseen waters, rang a mocking laugh and the soul-torn sob of a frightened girl.

EIGHTEEN
A SITUATION SQUARELY FACED

WARM RAYS of the morning sun falling aslant his face as they slid over the ravine's eastern wall must finally have awakened Lawler. For long minutes his aching head was in a whirl and his intellect seemed dazed and dormant. He could comprehend neither where he was nor how he came to be here. Objects seemed strangely distorted when he turned his bloodshot eyes upon them. He seemed to have a double sight. He could see two separate groves of trees, two separate gurgling creeks. But presently this handicap passed and his vision grew somewhat clearer.

With an effort he turned his head. A dead horse—a long-legged bay—lay beside the trail in a grotesque heap.

Sight of the animal brought a sudden rush of memories. Fearful thoughts engendered by his illuminating return of memory served to rouse him from his stupor. He had been hurled from his horse when the bay took the bullet that had been meant for its rider. He realized that his head must have contacted something hard.

Raising an exploring hand he discovered a lump on his scalp and a large patch of hair matted and rough with dried blood.

He saw his hat beside a rock and shivered. Only that hat could have saved his life. It seemed a miracle—but perhaps he had not struck the stone. He could recall the burst of light in his brain and a flash of terrific pain. His exploring hand touched again the ragged wound. "Couldn't 'a' been much closer, I reckon," he muttered, eyeing the flat-topped rock.

He recalled now that streak of flame among the trees and the crash of the shot. Then his eyes fell upon a patch of sunlight and he groaned. He'd been unconscious several hours! It must be early morning now—the killer would be far away in the maze of badlands to the south.

A damnable thought, yet Lawler did not see how he could do anything about it now. Certainly he had not hankered to have the killer shoot his horse from under him and bash his head against a rock!

Thought of the killer getting away with Sara Tranton brought new strength surging through the sheriff's veins. His head was clearing fast. Instinctively he began to seek the extent of his damage. Aside from the jagged, swollen wound in his scalp, a bruised shoulder and several minor lacerations due to his spill, he found that he was not badly hurt.

He got to his feet and stood swaying dizzily for several moments. Then his head cleared. He looked around then returned his glance to a brooding contemplation of the bay —his borrowed horse. It would be no deader.

"I'm gettin' to be hard on horses," he muttered

gloomily. "Expect I'm due for some more shanks' marein' 'f I aim to get outa here."

It was then he became aware that his holster was empty. He searched the nearby brush but did not find the weapon. "Looks like I've got to start after that killer with neither a horse *nor* a gun! Reckon Obe Kringle was right at that I'm sure one hell of a sheriff, an' no mistake!"

He approached the dead bay to see if his rifle were worth salvaging. It was not. The bay had fallen on its left side and the rifle, having been in the saddle scabbard, was smashed beyond possibility of repair.

Lawler shook his head morosely. Picking up his hat he put it on carefully so as not to reopen the wound in his scalp, and then set off slowly down the trail. He waded the creek which was quite shallow at this point and, passing up the opposite slope, got out of the ravine.

It was half a mile to Tawson's Bar 2, which lay in plain sight and looked to be about a stone's throw away. He could see no sign of anyone moving about the buildings as he struck out for them with long strides. The early morning air was cool and invigorating, yet he well knew that in less than an hour this semi-arid stretch of country would be blistering hot. He was glad he'd knocked the heel from his left boot after that rifle bullet had torn the one from his right. He dreaded to think of having to walk this distance in high heels.

Approaching the headquarters of Bar 2, Lawler circled the buildings warily. But he saw no sign of human presence, which might or might not mean anything. He *did* manage to get behind the stable without, he sincerely hoped, having been seen.

Shoving up a window he pulled himself inside.

Tawson's horses were not in sight. Believing there was no longer any need for caution he passed quickly through the stable and out through the open front doors. There he received a shock, for the corral was in his vision. Inside the pole enclosure stood a dejected-looking pair of broncs. Lather-like sweat had dried on their hides. Lawler saw marks of the saddles which had been hurriedly stripped from their backs at no far distant date.

"Hell—those ain't Tawson's nags!" he exclaimed hoarsely.

"'Those broncs belong to Captain Dan and—" he broke off with a second oath and went sprinting toward the ranch house. A lamp was burning in the window.

He reached the porch and dashed across it, threw the front door wide and stopped. Once more he had arrived too late!

Face-down beneath the window Tawson sprawled. A dark smear between his motionless shoulders told the story. With crushing impact it came to Lawler that his hours of unconsciousness in the dark ravine had cost the marshal's life.

Tawson's pockets showed inside out. The drawers of the dresser in the far corner of the room lay upon the floor, their contents scattered round about. The killer had been after something beside the marshal's life. Had he found it?

Lawler thought it likely, if the sought-for thing had been here.

Spying the phone-box above the dead officer's bunk, he jerked the receiver from the hook and raised it to his ear. The line had not been cut, attesting to frantic hurry on the killer's part. Lawler called the telegraph office in Pecos.

Positive he knew the killer's identity, Lawler could not but hope that he was wrong. This call, he felt, would definitely discredit his suspicions or confirm them beyond all doubt.

Holding his lips pressed close to the mouthpiece he spoke slowly, distinctly, explaining to the operator that he was Sheriff Lawler. As proof of the fact he mentioned that yesterday afternoon he had sent off a message by Pony George to which he was expecting an answer. Would the operator kindly read said answer?

The operator would not. "You're not identified as Lawler yet," he gruffed. "Who was your wire sent to? What did it say? . . . Yeah—word for word!"

Lawler gave the desired information. A red mist floated before his vision as, satisfied, the operator quoted:

"'Man described undoubtedly Rowdy Joe Raine, former leader Toyah Lake Gang. When last in operation Raine's hair was black, not white. So far as we know them, all other points tally.'"

Mechanically Lawler hung the receiver back upon its hook. The last remaining vestige of hope was drained from him. His suspicions had proved well-founded indeed—too damned accurate by far!

Naught but dread, despair and duty lay before him. Dread of the future; despair of the mocking horde of lonely hours stretching without end down the lane of future life— cold dark clutching dread of the duty that must be his.

He was convinced at last that Dan Tranton, self-styled "sea-dog," was the infamous Pecos Killer!

Before Lawler had been placed a vast jigsaw puzzle of murder, mystery and sudden death for solving. And now he had it solved. Each last piece slipped neatly into place to reveal an all-but-perfect picture when Captain Dan Tranton was cast in the killer role. There were a few loose ends but Lawler reflected morosely that when those ends were tied the picture would be perfect.

Tranton had tried to persuade him, through the unwitting employment of Sara, that someone had tried to take his life two nights ago by hurling lead through the window of his illuminated office. As further proof the Captain had offered, reluctantly, the wound in his side—which had certainly been made by a bullet. That wound, Lawler now believed, was self-inflicted by the cunning Captain in the hope that wool would be drawn across the eyes of Lawler and any other lawmen who might become interested. That wound was to help the sheriff come to the natural conclusion that Tranton was one of the men marked by the killer for death. Under such an hypothesis it would be assumed impossible that Captain Dan was himself the murderer.

Slick, thought Lawler grimly; cunning and adroit. Quite worthy of the fertile twisted brain of Rowdy Joe, the pseudonym under which Tranton had led the renegades of Toyah Lake.

This explained the mystery of the missing bullet. The second shot was the one whose bullet had torn that splintered hole in Tranton's desk, described by him as the first shot—the one with which he had been wounded. The *first* shot was the one with which the scheming Captain had, upon the ridge-top, inflicted the wound in his side which was to establish for himself an airtight alibi.

He had carefully, Lawler figured, swathed the muzzle of his pistol in his neckerchief so no powder-marks would show about the wound. Last night he had left that bullet-ridden handkerchief blood-stained on the floor of Sara's room to make it appear that in defense of his daughter he had been killed, and his body hidden someplace about the house by the murderer who later had forced Sara to accompany him in his flight. Thus Tranton had again knocked down two birds with a single stone, and had at the same time furthered the illusion that he could not possibly be himself the infamous Pecos killer.

After inflicting his wound, two nights ago, on the ridge behind the house, Tranton had fired his second shot through the office window in such a manner that it struck his desk at the appropriate angle; had then sprinted to the window, climbed through it into his office barely in time to jerk the window down as Sara pounded on his door. Thus he had proved himself within his office while the shooting outside was going on.

The running footsteps Sara claimed to have heard moving toward the house were the footsteps of the Captain making that hurried return from the ridge. He, in turn, had described those footsteps as "horse's hoof-beats" and had said they were moving *away* from the house. This must have been what originally had shown Sara that her father definitely was up to something which he did not want found out. This lying explanation must have aroused Sara's suspicions to a fever heat and forced her, in his defense, to break her engagement.

Lawler mopped his brow. His expression was dark and scowling as he sat there summing up on Tawson's bunk. His big hands were clenched and knotted at his sides.

Two nights ago, at eight-thirty, it had not been quite dark.

Leastways, it had not been so dark but what Sara *might* have seen some part of the Captain's strange performance. If she had seen such a part, it was Lawler's surmise she could have guessed the rest with reasonable accuracy and so have known her father as the killer. *That* certainly would have explained their broken engagement!

Lawler recalled that no one in Pecos or its vicinity knew for fact one blessed thing concerning the Captain's past. They did not *know* that he was or ever *had* been a captain. Though they had accepted his word for it, he had never offered proof, other than, the very briny slang he seemed to sling about with ease. And if he had committed blunders in the use of sea-goingese, who had there been to point such blunders out?

Yes, Lawler admitted to himself, Dan Tranton was a slick customer from 'way back! Five years after bringing about the break-up of his gang of stage and bank robbers, Tranton had come with his gangling ten-year-old daughter to Pecos, center of the zone of his former crimes, and here had brazenly settled down to the diverting business of putting beef on steers!

One had to admire the man's ingenuity and nerve—these, Lawler told himself, and the love Tranton apparently bore his daughter were the only things about him which an honest man could admire.

And right now Lawler was thinking that the pseudo-captain's apparent love for his motherless girl was just that —*apparent*. Could any father who really loved his daughter force that daughter to share with him the hardships and hazards of a life on the Owl-Hoot Trail?

She had kept her suspicions of him to herself out of loyalty —had made herself an accessory after the facts of Tranton's murders. That had been the meaning, Lawler reflected, of her talk last night about loyalty and duty. She' had, in roundabout way, sought Lawler's advice upon the subject. And he —blind fool—had as much as told her that in a man's eyes loyalty and duty were of prime importance!

He swore whole-heartedly, blaming himself that he had not at that moment really begun to suspect the Captain. He should, he bitterly thought, have suspected the suave old scoundrel from the first!—from the very moment when his explanation of the shots and foot-steps had differed from the girl's!

Now Lawler saw the meaning of the single initial signed to the note Pony George had found at Reede's. That "T" had stood, not for Tawson, but for Tranton. Reede must have been the second man to have discovered the Captain's true identity, and have been offered hush money to seal his lips.

To seal them until such time as Tranton could get around to sealing them for good!

Lawler realized now how easily that "Justice" note had come to be found by Kringle in Doak's pocket after Pony George had finished searching. Dan Tranton had been present at that searching; when it was over and the deputy had been looking elsewhere it had been child's play for Tranton to get the note into the dead man's clothes.

Now the reason for Sara's determined defense of

Link Holladay was explained. Lawler now. understood that at that time Sara must have known that her father was the killer and that palpably Holladay could have had no hand in Toreva's sudden demise.

Toreva, however, must have known all along that Tranton was the murderer of Doak. Very likely the Captain had given the Mexican his split long ago, so had nothing to fear from him. Then, perhaps, after Doak's killing Toreva had demanded hush money. If so, Toreva had made a fatal mistake in psychology.

Lawler's thoughts next turned to the man who lay so still upon the floor. Tawson had undoubtedly been recognized by Tranton for what he was—a U.S. Marshal. Tawson was in the country to get him: Tranton had simply beaten the marshal to the jump. Having planted the bit of braid in Sara's room last night to implicate Tawson, the Captain evidently had later found reason to close the marshal's lips for good with one quick stroke of a knife.

Perhaps he had hoped that the authorities, investigating the marshal's death, would become inextricably tangled in a web of close-spun suspicion when knowledge of that bit of braid in Sara's room, together with the bloody, bullet-pierced neckerchief of the girl's father, came to their attention.

He had been pretty certain, at any rate, should the Law ever stumble on a correct interpretation of events he would by that time be safely beyond its reach.

A far worse thought abruptly burst on Lawler's consciousness: Tranton, now, would never dare turn Sara loose—he must keep her with him constantly or seal her mouth forever! For free, Sara would place him in the shadow of the noose!

Lawler wiped cold perspiration from his forehead. Tranton had plotted well, had covered his tracks with consummate skill. He would have been caught red-handed last night but for his infinite care of detail. Tranton had known the sheriff for a man of dogged tenacity and stubborn determination and had left nothing to chance. He had expected Lawler to follow him and had awaited him in the spot of greatest vantage along the trail he was sure Lawler would be taking. Crossing the blackness of that stretch of ground beyond the creek, Lawler had been plainly silhouetted against the glowing moonlit wall behind. Only for the sudden upflinging of the bay's head, Lawler would have died—and it was patent that the killer thought he had!

Swiftly the sheriff reviewed his case against Dan Tranton. The Captain, recognizing the marshal as soon as Tawson had appeared in Pecos, to save his neck had figured upon a succession of ruthless killings. There were too many witnesses against him; he had to whittle their number down—for killing Tawson alone would do no good. Another marshal would be sent to take his place. Desperate, his hiding place at last discovered by the law as well as by members of the gang he had betrayed, Tranton had sent for Max Smith. Then he had killed Doak, who was already on the ground. Next had come the faked attempt upon his own life, designed to turn suspicion elsewhere. This illusion he had promptly strengthened by giving out an impression that he knew the would-be assassin and was determined to keep the fellow's identity to himself.

Next in Tranton's ruthless campaign to gain for himself impregnable security had come the murder of Manuel Toreva. A bleak smile quirked the sheriff's lips as he reflected that Big-Ear Lester's testimony against Holladay, save for mention of the latter's name, would have fit the Captain equally well. Then Smith had arrived and ridden blithely to his doom. Reede's death had followed swiftly and on the heels of that Tranton had staged the false struggle in Sara's room to plant suspicion on Tawson and lure Red Lawler to his end. That Lawler had not met his end in the dark ravine was certainly no fault of Tranton's.

And by now, he reflected darkly, Dan Tranton and the daughter he was kidnapping must be far away among the maze of draws and canyons that gouged the country to south and west.

Stepping from Tawson's shack out into the sandy yard, the sun's hot smash struck Lawler like a hammer. The near-noon air was filled with a dry heat that scorched the nostrils, that drew all moisture from his body.

For long moments, nevertheless, he stood staring out across the shimmering layers of heat that lay in stratas above the yellow earth. His gaze went out across the rolling range, the distant ranches, the sand and desolation. This was his kingdom. Nearly as far as he could see in any direction his word was law. With Tranton riding clear, and each moment taking Sara farther from him, the thought was a mockery that made him squirm with its torture.

Then his lean jaw clenched and he squared his broad shoulders with resolution. Though it be the last act he performed in life, he meant to catch Dan Tranton and make him pay.

NINETEEN
"I GOT TOO MUCH RESPECT"

PONY GEORGE KASTA looked but little the worse for wear on the morning following his harrowing experiences at Joe Reede's Lazy R. He sat with his spurred heels resting comfortably on the sheriff's desk, a pad of finger-marked white paper on his knee and a stubby pencil gripped in hand.

To be sure, there was a home-made bandage about his head that peeped forth a trifle beneath his hat and aroused considerable speculation on the part of those who saw it. It had, in fact, surprised a comment from no less a personage than Obe Kringle, the coroner, when Pony George had stopped by to tell him there was a chore for him at the Lazy R. But the deputy could not be led to talk about the manner in which he had come to require the need of a bandage about his cabeza. Nor had he a great deal to say anent why Obe Kringle was needed at the ranch of Reede.

"But what in the heck do I wanta drive 'way out there for?" complained the coroner.

"Couldn't say."

"Well, what's out there?"

"Reede."

"I can see him in town without stirrin' from my porch," objected Kringle.

"Not no more, yuh can't."

"Why—"

"He's the one that's needin' yore attention."

"You don't mean to tell me Reede's dead?"

"He'll never be no deader!"

"My soul!" gasped the startled coroner.

"An' Reede's body," finished the deputy drily, "oughta make a dang good pair!"

And now here was Pony George safely ensconced in the sheriff's office inside the Pecos courthouse where he felt reasonably safe—for the moment. But though he did not believe the Pecos Killer would come seeking for him here, he was a man who believed, likewise, in taking no more chances than were absolutely necessary.

In the furtherance of this commendable philosophy he had placed with considerable effort a pile of tin cans, one atop the other, behind the closed office door in such, a manner that they formed a hazy resemblance to the famous Leaning Tower. A person opening that door from the hall side would be bound to announce his coming, intentionally or otherwise.

Besides this ingenious alarm system, Pony George had also taken the liberty of moving Lawler's desk from its accustomed position so that, from where he now sat behind it, he commanded an unobstructed view of both windows.

"One thing that corpse an' cartridge occasion did fer me which I got tuh admit is right helpful," he muttered thoughtfully. "It sure give me some right smart ideas fer m' Ballad of Kyote Cal."

He looked pridefully down upon the four scrawled lines of writing soiling the virginity of the pad's top sheet:

> *"He was tall an' slim an' quick as a cat,*
> *An' like a cat he walked—*
> *His clothes was black, an' black was*
>   *his hat;*
> *Like honey, his voice when he talked.*

"George," he complimented himself modestly, "that there verse is sure a dinger! Why, gosh—it's good as the stuff that fella Shakespeare used tuh write." Re-reading the verse he added, judicially: "In fact, I expect it's a little better."

For several moments longer he continued to regard his masterpiece with all the fond pride of a loving parent. Then once again he wet his stub of pencil on the tip of his tongue and made ready to get down to the serious business of composing another four lines.

But the Muse must needs be coaxed, he found. It was slow work, yet little by little new thoughts began to form. Word by word and phrase by phrase, with many a muttered oath and grunt, he managed to tabulate another quatrain:

> *"One hand, long an' lean, clung close to*
>   *his Colt;*
> *As he chuckled right nasty an' grim*
> *"Jest lissen tuh me, yuh dirty Paiute;*
> *That dame yuh been neckin's my bim!"*

Pony George pursed his leathery lips as he scanned appraisingly his latest jingle for posterity. From the expression that began slowly to dawn on his ugly countenance it was obvious that the verse afforded him a good deal of quiet satisfaction. Forgetting for the nonce to keep a look-out for his playmate of the previous night, he tilted his hat rakishly and stroked his long nose.

"'That ain't so bad," yet his voice was dubious. "Still —it ain't so dang good. Leastways, it ain't in the same class with that last 'un. *That* verse is sure gonna be right-down hard tuh beat, an' I ain't meanin' *if* or *perhaps!*"

He regarded the two quatrains pensively. "Now le' me see. Cal hadn't ort tuh stand fer any talk like that from a stranger. Cal's a real tough hombre—like m' boss, Red Lawler. Only Red ain't so orn'ry as Cal. Trouble with Red is he ain't got no poetry in his soul. He can't sabe it's poetry makes the world spin round!

"Hmm. Now what the hell was I thinkin' about when Red got me off the track? . . . Oh, yeah—Kyote Cal. Wal, it's plain that Cal ort tuh have some sorta comeback fer this obstreperous stranger. 'Course, Cal don't savvy what a mean jasper he's buckin' up against, so he'd be feelin' pretty mean, seems like. Le's see, now …"

> Cal whirled around quick, an' he sez
>   "Looky here,
> Pilgrim, yo're headin' fer hell
> I don't give a damn if yo're mean as a
>   mule;
> It's time someone sounded yore knell!"

A tremendous rattling crash jerked Pony George's startled eyes to the door. It was standing wide open and, framed in the opening stood a man. George gulped uneasily, for the man was Red Lawler and Lawler's expression was not, by any stretch of his duty's ready imagination, one of amusement.

"Well, what happened to you?" Lawler gruffed, eyeing the bandage that showed from under George's hat. "That the result of them shots I heard when you called me the second time from Reede's? Looks like you been in a fight."

"Fight!" snorted Pony George, indignant. "Lemme tell yuh. Red Lawler, yuh dang nigh lost yore best depity las' night! Do yuh realize I dang near got massacreed? An' speakin' of fights—yuh don't look so durn festive yoreself."

"I ain't feelin' festive neither," Lawler's tone was curt.

"Looks like yuh been playin' tag with a mountain lion."

"Playin' hell would be more like it! George the Pecos Killer's pulled his picket pin an' sloped—with Sara Tranton."

Pony George's lower jaw dropped open; his eyes grew big and round.

"The Pecos Killer," Lawler told him, "is Dan Tranton—"

The next morning posses under the direction of Sheriff Lawler and Deputy Kasta set out from Pecos to comb the surrounding country in an effort to run to earth, dead or alive, the notorious Pecos Killer.

Aside from the forty-one men armed and outfitted by the sheriff's office, there were innumerable smaller parties unofficially scouring the vicinity in the hope of gaining some part of the seven-thousand dollar reward offered by Reeves County for the capture or death of Dan Tranton. It was a red-letter occasion in the history of Pecos.

But the man-hunters did not come up with the elusive and much-sought Captain, neither that day nor the next, nor the day after that. For two weeks hard-riding posses under the grim-lipped sheriff and his poetic deputy searched Reeves County from end to end.

They combed the desert country and all that rolling stretch of range south of Pecos to Balmorhea in ever-widening circles. But to no avail. Dan Tranton had completely vanished. Either he had made good his escape and left the country, or he had found some hole-up never previously brought to the attention of the forces of law and order.

Kringle brought his juries together and returned verdicts of murder against Tranton for the deaths of Joe Reede and Buck Tawson.

During the following two weeks the reward-hungry posses and many private citizens, all searching with the same motive, labored mightily in a hunt that wore their leathered horses down to skin and bone.

With unwearying persistence they combed the bad-lands and mountain areas again and again. With dogged tenacity they fought the stinging grit and stifling heat of the desert country in a wallowing, wide-flung search across the shifting sands. But they did not cut sign of the wanted man, though occasionally Link Holladay and other lesser fry were seen watching them with mocking grins. Once or twice Holladay even helped, though most of his time was given over on such occasions to razzing the other searchers.

It was exasperating, the way Dan Tranton evaded their far-flung net. The search had gone from Kent almost to Angeles; from Orla to beyond the town of Sand Hills; from Sand Hills in a straight line south to a junction with the Pecos River; westward along that river to a certain spot where they swung southwest to the southwestern boundary of Reeves County, returning through Balmorhea State Park to Toyahvale, thence to Kent and back to Pecos.

On the fifteenth day Lawler gave it up and disbanded the posses.

But he did not give up his intention of bringing the killer back to face the penalty for his crimes.

"Can't see what yuh're goin' to do about it," Pony George told him cheerfully as they sat in the sheriff's office that afternoon. "Looks like tuh me we been pretty well all over this county. Yuh've warned all the surroundin' counties an' we've plastered pictures of 'im all over the whole dang estate. Reeves County has sure been raked with a fine-tooth comb."

"Yeah," Lawler hunched his broad shoulders, took a turn or two about the room, "an' it ain't done a mite of good. Tranton's still ridin' free an' easy an' Sara ain't been heard from." He thrust his hands deep-down in his pockets. Eyeing George intently, he added, "But we ain't hunted none outside the county."

Pony George squinted owlishly. "Y'ain't figgerin' tuh go clear tuh Mexico after 'im, are yuh?"

"If necessary—yeah." Lawler's tone was flat and serious. "Get it into your head, George, that I'm gonna get Dan Tranton, one way or another. It's my duty to apprehend him for these killin's. What do you think I feel like when I recall how he's forcin' Sara to stick with him through all the hardships his flight must be facin' him with?"

"What do yuh think," George countered, "Sara'll feel like when yuh bring her ol' man back tuh face a hangman's rope? Ever spent any thought on that?"

"Do you think I'm a fool?" Lawler growled.

"Why don't yuh turn yore star in then an' give it up? If yuh ain't sheriff no more, folks can't expect yuh to risk yore neck huntin' Tranton an' tryin' tuh bring 'im in."

"I'm not dodgin' the issue. I ain't the side-steppin' kind. What's more," Lawler said grimly, "Tomorrow mornin' I'm headin' for points south."

"Yuh mean—Mexico?" George's eyes were round.

"I mean . . . Well, mebbe it'll be better if you don't know. But I'll say this much; I'm figurin' to go where my star'll be a damned sight more of a liability than a asset. An' I ain't aimin' to come back till I've found Tranton an' Sara— if Sara's still alive."

"Suppose she ain't?"

"Then," said Lawler darkly, "I'll be comin' back alone."

TWENTY
"WHAT'S YOUR HURRY, MR. HOLLIDAY?"

IN THE ONE-ROOM shack serving the Bar 2 for a ranch house since the advent of Buck Tawson, a group of hard-faced men were gathered about the rough plank table leisurely finishing a supper of beans, bacon and biscuits. Chief among this group was the burly Holladay—gentleman of the Hungry Loop.

Rubbing his bottle-like nose with a calloused hand that was none too clean, Holladay gave his companions a hard stare.

"Tonight," he said, "I'm figgerin' to take a pasear into Pecos. I got a long chore in a dark suit what's needin' tendin' bad."

"But," began one of the men. Holladay's rough growl rode through his voice:

"Account's too long past due right now. I ain't figgerin' to wait no longer. I'm gonna make that slat-sided son of a rattlesnake's grandmother wish to hell he'd never been born!"

"Kringle, yuh're meanin', I take it?" asked one of the others thoughtfully. "Be kinda risky, won't it?"

"Risky? What of it? You ain't figgerin' that mealy-mouthed windbag could ever beat me to the draw, are yuh, Tierny?"

"Wal, look—" said Tierny soberly. "Pecos is kinda on the prod right now. Be better tuh wait. S'posin' someone should recognize yuh?"

"What if someone does? Hell, they got nothin' on me!" sneered Holladay, wiping a greasy hand on the scarred bat-wing chaps he wore. "ı been weaned for quite some spell an' figger on bein' plumb able to take care of any little thing what comes along."

"Yuh can't lick the whole damn town!"

"Whole damn town won't try pickin' on me. Least-ways, not all to once't."

"But what'll it get yuh? Seems tuh me you are gettin' kinda reckless, Link. That Kringle gent ain't worth a two-bit ante in this game. Anyways, he's the one what fixed yo' getaway."

"What's that got to do with it?" Holladay scowled. "He's the one what got me slapped in gaol in the first place, the lyin' hound! Did you ever know me tuh own a blackjack with my name burned on it?"

"Jest the same," Tierny observed quietly, "I can't see no sense in riskin' more of the same jest tuh take a whack at the fella what got yuh out."

"Look," growled Holladay viciously. "That skunk tried to frame me with the murder of Toreva. There can't no gent frame Link Holladay an' go round blowin' about it. I'm figgerin' to beat that coroner up so bad he'll think a Kansas twister struck him. After that, he'll mind his own business, mebbe."

"Wal," shrugged Tierny. "It's yore funeral, I reckon."

Holladay laughed. "If there's any funeral it won't be mine. I'll be back 'fore mornin' an' we'll strike out for the Barrillas. Keep yore eye on."

"What yuh want us tuh do with—"

"Jest keep on like we been doin'," Holladay cut in, "an' see that yuh keep these hellions in hand."

Shoving back his chair Holladay got to his feet and went out to the corral where he roped himself a bronc, slapped a saddle on its back, slipped on a bridle and went loping off toward town.

Coroner Obe Kringle was a man who held a high opinion of himself. He knew that the best way to get ahead in a world of more or less competition was to play politics and make it a habit to grease the right palm. He had no scruples; his motto was "Every man for himself." He had done quite nicely with this system.

On this particular evening he was feeling very much at ease as he sat rocking in his comfortable adobe house on the outskirts of town. He was taking a deal of pleasure from the fact that Red Lawler and his posses had returned empty-handed this afternoon from their two-weeks' search for Dan Tranton.

"Damn young squirt!" he growled, then chuckled as he thought of the discomfiture that must be Lawler's as a result of his vain efforts to apprehend the Pecos Killer.

"Won't be long now," he reflected smugly, "till the county commissioners ask for Lawler's resignation. When that welcome time arrives, perhaps this county'll see a real gent packin' that star—Obe Kringle, mebbe." And he smirked in anticipation.

Rising presently from his easy chair by the window he crossed to the table and lit the lamp. Dusk had fallen outside and the coroner was a man who preferred much light; he had no use for shadows. He closed the door too, for the evening air was cool and invigorating and Kringle was a man who liked his ease. Oftentimes of an evening he would have a few friends in for a game of stud; Zeb Hartley, who ran the general store, and other prominent townsmen. Obe particularly enjoyed these "friendly" games as he nearly always won—due, perhaps to the fact that most of his companions played according to Mr. Hoyle while Kringle was a man who believed in making his own rules.

"Reckon I'll call Zeb up now an' see if him an' some of the others don't want to drop over for a little stud tonight," he thought. And going to the phone he called Zeb. And Zeb said they'd be glad to "set in" for a spell. Zeb promised to round up some other boys soon as he finished figuring on his accounts.

The coroner returned to the comfort of his easy chair by the window.

He must have been dozing. For he roused to the thump of steps crossing the porch. He hastened to the door and flung it open. He was expecting to see Zeb and the others, but what he *did* see gave him much the same sort of shock he would have realized had someone struck him unexpectedly across the head with a crowbar. He was almost floored, for Link Holladay stood there grinning.

"Howdy, Obe. Ain't got company, have you? Like tuh palaver some."

"I ain't got company," Kringle said, "but I'm expectin' some any minute."

Holladay forestalled his attempt to shut the door by thrusting between it and its frame a booted foot. Then pushing Kringle before him he stalked into the house and shut the door.

"Wal," he said, looking curiously around, "nice place yuh got here, Obe. You must be doin' pretty well. You givin' the killer a cut?"

"What do you want?" Kringle's tone was not quite petulant. He was beginning to wish he'd left the big rustler in gaol.

"Come tuh thank you for all yuh've done for me, Obe. Special-like fer producin' that blackjack at the inquest the other day an' claimin' yuh found it under Toreva's window. Mebbe you did find it there. But yuh never found it like it was when yuh showed it tuh that damn jury 'cause I never put my name on a blackjack in my fife."

"Why—why—" Kringle stammered and fell abruptly silent.

"This here's a swell night for a murder, Obe," said Holladay pleasantly.

A hoarse cry broke from Kringle's throat as he backed away. "Wh—what you want with me?"

"Why, look, Obe—I ain't forgotten the way yuh run on me at that inquest you held on Toreva. Kinda figgered mebbe I'd swing for Toreva's death, eh? You yeller cur! I'm gonna take you apart, fella, an' throw the pieces out the window!" Kringle could see the rustler's eyes glowing like smoldering coals beneath the down-turned brim of his shabby hat. The rustler's thin lips were stretched tight across his huge buck teeth in a grimace that sent a wave of fear up the coroner's spine. A feeling of helplessness seemed to have him in its grip; the blood surging through his arteries seemed to curdle as he stared at the advancing Holladay.

A wolfish growl left the rustler's lips. There was murder in his glance.

"Gawd's sake, Link!" the coroner screamed. "I never done it, I tell yuh!"

"Him as sups with the Devil needs a damn long spoon," jeered Holladay. "You ain't got the guts for the kinda stunt you tried to pull. A single-barrel squirt like you, Obe, ain't got no business on the river side of the corral. If yuh know any prayers now's the time tuh say 'em."

Leaning forward Holladay reached out a calloused hand toward Kringle's collar.

With sudden, desperate leap Kringle avoided that outstretched hand and sent his own diving beneath his frock coat for the weapon he always carried in a spring holster beneath his arm.

"Why, you drivelin' nit!" snarled Holladay. His reaching hand dropped hipward. As it struck, a burst of flame sheared outward from his thigh.

Obe Kringle reeled against the wall, jack-knifed and slid forward on his face as the shot's concussion snuffed the lamp and sent wild echoes smashing through the dark.

Gun gripped ready Holladay whirled, flung open the door and went sprinting out across the porch making for the horse that stood with grounded reins just below the railing.

Shouts rose from a group of shadowy figures sprinting toward him from down the street. Holladay's gun whipped up; flame spurted luridly from its weaving muzzle. A man reeled screaming from the running group. A second sprawled headlong. A third clutched an arm and staggered, Shouts— curses—pandemonium!

Someone in that milling blur of figures produced a pistol and opened up. Lead splashed the adobe at Holladay's back. Jumping the rail he landed in the saddle, thrust an arm beneath his horse's neck and gathered in the reins. Viciously his star rowels jabbed the animal's flanks. With a frightened squeal it bolted for the open range.

Three hundred yards it covered at rocket speed. Then Holladay sawed the reins back savagely, jerking his animal's head back forcibly against its chest. On braced legs the horse skidded to a stop. Broadside before it loomed the dark blur of another horseman and the town lights glinted on the carbine across his lap.

"What's your hurry, Mr. Holladay?" came Lawler's cold drawl through the gloom.

Holladay cursed bitterly. "What the hell you doin' out here?"

"Might be I was enjoyin' the evenin' breeze. Then again I might have been waitin' here for you. Take your choice."

"Some day," Holladay snarled, "I'm gonna have to gut-shoot you!"

"You've certainly been takin' plenty of practice— must be your eyesight's failin', Link."

Had Holladay's pistol not been empty at that moment, he looked as though he would have shot it out with Lawler then and there. Even as it was he appeared sorely tempted to chance his luck and jerk his Winchester from the saddle. But what he did was" to grunt, "Expect yuh're figgerin' to pull me in fer breakin' gaol ... ?"

"When a rim-fire man like you breaks gaol I never let it bother me," Lawler drawled contemptuously.

"Was aimin' to let you loose in the mornin' anyhow. No, I ain't after you for breakin' gaol—'f I had been I coulda grabbed you before when you was helpin' some of my men hunt Tranton."

"Then if you ain't wantin' me choke off the blat an' git outa my way!"

"Hold on a minute, Link. Seems like you might know what's all the commotion about down yonder. Seems like it might be in front of Kringle's place. Seen Obe lately?"

"What if I have?"

"Be kinda tough, say, if you'd seen him to-night an' it was found that he'd been killed," said Lawler softly. "Mebbe you an' me better ease down that way an' see what's up. Seems like I heard shootin' a spell back. Got any burnt shells in your hog-leg, Link?"

Holladay shoved his horse in close beside that of the sheriff, as though to hand his pistol over for inspection. Instead his clenched fist drove abruptly at Lawler's head. Lawler ducked, and the carbine roared. A streak of flame tore past the rustler's shoulder. Then Holladay swayed in, got his hands about the weapon's barrel and wrested it from Lawler's grip. Aloft he swung it, and downward in a flailing arc at the sheriff's chest as Lawler flung himself backward over his horse's rump. He lit rolling and, bounding to his feet, jerked the pistol from his holster.

Holladay sank the spur as Lawler fired and missed. Lawler emptied his pistol. But Holladay stayed in the saddle and his pounding horse soon vanished in the black of the open range.

TWENTY-ONE
PEACEFUL INTERLUDE

BY THE TIME Lawler had caught his frightened mount he saw no sense in trying to overtake the fleeing rustler. He believed he had wounded Holladay, basing his opinion upon the way Holladay had seemed to sway in the saddle. At any rate, just now it was Lawler's business to see what had happened down the street.

So turning in that direction he jogged along till he reached the coroner's house. There he stopped. A crowd of angry, gesticulating townsmen before the porch fell silent as Lawler swung from the saddle and strode through them to the porch and up the steps and on inside.

At one side of the room Zeb Hartley and his friends stood motionless. The light from the rekindled lamp clustered the floor with shadows. But as Lawler approached he saw the limp figure of a man upon the floor. It was flat upon its back staring ceilingward with sightless eyes. Obe Kringle.

"He was on his face when we came in," explained Hartley. "We turned him over to see was there anything we could do. There wasn't. The fella what shot him jumped out the door as we came runnin' up. He threw down on us. Shot Bill Townsend deader'n hell. Nicked Zeke Loftus an' Ray Branton. He jumped to his saddle an' made a getaway. I had a gun an' done some firin' but I don't guess I hit 'im."

"Who was he? Anyone see his face?"

No one answered. Then Hartley said, "Too dark tuh make out his face from where we were. We oughta have more lights down here. This end of town's dark as the inside of Jonah's whale. I've said it afore an' I'll say it ag'in. Damn shame! 'F it hadn't been so dark Obe might be alive this minute. Who knows?"

Another man said, "Gettin' so a fella ain't even safe in his own house no more."

Lawler made no examination of the coroner. He'd seen too many dead men before not to know when life had departed. Obe Kringle he knew had been dead some minutes. And the chances, he thought, were about one hundred to one that Link Holladay had done the killing.

But he saw no reason for telling the townsmen that.

"First thing in the mornin'," he said, "I'll get on the killer's trail. Can't see to do anything before mornin'. One of you gents can call ol' Doc Shantert in to look at the body, then you can put it on the bed."

After putting up his horse, Lawler went directly to his office. Pony George was holding down the shrieval chair.

George looked up when Lawler came in and flung his hat on the desk. "Was that shootin' I heard a while back?"

"Think mebbe it was thunder, George?"

"Wal, there ain't no call for yuh tuh get sarcastic. *I* couldn't tell from here what it was, could I?"

"I don't expect it occurred to you to get out of that chair long enough to find out, did it?"

"Wal, sufferin' snakes!" Pony George protested. "I figgered *somebody* oughta stay in this office in case there was a robbery or another murder in town an' some gent come lookin' for the law!"

Lawler sighed. "No use, I reckon," he said resignedly. "You're you an' Gawd himself, I expect, couldn't change you." After a moment of disgusted silence he told of the happening up town and of his brush with Holladay.

"That fella's bad medicine!" Pony George declared, pounding the desk with his fist for emphasis. "Somethin' oughta be done about gents like him. They give this county a bad repitation."

"Yeah," said Lawler drily and, thrusting his big hands deep into his Levi's pockets, fell silent, staring gloomily at the floor.

"D'yuh know what?" Pony George asked after a time. "I think that durned rustler has some kinda connection with Dan Tranton."

"It's an idea," Lawler agreed. "Considerin' its pedigree I reckon we ought to treat it kindly."

Pony George sniffed. "Anyhow," he said, "Link Holladay showed up around here just a short spell before Doak an' the rest of them jaspers." He regarded the sheriff somberly. "Do you reckon Link was bad hit?"

"Couldn't tell. Might not have been hit at all. It was damn dark out there an' I had to do my triggerin' by guesswork mostly. Look like he clutched at the horn once but I might been mistaken. I'll give Link credit—

he's crafty as a lobo. If he figgered I'd quit shootin' he'd act that way, anyhow."

Pony George nodded. "I expect you hit him. But I'm bettin' we don't find him layin' round anyplace in the mornin'. Reckon this'll sorta put a crimp in yore plans for leavin' town, won't it?"

Lawler pursed his lips thoughtfully. "No," he said at last. "Reckon I'll be leavin', anyway. You can ride along a spell an' we'll keep our eyes out for Link's carcass. 'F we find it you can pack him back to town."

"Shucks," said George. "I was sorta figgerin' tuh trail along."

"Where?"

"Why, huntin' Tranton, of course. Wherever yuh was figgerin' tuh go."

Lawler shook his head. "Be too dangerous, George. You better stay here. I gotta leave a deputy here anyhow. No tellin' what I'll bump into."

"How about appointin' Zeb Hartley's kid depity till we get back?"

Lawler looked at George in some surprise. "I can't see why you're wantin'—"

"Flip a coin," cut in the deputy, anxiously. "Heads I go, tails I stay."

"All right. If you wanta be buzzard bait," said Lawler wearily, "far be it from me to stop you. Here goes," and he flipped the coin. It landed heads.

"Now," said Pony George jubilantly, "Mr. Kasta's li'l boy gets tuh go!"

"I'm some surprised you wantin' to go this way. Thought you was puttin' in all your time on that coyote ballad?"

"I've done finished that. Can't think how to start

another'n so I might's well go with you. Might be I would get some new ideas," George said hopefully.

"Finished that thing, have you?" Lawler said. "How's it end? Cal get killed?"

"Wal—ef yuh insist on knowin', I'll read 'er," said George, and dug hastily in his pocket for the pad.

"I wasn't insistin'. But if you want an opinion, I'll listen," Lawler said. Leaning back in his chair he closed his eyes. "Better read that last verse over again so I can catch on where you left off."

"Wal, sure," said George, and—

> " 'Oh, yeah?' says the stranger, 'Yuh son
>   of a Chink!
> Git yore paws up an' keep 'em right
>   still—
> Don't gimme no sass, yuh mangy Kyote,
>   'Cause it's you thet I'm pinin tuh
>   drill!'
>
> "At this orn'ry insult Kyote Cal swore,
> An' his hand to his holster did flash—
> The stranger's gun spoke, an' the sound
>   of Cal's fall
> Was drowned in the thunderous crash!
>
> "Cal uttered a sigh, an' his eyes they
>   got dim,
> As he slumped to the sawdust-spread
>   floor—
> An' the stranger's harsh laff rang out
>   like a blast,
> As he crouched, gun in hand, by the

door.

"Swift his narrow-eyed glare flashed
     round like a curse,
As he looked for Kyote Cal's dame—
She stood there by the bar, with her hand
     on a knife,
An' her charms standin' out like a
     flame.

"All the folks in that place stood back
     wooden-faced,
As the stranger cat-stepped toward our
     Lou——
From his lips burst an oath, an' his eyes
     filled with fear
As her hand flung the knife straight an'
     true.

" 'Tis a saga of sorrow, a tale bold but
     true.
That yuh've heard of ol' Kyote Cal-
An' the moral this saga has tried tuh
     drive in, is
'Don't be a fool fer a gal!'"

Despite his troubles Lawler chuckled.
"How'd yuh like 'er?" Pony George
     anticipated praise.
"So-so," said Lawler. "Reminds me of
     the curate's egg."
"Was it good?"
"Yeah—in spots!"

TWENTY-TWO
"TWO FELLAS HELD THE STAGE UP"

CHILL DAYBREAK WAS in the air and beneath the heavens the range lay grey and lifeless when Lawler and Pony George rose on the following morning. After a cold breakfast of beans and biscuits, wolfed down with scalding java, George went to the stable for their horses while Lawler washed the dishes.

Great scarlet streaks appeared in the eastern sky. The light grew steadily stronger and crimsoned along the far horizon as the sun got out of bed.

Old Sol's beaming face was just commencing to peep above the rim of the world when the sheriff and Pony George, rifles under their stirrup leathers, food in their saddle pockets and blankets rolled in slickers behind their cantles, struck out on the trail of Link Holladay.

The air was cold and invigorating and the breaths of horses and men shot out in smoky plumes before them though both lawmen, experienced desert men, knew that in hardly more than an hour it would be stifling hot.

"Reckon he's got a pretty good start by now," offered Pony George.

"If he was badly wounded, we'll find him," said Lawler grimly, "because we won't have travelled far. Somehow, though, I kinda think mebbe he was funnin' me when he reeled in his saddle las' night. If I hit him at all it prob'ly was only a nick—mebbe caught him in the arm."

"Hope it was his gun arm, then. That jasper can shoot! Took four shots at them fellas last night; killed one an' nicked two others. That's shootin', if anyone should ride up an' ask yuh!"

"Yeah—not bad. Mighta been luck though. Somethin' tells me we ain't gonna come up with Link today. Let's shake it up a little. These tracks are pretty plain."

They increased their pace to an easy lope, Lawler watching the trail, Pony George keeping a nervous eye on the surrounding country. They wanted no ambushes this morning.

Trail-lure gripped them. For a time, the set of hoofprints they were following, representing as it did the flight of a killer, was all-engrossing. The sun's rays grew hotter and hotter, yet they did not notice.

"This is Link's trail, all right," Lawler muttered presently. "He's ridin' that hog-back roan; I'd recognize them tracks anyplace. Two-year-old whittler."

"Reckon that's so, Red. That sign is big as soup plates." Pony George shot a sidelong glance at his superior. "Mebbe we better ease up a little."

"What for? These broncs can hold this pace all day."

"I wasn't thinkin' 'bout the nags. Looks like Link's

headin' straight fer the Bar 2. What we gonna do if his gang's holed up there?"

"Do?" Lawler laughed grimly. "We're goin' in an' arrest him.—that's what!"

"Yeah, but—mebbe his gang won't like it."

"Mebbe they won't. That's *their* lookout. If they wanta put up a scrap they got nobody to blame but themselves if they get hurt."

"Yeah—but these corpse an' cartridge occasions is hard on weak hearts."

"Shouldn't worry you any. Fella what smokes chewin' tobacco in his pipe hadn't oughta do any complainin' "'bout a weak heart."

George frowned and pulled the rifle from his scabbard, rode with it across his saddle. "If they's any shootin', all I hope is I get first shot!"

Talk fell away as mile by mile the sign showed fresher. The lawmen grew more alert, more cautious, seldom topping rises without first spying out the land afoot. Around nine-thirty they drew close to Tawson's former shack. There was no sign of life about the place. The pole corral was empty.

"Gone!" growled Pony George, as though disappointed, and thrust his rifle back in its scabbard viciously.

"The roost sure looks a heap empty for a fact," Lawler admitted. "George, you take the southeast side an' I'll scout northeast. 'F you see fresh tracks sing out."

They parted, George reluctantly. Lawler scouted the ground to the north and west of the Bar 2 shack in a wide half circle. Abruptly Pony George let out a howl that brought him pounding up.

Four sets of hoofprints led due south. "That's

them," said Lawler softly. "Look—there's the tracks of Link's roan whittled. He's joined his men an' they're headin' south. Prob'ly got some hide-out in the hills. Those tracks ain't more'n four hours old—five, at most. C'mon, let's go!"

They struck off along the trail at a fast lope.

"Where yuh s'pose they're aimin' fer?" yelled Pony George, after half an hour of steady riding. "Reckon they're headed fer the Injun Paintin's?"

Lawler shook his head. "Trail's gonna swing east or west right soon. You'll see. Might be figgerin' to hole up in the Glass Mountains. Be able to swing from Pecos County to Brewster without much trouble. Seems like they're hittin' a faster pace, too. See them puffs of earth before an' behind each print?"

For two more hours the trail led south, southwest. The sun climbed higher, its rays grew more fiercely hot. Then abruptly the tracks swung dead southwest.

Pony George shot a look at Lawler. "Headin' fer the Barrillas, surer'n sin!"

Lawler nodded. "Right. Us, too. Barrillas ain't what you might call the property of Reeves County, but we're goin' there anyhow. I think we're gainin' a little, George. We may catch him by nightfall—sight him anyway."

"Bad business, fightin' in the dark," muttered Pony George. "Seems like we oughta give him more of a lead so's we'll come up with him tomorrer when there'll be plenty of light tuh line a sight with."

"We can't afford to give him any more of a lead than he's already got. We're gettin' into buscadero country now. We gotta mind our P's an' Q's or some gent is goin' to tag us with a lead plum. We gotta get Link quick or we won't get him at all. Once his bunch gets holed up in them mountains they could hold us off for months mebbe. We gotta push on, George. Shake it up."

"I'll hev to agree with whatever you and yourself decide, I reckon," George said resignedly. "But it looks like tuh me these nags'd appreciate a little rest."

"We'll stop a spell in that grove of pig-locusts up ahead. Give us a chance to grab a bite an' the broncs can get their breath."

In a few minutes they pulled in beneath the shade of the twelve-foot trees Lawler had mentioned and pulled the saddles from their mounts. Lawler cuffed the dust from his clothes.

"Seems tuh me," Pony George mentioned between bites, "I heard there was a cantina round this stretch of cactus someplace. I could do with a spot o' likker."

Lawler's lips quirked queerly. "You're thinkin' of a place called the Saloon of the Hawk. It's a damned tough layout from all I've heard. Put up 'bout ten years back by a Mex breed. He's had his finger in every bit of deviltry inside a hundred miles ever since."

"Don't look like he'd get a whale of a lotta business round this stretch of hell," George commented. "Shouldn't think he'd get trade enough to pay fer haulin' his—"

"Don't say liquor', George," the sheriff cut in. "He makes his own, an' from what I've been told it's the sorta stuff that would make a grasshopper fight a curly wolf—an' lick him!" He gave his deputy a sidelong glance and chuckled. "Guess I'll buy you a coupla gallons."

Pony George snorted. "I hope yuh ain't figgerin' tuh compare me tuh no damn grasshopper! I'm a hard-tie man, by cripes, an' I won't take such talk from no man!"

The trail they presently followed twisted through many ravines and coulees as they pressed constantly into rougher country. Over hog-backs and eroded hills they went. On the rocky ridges which it crossed occasionally the trail became harder and harder to follow. Here Lawler's expert knowledge of reading sign stood them in good stead.

The sun's slanting rays cut down through a haze of dust stirred up by a vagrant breeze as the stifling afternoon wore along. Half an hour after their last conversation they lost the trail in the stony bottom of an arroyo. Right and left they cast looking for sign, but did not find it. Through the arroyo they finally pressed, hoping against hope to find tracks leading out of it. But the sandy ground outside yielded no faintest picture of riders having passed.

Lawler nodded grimly. "This," he said, "is it. I been expectin' for quite a spell they'd try somethin' like this. Link Holladay's no man's fool. We're wastin' time here, George. We could hunt from now till Kingdom Come an' not find a trail within three-four mile of here. We'll push on for that *El Gabilan* establishment."

"Now yuh're soundin'," Pony George approved. He wiped his streaming face with his dusty neckerchief. "Rest an' shade —beautiful shade—fer man an' beast, an' a drink fer ev'ry gent."

As they jogged along they noted abruptly the head and shoulders of a strange horseman coming over a distant rise. He saw them at the same time, but kept coming. They pulled up and waited. The stranger approached them slowly, hand raised in the peace sign.

There was a sparkle of braid on his fancy vest and, as Pony George remarked under his breath, "Looks like a dang potato bug—I mean uncommon gaudy." As he drew near, reining in a matter of twenty feet or so away, they saw him to be a broad-shouldered man with a stoop. His was a stubborn chin, Lawler noted, and a hawk's beak nose curled predatorily above his thin, trap-like lips. His piercing eyes rested on them with suspicion.

"Howdy," he drawled and smiled.

"Howdy," Lawler replied. He was glad he'd had the foresight to remove his badge some time ago. And glad that Pony George had done the same. To all intents and purposes, he and George were just a couple of drifting range hands.

"Thirsty weather," grunted Pony George. "Don't s'pose yuh know where we could get a drink, do yuh?"

The stranger's eyes swung to the deputy. "You pilgrims know anyone round this country?"

"No," answered Lawler, "we're just driftin' through. Might take a job of work if the pay looked right. You acquainted round here?"

"Wal, it's a swell country to drift through," the stranger's words were pointed.

"We'd rather get a job," said Lawler hesitantly. He had to be careful what he said and what sort of questions, if any, he put. These were trails seldom ridden by honest men—buscadero country where a throat could be slit for ten dollars up, and for nothing if one offended the inhabitants.

"Work's scarce in this man's country," returned the hawk-nosed stranger, gruffly. He tried to maneuver into a position from which he could get a look at the brands on their horses. But Lawler was not minded to have him do so, and shifted his own to match the other's movements. Pony George did like-wise, cagily.

The stranger grinned, relaxing a little, and shot a questing look along their backtrail. "Don't see any dust cloud—yet."

"Was you expectin' to?" Lawler countered, playing up.

"Lots of gents sift through here with fellas raisin' dust behind 'em," said Hawk-Nose meaningly. "I take it you ain't that kind. So I won't tell you that I'm Hawk Bellero, what owns a cantina not far from here. Nor I won't be tellin' you that said place is two-three miles due west. What did you say yore handles was?"

Lawler growled, "We didn't say. But you can call me Redson an' my pardner's known as Han'some George—account he's so homely even a hoss-fly wouldn't look at him twice." The stranger chuckled thinly. But not Pony George, who was touchy about his looks.

"Don't expect you could put us up for the night?"

"Don't reckon. But I might find a mite o' feed for yore nags."

"I could do with a long drink of somethin' that ain't got alkali in it," said Pony George with a gusty sigh. "I ain't the kind tuh enjoy these long fast rides."

Bellero shot him a glance and grinned. "Might be I could find a odd pint or two—if the price was right."

"I expect we could scrape up six-bits, mebbe, between us," Lawler said. At which Bellero laughed. It had a grating sound, was knowing. "Let's go," he said.

Turning their horses all three jogged due west, picking their way between the patches of prickly-pear, boulders and tall, yellow-stalked sotol adorning the surrounding landscape. Long cobalt shadows leaned down from the mountains and lapped across their path.

The vast silence of the country lay unbroken save for the soft thudding of the animals' hoofs until Bellero, after several covert glances at Lawler's inscrutable countenance, said casually:

"Must be quite a bit of excitement over Fort Stockton way since them two fellas held the stage up."

"Do you reckon?" Lawler's grin was satanic, so Bellero let it go at that.

TWENTY-THREE
TURPENTINE GULCH

HAWK BELLERO'S place was not by any means the only building in the little gulch where it was situated, the lawmen found when they arrived. But it was the largest of the group of shacks constructed from scanty timber and plenty of good, tarred paper. It bore a sign above its door which read: SALOON OF THE HAWK.

"What's the name of this place?" Lawler asked as the three stopped their horses before Bellero's cantina.

"Most folks in this man's country calls it 'town'," the hawk-nosed man replied. "But us that lives here calls 'er Turpentine'."

"Turpentine?" Pony George's jaw dropped. 'That's a hell of a name to wish on a town. What's the idee?"

"Likely 'cause it's more'n average hot," Bellero grinned. "Most of the boys round here is gents of unkempt hair an' lightnin' draws. They got shifty habits an' itchy trigger-fingers. The name seems to fit us like a glove."

"Outlaw roost, eh?" Lawler scowled.

It was plain to him that Bellero regarded them as a

couple of promising stage robbers, for he said sooth-ingly, "Don't let that bother you. We're one big happy family, as the sayin' goes. All jolly good jaspers," he added gravely, "long as a man tends his own business an' don't show too much interest in his neighbors. You'll get along. You'll find my boys'll do tuh ride the river with."

Pony George muttered under his breath as Bellero dismounted, "I got a feelin' like a gol'fish in a bowl."

Bellero looked up and his steel-trap mouth quirked slightly at the corners. "We're all gentlemen here," he said. "We got a rule that keeps fellas from robbin' their compadres."

"Yeah, but what happens if some excitable gent forgets the rule?" asked George.

"He gets a hole dug for him the follerin' morning."

Lawler and Pony George dismounted and tied their horses to the long rack that fronted Bellero's saloon. Bellero then led the way inside.

The two lawmen beheld a long main room with a crude bar fixed up along one side. It was made with a rough plank and a couple of barrels. Behind it was a short shelf holding four big demijohns filled with an almost colorless liquid and alongside which were several labeled bottles. Along the opposite side of the room were six rough plank tables and a couple of dozen three-legged stools. At two of the tables a number of men were playing cards. That is, there were cards and money scattered on the tables, but the players were at the moment absorbed in a fight that was in progress in the center of the room.

The two fighters did not appear very evenly matched and Queensbury rules had evidently been unheard of. One fighter was a big, brawny roughneck while his opponent was short and had a cast in one eye. But the short man seemed to be giving a good account of himself. Although his nose was bleeding and his good eye was shut tight, the big man looked as battered as though he'd been fighting six instead of the one puny fellow who crouched before him.

As Bellero and the two supposed stage-robbers entered, the hairy giant went back and down before a terrific crack from the blackjack held in the little man's right hand. He went down slowly, shaking his whiskered face from side to side as if to clear his head. There was blood drooling from his heavy lips.

"Now's yer chance, Pot-Eye!" shouted one of the gamblers. "Kick his damn face in!"

"That's about enough of that," said Bellero softly. "Lay off, Pot-Eye—you know the rules of my camp."

"Tuh hell with yer rules!" snarled the little man, and started for the fallen giant. He had one booted foot drawn back, preparatory to polishing off the fight in his own individual manner, when Bellero's right arm snapped forward in a short arc. A knife struck the little man hilt-first behind the ear. He went down and stayed down.

Bellero picked up his knife, returning it to the sheath inside his collar.

"Some of these boys are kind of slow in heedin' the rules," he apologized as two other men dragged the unconscious combatants outside. "But I teach 'em pretty fast, all things considered. Step up to the bar, gents, an' name yore favorites. This 'un will be on the house."

"Let's get outa here," muttered Pony George,

nervously tugging at Lawler's arm. But Lawler ignored him, knowing it would be as much as their lives were worth to back down now. "We'll take whatever you recommend," he said.

Bellero stepped behind the bar and poured three glasses from the contents of a demijohn. They raised their glasses.

"To a short life an' a unknown grave," said Bellero.

When they set their glasses down empty, Pony George was still trying to get his breath. Several of the gamblers guffawed. "What'n time is this stuff?" demanded Pony George, huskily, when at last he found his voice. "Tobacco juice an' lightnin'?"

"Wal, that's comin' close enough. It's my own product," said Bellero modestly. "I got a secret process."

"Wal, don't never worry 'bout anyone tryin' to hook it," said Pony George, and felt tenderly of his lips.

After the two lawmen had eaten a passable supper at one of the smaller shacks, they returned to the saloon. Dusk was rapidly settling over the gulch and one or two stars were peering timidly forth from high above.

"This place ain't my idee of a good place tuh be," muttered George as they drew near the saloon. "Let's shove on 'fore we get shoved under."

"We'll stay tonight, anyhow," Lawler decided. "This is the best place we're like to hit for gettin' news of Holladay— or Tranton, either, if he's in the country. Keep your lip buttoned an' your ears skinned."

The saloon, they saw on entering, was crowded now. The gambling layouts were being patronized heavily; around one game the onlookers stood three deep.

A number of men were bellying the long plank bar.

Lawler and Pony George sauntered toward it. Pony George regarded the demijohns dubiously.

"I'll try one of the bottles," he told the man in shirt sleeves who was serving as bartender.

"Me, too," Lawler spoke. He was aching to ask if any strangers had passed through recently but, being a stranger himself, knew that such a question would be distinctly out of order. It was necessary they move gently in this gulch of wanted men.

"I got a uncle and a girl cousin livin' in this country someplace," he said, as though to George. "You oughta meet the cousin—she's mighty easy on the eyes."

George looked blank but the barman grinned. "There ain't many," he said. "I reckon you're meanin' Sara—" He broke off as he caught a hard glance from the man next to Lawler.

"Frank," said this man coldly, "Dusty, down there, is waitin' tuh get served."

The loose-mouthed bartender took the hint and hurried off down the bar. The man who had cut short his conversation looked Lawler squarely in the eye. "Seems like I've seen yore face before somewheres. What did yuh say yore name was?"

"Redson—Flash Redson."

"Flash in the pan, I guess yuh mean, don't yuh?"

Lawler did not argue the point. His right fist whipped up in a mighty hook to the angle of the fellow's jaw. The belligerent one went over backwards and did not immediately rise.

The rattle of glasses and clink of coins abruptly hushed. Talk fell away as heads craned toward the lawmen. "Frank," said Lawler smoothly, "I'll take another glass of this tarant'la juice."

The room had grown very quiet, and in the stillness the sound of the barman's boots on the hardpacked ground seemed intensely loud as he came toward Lawler and thumped a pint bottle on the plank beside his glass.

Lawler gave him a grin as he poured a drink. Fishing a silver dollar from his pocket he laid it beside the bottle. Downing his drink and, followed nervously by Pony George, he headed for the door. The eyes of every man in the room, save those of the gent who still lay unconscious on the floor, seemed to be on his back. But—

"I think," he said casually, yet loud enough to be plainly heard, "we'll hunt up Bellero, George, an' have a little talk."

Some of these men, at least, had seen him and George enter with Bellero before supper, and Lawler was banking heavily that Bellero had not given out any information concerning them as yet. In which case he and George might be permitted to leave the saloon without further trouble.

Evidently such was the case for no overt move was made as they passed outside.

"Whew!" Pony George wiped his forehead on his dusty sleeve. "Me, I'm headin' outa this gulch fast as m' hoss will travel."

As they moved down the dusty lane that ran between the rows of tarpaper shacks, Lawler was glad as the deputy to be out again in the cool night air.

'Tell you what you do, George," he said softly as they paused. "I'm figurin' to stay a spell in spite of havin' had to knock down that suspicious gent. But I ain't figurin' to stay all night. You get your bronc an' fan dust. I got a hunch mebbe Sara an' Tranton are round here someplace. I'm goin' to try an' find out. You go to Toyahvale an' raise a posse; get a good-sized one if you can an' bust right back here. If you don't spare your horse, you oughta make Toyahvale in two-three hours. Figure half an hour or so to get your men an' 'bout three hours to make it back here—"-that'll get you here round dawn. I'll try an' meet you outside town someplace." He gave George a shove. "On your way!"

As Pony George hurriedly vanished in the gloom Lawler, turning, saw another man coming toward him from the opposite direction, just a blurred bulk dimly discernible against the deeper black of the starlit night. There was no moon, for which the sheriff felt extremely thankful.

When the man came abreast, Lawler spoke. "Say, pard! Can you tell a fella how to locate Bellero when he ain't in his bank?"

"Sure," said the other. "You must be kinda green round here. End shack. West end of the gulch," and off he jingled, headed toward the saloon Lawler had termed Bellero's bank.

"Further complications in the event of trouble," Lawler reflected grimly. "Me at one end of this town an' my horse at the other. This is gonna be no picnic if I have to make a run for it."

He thrust his big hands deep in his pockets, clamped his jaw determinedly and went striding along toward the shack the man had indicated. If possible, he meant to wring the information he was after out of Bellero—even if he had to do it at gunpoint.

He knocked when he reached the shack and Bellero's voice bade him in.

It was a much larger place, he found, than it had looked to be from the outside. He shut the door. There were two rooms, he saw; the second room opening off the wall across from that beside which the hawk-nosed boss of Turpentine was seated. Bellero peered up from the tally-book he had been examining.

"Howdy, Redson," he said, thrusting the book inside his coat. "Have a chair." For a time he sat regarding Lawler with his head on one side. Finally a slow grin quirked his lips. "Where's your pardner?"

"Left him buckin' the tiger," Lawler lied without hesitation. "I got in a quarrel with one of your boys an' decided the atmosphere in your saloon was not conducive to the Redson health. Thought I'd come up an' chin with you a spell."

Bellero grinned. "You don't wanta mind my boys. They're a little rough an' loud-spoken sometimes, but they mean all right. How d'yuh like my camp? Care tuh make it yore headquarters for a while?"

Lawler took plenty of time for his answer. This was delicate ground. "I ain't so crazy 'bout this camp," he replied slowly, "but I could get along with you first rate. I think you an' me could hit it off fine together. I'm aimin' to take a little pasear over the Barrillas in the mornin'. Got to see some gents. Small outfit run by a guy named Holladay. Don't s'pose you know him?"

"Holladay?" Bellero creased his brows. "Holladay—le's see, now. Seems like I've heard that name some-place." He squinted up at the ceiling poles reflectively.

"Dog-gone! You remind me that I *did* know a Holladay one time. Big, burly fella with fence-post legs an' a tight—"

"Was his name Link?" Lawler asked him swiftly.

"Yeah—his name was Link!" From behind the sheriff the words purred ominously across the silence. Lawler whirled.

Link Holladay stood gloating in the open door. A levelled gun was in his hand.

TWENTY-FOUR
THE WHEEL OF FORTUNE SPINS

LAWLER DID NOT NEED anyone to tell him he was trapped; he knew it! If he chanced a draw, Death inevitably awaited him. He could not take but one of these outlaws with him, and there was no profit to him in that. If he stood motionless and allowed events to take their natural course the same end stood plain in view for him. Holladay grinned with his naked gun held ready. From behind his back came the grating chuckle of Bellero.

Lawler held his cheeks smooth, emotionless. He remained moveless, his massive shoulders hunched a trifle forward, his big hands hanging at his sides. He knew his danger fully yet no sign of fear marred the level directness of the glance he turned on Holladay. His eyes were like chilled jade.

Holladay's mocking lips framed a grin of triumph. "Gotcha!" he chuckled wickedly. "That damn coroner hit the nail plumb on the head, Lawler—you're too young an' tender green to ever be worth a row of shucks as sheriff. Hell, you're jest a damnfool kid!"

"I expect, Link, time will remedy that."

"Not in yore case it won't."

Lawler grinned easily. "Threatened men live long."

"Not the gents Link Holladay threatens. They got a habit of dyin' quick!"

"Yeah?"

"Yore hearin's good. This here's *my* camp you're in, young fella. We been drivin' rustled stock in here fer months. Hawk Bellero's boys takes a cut fer shovin' it crost the river."

"I can't see no sense," Bellero said, "spillin' yore guts to a sheriff."

"I'm doin' the talkin'," Holladay's tone grew ugly. "You an' me, Hawk, have got along so far because yuh had sense enough to mind yore own business. Keep on mindin' it or you'll wake up one o' these mornin's to find yoreself shovin' up daisies! Get his gun while I keep him covered."

Lawler, though his heart beat fast, offered no resistance when Bellero reached round and lifted his Colt from its holster.

Holladay directed, "Better look him over fer a hide-out gun."

"He ain't got none," answered Bellero, patting Lawler up and down.

"All right. Take that flour sack over there an' tear it into strips an' tie his wrists behind him. Lash 'em good so's he can't even wriggle a finger."

Bellero did so; tying the knotted strips so tight they hurt. Yet Lawler was not noticing the pain. He was wondering if Pony George had gotten clear.

As though reading the sheriff's thoughts, Holladay grinned. "Don't figger too large on gettin' help from that clown depity of yores, I give the boys their instructions about *that* hairpin. By this time he's likely swingin' at a rope's end!"

Lawler's face remained unreadable.

"Set down on that stool over there," came Holladay's next command. "Jest one false move an' I'll bend this gun over yore scalp. Now *set!*"

Lawler, needless to say, sat.

"Hawk, tear up them other sacks." The burly rustler strode near to stand leering down at the trussed-up sheriff. "Wal, how do yuh like bein' the under-dog fer a change?"

Lawler made no reply, nor did his features express his feelings. He was watching the shadow of Bellero as the man tore flour sacks into strips. The shadow straightened. "Ready, Link."

"Lash his ankles to the legs of that stool. . . . Now run a coupla strips from his wrists underneath the seat an' then fasten the loose ends to his legs. There, that's fine," Holladay approved as Bellero finished his work and stood back. "If yuh get loose now it'll be by one of them there 'acts of Gawd'," he said with satisfaction.

Lawler saw scant likelihood of his getting loose. He wished now he had taken his chance on a gun battle, suicide though he had known it to be.

A rattle of shots went up from the far end of the street He saw Holladay stiffen and felt Hawk Bellero go tense behind his back.

A startled curse fell from Holladay's lips as hurrying boots pounded near. He started to the door. Before he reached it, it was flung violently back against the wall. A wide-eyed man stood framed in the opening. He was breathing fast.

"'Talk up!" snarled Holladay. "What's gone haywire now?"

"'That blasted depity yuh told us tuh round up musta slipped away before we started huntin' him. We found that his nag was gone right off, but we figgered mebbe he'd moved it some place else, mebbe thinkin' tuh make a quick getaway. But we've searched the whole dang gulch an' neither the horse nor him is here!"

"What was that shootin'?" Holladay's tone was ominously quiet.

The man shivered. "Jest as we'd about concluded the depity had got away, Jed saw somethin' movin' in the shadows back of one of the shacks. He opened up an' so did the shadder. Jed went down, hit bad, clawin' at his stomach an' screechin' like a stuck pig! Me an' Ed an' Tanner joined in then an' got the fella, thinkin' it was that damn depity. But when we got a light an' went over there it was Bud Hennley we'd potted. There was six slugs through him an'—"

One blow of Holladay's gangling arm swept the speaker from the doorway. The next instant the burly rustler was outside and sprinting down the street. Lawler could hear the fast clump of his heavy boots. He grinned at Hawk Bellero.

"So George is gazin' at the stars from the end of a rope, eh?"

"You better sing low, Mister," Bellero said ominously, and turned to the man who had brought the news. "Go down an' keep an' eye on that girl. If she gets away the Chief'll have yore ears!"

After the man had gone Lawler grinned again at the scowling Bellero. "Better get on with your gut-shootin'.

If Pony George gets to Toyahvale he'll have a posse back here before mornin'.'"

"If he does get through," Bellero snarled, "he won't be doin' *you* any good! The Chief'll fry *yore* bacon long before mornin'!"

Returning to his chair beside the wall Bellero sat down, not troubling to take his gun from leather. It would not be necessary and he knew it. He was too expert a thrower of the far-famed diamond hitch.

"If you got any prayin' tuh do," he pointed out pleasantly, "you better be gettin' on with it. Yore Sands of Time are due tuh run gosh-awful short."

From without the shack a soft *clink-clump* of spur rowels and high bootheels drew near. Again the door was flung open and Link Holladay came striding in, pushing before him a slender booted and belted figure that Lawler thought somehow familiar.

A girl in man's clothing! Lawler's cheeks went white as he saw her face.

"*Sara!*"

" 'Lo, Red. Going to join our happy family?"

Slim and virginal she stood before him. Yet staring at her Lawler felt a wave of fear grip him.

She seemed thinner now, more fragile than he remembered her. Her golden hair was a tangled mane. Her face was pale and there were deep, dark circles beneath her eyes. Yet these things but enhanced her beauty. It caused a hungry pounding of the sheriff's heart.

She faced him squarely; stood before his scrutiny with head uplifted, her eyes wide and level and unafraid. Whatever the hardships, the brutal contacts, she had been forced to undergo, they had not daunted her spirit. It burned in her eyes like a silver flame.

She spoke abruptly. "Red, I was wrong—terribly wrong. I thought—"

"Choke off the blat!" roughed Holladay. "Who cares what you thought? You got more damn lip than a muley cow!" And to Lawler: "Go on—look yore fill. She's *my* woman now, an she's gonna stay mine till I get sick of 'er an' find a better!"

Sara tautened; her dark eyes flashed.

""That's a lie!" she cried, and struck him with her open palm. "I never was your 'woman'!"

Holladay bent her a sweeping bow and chuckled at Lawler's futile anger. "Our Sara's a little wildcat. But I'll tame her—she's the kind I like in my string."

Sara darted to Lawler's side. Her stare at Holladay was defiant.

"Family tintype!" he jeered. "Make the most of it, m' dear, 'cause in a few hours you an' me'll be headin' for a nice long honeymoon in Manana Land." Then his mood abruptly changed; grew ugly. "Don't be gettin' so damn familiar," he rasped as Sara flung her arms about Lawler in sudden desperation. "I don't enjoy havin' my loot pawed over—"

"You won't enjoy havin' a rope around your neck, either!" Lawler gritted above her shoulder. "But I'll live to put one there."

Flecks of flame coalesced in Holladay's glare. He took a half step forward.

"Where's Tranton?"

Holladay's head went back in a mocking laugh. "You still huntin' *him?*"

A chill swept over Lawler as Sara pressed close against him. The chill was warranted.

"Hell, Tranton's been dead damn near a month," jeered Holladay. "I said you wasn't fit to be no sheriff—a gent with sense woulda figgered long ago that he wasn't the Pecos Killer!"

Lawler's startled glance swept Sara's face. "It's true," she said with trembling lip. "*I* thought Dad was the mysterious killer, too. So many little things seemed to—"

But Lawler was not listening. "Tranton . . . dead . . ."

"Sure he's dead," Holladay sneered, and then to Sara: "Go ahead. Tell the fool; he'd never learn no other way. What he learns now won't do him a heap of good, anyway. I'm settlin' his account."

Sara ignored him. "Some time before the killings started," she said to Lawler, "Holladay showed up. Dad seemed to change almost overnight; he acted strange, uneasy, morose, abstracted. And then one night he told me he would be pleased if I married Link—"

Holladay's rough chuckle broke in on Sara's words.

Lawler's cheeks were grey beneath their bronze. He guessed what revelation was to follow and his square jaw clenched till the muscles stood out like ropes.

"To cut it short," Sara's tone was weary, "Dad said that Holladay was an old friend of his and I'd oblige him by marrying Link as soon as possible. He said he had a hunch it wouldn't be for long, and for that time in name only as I was to stay on the ranch. I could see that Link must have some fearful hold that needed time to break, so I married him. In Toyahvale—secretly. It was hard. But I couldn't let Dad down—he'd done so much for me.

"The next day the killings started. Dad and Holladay had a fearful row in Dad's office. I couldn't hear much of what was said. But I could tell that Dad was furious. After Link had gone he stayed in his office and wouldn't even come out for supper. The next few days he was gone most of the time. He never mentioned where he went but always came home late at night.

"Then one day I found some papers that had fallen from a pocket of his coat. They were things about the Toyah Lake gang—accounts. I guessed then that Dad was Rowdy Joe. Link had been a member, too. He had been hunting for Dad a long time—"

"That ain't no lie," Holladay growled. "When I found out where he'd been hidin' out I got in touch with the other boys an' put 'em wise. We fixed it up between us to get our splits or croak him. We drew lots an' I got the job of collectin'.

"I got my split right off. Tranton didn't want no trouble. He was gettin' along too well here. I told him if I got Sara I'd keep the other boys off. He finally saw the light. I reckon he was figgerin' to get me planted sudden but I kept outa his way.

"I sent for Doak an' when he showed I dropped Tranton a letter tellin' him to pay off quick or else. He paid—but swore to cook my goose." Holladay laughed. "He never saw the day when he could outfigger me. I rubbed Doak out that night and pocketed his split."

"When I saw how nice it all worked out an' what a cinch it was, I wrote the other boys to start filterin' in an' I'd get their shares for 'em. I gave 'em the same share

Doak got." Holladay sneered, "It was like takin' candy from a bunch of kids!"

"What was the idea of the 'Justice' notes?" Lawler asked.

"Just a red herrin' to throw folks off the trail. The gang thought Tranton was bumpin' 'em off. Reede got suspicious though. He was fixin' to clear out the night I stopped his clock. Them notes an' what follered 'em had scairt him pink. He'd just got one himself."

"What about Tawson?" Lawler was unable to keep the loathing from his voice.

Holladay sneered. "Tawson was jest damn fool enough to show he was gettin' wise. He figgered whoever was doin' the killin' would eventually get to Reede an' as he reckoned it was the Toyah Lake crowd gettin' rubbed out he played hands off, aimin' to nab the killer when he went for Reede. But he got to Reede's too late that night. The job was finished when he came."

An idea came to Lawler then. He asked, curious, "How about those shots at the Captain? That time he claimed someone had shot at him through the window?"

"I took those shots at him for a warnin'—he was threatenin' to kick over the traces an' spoil my show."

"All he had to do to wreck your plans," Lawler growled, "was to refuse to hand over the money you were supposed to be payin' them others."

"He didn't dare. He wasn't a heap anxious to get himself a harp. An' besides I told him I'd get Sara sure as hell if he didn't kick through."

"Why bother with those others, though? Why

didn't you save time an' risk by forcin' the Captain to fork over all the loot at once?"

"No fun in that," Holladay explained, and laughed. "I aimed for him to see them others gettin' rubbed out one by one. He knew his time was comin', but I got a deal of pleasure outa keepin' him guessin' when. I tell you, I made them hombres sweat!

"Tranton knew what was goin' on, of course, from who laid the chunk. *But*—he couldn't figger no way of stoppin' it outside of killin' himself; I'd fixed things so that was the only out he had. An' he an' me both knew he'd never kill himself. He was too big a coward—had a yeller streak up his back three inches wide!"

"You mean," Sara corrected hotly, "that he was afraid to take his life for fear of what you might do to me!"

"Have it any way you want, m' dear," Holladay smirked and swaggered nearer to stand with arms akimbo, grinning down at Lawler. "Might's well quit gnashin' at the bit," he told the straining sheriff. "When I'm ready to pull stakes I'll see that yo're put outa yore misery. Until that time you might's well take it easy. You won't find no broken bottles, or handy knives, or jagged stones or tin around here to help you to get yore-self loose. You are pig-tied for slaughter, Sheriff, an' you might's well make up yore mind to it."

A wave of despair swept over Lawler. A keen appreciation of his helplessness was in him. This was to be the end—the end of all his plans and hopes and purposes. Desperately he forced his mind from such thoughts. He dare not contemplate the end with Sara in this renegade's power. Perhaps Pony George would get back in time with help . . .

"Bellero," Holladay's growl interrupted the sheriffs abstraction. "Get them boys of yores started off with the cattle. We're gonna have to quit this place 'fore that blasted depity gets back here with a posse. Get 'em started pronto! It's gettin' close to daylight. Sun-up ain't more'n one-two hours off."

Bellero rose and started for the door. "Think you can handle the filly?"

"You're damn well right I can! If there's any time Link Holladay can't hold his own against a female critter, it's time he was planted in his gravel."

With a chuckle Bellero left.

Holladay caught Sara by an arm; caught the other as she sought to strike him. "C'mon, yuh hellcat! Show sonny-boy Lawler how you kiss a real hard-tie man like yore lovin' husban'."

Her struggles suddenly infuriated him; letting go one arm he struck her across the face. In a twinkling he had both her wrists imprisoned in one big paw. He slid the other about her waist.

"C'mon, now—show 'im how you snuggle to yore Link!"

Lawler's jaws clenched hard. His sweat-beaded face was a lamplit mask as Sara put up a valiant but impotent struggle against the burly killer. Rage ripped through Lawler like jagged veins of fire; the room reeled redly before his eyes.

"Let go that girl, you swine!"

Holladay turned his head and leered.

"I'm gonna kill you like I would a snake," Lawler's words were thick with fury, "first minute I get loose!"

Tightening his grip on Sara's wrists, Holladay dragged her close to Lawler. "Yeah?" he jeered, and smashed his free fist into Lawler's chest with a force that sent him tumbling backward, stool and all.

"Yeah?" He swung a booted foot at Lawler's unprotected ribs—hard. A groan slipped through the sheriff's lips.

Sara kicked at Holladay's shins. With a snarl he flung her from him and again launched his booted foot at Lawler's side, more viciously than before.

But this time Lawler managed to roll sufficiently so that instead of thudding against his ribs, Holladay's blow caught one of the stool's legs and snapped it off clean! And that moment, out of the tail of his eye, the killer saw Sara making for the door. He went after her with a curse.

Lawler's pulse abruptly pounded; hope renewed surged through him like a heady wine. The lashings that bound him to the stool were loose! Link Holladay's brutal kick had proved a godsend!

Lawler worked one foot free and got to his feet with desperate haste. His wrists were still lashed behind him, but he could move—and that was something!

The debris of the stool lashed to one leg did not prevent him from limping toward where Holladay struggled with Sara beside the door. Yet just as he came within range the killer, catching the startled light that blazed uncontrollably in Sara's eyes, whirled.

One blow of Holladay's big fist sent the girl lurching across the room while his right hand dropped to his gun. With the weapon clearing leather Lawler's right foot, with the debris of the broken stool, came up in a smashing arc, struck Holladay's arm and sent the pistol spinning from his grasp.

With a smoking curse Holladay slammed his huge

frame forward, both fists swinging. His rising right caught the sheriff full in the face. He brought his left in flush behind the sheriff's ear.

Lawler dropped.

Whirling, again Holladay made for Sara. But he brought up swiftly when he saw her hand was closing about his fallen gun. He dashed for the door, yanked it open. He went leaping through just as Sarah fired. The next moment he was gone from view.

Sara slammed the door and dropped its oaken bar in place. Crossing to Lawler's prostrate form she dropped to her knees beside him. Frantically she fumbled at the knots that held his wrists. He was conscious by the time she had the lashings off.

He struggled groggily to his knees. His head cleared swiftly as she worked to extricate his right foot from what was left of the wrecked stool. He commenced chafing his arms and wrists to dissipate the sensation of pins and needles coursing through them.

"Gosh . . . I—I don't know what to say," he stammered, embarrassed. "I—I—Sara, you're a brick!"

"You can save the compliments till we're out of this," she told him practically. "Here, take this gun and watch the window. Link Holladay won't be gone any longer than it will take him to get another pistol."

His mind was functioning more smoothly now. "Better put out that light," he whispered, as at last she freed his foot. "Hurry! His bunch may try to pick us off with rifles!"

With the room plunged in darkness Lawler's glance searched the sand beyond the window. There had been no moon and now the stars were not bright enough to dispel the heavy shadows that filled the outlaw gulch.

Sara stood beside him and when he realized it, he slipped his arms about her hungrily and for a long moment held her tight. For that blissful interval of time her lips were pressed deliriously to his. The spell was broken when Sara freed herself at sound of running feet in the night outside.

With new life pouring through his arteries in a heavy tide, Lawler steadied the captured pistol on the window sill and waited.

TWENTY-FIVE

POWDERSMOKE SHOWDOWN

THE SHEER HOPELESSNESS of their position gradually absorbed the tonic of Sara's kiss; gloom again flooded Lawler's mind. To be sure, he had heard Hawk Bellero's men go off with the stolen stock and knew, therefore, there could be but few men left within the gulch. But even a few were like to prove several gents too many—especially as Link Holladay and Bellero both must be numbered among that few.

No moon shone down from heaven's blue bowl and the dying stars gave off but a sickly glow. False dawn's pale grey would soon be permeating the gulch. For such time was Lawler waiting, yet he knew the outlaws would strike before.

Black shadows filled the shack. Muffled whispers drifted in through the open glassless window. Lawler's eyes, keened by many a night hunt, saw a flitting shadow cross a lighter space somewhere between the shack and Hawk's saloon. A grim smile crossed his lips. He had no lead to waste; each shot must be made to count, A wind had sprung up and Lawler, his nerves strung taut, could hear the dismal swishing of the sage and rabbitbrush. Sara huddled against him, shivering.

"Red!" she suddenly clutched his arm. "*Red!*" there was hysteria in her voice. "We can't stay here! They'll burn us out! These tarpaper walls are no protection! They'll blaze like tow! *Quick*—unbar the door!"

"Sara!" he shook her roughly. "Come out of it! You can't let go like that!"

She started to scream. He saw it coming and dropped his pistol on the sill to clamp one hand across her mouth. She tried to bite and he slapped her sharply across the cheeks with his free hand. "Stop it! Get hold of yourself, Sara!"

He could feel her shaking in his grip. He shook her fiercely. "Stop it!"

"I—I'm all right now, Red. I'll behave," she told him huskily.

Releasing her, Lawler felt for his pistol on the sill. Feverishly his hand swept it from end to end three times before he would let himself believe that it was gone. Then, the implications of the fact breaking over him, he softly swore.

"What is it, Red?"

"My gun—it's gone. I must have dropped it out the window. I'm gonna climb through after it. We wouldn't have a chance without a gun." He did not think they had a chance anyway, but could not bring himself to tell her so for fear she'd realize she was hampering his movements. "Down on the floor now. Quick," he muttered, "them birds may open up any second. I don't want you hit!"

"Don't leave me, Red!" Sara cried as he thrust a leg

across the sill. "Please—I couldn't bear to lose you now .
. ."

"Don't be silly! I gotta get that gun!"

"Red, please—"

"Git down!" he growled, and dropped to the ground
outside. Almost instantly one groping hand came in
contact with the cold steel of the errant pistol. As he
picked it up a spur rowel clinked against a stone. A
burst of flame sheered the mark to his right and lead
splashed whining off the rock!

Motionless Lawler crouched there. He did not dare
return the unknown's lead for fear of drawing a leaden
hail upon the shack. Bullets would sail through those
flimsy walls like cardboard—and Sara was inside.

A brittle hush closed down; a stillness far more
sinister and disturbing than ever could be the natural
silence of this land. It seemed as if the entire world
were waiting breathless.

With infinite caution he slowly straightened. For
long moments he stood there motionless, one more
shadow among the multitude. Then swiftly thrusting a
leg across the sill, he pulled himself inside and drew the
other leg in after him.

Something was wrong—*he knew it instantly!* What
it was he could not tell, but something— Danger cocked
his muscles, held his big frame tense. Then his voice
crossed the silence recklessly:

"Sara!"

He knew then what was wrong. No answer came,
yet he sensed a stirring of the shadows by the door
leading into the back room. He dropped to the floor so
he would not be silhouetted against the window's lesser
gloom.

Something had happened to Sara while he'd been outside. That back room must also hold an exit from the shack! Someone had entered this place—

A faint scuffling came from the deepest shadows across the room. Lawler drew back the hammer of his pistol to full cock. In the strained hush the sound was like the striking of a gong! Tense, he drove his voice across the darkness:

"Who's there?"

Came a faint creak of leather, a *swish-h-h!* and something that even in this murky light gleamed dully slithered past his cheek and struck the wall behind with a sharp *thwunk!*

A knife! Hawk Bellero was across the room!

Lawler flattened—and just in time! A streak of flame speared out above him. He worked his trigger feverishly, angling his shots upward into the clustered shadows near the back room door. Dimly in the thunder he caught Bellero's ripped-out curse and knew one shot at least had scored. Then came the thud of bootheels crossing the back room floor. A cold dank silence crept shivering back as sounds of his shots dimmed out.

Fumbling in the gloom Lawler shoved fresh cartridges into the emptied chambers of his smoking gun. Then, despite the crazy danger of the thing, he struck a match. Bursting orange against the wavering shadows it showed an empty room. Bellero, if Bellero it was, had gone.

The man would not be fool enough to linger now in that back room, so Lawler did not look. He dropped the match into the pile of discarded flour sacks from which Bellero had torn the strips to lash him, scooped the igniting material against a wall. He watched for a moment while the yellow flames licked up. Then—pulling the bar from the door—he slid outside.

Sprinting thirty crouching feet he dropped behind a clump of sage.

The tarpaper shack burned with a fiercely wild abandon; the red-tipped flames licked up its flimsy walls with hissing fury. For a hundred yards the towering blaze lit up the surrounding earth as bright as noonday, picking out each stump and bush with crystal clarity.

Lawler, belly-down behind his bit of sage, waited with levelled pistol, his narrowed glance probing the brightened area in searching stabs.

Abruptly his vigilance received reward. A man bounding up from a nearby thicket commenced to run. He was headed for the shadows bulking large beyond the radius of the flames.

"Halt!" snapped Lawler grimly. But the man ran on unheeding. Maliciously Lawler's finger squeezed the trigger of his levelled gun, relaxed when the runner, clutching wildly at his side, spun half around and went to his hands and knees. A moment he swayed there crazily in the fireglow, then pitched suddenly forward on his face.

"One," Lawler said deliberately.

Not far to his left a man jumped swiftly to his feet and whipped a rifle to his shoulder. Flame belched instantly from its muzzle, whining lead cut twigs from the bending sage.

"Close," Lawler grunted, and let the hammer drop again. The man with the rifle went over backward, sprawled motionless against the yellow earth in the light of the leaping flames.

"Two," said Lawler grimly, and replaced the spent shells with fresh ones from his belt. "These polecats will soon learn they're pawns in a damn bad game!"

At the dim edge of the firelit circle nearest the Hawk's saloon, Bellero sprang from his place of concealment. He went dashing toward the saloon, unnerved by what he had seen.

Knowing the distance far too great for accurate pistol work, particularly in the present circumstances Lawler held his fire and went plunging after the fleeing outlaw. It was in the sheriff's mind that if he could keep the fellow in sight, Bellero would probably lead him to Holladay and the girl.

He yelled at the rustler to stop. Bellero did—but only to turn and fire. His lead went harmlessly overhead and to the side due to his hurried aim and, seeing Lawler cutting down the distance, he turned and ran again. Ran until he reached the corner of a shack, round which he dashed with unabated speed.

As Lawler drew near the spot he slackened pace. It was darker here and Bellero might be lurking round the corner hoping for a finishing shot. Lawler stopped and listened. But he heard no sound save the crackling of the flames behind.

Crouching lower against the earth he worked cautiously closer to the place where the Hawk had vanished. He wanted to angle out so as to command a view of that hidden corner before coming too near. But to do so would bring him uncomfortably close to the adjacent shack. And Holladay might be laying for him there.

He caught abruptly a blur of movement and there was Bellero crouched before him in the open.

"This is *it!*" the hawk-nosed outlaw snarled, and a burst of flame belched outward from his levelled gun.

Even as Lawler hurled himself aside, from the tail of one eye he saw a second crouching figure rock into view from round the corner of the opposite shack.

Shot upon shot choked the gulch with smashing echoes. Lead ripped through the brush back of Lawler in a thumping hail of sound. A blow rocked against his head and he felt himself sagging as red flame and whirling lights danced pin-wheel-like across his vision. He staggered and went down, the gun in his hand still spitting.

But consciousness did not leave him. He got his chin up on a fist and saw Bellero slumping down against a shack. A red mist swam before his eyes yet did not obscure Holladay's burly form lumbering toward him through the half-light, big pistol gripped in hairy paw.

Pulses slowing, Lawler fumbled with the cartridges in his belt, striving doggedly to jam fresh ones into the empty cylinder of his gun. He knew that the end had come yet inside him something whispered that he was glad it was to be like this. Though he died for it, he was glad to be here now facing Link across levelled guns.

Wiping the blood from his eyes he struggled to his knees. The pain the effort cost him was excruciating yet he managed to lurch erect. "Come an' get it, polecat," he whispered.

Holladay lumbered closer, watching his enemy through slitted lids. With twenty feet separating them, light from the burning shack picked out his snarling features—showed blood drooling from his mouth.

There was something fierce and blazing in the outlaw's slitted eyes. Whether it was jealousy, hate or envy Lawler could not tell; perhaps it was none of these, or a mixture of them all. But there was unswervable stubbornness in the forward throw of his jaw.

Lawler's gun hand hung at his side. "Say when," he whispered hoarsely.

"Now!" cursed Holladay, and his pistol rose in a bursting arc of flame.

With lead tearing through his hat Lawler's gun bucked his palm in sharp recoil—just once.

Features twisting with incredulity and rage, Holladay's forward lurch abruptly stopped. His thin lips writhed back from his great yellow teeth in a savage snarl. His yellow neckerchief grew red in the firelight as he stood there swaying, trying again to work the trigger of his gun. He swore thick drooling oaths when his failing muscles refused the dictates of his stubborn will.

Swiftly then his twisted features reflected the ghastly realization that he was done, was dying on his feet—was shuffling as he'd shuffled others. His legs let go at the knees and pitched him forward on his chest, shoved his face in the yellow dust. Limp and motionless he lay there, one arm out-flung, the other crumpled under him.

This much Lawler saw, and then the world blacked out to the drum of approaching hoofs.

He came reluctantly back to a world made noisy by stamping feet and shouting voices. His head throbbed as though he'd bumped it on some rafter. His body burned with shooting, fiery veins of flame. Some damned fool seemed to be hammering a dull knife into his shoulder and turning it round and round.

Gentle hands now were turning him over. One cool hand was smoothing back the red hair from his forehead. It was soft and cool, that hand, and soothing. He felt grateful for its touch and, wondering whose it was, opened his eyes. He shut them almost instantly for he was in some place that was bright with light—sunlight!

After a time, the sound of voices and other noises became more distant. He ventured to open his eyes again. He did so, tensing. Hair like spun gold framed a familiar face above him—it was like the face of someone he had known in the distant past Then realization came flooding back to him. This was the inside of a shack in Turpentine Gulch—*it was Sara's face above him!*

"Sara!"

"Red—I'm so glad!"

He could see now there were tears in Sara's eyes. Oblivious to the pain that racked his bruised and battered body, Lawler struggled to a sitting posture beside her and, slipping his good right arm about her, drew her close.

"It's all over, hon," he whispered with his lips against her hair. "Link Holladay is dead."

She nodded, hid her face against his chest and sobbed. He saw his ring upon her finger and guessed with quickening pulse she must have got it from his pocket. It gave him courage to say:

"Soon's we get back to town we're gettin' married, Sara."

"You wouldn't want to marry the daughter of Rowdy Joe—"

"Reckon you don't know much about me then—I can't think of anythin' that would please me better. I—"

He broke off as boots with chiming spurs came creaking up. A nearby door popped open and a long swift ray of sunlight sped across the floor and then was blotted by a shadow as a man stopped in the opening. He had a drawling nasal voice and used it now to say:

"Wal! Wal! I was gonna make a report to—but shucks, m'boss Red Lawler wouldn't be found in no place like this-here! 'Seems like I've done busted into the ward for the incurably romantic—"

"That ain't funny, George," said Lawler, as Sara snuggled closer.

"Wal, cripes!" said Pony George, "even Homer was knowed tuh nod!"

THE SHOOTIN' SHERIFF

ONE
WILD BILL DORNE

DOWN UPON THIS man-for-breakfast cow town of Spavined Nag, the Arizona sun hurled its brassy, smashing rays with a definite fury. This was the hottest, lowest-ebb hour of any day—a time when gentlemen and roughnecks alike took their respite from the heat in whatever spots of coolness might be found.

Dorne knew it was this hour; knew it and did not care. Indeed, the knowledge of this very fact was what had sent him trudging through this burning, hock-deep dust of the deserted main street. It was his firm belief that this would be the best hour of the entire twenty-four for the doing of the chore he had in hand.

So it was with a definite purpose that he now was heading through the stifling dust between these gaunt flanking rows of bleached frame buildings towards the combination saloon, dance hall and gambling hell upon whose flaring false front was painted a fading legend: GOLDEN STACK *Pecos Borst, Prop.*

And this purpose of Dorne's was not a thing born on the spur of the moment; it was the thing for which yesterday he had been elected by a scant majority to pack the Sheriff's star. It was more—a purpose of prime importance to those "solid" citizens residing in this wild, raw town; a thing they had cherished in their secret hearts for many months.

"Wild Bill" Dorne they called this newly-elected sheriff. Lean of hip he was, and long of leg; a tall young giant with a slender wiry body holding immense reserves of strength and topped by the broad, tapering shoulders of a born fighter. A man who was held to be something of an expert in the old and gentle art of "draw-and-shoot."

Redheads, as a rule, are florid, or light of skin. But Dorne's was deeply bronzed, though his flaming mane was the color of the adobe banks of the Little Red River. The eyes beneath this brilliant scalp adornment were a cold, clear blue, level and disconcerting. They had been known to hold a twinkle upon occasion, but were more often to be seen fairly glittering with frost, or with that wanton blazing reflection of a fiery temper out of leash. Below Bill Dorne's eyes was set a long Roman nose which more than once had been compared to a vulture's beak— though not within his hearing. Beneath this highly prominent and much advertised proboscis, a pair of long wide lips gashed his face above a rugged chin which, more often than not, could be seen swung forward at a stubborn jut. His cheekbones, to complete the picture, were high and flat, and the cheeks themselves a bit tight-pinched from the same source that had etched those radiating wrinkles about his eye-corners— long hours of saddle slicking beneath a broiling sun.

He was dressed in a somewhat ostentatious manner, as befitted a man with a name like his. His black J. B.

was a ten-gallon hat, and a black-and-red checked flannel shirt covered the long rippling muscles of his upper body. Scarred black batwing chaps encased his long legs, and fancy Hyer boots peeped from their flaring bottoms, from the heels of which protruded huge silver gut-hooks with Texas-star rowels and pear-shaped danglers which, in the words of Bill himself, "shore tinkled one lovely tune." A lavender neckerchief was knotted loosely about his neck, and his wrists were covered by five-inch leather cuffs set off with silver wire.

But Bill was no dandy; he dressed this way because it suited his fancy; the things he wore were built as much for use as for appearance. Their use, as any man with half an eye could tell at a glance, had been long and steady. And the thick greasy cartridge belt girdling his lean hips looked as much a part of him as anything he wore, and the hickory stock of the heavy pistol, protruding from his low-slung, half-breed holster, was shiny from an excess of handling.

Wild Bill Dorne most men named him, though there had been some—long since planted—who had been thoughtless enough to call him a thing less complimentary. And Dorne was a man who believed in meeting his obligations, no matter what their nature. He placed great value on his reputation for keeping his word.

It was that word which had placed him yesterday in the Sheriff's Office. And today he was starting out to make it good.

He was nearing the Golden Stack now, and could see the line of weary cow ponies chesting the peeled aspen rail beneath the warped wooden awning that crossed the boardwalk above the main entrance to Borst's resort. He was nearing it at the steady rolling gait of a man in whom determination was a definite thing.

Pecos Borst, as Dorne well knew, was overlord of this outlaws' paradise which a special meeting of legislature had defined on the maps as Spavined Nag. Well aware, too, was Dorne that Borst was one *cultus* hombre — "crooked as a dawg's hind laig." Suave and cunning, Borst was, as cunning as they came, and so damned suave that "butter wouldn't melt in his mouth."

It had long been hinted, as Dorne had heard, that Borst was taking a goodly cut from the wholesale activities being carried on by a band of unusually well-informed rustlers. Indeed, there was one rumor rife that Borst was not only the brains of the gang, but actually rodded it and led it upon its exasperating midnight forays.

But be that as it may, Bill Dorne knew from personal observation—as many another gent likewise knew—that Pecos Borst was the "dawg with the brass collar" in this man's town. All things, by the salty and hard-case gentry who made this town their hangout, were deferred to Pecos Borst, who passed upon them or vetoed them according to the measure of profit in them for himself.

It was a fine state of affairs, as the solid citizens had pointed out more than once. It was, in fact, such a state of affairs as made the packing of the Sheriff's star one job most terrifically undesirable. Especially as the former incumbent had survived his election but a scant two hours.

But Wild Bill Dorne was packing the Sheriff's star

now. And that made things a little different. For Dorne was a man—as the saying went—who had killed his men and buried them, and was like to do it again.

Bill packed the star and he aimed to perform. And right now, as he had declared to himself, was as good a time as any.

He crossed the walk and shoved himself through the swinging batwing doors and placed his back against a wall. There he stayed until his eyes had accustomed themselves to the dim light of the indoors after the change from the blazing sun outside. While standing thus, Bill Dorne took note that there was no sound in here save the droning of the flies and the ticking of the fat clock above the back bar.

Another man might have judged from this that the place was deserted save for a sleepy bartender or two. But not Bill Dorne; he reacted properly to such an unreasonable state of stillness. He figured that there were plenty of people filling the shadowy corners of this long main room—people who were holding their breath for the explosion of leaping weapons.

His vision cleared abruptly and he saw that he was right. At least twenty people had been lolling here upon his entrance; they were still here, but they were no longer lolling. Now they sat straight and rigid in the chairs about the gambling layouts; stood grimly motionless where they bellied the ornate black bar.

A faint grin quirked Wild Bill Dorne's wide lips as he glanced about him. Many times had he entered this place in the role of boisterous customer. And he knew many of the gathered assembly by their first names. But none smiled back at him now. They were woodenly noncommittal while waiting to learn what was up. For

Wild Bill was the Sheriff now, and that was right apt to make some difference in which side of the fence a man had ought to be on.

Dorne's glance swept the room in one full comprehending stab. Borst's tinhorns, lookouts and bouncers were in their accustomed places. Lola, too, sat inscrutably behind her faro table, sheathed today in a pale blue gown that brought out the richness of her tall blonde beauty and made the most of her full lithe figure that seemed as if it had been poured into the thin fabric of that low-cut dress.

But there was a difference here, today. Dorne recognized at once that Borst was ready for him. His flashing glance had noted where the hands of Borst's men hung. And he had noted, too, how men were unostentatiously slipping away from close proximity to himself and to Pecos Borst, where he stood with thumbs hooked into the armholes of his elaborately embroidered vest.

Bill's grin tightened a bit, but it stayed right there on his lips.

Pecos Borst was smiling, too; suavely, smoothly, dangerously. He rolled the fat cigar across his thick mouth and chuckled deep down in his great bull throat.

"Howdy, Bill. How's it feel to be the Sheriff of this man's town?"

"Can't tell yet," Dorne said. "Ain't been in office long enough. Guess you know what I'm here for, Pecos."

Borst drawled, "Sure. An' thanks, Bill. You came over here to spread the good news that you've got everything fixed, an' that the Golden Stack can go right on like usual."

Dorne's easy laugh mocked the tightening stillness.

"Why, no, Pecos," he said. "I came over here to serve you warnin'. This town is plumb fed up with the way you've been runnin' things. You can shoot it out or you can hoof it out. But out you're goin'. The choice is up to you."

TWO
TWO GIRLS

BILL DORNE HAD LONG BEEN KNOWN as a wild and reckless ranny to the folk of Spavined Nag. But it took an inordinate amount of gall to stand up here and tell Pecos Borst to his face that he had to get out of town. The whiteness of listening customers' faces and the rigidity of their bodies amply testified to this.

Borst's big rock-like figure did not shift its posture by so much as a twitching muscle. Nor did the expression change on his beefy, florid face. But his eyes showed suddenly smoky behind his sleepy lids.

"You surprise me, Bill," Borst said, and his head moved restlessly, throwing his long-eyed glance around the room. This sizing-up of the crowd was a constant thing with him. A habit it was, and unbreakable. For it rose from long-grounded instincts of self-preservation. "In fact, Bill, you disappoint me. I figured you for more sense than that."

"You're a cool one," Dorne commented, laying his regard upon Borst closely. "But cool or hot, you're goin' out. Them's orders, an' you better make up yore mind to seein' they're carried out."

Borst's voice was soft as the purring of a cat: "Are you allowin' you're man enough to give me orders, Bill?"

"We won't be goin' into that. You've got yore choice. See that you take it before sundown. Because after that you won't have a choice any longer," Bill Dorne concluded, and a wide grin fired up his face.

Ignoring Borst then, Dorne tilted his hat to a rakish angle and moved off towards the girl at the faro layout. It was like a slap in the face to Borst. But the overlord of Spavined Nag turned away, on his beefy face a look that was reserved and thoughtful. Whatever move he had in mind, one thing was certain: it would get no advertising in advance. For he was like that—sudden.

* * *

BILL DORNE STOPPED before the faro table. It was deserted now, save for the lithe blonde goddess who sat behind it. Her eyes were on his gravely, inscrutably. No one had ever known Lola's face to betray the secrets of her head. Or heart. She kept things to herself, exhibiting to the world a cold smooth face whose pallor and poker calm could not be pierced. And, though her figure was like a living flame, and as easily seen, men treated her with respect. For Lola had been around and knew a thing or two about keeping gents in their places.

In her eyes and poise, in her impenetrable calm—the very atmosphere about her, Bill had always found a quality hard to define. Accurate description would have labelled her exotic. But she was more than that; in Bill she awoke an eagerness, a pulsing excitement, he could not understand.

As she returned his steady glance, her red lips made a long and wistful curve against the alabaster pallor of her face. And slowly, under his close regard, her cheeks took on a tint of rose.

Bill saw this change and was flattered by it. But he would have been hard put to give the reason for his feeling. He could, however, have offered many reasons as to why he should give this woman a wide berth. He didn't, though; not even to himself.

He felt again that sense of wild elation which she always stirred in him. Perhaps it was because unconsciously he sensed in her, a kindred nature, an equal love of wild abandon—a deeper, fuller hunger for the fierce emotions of a dangerous living. Though God knows she never had given him cause to sense such things.

She kept herself to herself, and always had. So far as he knew. And she treated him no better than other men who had looked upon the wine when it was red, and had gambled away their money at the beckon of her rare smile. She treated them all alike and screened herself behind a cold hard barrier of aloof reserve. A reserve that hinted there were certain limits to the familiarity a man might attain. And that beyond those limits a man would travel at his own risk. And that it would be a risk was evidenced quite often by the wicked light that flashed far back in the jade-green depths of Lola's eyes when men tried to lay foundations for a more intimate relation. Those eyes of Lola's warned that she would feel no compunction about using that pearl-handled little derringer that always peeped from her bodice.

"How are you, Bill?" she said. "We haven't seen you for a full twelve hours."

"I been busy," he said, sighing. "This sheriffin' keeps me busier'n a dawg with fleas. 'F I'd 'a' knowed there was so danged much deskwork to runnin' this office I sure wouldn't 'a' let 'em put my name on that durned ticket. I got to get me some help befo' I bust a gut, or somethin'."

She gave him a little smile. One of the few he'd ever seen upon those ripe, red lips of hers. It transformed her instantly. Brightening her features. Adding fire and zest, and hazing a luring sparkle into the hard green of her eyes. Bill thought her teeth the whitest he had ever seen, and the most even. Then the smile was gone and the old inscrutable mask was back upon the alabaster whiteness of her cheeks.

"How's your engagement getting on?" she asked. "Got the date set yet?"

Embarrassment put a dull glow across Dorne's face. And her words brought conflicting emotions to the surfaces of his eyes; amazement, chagrin and anger.

"How'd you know about that engagement?" he growled softly.

She regarded him gravely, wistfully almost, one might have said. "Shucks, Bill. You're too important a figure in this community not to have all your comings and goings vigilanced. Shucks, I'm betting they knew it here five minutes after you'd popped the question. Last night it was, wasn't it? Right after you'd been elected?"

Bill swore, and then apologized. "It's sure got me fightin' my hat," he growled, "how Borst gets onto things so quick. It sure is amazin'. I reckon you know—"

"Who she is? Of course. Marcia Globe, the Mayor's daughter. You've got a keen eye, Bill. I congratulate you.

He took her small pale hand in his big brown one, and held her fingers as though they had been eggs. He was wondering if he had detected a catch in her voice, or if he had just imagined it. Desire, he thought irrelevantly, sure is the pappy to a peck of things.

"Well that's right nice of you, Lola," he said. "I don't know anyone whose congratulations I'd rather have."

He became conscious abruptly—as she sought to pull it loose—that he still held her hand. He released it with another flush. And had difficulty smothering an oath. Why was if, he wondered, that he blushed so dash-burned easy? It usually happened, he recalled, when he was around this Lola girl.

"Have you set the date yet?" she repeated, affecting a show of interest he was sure she did not feel.

"Why, no," he said. "I'm lettin' Marcia tend to that. Women like to do them little things, some fella told me once. I wouldn't wanta cut her out of any of the fuss an' fixin's."

But very seldom had Bill ever penetrated the poker veil of opaque green with which her eyes screened away her thoughts. But he read something into the expression of her eyes right now, a pure emotion—fear.

It spun him wickedly on his heels and sent his right hand slapping towards that pistol slung in the half-breed holster at his hip. The pistol's detonation and leaping burst of flame seemed identical with another. But it was the man across the room whose hands clutched frenziedly at his chest while he tottered there swaying, before he crumpled on his face.

Bill's gun weaved slowly back and forth. His eyes

raked those faces turned to his with slashing contempt. Eyes shifted and slid away before that icy glance. "Anyone figurin' to take up where he left off?"

But under that pistol's steady stare and the reckless challenge in the smoky eyes of Dorne, no man moved. Several had got their hands above their heads, and they kept them there, fearfully. Dorne looked straight at Borst.

"You wantin' any?" he asked.

Borst slowly moved his head from side to side in a negative gesture. He did not look scared. Merely amused. For his heavy face showed a thin smiling.

Bill Dorne sneered, "Caution can sure be learned quick by the misfortunes of others."

Borst chuckled deep down in his throat as though amused by some secret thought. Then abruptly he quit smiling; the change threw a shadowed light across the brightness of his eyes.

"One of these days, Billy boy, you're goin' to go too far. When that day comes—"

Malicious desire spread a reckless look across Bill Dorne's cheeks. "When that day comes, you ain' goin' to be around, Borst. Not unless you make yore play right now."

Borst's crag-like, beefy face did not change expression. "I'll even that score in my own good time," he said, and lit a new cigar.

"Yore time," Bill reminded grimly, "is gettin' mighty short."

But Borst just grinned. "I'm the best judge of that, Bill," he answered, and turned away, catching the eye of the white-faced piano player. "All right, Professor. Strike up a tune."

* * *

BILL LEFT the Golden Stack and, crossing the dusty street, chimed his spurs down the opposite side. When he came before a white frame house trimmed with green, he turned in the gate. A couple of steps later he was mounting the wooden steps to the veranda. This was the home of Mayor Globe, one of the only two buildings in town to be garnished by a coat of paint (the other building was the church). It was on the outskirts of the town.

As Dorne stepped upon the veranda, the door opened and in it stood framed a girl of rare loveliness. Her oval face was softly tanned and there was a natural color in her cheeks. Her eyes, of a soft clear brown, were topaz bright behind her curling lashes. They were smiling, level eyes—eyes which always filled Bill Dorne with a new calm and smoothed the turbulence from him like a wand of Peace. They did it now.

"Bill!" she said, and he thought it lucky guns were fired so often in this town that she did not think to ask him for an explanation of the shot she must have heard a few minutes back. "I'm glad you came. It's so lonely here when Dad's uptown. Stay awhile, won't you?" And, at his nod, "Come on inside; it's cooler there."

He could not help but admire her as he sat in a chair facing hers across the room. It did not seem possible, he told himself, that she could be engaged to him. Such luck was hard to realize.

She was dark, and her jet black hair held a soft blue sheen where light from the open window struck across it. She rose to her feet abruptly and came across to him.

He stood up, wondering. And blushed like a schoolboy when she offered him her lips.

He kissed her awkwardly and somehow felt a little guilty. Why, it would be hard to say. No one ever would have thought of Marcia Globe as any goddess that a good strong kiss would sully. There was too much light and laughter to her.

They talked some while of this and that. And then Bill rose to go.

"Gotta be gettin' back to the grindstone," he muttered, self-consciously. "You mightn't think it, but there sure is a pile of deskwork connected with sheriffin' that I never woulda believed before I got this job. Kinda makes a fella wish he'd stuck with cows. I gotta good mind to call Dave Kierny, or one of the other boys in to help me."

"But Kierny's your foreman," Marcia protested. "Who'd run your ranch if—"

"Oh, I couldn't spare him from the outfit," Bill Dorne answered. "But I sure wisht I could. Wonder how a fella goes about gettin' a deputy? Reckon I could advertise for one? Like city folks do when they want a house?"

Marcia shook her head. "I don't think so. I can ask Dad. He'd know."

Dorne nodded. "Well, I'll be seein' you after a while."

"Yes, of course. You'll come to supper, won't you?"

"I ain't right sure that I'll be able," Bill said, flushing again. "But I'll sure come if I can find a chance."

Leaving the Mayor's house, Dorne started back up town. On his way he got to thinking over that business in the Golden Stack. He would, he reflected grimly, be willing to bet his first month's pay as Sheriff that Borst had put that tinhorn up to trying to pot him in the back. It had the mark of Borst's methods. For Borst believed in never doing himself anything he could get some other gent to do for him. Especially if there was apt to be any risk attached to it.

It was uncommon odd, he mused, that Borst's pet pair of gunslammers had not been around to scare up a little excitement when he'd called. Uncommon odd. For Borst hired Smoky Leupp and Joe Fuddabaugh solely for their proficiency with pistols. And Borst was not a man to pay out good money to gents who weren't around when they were needed.

As he came in sight of the Sheriff's Office, he slowed down his long-legged stride. A man was lounging near the door. An unsavory looking customer. Shabbily dressed. And with one hand hooked into the greasy gun belt that sagged from a lanky hip.

THREE
A MAN WANTS ACTION

"WELL, PILGRIM," Dorne said. "What can I do for you?"

"What would yuh be expectin' tuh do?"

Dorne looked him over carefully. The fellow was dressed in a patched orange flannel shirt, over which he wore a greasy vest, and a pair of frazzled corduroy trousers stuffed into scuffed half-boots with run-down heels. These boots were equipped with tin-belly spurs whose rowels were missing. A faded blue scarf was pulled tight about his scrawny neck, and a floppy-brimmed sombrero was shoved far back on his shaggy head. His face was gaunt and wrinkled, and was covered by a three-days' stubble of beard.

Dorne said, "From the look of you I'd say you was lookin' for a night's lodging at the expense of the county."

The ragged stranger grinned widely. "Wal, yo're right in a way. I am—but not jest like yo're figgerin'. I'm lookin' for a job."

"Job?"

"Yeah. I hear yo're aimin' to curb the wickedness of this hell-roarin' town. Brother, yo're goin' to need some depities. Fact is, yo're lookin' at the first candidate right now.

"You think so?"

"I know it!"

"What qualities you got that make you think you'd be considered as a possibility?" Dorne asked skeptically. "You don't look so hot."

"Hot!" the stranger snorted. "This is the thirstiest country ever I hit! I'm hotter'n the hinges of hell—which goes to show appearances is some deceptive."

"I'm talkin' about qualifications for this deputy job you mentioned."

"Wal, Mister, yo're lookin' at the shootin'est ranny what ever come down the pike; a pistol-slapper on which yuh kin smell the powder smoke an' brimstone! Brother, if yuh don't take me on—"

"It won't do you any good to hand me any sob stories," Dorne cut in hastily. "I came from Missouri an—"

"Yuh did! Wal, I'll be a purple prairie dawg! So'd I! Shake, Missouri!" and the stranger stuck out a grimy paw.

But Bill Dorne looked it over suspiciously. "I ain't bitin' on that one," he grunted. "You wouldn't be the first gun man—if you *are* a gun man—to shoot down the gent whose hand you grabbed."

"Wal, prancin' prairie chickens! *If I am* a gun man says he!" and the stranger's right hand suddenly spouted flame and lead. And while the echoes of his shots slammed back and forth between the sun-bleached buildings, Dorne stared incredulously at the outline of himself which, with six leaden slugs, the ragged stranger had blasted against the adobe wall!

He smothered an admiring oath and said, "What handle do you go by?"

"Tranter's my name—Buck Tranter. Though there's some as calls me Brimstone."

"Well, Tranter, you're a pretty good shot."

"Pretty good!" Tranter snorted. "If you kin do better, an' in quicker time, I wanta know! Brother, that shootin' of mine's DAMN good! You can take it from a man what knows."

"You sure ain't shy on brag," Dorne chuckled. "But will you work?"

"Work! Why, Mister, I'm the hardest workin' cuss you'll meet up with in forty-eight states—bar none. I'm a genuwine early riser what don't bed down until the wee small hours, account I'm so dang scared that some 'un might say Buck Tranter ain't a-earnin' his keep!"

Dorne eyed him skeptically. "Don't look much like you been garnerin' the rewards of such steady an' ga'ntin' work."

"It's 'cause I ain't had any work for a calendar of Sundays," Tranter said, and bit himself off a chew from the plug of Brown's Mule which he took from his right hip pocket. "Honest work is sure scarcer round this country than hen's teeth. Never saw such a place. Arizony ain't what she used ter be. Why, I can remember the time when all a fella had ter do ter earn a livin' in this yere state, was ter swing a lass rope free an' easy, an' carry along a extra cinch ring in his saddle pocket. With a tolerable display of hawss sense an' a fair amount of labor a man could make quite a pocketful of change in a mighty few hours."

"Bein's you're puttin' in yore bid for a deputy's job, I take it you've reformed a bit since them days," Dorne suggested.

"Reformed?" Tranter scowled. "Hell, yes! I sh'd say I hev. I goes to church reg'lar now, ever' Sunday. Don't smoke, don't cuss, don't chew an' never slap m' brand on another man's steers. Brother, I've reformed so dang much it hurts!" Tranter's scowl grew fiercer. "Why, dang it, Mister, I've even took ter usin' soap an' water since I got the Word. I never thought I'd see the day when I'd lay my cheek ag'in' a chunk of soap! But there it is. I'm a reformed character, as they say in the book."

"I think I could use a gentleman of yore type," Bill grinned. "But there's one thing I gotta tell you first, Brimstone. This here's a tough town. I'm goin' to tame it if I have to bust a gut. Goin' to gentle 'er so she'll eat right outa my hand, so's to speak. But right now she's hotter than hell on wheels. Eats herself a man for breakfast every mornin' reg'lar. If you want the job, knowin' that, then she's yores."

"Brother, she is mine," said Tranter, and stuck forth his grimy paw again. This time Bill took it, and was surprised at the strength in Tranter's hand.

"You've got a grip," began Bill.

But Tranter interrupted with a dismal smile. "Not bad. But yuh can't have one thing without yo're missin' someplace else. With me it's a strong back an' weak mind. But it really ain't my fault. I got dropped out of a prairie schooner along the River Pecos when m'folks was migratin' from Missouri. Saint Louis is where I hail from, Brother. Good ol' St. L! I was right tender at the time."

Looking at him, Dorne could hardly imagine a time

when this lanky, grimy, wrinkled-faced specimen had ever been tender. But he just grinned. "Well, hang yore hat up in the Sheriff's Office—just inside the door here, Buck—an' get busy on that pile of papers you'll see on my desk. I'm goin' down the street a spell to wet my whistle."

Tranter stuck his head inside the door, took a look at the papers,and hurriedly pulled it out. "Say!" he wailed. "You don't expect me to mess around with no damn papers in this heat, do yuh?"

"That's what I'm hirin' you for."

"But I got a whistle, too," Tranter objected. "An' this godawful heat has done curled 'er up like a dry leaf."

"Little more curlin' won't hurt it, then," Bill decided, and started off.

Tranter swore disgustedly. "An' here I thought this was a hell-bendin' town plumb sufferin' from the lack of a two-fisted gun-slammin' depity which knows which end of the tube the smoke curls outen! Hell! There ain't no justice any more!"

Bill Dorne turned round, a cold gleam sparkling in his eye. "Do you want the job, or don'tcha?"

"Course I want the job—"

"Then quit gripin' an' stick up yore right paw while I swear you in."

Tranter did so and was sworn in without further waste of time. Bill got a deputy's badge from the desk drawer and handed it to him. Tranter looked it over admiringly, spat on it, and shined it up on his shirt tail. After which he pinned it on. Thrusting his arms akimbo, he stood considering it with a peculiar expression.

"First time," he said, "I ever wore one of them. I can

picture a coupla gents which would spin round in their graves like a top, was they to see me now. Buck Tranter, Depity! Cripes! I feel plumb dolled up like a little red waggin."

In the combination saloon, gambling hell and dance hall behind the faded sign bearing the words GOLDEN STACK, Pecos Borst was in earnest conversation with a pair of his trusted smoke-and-lead experts. To wit, Messrs. Leupp and Fuddabaugh. His tone was lowered and what he said was evidently to the point, for leers of pleasant anticipation overspread his listeners' evil countenances.

They moved to the door. "An' be sure there ain't no slips," Borst sent purring words after them. "An' on yore way out, send in Phoenix John Muroc an' Mendota."

While he was waiting, Borst entered a few figures in the little black book he always carried in the left breast pocket of his coat. Then he peeled the cellophane from a fat cigar and, biting off an end, placed the weed between his lips and lit it. With spirals of pale blue smoke wafting ceilingward, he settled comfortably back in his padded chair.

Came a knock on the door.

"Come in."

Two men entered the room. The first, Phoenix John, was dressed in the dark funereal garments of a professional gambler. He wore a diamond in the starched front of his white shirt, and there were lacy ruffs extending beyond the black sleeves of his coat. And a string tie at his throat. A stovepipe hat sat jauntily upon his head, and the face below it was a somber unsmiling mask.

Behind him appeared a Mexican breed, handsome

despite the tight-pressed gash that served him for a mouth. Pedro Mendota's forbears—on his mother's side —had walked in moccasins. And it was plain, by the dark little eyes alive with flashing sparkles, that Pedro felt no shame for the fact. He was clad in a tight-fitting jacket of blue velvet, and wore Mexican chaps over his leg-clutching trousers of green corduroy. A high-peaked straw sombrero, a-glitter with thread of gold, was thonged to his head by a chinstrap that was looped through a silver concho. The cartridge belt circling his panther-lean hips sagged in the middle to the weight of the bone-handled Colt that filled its flapless, brass-studded holster.

"Mendota," Borst said softly, "how long'll it take you to round up the boys?"

Mendota rasped a smooth brown hand across his chin, then grinned in a way that displayed to advantage his flashing teeth. "Mebbeso three hours?"

"That'll do," Borst nodded. "Take 'em over to Globe's ranch tonight. Cut his fences all to hell an' run off every two-year-old you can get yore hands on. Savvy?"

"Si, si!" Mendota chuckled slyly. "Thees Jefe, he weel be the one mad hombre, no?"

"I'm gonna own every decent spread in this county before I get done," Borst said in a way that took the brag from his words. "You fellas string along with me, an' by Gawd, we'll show some folks a thing or two! I'm figurin' to go places, an' them that trails with me are a heap likely to get their pockets lined."

Phoenix John eyed him dourly, saying nothing. Mendota grinned.

"All right, Pete. Get started. We're hittin' Globe

hard to-night. Globe is the one that put Dorne up for sheriff an—"

"What about Dorne," interposed Phoenix John drily. "Ain't you sort of leavin' him out of your calculations?"

"I'm not leaving anything out—or anybody," Borst said. "I'll take care of Bill Dorne when it suits my book."

"Take the cattle to the usual place?"

Borst nodded. "An' don't be afraid to use yore guns if any of Globe's half-baked punchers try to interfere. But keep yore lead clear of Polsky. I ain't through with him yet."

Mendota nodded and left the room, dragging his spurs.

"Shut the door," Borst told the gambler, and when the door had been closed: "Sit down. I got a few things I wanta say to you."

Phoenix John was settling himself in his chair when Borst stepped on a buzzer. A moment later one of the bartenders stuck his head in the door. "Call Lola. I want her in here," Borst said, and the white-aproned man disappeared.

Borst turned his smoke-grey eyes on Phoenix John. "If Dorne, or any of his friends, play in here I want you to see that they get cleaned proper. But don't pull anything crude; I don't want Dorne makin' a sieve out of you. Understand?"

"Yeah."

"All right. Pass the word around. When you go out, send in Gleed."

Phoenix John stared at Borst for a long silent moment, then got carefully to his feet and left the room.

Gleed and Lola came in together. Borst scowled at the girl. "Took yore time, didn't you?"

"Were you in a hurry? Ed just said you wanted to see me when I got through. I was racking the chips for tonight's game—"

"Never mind the alibis. That ain't what I'm hirin' you for." Borst's smoky eyes fastened on her face with a close regard, with a probing, penetrating stare. "Dorne stops by to pass the time of day quite frequent with you, I been noticin'. You ain't pullin' no fast ones on me, are you?"

"What do you mean?"

"Like, mebbe, tellin' him to lay off my game. He ain't been playin' at all lately." His glance grew opaque and flintlike. "If I thought for one minute—"

He let his words trail off, but his cheeks were harsh with the unspoken threat.

Lola looked at him and laughed, a swift tinkle of mirth. "Don't be a fool," she said. "What do I care about Wild Bill Dorne?"

"That's what I'd like to know," Borst said, and turned to Gleed.

"Put everyone to work gettin' the stuff packed up. Send somebody down to the freight office an' have 'em get a coupla their biggest wagons up here right away. We're movin' out."

Gleed's pugnacious jaw fell open and he stared at his employer with a look of stunned surprise. Then his jaw swung shut with a heavy snap and he growled an incredulous oath. "By cripes, I alius knew Bill Dorne was plenty tough, but I'd never believe he was tough enough to put the Injun sign on you!"

"Save that wind to cool yore beans," Borst growled

softly. "He ain't puttin' no Injun sign on nobody—me, least of all. I been contemplatin' this move for some while, an' this gives me the chance to put it through without no questions bein' asked. We're movin' to that ol' Seldies place three miles out. You know that ol' 'dobe?"

Gleed, Borst's head bouncer, nodded. "I know the place all right, but I'll be damned if I know what you're wantin' to shove way out there for! You may be doin' this for yer own good reasons, but this whole damn town's goin' to say we moved 'cause Dorne run us out. We'll never live it down—we'll be the laffin' stock of the whole blame country!"

Borst was a man who knew the value of a long silence; more than once he'd made silence worth its length in gold. He tried it on Gleed now, while he held the man with his smoldering, opaque eyes.

Gleed was a hard case; a bar-room bruiser who was an expert in his line. A man with sledgelike fists and gorilla torso. Six-foot-four he was, and weighed around two-sixty. Cauliflower ears adorned a face that was huge and flat, a bullet-headed face with a broken nose and a jutting, pugnacious jaw. Yet under Borst's fixed regard he shifted uneasily.

Borst's voice, when at last he spoke, was smooth and cool: "You doin' the talkin' round here now?"

Gleed shook his bullet head hastily. "Not me, boss. I was on'y—"

"Then shut up," Borst said, and peeled three-four bills of large denomination from a roll he pulled out of his pocket. These bills he tossed across the table. "Get busy. I want this joint moved out of town before sundown. An' I want our new location ready to open up in time for the evenin' trade."

Gleed took the bills, stuffed them in his pants and went out, shutting the door softly back of him. When the door was thoroughly closed, Borst turned back to Lola.

"Well," he said, "that's that. We'll open up tonight in the old Seldies place. Dorne'll play hell runnin' us out of there."

Lola was looking at him thoughtfully. "It all depends ... I wouldn't be too sure. Bill Dorne's got a mind of his own and he's a man who don't know the meaning of the word fear."

Borst scowled. "He'll know what fear is 'fore I get done with him! Who the hell's Bill Dorne, that he can give me orders? He's crossed me more'n once. But he ain't crossin' me no more—not after we move outside the town—"

"Bill Dorne's the sheriff," Lola reminded him. "Town boundaries don't mean anything in his reckless life—nor county boundaries, neither."

Borst swore vividly. "That fella's huntin' a quick grave if he messes with me any more! I'm fed up! He'll keep his hooked beak outa my business from now on or he'll get himself rubbed out! We're goin' to run the Golden Stack wide open. Everything goes. An' another thing I've meant to *habla* to you about, sister—from here on out I wanta see the percentage of profits from yore game go up. Either they go up, or you find yourself a job some other place! I want some action—an' I'm goin' to get it!"

FOUR
TUMBLEWEED

WHEN DORNE LEFT his newly-hired deputy in the Sheriff's Office, with orders to clean up the neglected correspondence and other papers littering the sheriffs desk, he set out down the street at his easy, swinging stride with no definite purpose in his mind—unless the dodging of that detested deskwork could be so described.

Tranter, he had a hunch, was going to be a great comfort.

He found himself wondering, as he wandered aimlessly along, just what section of the country Tranter hailed from. The new deputy, in Dorne's not unconsidered judgment, had the look of a tough hombre. He looked to be the kind of man who lived by his wits, rather than the sweat of honest toil—to be exact, like a Rider of the Hungry Loop and Ready Cinch Ring. It was a fraternity which Dorne, when he took his oath of office, had sworn to rout. And he meant to do so with Tranter's aid.

Tranter might, of course, be just a drifting leatherslapper. He sure could slap it, Dorne reflected, like nobody's business. Yes, all things considered, he believed the new deputy was going to be a good man to have around. If he could only meet up with another drifting gunslammer open to the argument of good wages in exchange for a little sleight-of-hand, he opined he'd have this town plumb gentled inside a week.

It was with this thought in mind that Bill Dorne was suddenly brought up short in his stroll by the advent of a bechapped and spurred buckaroo who had just bulged unexpectedly from the doorway of Manuel Venta's Broken Harp Saloon and gambling joint.

Dorne stared at the man, and the fellow stared back. There was an expectant look in this stranger's eyes that made Bill pause. The man had collided with him and, had Bill not been a cat on his feet, both of them would have gone down in a heap. Now the fellow seemed waiting and cocked for some sign of resentment from Bill.

Bill gave none. He just stood there hipshot, looking the other in the face. And the face was none too hand-some, either. It was an ugly, jeering face, packing a knife-scar that ran from chin to ear along the left side. A face that held the pale, intense eyes of a killer. But a face, none the less, having a high, broad forehead denoting intelligence. The face of a man who had seen better days. That he was from the north—Colorado, Wyoming, Nebraska or the Dakotas—was evidenced by his goat-skin chaps; things much too hot and itchy for this part of the country.

"Wal, why don'tcha say it?" the fellow jeered.

"Say what?"

"Aw—hell! They sure raise 'em panty-waisted

round this here stretch of cact—" the fellow began. And ended. For just there, Bill's right fist—coming up from his bootstraps—took him under the chin and stretched him flat on his back, spreadeagled neatly across the plank walk.

Bill reached down with a long left hand, which he snagged in the fellow's shirt-front, and hoisted him to his feet as though he'd been a child. Bill let go and, before the fellow could fall, struck him a second pile-driver blow beneath the ear. The man in the hairy pants folded up without sound.

Bill heard the thud of booted feet and knew a crowd would be collecting fast. So, reaching down with both hands this time, he picked the fellow up, deposited him over one shoulder and started for the jail.

The place where Spavined Nag was wont to incarcerate its unruly citizens was a small adobe building to the rear of the Sheriff's Office. Towards this place Bill now packed the luckless buckaroo. A group of curious townsmen followed along at a discreet interval until Bill, with a fearful scowl, spun round on a heel and said: "*Git!*"

At which the curious *got,* and stood not upon the order of their getting, but got at once—complete and final. Bill grinned as he swung round and resumed his interrupted cruise toward jail.

Tranter saw him coming and met Bill before the Sheriff's Office.

"What'n seventeen purple prairie chickens you got there? A hair mattress? Or is it a new kinda caterpillar?"

"Ain't right sure," Bill Dorne grunted. "But I aim to find out. Shall I take him into the office or dump him in the jail?"

"If yo're askin' me, I vote yuh bring 'im in the office," Tranter said. "Seems like I've met that coot before, someplace or other. I got a great mem'ry fer faces," he added solemnly. "I can even recollect the fella what baptized me when I was two weeks ol'! A big fella he was, with fiery red whiskers an' a black patch over one eye. He was a great fella fer swappin' jokes. I recall as how he tol' me one about the—"

"Save it for some other time," Bill cut him short. "Right now, we got to learn who this hellion is an' where he's drifted from. He's got a mean eye."

Tranter said, "What happened to him? Did 'e get shot? Or what? Where'd yuh find 'im, anyhow?"

"On the sidewalk front of the Broken Harp."

"Sleepin' off a drunk—"

"Sleepin' off a good sock on the jaw I gave him," Bill Dorne snapped. "By cripes, how long you think I'm gonna stand here holdin' him? Git out of the way so's I can take him inside."

Tranter moved, preceding Bill and his burden into the — office, where Bill dumped the latter on the floor in front of his desk, thereby eliciting from the luckless northerner a doleful groan. Seconds later the fellow opened his eyes cautiously, blinked, winced and came to an elbow. "My Gawd!" he muttered. "You got a fist, Mister, that packs a slug like a shot of hundred proof! Don't hit me no more—I couldn't stand it. I ain't had a square meal in a week."

"What did you get thrown out of that saloon for? Tryin' to rob it?"

"Rob yore gran'mother! I was tryin' tuh bum me somethin' to eat!"

"Well, you'd ought to 'a' looked where you was

lettin' 'em pitch you. I've a good mind to throw you in jail for shootin' off your mouth the way you did. I'm waitin' for your apology."

"You sure got it," the Long-Faster said with alacrity. "I don't want no more argyments with *you!*" He stood rubbing his jaw tenderly with one hand, while cautiously caressing the bump behind his ear with the other. He eyed Bill Dorne reproachfully. "Whatja hit me with, anyhow—a hawsshoe?"

Bill Dorne grinned. "Them was just love pats I gave you," he chuckled. "Bear with me for a bit till I get warmed up an' I'll show you some hittin' as will make yore eyes bulge out!"

"No thanks. I know w'en tuh quit," the buckaroo protested vociferously. "This is the toughest burg I ever struck. What I'm needin', Mister, is a square meal. I ain't had nawthin' ter eat fer six days. Golly Moses but I'm hungry. Why—I'm so danged hungry I could eat a skunk an' like 'im!"

"Folks in this here town has tuh work fer their grub!" Tranter growled righteously. "We don't want no bums round here!"

Dorne grinned a little. Then he said to the stranger, "What handle do you pack?"

"I'm most generally known as Tumbleweed," said the man in the hairy chaps.

"Tumbleweed, eh?" Dorne considered. "Well, Tumble, can you manipulate that Peacemaker you got stashed in yore holster?"

"I sabe which end the smoke comes outa."

"Where bouts do you hail from, Brother?" Tranter popped a question.

The drifting buckaroo slapped his pale-eyed glance

on Tranter disapprovingly. "Where I come from folks don't ask strangers that kinda question—not onless they're lookin' for a fast grave. Further, Mister, they have learned in my part of the country that them that don't ast no questions, don't git told no blasted lies."

"Now listen, fella," Bill broke in earnestly. "Unless you're wantin' to spend time in my calaboose, then you better answer all questions we see fit to ask. I'm the Sheriff of this county, an' Tranter here is Chief Deputy. We—"

"Glad ter know yer, gents," Tumbleweed butted in. "Can either of yer spare a dime?"

Tranter snorted. "You got some nerve—"

"I got some speed, too!" Tumbleweed purred, and Tranter found himself staring down the muzzle of this stranger's short-barreled .45. That this was an unprecedented situation for Tranter was evidenced by the way his eyes bulged out and the slackness manifested in the longitudinal position of his lower jaw. Dorne, too, stared at this drifting buckaroo in amaze. If Tranter was fast— and he most certainly was—then this belligerent Tumbleweed shamed lightning by comparison.

"Balance of the power is now vested in the minority," Tumbleweed drawled wickedly. "Empty out yore pockets, gents, an' empty 'em pronto onless yer wants ter view the daisies from a worm's altytood!"

Dorne and Tranter exchanged chagrined glances. This was pretty bad. Stuck up by a hairy-pantsed stranger right in the Sheriff's own office! If the town ever got wind of this they'd be the laughing stocks of the whole county. Unless they could swiftly get the upper hand.

"Shell out, gents! Shell out an' make it snappy!

Why, yer pore deluded gophers! There ain't no man alive can sock Tumbleweed Shane under the button an' behind the ear, an' git away with it. Nor there ain't no ragbag on Gawd's green footstool what kin sneer down his nose at me!" His pale, killer eyes glared fiercely. "Shell out, yer dang tin-belly star-packers!"

Bill and Tranter turned their pockets inside out; Bill philosophically, Tranter with unconcealed malignance. "He what laffs last—" Tranter began.

But Tumbleweed's hoarse chuckle cut him off. "Wall, I'm doin' the laffin', sonny, an'—"

But Tumbleweed's words and Tumbleweed's laughter both abruptly ceased together as Bill Dorne's booted foot came up like the sun out of China, batted the pistol out of his hand and sent it spinning across the room. Before it landed, Tumbleweed was gazing viciously into the gaping bore of Tranter's hog-leg.

"The worm has turned," Tranter sneered, and spat at a knothole a scant half inch from Tumbleweed's left boot. "What'll we do with this ingrate, Bill?"

"What we'd ought to do by rights," Bill said, "is shove him in the jail an' forget about 'im." He stared resentfully at the glaring Tumbleweed. "What was the big idea?"

Tumbleweed's scowl vanished in a sudden grin. "Jest havin' a little fun with you boys, that's all. Wanted ter see if I could beat yer to the draw." He chuckled. "It was like takin' candy from a kid."

"Yeah?" said Tranter, advancing with an oath. "Well, if I swipe this gun's muzzle acrost yore homely mug yuh won't be thinkin' it's so dang funny, I'm bettin'!"

"Hold on, Buck," Dorne interposed, picking up his

belongings and stuffing them back in his pockets. "Do you want a job, Tumble—a good job that packs excitement an' forty bucks a month?"

"Where is it?" Tumbleweed looked skeptical.

"Right here," Bill explained. "I need another deputy an' you sure got all the signs of makin' just the kind I'm lookin' for. What do you say?"

Tumbleweed appeared to consider, rasping a none-too-clean hand across his stubbly jaw. At last he admitted, "Wal, I might sort of give it a whirl."

"Good," said Bill, and swore him in, Tranter looking on disgustedly. Bill then gave his new deputy some money and told him to go out and fill his aching cavity. When he had gone, Tranter growled lugubriously:

"Jest pilin' up trouble for us, that's what you're doin'. That li'l scorpion's plumb cultus, if I know the breed! Yuh should've put yore heel on 'im, Bill. He'll live tuh sting us yet."

JOB FOR A BUCKAROO

AN HOUR or so later when Tumbleweed returned, it was to find Bill Dorne comfortably tilted back in a chair behind the Sheriffs desk, with his spurred boots reclining inelegantly upon its much-pitted surface. Tranter had left the office, having been sent by Dorne to keep an eye on the resorts which already were dusting off their tables and polishing up their glasses for the evening trade.

Dorne said, "Take a chair, Tumble. We're gonna *habla* a spell."

Tumbleweed pulled up a chair and perched himself gingerly upon the extreme edge. He looked enquiringly at the sheriff.

"What kind of work do you do? I mean," Dorne elucidated, "what's yore profession—cowpuncher, buckaroo—"

"That's it."

"What?"

"Buckaroo," said Tumbleweed succinctly.

Bill Dorne let his blue-eyed glance play over his

newest deputy in a manner that was closely speculative. "Work on the theory that a man who wastes no words wastes no breath, and that silence is worth its weight in gold, I reckon," he commented. "Now s'pose you loosen up a mite an' get confidential. Where'd you work last as a rider?"

"Box O B, Salty Crick, Nevada."

"Never heard of it."

"Wal," grunted Tumbleweed with a sly smile, "I reckon even the Sheriff of Spavined Nag ain't heard of ever'thin'."

Bill snorted, and eyed the hairy-chapped man more closely. "There's more to you than meets the eye," he opined drily. "So you worked for the Box O B. What kind of monicker did you give the ramrod for a last name to stick on his payroll?"

"Tumbleweed—just plain Tumbleweed. I ain't one of them high-minded aristocrats what has to have two handles to git called to grub with. Plain Tumbleweed's good enough for me."

"Yeah. Tumbleweed, eh? Ever been a bronc peeler, Tumble?"

"Oh, I've gentled two-three rough 'uns in my time," the new deputy admitted modestly. "How come all this curiosity? If I might ast?"

"Vital statistics for the Sheriff's Office," Dorne answered. "We have to know who we got workin' for us, an' why." The blue of Dorne's eyes grew thoughtful as he sat regarding his newest deputy, who was softly whistling a tune the while his pale eyes roved the raftered ceiling. "You're pretty fast at gettin' out that hog-leg you're totin'. Ever hire it out?"

"Yer mean am I a perfeshional gun slinger?"

Tumbleweed queried innocently. And at Dorne's nod, "Hell, no—I'm a buckaroo, like I told yer."

"Let it go," Dorne said. "Where'd you work before you got that job at the Box o B?"

"Deer Lodge—I was workin' fer the government."

"I see," Bill said, though he didn't. But he decided not to push his questions any further in that direction before this man who had worked for the government, for fear of making himself appear ignorant of Sheriff procedure. Instead he said, "Can you read sign?"

"Shucks, that ain't my long suit," Tumbleweed admitted with a wry grin. "To tell yer the truth, I couldn't find a baseball in a termato can."

Bill thought awhile in silence. When he spoke, finally, it was in a greatly lowered voice. He was a great believer in the saw that even walls have ears. "I'm going," he said, "to give you a risky job. But it's an important one an' I hope you won't turn it down."

"What kinda job?" Tumbleweed asked suspiciously. "I hear that yer done ordered Borst ter get shut of this town. Don't give me no job seein' that he gets shut of it, because I wouldn't be able ter git very enthusiastic about a chore o' that kind."

"Listen," Bill said earnestly. "What I want you to do is go over to Borst an' hit him for a job," and he looked at Tumbleweed intently.

Tumbleweed looked back, and just as intently, between his suddenly narrowed lids.

Bill said softly, "Do you get it?"

"'Fraid I don't. Better chew it finer."

"What I want you to do," said Bill briefly, "is to get on Borst's payroll where you'll have a chance to work yoreself into his good graces an' be in a position to act as undercover man for this office."

"Thought yer was orderin' Borst outa town?"

"I am. But I got a notion he ain't figgerin' to go very far."

"Wal, I don't wanta be no sneakin' spy!"

"Don't be a fool. What I'm offerin' you is a damned important job; it's a compliment to yore ability that I'm even askin' you to take it. An' the pay'll be sixty bucks a month. If you keep yore head the chances of you bein' caught will be pretty slim."

"Yeah—an' so'll my chances of gettin' out with a whole skin if I *do* git caught!" Tumbleweed snorted. "What do yer think I am? You got me mixed up with some other gent, Mister. Me, I ain't cut out ter be no martyr. I got a few things I want ter do yet afore I pass in my checks."

"Eighty," said Bill softly.

"Not on yer tinpipe!"

"A hundred."

"Huh? What's that?" Tumbleweed whispered. "Say that ag'in."

"A hundred bucks per month if you can cut it."

"Cripes!" Tumbleweed muttered, and: "I reckon I'm the world's champeen nit-wit ter even think about it. But ... a hundred bucks per month—Hell, I'll take yer up on that." Tumbleweed's leathery face was very solemn.

Bill shook his hand and got to his feet. "Fine," he said, simply. "Keep me posted."

Tumbleweed paused at the door and turned. "How would yer suggest that I go about gettin' this job with Borst? Is he lookin' fer some help?"

"Couldn't say. But he owns a ranch—cattle ranch—besides this dive in town. He oughta be able to use a good tough hand."

"Thanks," Tumbleweed said, and grinned. "Leave it ter me; I'll git on."

As he went out the door Tranter came in. There was a disapproving scowl on the ragged deputy's face. He put a hand to his nose and walked around in a circle. Then, stopping before Dorne, he shook his head. "Them as sups with the devil sure needs a long spoon."

"What you talkin' about?"

"You an' that two-legged polecat what jest went out. Don't never let it be said I didn't warn yuh! You'll get yore tail in a sling yet, foolin' with that hombre."

Dorne got out his pipe and filled its bowl. He lit it and inhaled gratefully. Then, expelling the smoke from his nostrils, he looked at Tranter closely. "What you so down on that fella for?"

"Don't like 'im," Tranter grunted shortly. "He's plumb cultus. You take it from a man what knows. I wish to hell I could recollect where I seen him before. It wa'n't no place good, I'll swear."

"What's wrong with him?"

"How in seven devils do I know?" Tranter demanded testily. "But he's a bad 'un. Didja git a look at his eyes?"

Bill grunted. "Trouble is with you, you're jealous. I told Tumble to get himself a job with Borst. He's goin' to be our undercover man."

"Yeah? Wal," Tranter scowled, "there's no fool like a young 'un. Speakin' of Borst, he's done moved. Pulled out bag an' baggage not ten minutes ago. I'm s'prised he fell for yore bluff."

"That wasn't no bluff," Bill said. "If he hadn't gone I'd have seen that he was carried out on a shutter. When I say somethin' I mean business. Borst knows it an' acted accordin'."

"Oh, yeah? Wal, that's one way of lookin' at it. I met yore preacher while I was at supper. Seems right discouraged. Called this place a sink of iniquity an'—"

"That sky-pilot's a pretty good egg. Only he's kinda impatient. Rome wasn't built in a day."

"That's what I told him," Tranter said. "He says as how he's been a-laborin' in this Lord's vineyard for goin' on six months an' ain't gathered one grape yet. He's pretty down in the mouth."

* * *

LEAVING THE SHERIFF'S OFFICE, Tumbleweed crossed the street and went into the place recently occupied by the Golden Stack. Finding the place empty, he came out again and asked a passing puncher "What happened ter Borst?"

"Sheriff bluffed him outa town," said the puncher. "Claims he's goin' to open up in the old Seldies place. Reckon you'll find him out there if yore business is urgent."

Tumbleweed wheeled and headed for the stable where he got his horse, and swinging into the worn saddle he had not bothered to take off, forked him out of town at a quick jog.

It was almost dark when he reached the Seldies place.

He could see it as soon as he had topped the first rise after leaving town, for the place was a blaze of light as Borst's men rushed to get it into order for the night's business, which he plainly expected to follow him to his new location. Guided by its beckoning windows, Tumbleweed located it without difficulty or further directions. Dismounting before the old place, he tied his horse—a hammer-headed roan—to the newly and hastily erected hitching rail, and clumped his spurs inside.

Borst's men had been working fast. The bar was in and the mirror set along the wall behind it. Three sweating bartenders were unpacking the bottled goods. The tinhorns were getting their games in readiness and a couple of swampers were sweeping the bar-room out, while six carpenters were swiftly putting down a dance floor in the room behind it. Two more carpenters were busily engaged, amid much cussing, in enlarging the connecting doorway.

Pausing a few moments, Tumbleweed surveyed these activities with a keen interest. Then he tightened the slack in his belt, spat on his hands and, rubbing them across his hairy chaps, went swaggering over to one of the gamblers.

"Borst around?" he asked.

The gambler nodded his sleek black head without bothering to look up. "Yeah—back room. The door on the right. An' you better knock."

But evidently Tumbleweed was not accustomed to knocking upon doors, for he entered the room indicated without troubling with such formality. There was a girl with Borst. A girl with vivid green eyes in a pale face framed by golden hair. Lola.

Borst looked up with a scowl. "What do you want?"

"A talk with yer."

Borst looked him over carefully. Then he said to the girl "Git," and she went out. Borst's smoke-grey eyes swung back to Tumbleweed. "Spill it."

'I been wonderin' could yer use another hand.'

"What's yore line?"

"Anythin' the other gents won't tackle."

"Hard guy, eh?" said Borst, with a glint of amusement in his look.

"I ain't makin' no brags," said Tumbleweed easily, "but I'm alius willin' ter demonstrate—alius hev been an' I alius will."

The boss of Spavined Nag permitted a grin to reach his thick-lipped mouth. "Sort of handy man, eh?"

"Alius hev been, an' there's a pretty good chanct I alius will. Don't you reckon?"

Borst's sleepy lids shut down a bit. "Couldn't say. What kinda job d'you want?"

Tumbleweed rasped his chin. "I ain't speshully partic'lar—jest so's there's plenty of dinero in it."

"Have you met our new sheriff? His name's Bill Dorne."

"I've seen him," a grimace crossed Tumbleweed's ugly face. "He's knowed as *Wild* Bill Dorne."

"Well, I might be able to use you," Borst said, looking him over. "I could use you all right if you could get yoreself a job in the Sheriff's Office. There would be good money in it, too. Money from here an' money from there. Do you think you could cut it?" Borst's eyes were on Tumbleweed's sharply as he asked the question.

Tumbleweed grinned and, taking his left hand from his pocket, laid a bit of metal carefully on the desk in front of the big resort keeper. A touch of deeper color came into Borst's beefy face. He straightened, still looking at that object Tumbleweed had set before him. Then his glinting glance flashed to Tumbleweed's face.

"You're hired," he said, and chuckled.

Tumbleweed chuckled, too.

When Tumbleweed had taken his departure, Borst called Gleed, the bouncer, into the back room. Gleed looked hot and sweaty. He had been working with the others, hurrying to get this new location of the Golden Stack ready for a celebration Borst had ordered in honor of the change.

Borst said, "If Bill Dorne comes out here tonight, let him be. My orders, for the present, are hands off. *Sabe?* Right now Bill Dorne is goin' to be a durned sight more use to me alive than dead."

Gleed looked back at him curiously. Then he shrugged his gorilla shoulders and a sneer slid across the lips beneath his broken nose. "Yer gettin' soft," he jeered. "Y'oughta join the Panty-waist Club. Cripes, it fair makes my liver crawl ter see yer knuckle under to thet blasted Billy-be-Damned Dorne. What's—"

"That's enough outa you," Borst purred. "I'm runnin' this, savvy? An' what I say goes. An' I don't want no lip from you! Get me?"

Gleed nodded with a surly grimace. "It's yer funeral."

"Funeral—hell! If there's any plantin' goin' to be done, I'll be the guy to do it. Bill Dorne has seen his best days, an' you can stick a pin in that. I'm takin' care of him when the sign's right. You do what I tell you an' you an' me will get along fine. When you go back outside you can pass the word around. All hands are to lay off Dorne until I give the word."

Gleed left the room and Lola returned. Borst looked

up from some papers he was sorting. "Listen," he said heavily, "you get hold of Bill Dorne an' keep him busy tonight—"

"What about my game?" cut in Lola.

"To hell with yore game! Someone else can tend to it. Yore job's to find Bill Dorne pronto, an' to keep him in tow for the rest of the night."

SIX

SCORE ONE FOR THE SPORTING ELEMENT

IT WAS some time after old mother night had draped her sable folds across the town of Spavined Nag that Bill Dorne put on his hat and left the Sheriff's Office with Buck Tranter for a tour around the various resorts fronting the main street. Business was good and all hands seemed busy whooping it up. This was a payday night, and plenty of punchers were in from the outlying ranches, boisterous, exuberant, and as willing to fight as to drink.

"Goin' to be a kind of tough night," Dorne remarked to Tranter, and did not dream that his words were to come so true as the morrow was to prove them.

Tranter nodded sagely. "Yuh shore said somethin' that time. It's goin' tuh be a thirsty night, too. An' all these punchers bulgin' intuh town ain't goin' tuh be satisfied till they've raised hell an' shoved a chunk under it. My advice, young fella, is tuh let 'em do it. An' keep plumb outen the way, so's it won't git dropped on yore pet corn."

"These joints are gonna have to close up by two

o'clock," Bill growled. "That's long enough for any gent to work the Old Adam out of his system."

Tranter got out his plug of tobacco and bit off a generous chew. "Well," he opined drily, "you're the doctor, I reckon. She's yore game an' I guess yuh kin play 'er as yuh please. But if I was you, I'd let these joints plumb alone to-night. Depend upon it; that's comin' from a man what knows! This is yore cue tuh step soft an' easy fer a spell. Yuh've run Borst out of town—don't try crowdin' yore luck too far."

Bill reached out abruptly and put a hand on Tranter's arm. "Wait a minute," he muttered. And Tranter, following the direction of his glance, saw a woman coming toward them through the jostling crowd. A girl, in fact. Lola. Men were backing aside right and left to let her pass, and looking after her with admiring glances.

Tranter snorted. "I thought I heard yuh was engaged tuh be married!"

Bill made no answer, but his cheeks got red. He kept his eyes on Lola, and there was a keen interest in them.

But not in Tranter's. "I'll be amblin' along," he grunted.

"All right," Bill said. "I'll see you later. Better make the rounds of these places an' see that there ain't no rough stuff." He did not look at Tranter; he was too busy admiring Lola's lithe swinging form. He was still admiring it when she came up with that grave smile she seemed to reserve for him alone. "Hello, Bill Dorne," she said.

"Howdy, Lola. Doin' the town?"

"Not really. Just out for a breath of air. One of the

boys is taking my game for awhile. How's the sheriffing business? Who was that range tramp you were talking with?"

"That's my new deputy," Bill said, gazing after the departing Tranter with a grin. "I reckon he's kinda woman-shy. He cut his stick soon's he seen you comin'. If you ain't busy, what say we take in the sights?"

"We-ll," she appeared reluctant, but let Bill hold her hand. "Perhaps we'd better not. After all," she smiled, "you're engaged to be married now."

"I ain't married yet," Bill said. "Come on," and linked his arm in hers. "How'd you get to town?" he asked after a few silent moments of battling their way through the crowded streets. "Didn't you move out with the rest of yore crowd to Borst's new stand?"

"Yes. One of the cowboys lent me his horse for the evening. I've left it at the livery."

They walked along in silence for a spell—silence on their part, that is. For the night itself was anything but quiet. Raucous voices called the figures of reels and jigs to the scrape of fiddles, the twanging of guitars, and the reedy notes of a windy mouth organ. Feet stamped in time. These sounds were only a background for other, nearer, sounds. Oaths, snatches of ribald tales, occasional guffaws and once a woman's high-pitched laughter.

Bill did not seem to be heading toward any of the resorts. Neither did he appear to be strolling aimlessly. Lola must have observed that they were walking toward the edge of town. But it wasn't the edge where the Globe house was situated. So she offered no protest. Content, apparently, just being in Bill's company. Her fingers made soft pressure as they lay inside Bill's bigger ones. The night was hot, but there was a cool wind springing up off the desert, and as their sauntering took them further from the noise of those boisterous pleasure-seekers, they could hear the steady chirping of the crickets.

They had reached a spot by now some hundreds of yards from the edge of town. Spavined Nag's garish lights did not spoil the night's beauty out here. Not if one faced the other way.

The dark eerie forms of tall saguaro made darker patterns against the desert's thinning black. Patterns appearing to fill this girl beside him with some vague dread or sense of disquietude. For she pressed closer to him and, before Bill knew it—or realized what the night and this girl's proximity were doing to him—he found his arms around her. Tight. And his lips on hers, and hers returning their pressure vividly.

* * *

BUCK TRANTER, with his Chief Deputy's star glinting proudly from its perch on the left breast of his patched orange flannel shirt, making his rounds of Spavined Nag's resorts, was being received with an apparent respect and cordiality that was surely royal. Never in all his long and checkered career had he been so wined and feted as he was this night.

Seemed like every dive he visited he was made to feel more welcome. At first he could not understand all this friendly interest, but after the twentieth glass had dropped its fiery contents down his throat, he made up his mind that he was quite a mixer and let it go at that.

At Ortega's Black Bottle Bar, he was served the best

on the shelf, and later invited to take a hand in a stud game that was in progress. The stakes were pretty steep and he sort of shook his head and opined that it was a wise man who knew when to let well enough alone. But after a bit of coaxing, he was wheedled into playing for about a long half hour. At the end of which time he got up from the table wealthier by three hundred dollars. And felt pretty slick.

At Venta's Broken Harp he was asked to swig from Venta's private bottle. Which he did with pleasure and much smacking of the lips. It was prime stuff, he allowed. And was given a bottle to carry with him—in case he got to feeling dry between stops.

At Venta's, too, he took a whirl at the wheel. Elated at a hundred dollar win, he let his money ride and doubled it. Again he left it on the board, and once again he doubled it. Other players were beginning to follow his leads and there was a ring three deep sweating the game when he finally raked in his profits, and with bulging, clinking pockets left the place.

He stopped for a spell in two-three smaller joints and emerged amply repaid for the pause. Standing outside the swinging doors of the last place, he scratched his shaggy head and stood groggily watching the noisy punchers trooping by. How long he stood there would be hard to tell, but finally, biting off a huge chew from his plug of Brown's Mule, he went masticating toward the livery stable at a more or less rolling gait.

The stable's proprietor was a handsome gent. And very obliging. He got out Tranter's flea-bitten crow-bait, gave it a rub and saddled it for him. And wouldn't take a tip. Moreover, had Tranter been strictly sober instead of slightly pie-eyed, he would have found some cause to wonder at the ridiculously low fee he was charged for the two-day care of his horse.

But he wasn't strictly sober after all the libations that had burned their way downward past his gullet. He slapped the stable-keeper on the back in jovial gusto, called him a good sport and handed him one of the cigars that had been pressed upon him as he made his rounds. Then, right pleased with himself and the rest of the world, he kicked his decrepit-looking nag in the ribs and pointed its head toward the Seldies place, three miles out on the desert.

Tranter crawled off his bonerack nag in front of the new Golden Stack and, not bothering to trail his reins or tie them, dragged his spurs inside. Things were pretty lively. Booted and belted buckaroos were whirling thinly-draped females round the dance floor at a most reckless pace, stamping on one another's toes to the fiddles' wail of Turkey In The Straw. The games, he could see, were well patronized and the long bar was lined with men four deep. As usual, it appeared, the Golden Stack—even though removed three miles from town—was getting the lion's share of business.

Tranter had hardly weaved his way inside the swinging doors when the bullet-headed, broken-nosed Gleed came striding forward, a grin stretching across his ugly map from ear to cauliflowered ear, and grasped Buck joyously by the hand. With his free paw he slapped Buck's shoulder.

Tranter gasped: "Hey! Dammit! Don't shake m' teeth plumb out. Ack civilized, can't yuh? Whatcha think this is? An' m'hand ain't no dang pump handle. So lay off 'n it, fella. Lemme get m' breath!"

"Ain't you ol' Slip-shot Tranter?" asked Gleed, as though surprised.

"Hell, yes! An' what ef I am?" demanded Tranter belligerently. "I kin lick m' weight in wildcats, an'll sieve the guy what says I can't!"

"Wal, they ain't no gent here what'll say so," Gleed assured him, grinning. "It sure warms the cockles of my heart to see you here in Spavined Nag, Slip-Shot. Gonna drop yore picket pin a spell?" And at Tranter's nod, Gleed's jaw abruptly dropped in simulated amazement. "Gosh! Fer the love o' Lizzie! Have you done reformed?"

Tranter's bleary eyes followed Gleed's hard gaze to the star pinned on the front of his shirt. "What'cha mean, reformed?"

"You shore didn't pack no star in the old days—"

"Naw. I'm jest wearin' this tin badge tuh show a coupla incredulous gents that ol' Buck Tranter can be any damn thing he wants."

Gleed chuckled. "Like any old fool could doubt it! C'mon, have a drink, Buck, fer ol' time's sake."

"Wal, I don't care ef I do," grunted Buck, and permitted the grinning Gleed to pilot him up to the bar. When they had downed three-four drinks— "to get the alkali out of their systems" as Gleed put it—Gleed led Tranter over to a poker game. And with a flick of his off eye, got a chair vacated for Buck so quick he never noticed that a man had been sitting there as they came up.

When Tranter finally quit the Golden Stack some three hours later he didn't have two coins left to clink together.

AND, during this same evening, out on the range where the Wineglass cattle ran, a group of shadowy, swift-working, horsebacked figures cautiously hazed all of Mayor Globe's two-year-olds that could be found without much dalliance, off along a trail that ran south toward the Mexican Border—the trail of no return. And these cattle were not what might be described by a Westerner as a little jag of beef; this was a wholesale maneuver, designed to break Globe quick.

And in town things were going on, too—things seen by neither Dorne nor Tranter. Things which Borst had no intention of allowing to reach their ears. Till the harvest was gathered, and his share salted away.

It was after two when Bill Dorne rolled into his bunk in the room behind the Sheriff's Office. The two saloons, he knew, had not closed at two. But right then he had too much else on his mind to care. And was to have a good deal more.

SEVEN
"'EEF YOU ARE LOOK FOR TROUBLE —'"

WHEN BILL DORNE returned from an early breakfast the next morning, he found Buck Tranter seated in his chair and with his spurred heels hooked atop the desk.

"Hey," Bill growled. "Get yore dang feet down off 'n there! What do you think this is?"

Tranter chewed in a morose silence for a while, then observed, "I've seen you sittin' this here way."

"What of it? I'm the sheriff!"

"Wal," said Tranter, and spat at a knothole across the room, "I'm the sheriff's helper."

Bill Dorne's face made a grimace. "A hell of a helper you are! Why didn't you close up them saloons an' gamblin' dives last night at two o'clock; like I told you to?"

"Yuh didn't tell me to. Yuh say as how yuh aimed for them tuh be closed by that time; but yuh never said I was tuh do the closin'. An' if yuh had," Tranter added flatly, "I'd 'a' tole yuh to yore face that yuh couldn't hire me tuh try pullin' no dumb stunt like that. Besides, these here fellas what runs them joints is plumb friendly towards me. The—"

"Friendly as a Gila Monster," Dorne said sarcastically. "Don't never trust the sportin' element in this man's town, 'cause they'll knife you every time. I ought to know. I've spent quite some time hangin' round them joints—before I got to be sheriff, that is. That fella Borst would just as leave order yore throat cut as order you a drink."

"Yeah—an' a whole lot lighter!" Tranter growled. "I went intuh his place about two-thirty with my pockets stuffed with money. Musta had three-four thousand dollars on me—"

"Three-four *what!*"

"Thousand dollars," snapped Tranter emphatically. "I'd been takin' them other dives down the road. But them fellas up at Borst's musta seen me comin', 'cause they shore had their axe out. An' brother, was it sharp! In three hours they cleaned me down to a dime! An' I thought I knew a thing or two about poker!"

"You dang fool," Bill said. "You'd oughta known better'n that."

"Yeah—that's what the alligator said when he took the swimmer's laig off!" Tranter regarded him slantways. "Speakin' of fools; I ain't the on'y one in these parts."

Bill, on his way to the water-cooler for a drink, swung suddenly round. "What exactly was the meanin' of that?"

"Wal, I guess yuh know. An' if yuh don't well then jest ferget it," Tranter said, and turned to look out the window. "There's some fella hot-footin' it this way like he was in a big hurry. Know 'im?"

Bill came over to take a look, and swore. "Hell, yes! That's Fisk—president of the Stockman's Bank."

Fisk came in panting.

"What's up?"

Fisk said, "Plenty!" and looked as though he meant it. "Somebody robbed the bank last night. I went in to open up, an' there was the vault door standin' open an' papers strewn all over the floor. They got every bit of currency. An' most of the silver. The gold, thank God, they didn't find."

Bill looked at Tranter and Tranter looked at Bill. Then Bill pursed his lips in a soundless whistle. And began to look proddy.

"Ain't that somethin'!" Tranter said.

Bill growled, "When'd it happen? How'd they get in? How come they didn't get the gold?"

Fisk grunted, "Last night some time, I suppose. Sawed the bars off one of the back windows an' busted in the glass. I had the gold cached in another place. And damn lucky. This robbery's goin' to put an awful dent in us, Sheriff. I think we can weather it. But it'll be a mighty close shave."

"Got any idea who done it?" Tranter asked.

Fisk glared at him. "What d'you suppose I came over here for? You gents have been put in office to apprehend criminals. Not to ask a passel of fool questions. What are you waitin' around for?"

"C'mon," Bill growled to Tranter, and led the way toward the bank, which was down the street five or six doors. Fisk strode angrily after them, muttering to himself.

They entered the bank, Bill's rolling shoulders

shoving a way through the crowd collected about the open doorway.

Tranter glared at the crowd. "What in seven blue devils you guys standin' round here for? Close yore mouths an' take 'em with yuh ter some other climate. *Git!*" he said, and reached for his gun.

With resentful growls the crowd broke up.

As Fisk had said, the interior was strewn with papers, ledgers, day books, securities, and here and there the contents of envelopes had been scattered as though the looters had pawed through them hurriedly.

"I'd say," Tranter remarked, looking round, "that a Kansas twister'd been in here."

Fisk scowled. "This is no time for pleasantries," he declared icily. "What I want to know is what you fellows are goin' to do about it?"

"Keep yore shirt on," Dorne said. "We'll get to the bottom of this business. May take a little time. But we'll get there. You can stick a pin in that!"

He looked into the littered vault whose door had been opened with nitroglycerine. "How much exactly has been taken?"

Fisk ran worried hands through his thatch of silver grey hair. "My God!" he groaned. "I can't tell offhand. Round forty thousand, I'd say roughly."

Tranter whistled.

"Pretty much dinero for a bank of this size to be carryin', ain't it?"

"This was payday night. Two or three ranchers just sold herds. Had a small shipment of dust from the Topekas Mine. We were aiming to send it to the capital this morning."

Dorne nodded. "Well, we'll do what we can. I'd like to look around now for clues."

For a solid hour Dorne and Tranter probed about, but their search availed them nothing. Then Tranter asked, "Whyn't yuh look fer fingerprints? I hear they're ketchin' plenty of hard cases that way now."

But Dorne shook his head. "This office ain't equipped for that. Besides, what I don't know about fingerprintin' would fill a volume. C'mon. We'll make a round of the saloons. Mebbe someone heard the blast. They used nitroglycerine to get that vault door off. Somebody oughta heard that explosion."

But though they canvassed the town systematically, questioned people adroitly, all they found was one man who "thought" he'd heard an explosion of some sort about three o'clock. He'd been sleeping off a jag in the alley back of the bank.

"This is a hell of a sitcheation," Tranter growled. "How'n heck we gonna ketch this bank-robbin' party when we ain't even got a reliable witness to the time, an' there ain't no clues?"

Dorne nodded. "The sum total of our knowledge is absolutely nothin'," he agreed morosely. "But we'll get that robber—we got to! You keep yore ears peeled, Buck. Sooner or later we'll find out somethin'. Bound to. The law of averages."

"Must be a new law," Tranter opined. "I hadn't heard of it before."

Dorne flashed him a disgusted look. "C'mon, I'm servin' notice on these joints. Hereafter they're gonna close by two o'clock or I'll know the reason why."

Tranter picked up his hat. "You'll know, I reckon," he muttered drily.

They returned to the Sheriff's Office after making their announcement. It had not been kindly received, as Tranter had predicted. Scowls and smothered oaths had followed them from each successive resort they visited. "It's a ordinance of this town," Bill said, "an' by Jupiter, it's gonna be obeyed."

Tranter sat down on the edge of his desk and mopped his forehead with the back of a sleeve. "It sure is thirsty weather! Never see such a place fer onregenerated heat—it's enough tuh cook yore gizzard!"

Dorne frowned gloomily at the floor. "I'd give somethin' to know who robbed that bank," he growled.

"So'd Fisk," Tranter chuckled. "It was a damn neat piece of work."

"I'm bettin' Borst had his hand in it," Dorne said grimly.

"You got Borst on the brain," Tranter said, and snorted.

"I—" Bill Dorne abruptly stopped and stared narrowly toward the door.

Tranter heard the clump and clink of spurred boots on the walk outside and followed Dorne's glance, just as one of Globe's cowboys stepped inside. His face was red and covered with powdered alkali and sweat, and there was a wild look in his eye.

"Listen, Dorne—listen!" he panted; "We lost a hundred an' fifty head of prime two-year-old Wineglass critters las' night!"

"Huh!" Dorne came out of his chair with a surge.

"So help me Hannah!" the puncher growled. "Rustlers worked our range an' ran off every two-year-old we got!"

"Didja see 'em?" Tranter asked. "Anybody hurt?"

"By cripes no, we didn't see 'em! They'd 'a' been somebody hurt all right if we had! One hundred an' fifty prime steers! By cripes, it's a outrage!"

"It sure is," Bill said, soothingly. "When'd you discover they was gone?"

"First thin' this mawnin' when we hit for the gatherin' ground. We been roundin' 'em up for a week. Globe's fit tuh be tied!"

"Let's get this straight," Bill said. "You been roundin' up two-year-olds for a shipment?" And, at the puncher's nod, "Then why wasn't a coupla nightherds ridin' circle?"

"They was!" the puncher said, and swore. "They was part of the gang, I reckon. They've hauled their freight— plumb vanished like our steers!"

"Names!" Bill snapped, reaching for a pad of paper. "An' description. We may be able to pull them jaspers in.

"Ed Krayson, tall, lanky, with a knife scar over his left blinker. An' Dode Harniss, a sawed-off gnat what needs a ladder tuh reach the chow table."

"Say," said Tranter, scratching his shaggy head. "I've met up with that Harniss gent before. He's a mean actor—plumb cultus, in fact."

"Good," said Bill. "You keep yore eye out for him. We'll run him in, first thing. Mebbe we can make him squeal on the rest of 'em."

"No chance," Tranter replied. "He's saltier'n Lot's wife."

"You ketch him," the puncher said, "an' I'll give him a workin' over that'll be right revealin'. I know a Injun trick or two what'll make that pelican holler calf-rope right sudden!"

"Did the rustlers leave any sign?"

"Hell, yes. The prairies cut up plenty. Boys are trailin' 'em now. But they won't have no luck. You wait an' see. These fellers is slick. They been messin' round with us fer quite a spell, nibblin' off a few head here an' there. This is the first time they ever run off so big a jag, though. Must be gettin' ambition."

"Or mebbe," said Bill, "yore two missin' circle riders are the ones that were doin' the nibblin'. My guess is they've joined up with big-time company."

"Might be somethin' in that," Tranter agreed. "This Harniss hairpin, though, is a old hand. He sabes plenty, believe me. An' he can use a gun."

"So can my ol' man," the puncher grunted. "If Globe ever gets his hands on them gents, mince meat's gonna be coarse beside 'em!"

"If—" Tranter began, and stopped with his mouth still open as from across the street some place came the sudden crash of gunfire. The puncher stared at Tranter, and the ragged deputy stared back. Dorne swung round with an oath and, snatching up his hat, made for the door with catlike strides. Tranter and the Wineglass puncher whirled and followed.

The trio reached the street in time to see a man lurch staggering from the swinging doors of Ortega's Black Bottle Bar. A whiskered desert rat. And there was a smoking pistol in one down-swung hand as he backed stumblingly down the steps and into the dusty street. A stain was rapidly spreading on his shirt.

Dorne, running toward him, scrutinized him well. But did not recognize him as anyone he had seen before. Some stranger, evidently. He lengthened his stride.

Yet before he had covered more than half the distance across the street the doors of the Black Bottle bulged outward again. A man came crouching through them. A man with dark swarthy face wrinkled now in a malevolent grin. A face that held eyes that were tiny and alive with flashing sparkles—a Mexican's face, and one that Dorne knew well. The face of Pedro Mendota, one of Pecos Borst's ace gunslammers.

The white teeth of him showed now against his coppery skin in a tigerish smirk as he fired three times into the falling sage-brusher. And one more shot he threw in as the old fellow swayed, coughing blood, on hands and knees.

Dorne had an instant of tautness, and his face went pale as desert sand. Then he said, all at once laughing and reckless, "The brave Don Pedro has shot hisself a man!" And the scorn dripped from his words like a visible thing.

The Mexican faced him alertly, his swarthy face handsome despite the snarling curl of his tight-lipped mouth. The gun was still in his hand, but with a sudden show of bravado he thrust it in the flapless brass-studded holster that sagged the front of his belt.

Dorne's narrowed eyes held a steely glint. "Bold as Billy-be-damned, ain't you, Mendota? Specially when it's a broken-down ol' man you're pickin' on."

Fighting words. But Mendota laughed smooth and easy. "Thees fella, he draw first, *si*. You can ask the patrons in thees Black Bottle, if you no believe. But I am not making for back down, señor." The white teeth flashed in a sneer beneath his tiny black mustache. "Eef you are look for trouble, *por Dios,* I give you belly full!"

EIGHT
THE ARKANSAS TOOTHPICK

DORNE CHECKED the rush of his lifting temper with difficulty. This Mendota always rubbed him the wrong way. Dorne hated his sneers and swaggering bravado. They had never cottoned to each other since that day, two months ago when—in defense of a drunken puncher—Bill Dorne had all but wiped up Borst's Golden Stack with the Mex gunman. Mendota, he had realized even then, was not the man to forgive such a public beating as Dorne had administered. Mendota had neither forgiven it nor forgotten it. And right now he seemed in a mood to even up the score. In his own way—with a pistol. But though these things flashed through Bill Dorne's mind, no slightest indication of his feelings was permitted to show upon his lean bronzed cheeks. Bill's temper was a fearful thing, unleashed. But now he held it under firm control and, striding past the sneering gun fighter, he strode determinedly inside Ortega's Black Bottle Bar, the customers giving back before him, frightened perhaps by what they read in his narrowed eyes.

"That dawg out there says the old desert rat drew first. Can any gent corroborate that statement?" His voice was clipped and cold.

The even clump of boots and the jingle of dragging spur chains told him that others had followed him inside. But Dorne flashed no look at the men who had crowded in behind him. All his attention was on this glowering crowd before him. Particularly on Jose Ortega, a crook-nosed fellow with a short, piratical spade beard.

Ortega took his time, even though he must have guessed the question was meant for him. He looked Dorne over coolly while he lit a cigarette in the Mexican manner—by holding its end to the flaring match.

"I can vouch for eet, señor," he spoke at last. "Thees whiskaired hombre pull the gon—whssst! An' call the Señor Mendota the bad name. Wot would you? Don Pedro had no recourse except his gon, eef he would save hees life."

"Yeah," growled Dorne skeptically. "Happened just like it always has every time Mendota adds another notch to his hawg-laig."

He whirled at a soft chuckle behind him. Mendota stood there, between Dorne and Tranter and the Wine-glass puncher. And it was Mendota who had chuckled. There was a feline grin still on his lips. He placed his glance on Dorne's face and held it there mockingly.

"What would you, señor?" he grinned, and shrugged, spreading out his long-fingered hands. "It ees the fate."

"Then yore fate better undergo a damn swift change," Dorne snapped. "Because the next time you're forced to kill a man I'm goin' to pistol-whip you outa town!"

Two days passed uneventfully, as they usually do in the south-west cattle country—save around places like Spavined Nag, where the isolated nature of the country attracts tough hombres with a craving for dodging necktie parties or long-term jails. But such apparent passiveness on the part of the hard cases composing the sporting element was certainly unusual there. It began to get on Dorne's nerves as no amount of hell-bending action could have. He was frankly worried, and said as much to Tranter as they met in the Sheriff's Office on the morning of the third day after Mendota's shooting scrap.

"Don't git roiled up about it," Tranter advised with characteristic imperturbability. "Ain't no use yore frettin'. Things'll be happenin' soon enough. You take it from a man what knows. Why," he ran a gnarled hand through the rumpled hair showing beneath his shoved-back hatbrim, "I recollect when I was down round the Pan-handle one year, I saw a sim'lar spell of sugar-coated calm. Boy, these calm spells is shore real trouble-breeders! This time, I recall, some gents was plannin' to rob the gold express. An' they shore did, too. Busted 'er plumb wide open an' made a fifty thousan' dollar haul! They-"

"What I'm interested in," cut in Dorne drily, "is who busted forty thousand outa the Stockman's Bank of Spavined Nag! That's what I wanta hear about. Put your recollectin' energy to work on that an' we'll be gettin' someplace, mebbe."

"Yeah—mebbe," Tranter said, but did not display any great enthusiasm in the possibilities. "Tell yuh what

I will do, though. Let's you an' me take another pasear over that there bank. Mebbe we overlooked somethin' the other time. Fella never knows. Now if we could get somethin' on one of these gunslammin' hellions round here it might give us the toe-holt we're a-needin'. I swear tuh Hannah, it sure looks like this yere bank-robber was one old hand at the game. I recollect the time Jesse James was a-tellin' me—"

"Tie up the little bull," Dorne said, "an let's get started. Not," he added, "that I got any hopes we'll find anythin'. But even movin' round is better'n settin' here."

"Yeah," Tranter mopped his beaded brow as he got to his feet, "this shore is the most thirstiest climate ever I see. Sun—sun—an' more sun; each minute hotter'n the next. Hell's hinges ain't got nothin' on Spavined Nag when it comes to downright heat an' general cussedness!

"Save some of that wind to cool yore porridge," Bill Dorne snapped, irritated at the lack of progress they'd been making concerning the mystery of the looted bank. More than that in fact was bothering him. He could not understand Borst's unusual calm indifference to the insult of being run out of town by an old customer on whom the badge of authority had been pinned. He had been expecting swift reprisal. Yet, aside from Mendota's gunplay, Dorne could not see but what the town's sporting element was on the way to becoming right down docile. It wasn't natural! Then, too, he felt a vaguely restless itch to go out and see how Lola was making out.

He did not like to think of her working in Borst's wolf den. He'd expostulated with her no later than the other night. But to no avail. She'd only laughed, and assured him that she was very well able to take care of herself. He followed Tranter to the door, still engrossed in his milling thoughts. But once outside in the hot smash of the morning sun he took the lead, swinging out toward the bank with springy, jingling strides.

Fisk met them in the lobby. Bank business appeared to be going on about as usual. Save for the worried lines in Fisk's pale face, one would hardly have guessed that the Stockman's Bank had sustained a forty-thousand dollar loss.

Fisk greeted them with the question uppermost in his mind: "Have you caught the robber?"

"Hell, no," Tranter growled, before Bill could frame a proper reply. "We got tuh give the cuss a decent chance tuh spend the swag he's lifted, ain't we? What the hell kinda law officers would we be if we nabbed that misguided pilgrim before he had a chance tuh blow his loot?"

A man came in through the open door behind them as Fisk turned his scowl on Dorne. "Is that the attitude you're takin', Sheriff?" he demanded indignantly.

"No," Bill's tone was short. "We'll nab yore man. Just give us time—"

"That's right," the newcomer interrupted. "The ways of the Lord in Spavined Nag are not only inscrutable, but downright leisurely. The only thing that moves in a hurry round this sink of iniquity, this cesspool of immorality, this den of thieves and assassins, this— this—well, the only thing that raises dust is the Devil's business, which goes on every minute. What's to be done, I'd like to know, about the funds of the Lord which I deposited in this mismanaged institution?"

The banker's pallid countenance purpled. Tranter's

jaw dropped open, then closed with a click of teeth. "By cripes, Reverend," he grunted admiringly, "yuh shore got the gift o' gab!"

Dorne turned to Gospel Jones politely. "How much had the Church on deposit here?" he asked, diffidently.

The sky-pilot of Spavined Nag grinned sheepishly. "Wal, Bill, you know the Devil's got a stranglehold on this here cowtown that's uncommon hard to break. The Lord didn't have but five measly dollars in this palace of the moneychangers."

"Shucks," Bill said, pulling a slender roll from his chaps pocket and peeling therefrom a ten-dollar banknote which he tendered to Gospel Jones. "Take this, Parson, an' give the Lord's funds a new lease on life."

"Wal, now that's what I call uncommon kind," said Jones heartily. "Bill, the Lord's grateful—almost as much as me, in fact. Strike me dead if the Lord's pickin's ain't almighty lean round this man's town, an' the doves which fetch the meat an' bread to His loyal followers has sure enough done got sidetracked in this thirstin' wilderness of unregenerated sin. I ain't et a decent meal in three days."

"Well, don't use that ten-spot tuh feed *yore* face," Tranter protested, hurriedly digging down into his own pocket. "It don't seem right that the Lord's funds should be used fer no such foolish purpose. If you got a itchin' fer the nose-bag, take this quarter down to the Chink's an he'll fix you up some grub that'll take the wrinkles plumb outen yore belly. You better put that ten-spot in the bank 'fore she burns a hole in yore pocket—"

"The Lord turns the other cheek," Gospel Jones said knowingly, "but I ain't got to be that much of a

Christian, yet, I reckon. I'll take this two-bits piece, Brother—an' thank you. But the Lord's funds'll be a dangsite safer in my pocket than in a bank what makes a specialty of extendin' a field of operations to the Philistines."

Banker Fisk's scowl followed him out the door. He muttered something under his breath that had the tone of being a trifle uncomplimentary. But Tranter could not quite make up his mind whether the remark had been addressed to the sky-pilot or the Sheriff's Office.

Fisk said, "Haven't you made any progress on this case at all?"

"Well, yeah," Bill replied sarcastically. "The Sheriff's Office has the case well in hand an' the public may expect an arrest at any moment."

"I don't consider this a proper subject for levity," Fisk grunted. "Things have been going from bad to worse-fast. An' your election to the badge-totin' fraternity ain't improved 'em enough to make a gnat's eye water."

"It ain't, eh?" Bill snapped, and returned the banker's scowl with interest. "Listen," he said; "listen—I'm the peacefullest jasper ever was foaled. When folks lets me have my way. But when gents gets to makin' the kinda remark *you* jest made, an' tries to order me round an' run 'my office, why I jest naturally cloud all up for a big rain. Fisk, you be careful or you're gonna get wet!"

And with an angry snort Bill Dorne started for the door.

But not so Buck Tranter. That ragged deputy—on whom, by his own word, you could smell the powder-smoke—was lookin' at the banker's left coat pocket, which was hanging rather oddly as though some object, too big to fit, were leaning in it slantways.

"How long since you taken tuh totin' a knife round with yuh, Fisk?" he asked, with a saturnine eye on the banker's face. "Yuh must be dealin' with some pretty tough customers when yuh find it necessary tuh—"

"This knife," Fisk cut in, pulling the weapon gingerly from his coat pocket, "was in the safe. I—I was about to call Bill's attention to it when that Parson Jones sidetracked me." He held it out and Tranter took it promptly, lest he change his mind. "In the safe, eh? Yuh mean, I reckon, in the vault that robber busted open."

"Yes," Fisk took off his glasses and polished them with a handkerchief taken from the left breast pocket of his coat. He peered through the glasses, then satisfied, put them back on and returned the handkerchief to his pocket, dropping in the process a tiny bit of paper. Which he failed to notice.

Tranter unostentatiously planted one big spurred boot upon it while saying, as he turned the Bowie over and over in his hands, "This here's right smart of a knife, Fisk. Reg'lar Arkansas toothpick. Whose do you suppose it is?"

"Don't know, I'm sure," said the banker testily. "How would I know? I just told you I picked it up off the floor of the vault."

"How d'you reckon it got there?" Tranter asked as, curious, Bill Dorne came back.

"I guess the robber must have dropped it."

"He sure picked a poor place," Tranter commented sardonically. "D'you know a feller name of Dode Harniss? He works with cows."

The banker's expression said he did not associate

with persons who worked with cows. But aloud he said, "No," and let it go at that.

"Hmm." Tranter let his glance rove beyond Fisk's shoulder, suddenly let it widen, depicting startled incredulity. Moved by instinct, the banker whirled. As he did so Tranter stooped, scooped something from the floor beneath his boot and straightened. He was innocently paring his fingernails with the bowie knife when Fisk turned round again.

Fisk growled, "What were you looking at?"

"Me?" Tranter seemed amazed. "Nothin' as I knows of. Why?"

With an impatient snort the banker, muttering something about the banker's business having to go on, departed. Dorne and Tranter did likewise.

When they got back to the Sheriff's Office, Dorne said: "Well?"

"Dang right," Buck Tranter chuckled. "That vinegar-oon claimed he picked this Arkansas toothpick off the floor o' that vault. Uncommon strange, says I. It wa'n't there when we went over the place two-three days ago! Where'd it come from? Bill, this thing's a snare an' a delusion— it's a plant!"

"What for?" Dorne's narrowed eyes were on Tranter closely. "Why should Fisk want to plant evidence in his own vault?"

"How should I know?" Tranter countered. "But I'm bettin' it's a plant though, jest the same. Anyhow, you know well as I do it wasn't there the other day."

"Whose is it? Do you recognize it?"

"This hawg-sticker," Tranter said impressively, "belonged to Dode Harniss the las' time I saw him, three-four years ago."

Dorne started. "You sure?"

"Plumb positive. I reckon I ort tuh know. He tried tuh lift my scalp with it over some skirt in Sante Fe!"

Dorne's face showed that he caught the significance of this. Dode Harniss was one of the two Wineglass punchers who had been riding circle on the night the rustlers lifted one-hundred-and-fifty prime two-year-olds from Mayor Globe's range—and since that night he had not been seen.

NINE
"A DUDE JUST GOT KILLED"

"YOU MEAN—?" Dorne said, coldly drawling.

"I mean it looks tuh me like that smug pelican of a Chessycat-grinnin' Fisk is mixed up in this dang lootin' somehow, an' is tryin' tuh lay the blame onto Dode Harniss!" Tranter growled with emphasis.

"But why?"

"Don't ast me foolish questions," Tranter snapped. "I ain't no blinking' mind-reader!"

"But didn't you tell me only yesterday that Dode Harniss was a tough hombre—plumb cultus, I believe you said?"

"An' what if I did? He shore was a ornery cuss when I knew him. What's that got tuh do with Fisk findin' his knife on the—"

Dorne interrupted: "It mebbe has a-plenty to do with it, Buck. If Fisk found this Harniss' knife on the floor of the bank vault—"

"But," Tranter cut in swiftly, " we didn't find it there! An' we shore looked for it like a Scotchman what's dropped a penny. Leastways, we was lookin' for anything we could find, an' if it had been there we'd 'a' found it!"

"I reckon we would," Bill said thoughtfully.

"It sure looks like Banker Fisk is pullin' a fast one. An' speakin' of fast ones, Buck, I been hearin' that Borst is gettin' pretty gay out there at his new location. S'pose you fork yore bronc out there now an' serve warnin' on him. Tell him from me that if he don't tone down an' start runnin' a decent joint, I'm comin' out there an' bust his place to kindlin' wood."

Reluctantly, Tranter got up and sauntered out of the door. It was hot outside—hotter that blue blazes—and Dorne didn't much blame the ragged deputy for not wanting to take a three-mile ride. But somebody had to do it. Borst must be kept in hand, he told himself. For Borst was one of those gents that take a mile every time you allow them an inch.

Left to himself, Dorne put his time to good use. He lined things up for review across the screen of his mind. This bank robbery business was beginning to assume unexpected proportions. Imagine Fisk pulling a stunt like that. Why, he must have robbed his own bank! Anyway, he very evidently had had a hand in the robbing, and was— "Ah!" Bill growled. "I'm bettin' he hired Harniss to pull that lootin'. An' now that it's over Fisk is figurin' to deal himself the pot by framin' up on Harniss. Ain't no other way he could of got Dode's knife, less'n Dode was 'sociatin' with him."

But as he thought it over, Bill came to the conclusion that this theory was anything but waterproof. He found hole after hole to his chain of reasoning. Disgruntled, he got to his feet and paced the floor, hands deepthrust in his chaps pockets.

Another notion came to him regarding the means by which Harniss' knife might have come into Fisk's possession. After all, he mused, they did not know that Harniss had joined the rustlers who had raided the Wineglass range the other night. Actually, he and his pardner, Ed Krayson, might have been captured somehow by the cattle thieves and, for some ulterior purpose not to be found by surface indications, forced to go with the rustlers and their stolen stock. Yet even so, if Fisk were honest, Dorne could not see how he had come by Harniss' knife.

But assume for the moment that Fisk *was* crooked, and things straightened themselves out beautifully. If the rustlers had taken the two Wineglass punchers captive, Fisk might have come into possession of that Arkansas tickler through his association with the man or men behind these rustling activities. And Bill would have bet his last shirt that man was Borst!

But there were still plenty of loopholes in his reasoning, as he was forced to admit. Ed Krayson and Harniss *might* have *somehow* been captured by the rustlers, but to Dorne this seemed mighty unlikely. And even so, what possible motive could the rustlers have had for forcing the two punchers into accompanying them? It would have been much more in character for the cattle thieves to have shot the Wineglass circle riders out of hand. And Dorne knew it.

Furthermore, assuming that Fisk *was* guilty of robbing his own bank (and this was a possibility that clung tenaciously to Bill's thoughts), why should he affiliate himself with the sporting crowd, thus forcing himself to share the proceeds of his own villainy? It didn't make sense—unless, and Bill's brow darkened, that sanctimonious old smug-face, Fisk, had been dealing from a crooked deck right straight along. In which case it would be natural for him and Borst to have an understanding. Crooks didn't operate around Spavined Nag without splitting their swag with Borst!

Somehow, the mutations of Bill Dorne's wandering thoughts swung abruptly to Tumbleweed, the under-cover deputy. Perhaps it was the association of ideas. But, anyway, his thoughts went now to his newest deputy. What was the fellow doing? Had he uncovered anything of import? Why hadn't he got some message to Bill as to his progress and present whereabouts?

Questions, questions, and *more* questions! But no answers. Dorne scowled. There was something about that Tumbleweed gent . . . He shook his head and turned his attention to Polsky, Globe's Wineglass fore-man. An odd stick. Close-mouthed as the proverbial clam. And handy with his hog-leg—uncommon handy for a peaceable, run-of-the-range ramrod. There were lots of things about "Hoot Owl" Polsky—so-called because of the extremely sober cast of his countenance —that Dorne would have given the loose change that clinked in his pocket to know.

Polsky had arrived one day some eight months past, and had been promptly hired by Globe as foreman. Why? The man knew cows—no question about that. He knew how to run a big spread, too. And appeared aware of the frailties of human nature. But how had Globe known this when hiring the fellow. What sort of credentials had Hoot Owl shown? How had he happened to hit Globe for the job in the first place. Globe hadn't been short-handed at the time; in fact he had fired his top screw without notice to make a place for Polsky. Dorne had often wondered about that. It looked almost as though the two—Globe and Polsky—were old acquaintances.

Dorne thought briefly of Marcia and determined sheepishly that it was about time for him to be stopping by the Mayor's place. He hadn't been there since the late afternoon of the night the bank had been robbed. He guessed an engaged fellow had ought to be a bit more attentive. Resolving to drop by and "visit a spell" with Marcia before the day was out, he turned his mind to other things—the jingling clump of booted feet now approaching along the plank sidewalk outside.

He nodded as Tranter stepped into the office. "You made good time," he commented, and got out his pipe and packed it. "How'd he take it?"

"Didn't see 'im," Tranter sighed, and mopped the perspiration from his forehead. "That Gleed fella told me Borst wasn't around. Said he'd gone out to the ranch. Does he own a spread sure enough? Or was that jest a gag tuh git me on m' way?"

"He owns one," Dorne admitted. "Good one, too. The Hashknife. Over in Gypsum Valley—which ain't as dry as it sounds. What did Gleed have to say about my orders?"

"Not s'much as I figgered he would," Tranter answered dolefully. "Fer a minute he sorta clouded up an' I was hopin' fer the best. Then he seemed tuh rec'lect that he was talkin' tuh ol' He-Man Tranter's li'l son Buck—same being a holster-hopper on which the brimstone shore does linger. He backed off then, like he wasn't wantin' no part in what I reckon he c'd see I was honin' tuh give 'im. He nods his bullet head an' says as how he'll pass the word tuh the Boss. But, yuh know,

Bill—I got a sneakin' idee that Borst was right there in that back room. I c'd hear voices. Couldn't make out nothin', but one of them warbles shore sounded like Borst's cooin' purr."

Dorne weighed this, then nodded. And his eyes were a deeper blue, it looked to Tranter. Dorne said, "Didn't see Tumbleweed round there anyplace, did you?"

"Wal, now that's a funny thing, Bill. But since yuh mentioned it—yeah. I seen him, but he seen me first—an' cleared out like he had urgent business elsewhere."

"Didn't see where he went, did you?"

"He went waltzin' right intuh that back room. Where I heard the voices," Tranter grunted, and scowled. "If yuh'd 'a' taken the advice of a man what knows, yuh'd never made that leather-faced hyena no propersishun. He'll make yuh rue the day yuh took up with him yet— yuh wait an' see. He's got a eye what's meaner'n gar soup. A killer eye, that's what he's got. An' don't say I didn't warn yuh, when yore friends is packin' yuh slow an' mournful-like towards Boot Hill."

Bill snorted. "Yuh can leave that crepe with Borst. Tell me, did you see that Lola girl?"

"I'd think yore mind would be occypied with that Marcia gal right now," said Tranter drily. "I'm tellin' yuh. This two-gal business don't never work out tuh no good end. Yuh'll hev each of them feemales a-thinkin' yo're sweetest on the other, an' there'll be hair flyin' shore, if yuh don't cut it out. One string's enough for yore bow at a time, son. Take it from a man what knows.

"I been around a fortnight or two. An' I've met women—plenty of 'em. Taken by an' large, they're the salt of the earth. But take 'em two at a time, an' hell beside 'em would be a quiet place! Anyhow, yuh've gone an' got yoreself engaged tuh marry the Mayor's daughter. Yuh better steer plumb clear of that Lola skirt. Onless yo're courtin' ol' man Globe with a shotgun."

Bill flushed, and being aware of the fact—and of Tranter's twinkling regard—scowled savagely.

"Borst's place," Tranter added, before Bill could frame a scorching reply, "has done got itself a new monicker. The Three-Mile House they calls it now. An' there's a dude out there what somebody orta keep his eye on. My Gawd, but that fella's green. Got money in every pocket. Hard money, too, judgin' by the jingle. Talk about your lamb in the wolfs den. Boy, ef Borst don't hang him out tuh dry, my name ain't Buck Tranter!"

"What's he doin' out there?"

"I ast him. He allows he come in on the stage this mawnin', an' seein' some of Borst's hangers-on lollin' round them outbuildin's, figgers he'd hit town, an'he got off. Time he'd realized his mistake, the stage was halfway tuh town. But accordin' tuh what I could hear, they been entertainin' him right royal. I tried tuh wise 'im up. But he tells me real indignant like, tuh mind m' own business an' re—*refrain* from callin' his friends op—opprobious ethipets. Cripes!" Tranter snorted, "he's prime fer a pluckin'—*an' he'll get one, too!*"

"Oh, I dunno," countered Bill. "You carried my message to them warnin' 'em to tread easy for a spell. I don't think they'll bother that dude overmuch. Might part him from some of this loose cash. But I don't reckon they'll roll him, or anything like that."

"Live an' learn," grunted Tranter, shaking his head. "There ain't no fool like a young 'un."

Bill Dorne grinned. "Cheer up, you ol' damp covering; times are gettin' better."

"Yeah?" said Tranter skeptically. "Wal, how about advancin' me somethin' tuh smoke, ag'in my wages? I done chawed m' Brown Mule plumb up entire. That there pipe yo're smokin' has a real lively smell. Ef yuh've got any more terbaccy like what yo're smokin', I wouldn't mind rollin' me a quirley."

Bill tossed his sack over and watched Tranter's knobby fingers expertly twist a pinch of tobacco and a brown rice paper into a perfectly smooth round cylinder. Lighting his smoke, Tranter calmly dropped the sack in his pocket, and changed the subject.

Squinting his eyes to keep the spiraling smoke out, he spread a crumpled scrap of paper on one corduroyed knee and smoothed it out. "This here," he grunted softly, "is what I picked up over to the bank. It dropped outa Fisk's coat pocket when he was gettin' out a nose rag tuh wipe his specs. I got a hunch he's gonna be some perturbed when he finds he's lost it. Yuh might look it over, " he added, and held it out to Dorne.

Bill took it, and the following instant let out a startled oath. His cheeks were taut and his wide lips grim as he read for the second time:

"Three-Mile House Wednesday night at 11:45."

There was no greeting and no signature; just those six words and four numbers—but Banker Fisk had been carrying the paper in his pocket. And the Three-Mile

House was the name of Borst's new resort. The inference was obvious. Bill swore.

"Were you out to Borst's place last night?"

"Yeah," said Tranter. "But later—must have been round one o'clock."

"Didn't see Fisk?"

"He ain't exactly crazy, is he?"

"Well—skip it, then. Did you see Borst?"

Tranter nodded. "He looked like the cat that licked the cream. He," the ragged deputy chuckled, "give me a ceegar!"

"Must have been feelin' pretty chipper," Bill growled viciously.

"That's what I thought," Tranter said, and sobered. "Now look, Bill—S'posin' some of Borst's hands ran off them Wineglass critters th' other night. An' s'posin', them two circle riders of Globe's threw in with 'em. Then—"

"That don't take a whale of a lot of supposin'," Bill grunted testily.

"Nope," Tranter said, "it don't. Then supposin' that much is true. What would *you* do in Borst's place, was you as ornery an' greedy as he is? . . . Wait—lemme tell yuh! You'd likely put them two hombres outa their misery once their use was over. Then, tuh make sure folks wasn't suspectin' you or any of yore gang of robbin' the Stockman's Bank, it would come in right handy to plant that knife of Harniss' on the scene of the lootin'. *That*" he concluded triumphantly, "is what that note was sent Fisk for, I'm bettin'. Borst got him out there, give him the knife an' told him tuh plant it. Only trouble was, we seen Fisk before he'd had a chance tuh cache it."

"Or," said Bill, thoughtfully nodding, "knowin' we'd been over the place pretty thoroughly, Fisk hadn't figured out a safe place to put it where 'twould be effective, an' still not give his hand away. Buck, I believe you've got somethin' there."

Tranter, about to add something to the conversation, abruptly shut his mouth and turned as fast-drumming hoofs beat down the dusty street. Both he and Dorne made for the door to see what was up. Dorne reached it first and pushed outside into the broiling glare of the nooning sun. A horse and rider were spurring down the main street as though the Devil was reaching for the mustang's broomtail.

Straight up to the Sheriff's Office the clattering rider thundered, hitting dirt on braking bootheels as he threw his pony back on its haunches in a slithering stop. He was a puncher from one of the outlying ranches, Bill thought, vaguely remembering having seen the fellow's face before.

"What's up?" Bill demanded tensely.

"Hell's crick!" the puncher gasped. "A dude just got killed at the Three-Mile House!"

TEN
HEAVY, HEAVY –

"WHAT'S THAT?" Bill grabbed the fellow by the shoulders. *"Who got killed?"*

"That dang dude what was throwin' his dinero right an' left out to Borst's new joint."

"Who killed him?" Bill drawled, dangerously soft.

"Cock Robin," Tranter interjected. "I told yuh somethin' would happen tuh that jigger! Never let it be said I didn't warn yuh!"

Bill paid Tranter no attention. "Who killed him?" he repeated ominously.

"Dam'fino! Fella called Tumbleweed gave me half a dollar to ride in an' wise yuh up to the killin'. All I know is what he tol' me. I was playin' poker. All of a suddent, I heard a shot in that back room. I started for the outside door pronto. An' just as I got to m' hawss, up comes this fella who gives his name as Tumbleweed an' says, 'Ride in an' tell the Sheriff that dude's been shot!'"

"How long ago was this?"

"Not twenty minutes."

Bill said, "Get our hawsses, Buck. An' don't stop to

pick no daisies." Still looking at the messenger, he added musingly, "Don't I know you? Seems like we've met up before someplace." He saw a film of caution spread across the other's eyes. But the man's expression did not change.

"You might know me," he admitted. "I been around this part of the country quite a spell. Been workin' for Ol' Man Hartley over on the north side of the Blue Range. Wagonwheel. Reckon I better be siftin' along now I —"

"How'd you happen to be out at Borst's?" Bill asked.

"I come in fer the mail. Stopped off at this Three-Mile House tuh wet m' whistle," the fellow said, reasonable enough. Yet somehow, Bill had a notion that the man was lying. Tranter arrived with their horses just then, however, effectively preventing him from questioning the puncher further.

"Drop in again next time you're in town," he said. "We'll talk this over again. I'd like to get a line on that Tumbleweed fella."

The puncher nodded. "Okay, Sheriff. Be seein' yuh," and off he went with a wave of the hand.

Bill climbed into the saddle. "Seems like I've seen that fella someplace, Buck," he said. "But I'll be danged if I can place, him."

"Wal, I don't know him from Adam's off-ox," Tranter said. "Let's go."

* * *

INSIDE THE BAR-ROOM of the Three-Mile House, Borst eyed his two chief gunslammers grimly. A dead quiet obtained within the place, although beyond the batwing doors the yard outside seemed astir with a methodical activity.

Borst said quietly, "Bill Dorne an' that ragbag deputy of his will be out here in about three shakes. Bill's got an undercover man workin' here an' I jest seen him pass a tip to a puncher about that damn nosey dude we jest gave a ticket to the Great Beyond."

The gunmen's eyes glistened at these words. Then—

"Mebbe—" Joe Fuddabaugh began, when Borst cut him off. "They'll be here, all right, an' you can bank on that. We're gonna beat Bill, but he won't take it layin' down. Remember," he paused to be certain he had their full attention; "remember that when they get here I'm countin' on you boys to earn yore keep. An' there'll be two hundred apiece in it for you if you don't gum the works. I don't want to slip-up. Bill Dorne's dynamite, in case you don't know. Get him first pop or you won't get him at all. I ain't real sure about that deputy, but you better get him, too. Wait till they shove in these swingin' doors, then give 'em all you got. An' that won't be too much. I want Bill stopped definite, once an' for all— plumb final!"

"But," Smoky Leupp, the second of Borst's pair of ace gundogs, protested. "Supposin' the undercover squirt yuh mentioned cuts in or spills the play?"

"He won't," Borst assured them with a wolfish grin. "I'm keepin' him busy someplace else. . . . Lola. You can forget him entirely. Jest keep yore minds fixed on rubbin' out Bill Dorne. That's all you got to do, an' I'll be takin' care of any thin' else that comes up. Get set now—here they come!"

* * *

PUTTING their broncs over the ground at a hard gallop, it was not long before Bill Dorne and the ragged Tranter neared Borst's new Three-Mile House. Looking toward it, where it lay sweltering in the sun's noontime blaze, Bill reflected that there was a look about the place that went uncommon well with murder.

He and Tranter swung lightly from their saddles before the hitch rail fronting the main building, ground-tied their mustangs and started for the newly-installed batwing doors.

Several men, working about the pole corral a short distance off, looked up curiously. But said nothing. Neither did Bill or Tranter—to them. To Bill, Tranter said, "Don't it never rain in this yere country? Cripes, I'm thirsty enough tuh put down ever' last bottle behind Borst's bar."

"Borst's bar," Bill told him grimly, "ain't goin' to be fit for nothin' but kindlin' when we walk out of this joint, Buck. He's gettin' plumb outa the resort business here an' now—plumb complete. I've warned him twice; this is the time I act! When I say a thing I mean it!"

"Seems like if yuh was fixin' tuh start a corpse-an' cartridge occasion out yere," Tranter muttered, "yuh'd oughta brung a posse. We're goin' tuh be outnumbered six or eight tuh one. Them there's pretty powerful long odds, ef anyone sh'd ride up an' ask yuh."

"If you're scared," Bill drawled scathingly, "yuh can climb back into yore saddle an' start throwin' dust."

"Scared! Who? Me?" Tranter loosed a flood of educating profanity. "Why, dang yore everlastin' tintype! How'n seventeen prairie-chickens do yuh make that out? I'll have yuh know a Tranter never backed down from anythin'—not even the flood! Scared— hell! Bring on yore durn lead-throwers; I'll show yuh how we washes 'em up back in Texas!" And the scowl that furrowed his countenance and the blaze in his squinted eyes told Bill that there was no fear in the lanky deputy.

"I was just joshin'," he soothed, and added: "Sure hope Mendota's here. I'm pinin' to ask him what he done the other day to make that fool desert rat drag a gun. He mebbe drawed first, like Mendota an' Ortega claimed, but I'm bettin' Mendota egged the old coot into it."

"Wal, here we are," Tranter said. "Who goes in first —the Sheriff or his deputy?"

ELEVEN
"FILL YORE HAND"

"THE SHERIFF," Bill said, as they paused before the steps. "But he ain't goin' in like no bull through a Chink shop, an' you can stick yore pin in that!" Dropping his voice and letting his words come from between lips that hardly moved, he added, "No sense in us takin' extra chances. A ounce of prevention is worth a pound of cure—that's a ol' Dorne sayin', Buck, an' we're gonna 'bide by it. You sneak round to the back door; you'll find one round there someplace. You slip in, an' when you're set say something' loud enough so's I can hear it. This may not be no trap, but I ain't figurin' to put m' foot in it just to have the satisfaction of findin' out—"

"I ain't a heap partial tuh puttin' my hoof in it neither," Tranter objected. "But I'll do it, bein' it's you what's askin'." And, spitting on his badge and polishing it with his sleeve, Tranter went striding round toward the rear of the Three-Mile House.

Bill bent down and pretended to be adjusting a spur while he waited for Tranter's signal. Out of the corner of his eyes he slantwise watched the group loafing about the new corral. They seemed to be paying no special attention to either him or the vanished Tranter. He was beginning to get a crick in his back from his bent posture when at last he caught Tranter's booming voice.

"Wal, suff'rin' sidewinders, Sheriff,' he said, "fancy meetin' *you* here!"

Straightening, Dorne pushed through the swinging doors into a room filled with a tight, electric silence—a room wherein Borst's chief pair of gunslammers were poised, one to either side of the bat-wings, in a coiled crouch with their hands gripping guns and their guns pointed toward the entrance. But Tranter was behind them, as they well knew without having to look, and they dared not move from their tracks.

Dorne streaked a grin. "Playin' a new game, gents?" he greeted the glowering gun fighters. "Or is it ring-around-the-rosy?"

Joe Fuddabaugh swore. But his pardner only glared murderously and his fingers tightened on his gun as though he were of half a mind to bring its muzzle up and use it. But he stiffened when Tranter from his easy slouch beside the bar said, suggestively:

"That bet yuh had with me, Bill, about pickin' off ears at twenty paces, still hold good? These here fellas would be jest about right, I'm thinkin'. That Leupp jasper has ears like a giraffe, an' his companero has the same kinda pointed fuzzy ones that usual grow on jack-asses. I don't reckon neither would miss 'em a heap was I tuh shoot 'em off."

This time it was Smoky Leupp who swore. And he did so viciously. "You better laugh while you got the chance, you addlebrained nitwit, because once you lose that drop I'm gonna perforate yuh like a sieve!"

"Shucks," Tranter said, "I ain't even got my gun out. What's the matter with you rim-fire dally men?"

"They ain't got no sand in their craws when a gent's lookin' at 'em, Buck," Dorne depreciated. But he watched them closely. "They're the brave kinda tinhorns what only plays with stacked decks. I wouldn't be surprised if they was layin' for some poor misguided pilgrim when we came in. Like that dude they jest bumped off—"

"That's a lie," snarled Smoky Leupp. "I never even seen the dude!"

"You'll never be able to make a jury swaller that," Dorne said. And Tranter added, comfortingly, "Not that it'll ever git to a jury."

Leupp made his play then, frightened by the shadow of the noose. And Joe Fuddabaugh was quick to back him up. Smoky even got in first shot. But it buried its bullet harmlessly into the floor, three feet in front of Dorne.

Dorne was firing from the hip, and driving each shot with a wicked coldness that could have but one end—and had it. Smoky Leupp was dead when he struck the floor.

Joe Fuddabaugh fared better. But not much. He had whirled, bringing his pistol upward in a swing for the third button of Tranter's shirt. But Tranter broke both his arms at the elbow before he could squeeze the trigger. Then, with professional indifference, Tranter sent in two more shots that knocked Joe's legs from under him and dropped him, a moaning heap of misery, not two feet from where his pardner lay in a motionless huddle.

"You was a little hasty Bill," Tranter commented judiciously. "We don't kill 'em down in Texas—we jest cripples 'em up fer life as a object lesson to others of their ilk." He grinned, then adding:

"Statistics proves it works out better thataway. Texas ain't got no ring-tailed hellions anymore, except what's too crippled to practice—the rest has all moved into Arizony."

Bill could hear the pound of running feet now as men converged excitedly upon the place to see what had happened—probably, he thought, to look with satisfaction upon his and Tranter's corpses. They were due for quite a shock, he reflected sardonically, and turned to face the bat wings.

But it was not from the front entrance that visitors of import came. He swung round again as Tranter said, "Afternoon, Mr. Borst. Nice day for thirsty weather. How 'bout settin' 'em up on the house? These corpse-an'-cartridge episodes alius make me thirsty 'nuff tuh drink the Injun Ocean."

"What the hell you birds been up to?" Borst exploded as Bill faced him.

"Oh," said Bill, "we just been givin' a coupla side-windin' killers their marchin' orders. One of 'em's marched his last, an' the other 'un's goin' to do the rest of his marchin' on crutches. *Know* em?" he snapped the last two words at Borst like the crack of a whip.

But Borst had himself in hand. His face did not shed its expression of indignant horror by so much as a fraction. "You can't get away with this," he growled. "This town's had all the legal homicides it's goin' to, if I got anythin' to say about it. I'll have your badges before the sun sets."

"Yeah? You an' who else?" sneered Tranter.

Dorne said, before Borst could round up a suitable reply, "Do you know these hombres?" and the gun that still was in his hand made a brief gesture to the two luckless gunmen prostrated on the sawdust floor.

"No, I don't know 'em," Borst snarled. "D'you think I keep tabs on all the riff-raff that use my place to loaf in? You can't talk to me like this, Bill Dorne! There's a law in this country an'—"

"Don't make me laff," Bill drawled. Backing closer to the bar so that he could keep his eyes on Borst and the group of men standing huddled between the bat wings, he flung out his order tersely:

"I want every man an' woman cleared out of this buildin' pronto. Get 'em out, Borst."

"I'll be damned if I will! You ain't runnin' my place! You ain't—"

"Save a part of yore breath for breathin'," Dorne advised. "You're listenin' to the voice of authority, Mister. Get busy!"

"You can't—" Borst began again.

"Listen," Bill said flatly, and there was that in his tone that showed he would take no more lip from any man. "Before you get shut of me you're goin' to find out that there's a powerful lot of things that I can do. The word *can't* ain't in my dickshonary. Are you gonna clear them yaps outa here, or shall I do it?"

"Vamoose," Borst said, with a smothered oath, to the men who filled the doorways. "You heard the Sheriff orate. Must think he's Gawd A'mighty. But you better do like he says. It don't pay to argue," he added sneeringly, "with the man that's got the drop."

Like a flash Bill's gun was back in leather. "I don't need no drop when I'm bent on herdin' polecats. Anyone in them back rooms, Borst? If there is, get 'em out!"

"What's the big idea?" Borst asked, curious despite himself.

"I allow you'll be findin' out before a powerful great while shags along. Got an axe around here anyplace?"

"Might be one out in the cookshack—"

"Get it, Buck."

From where he stood, Bill caught sight then of Tumbleweed and Lola eyeing him curiously from outside through one of the open windows. But he gave no sign of being aware of their presence, and not for a moment did he turn his shoulders away from Borst's big rocklike figure.

"Get it, Buck," he said, and heard Tranter drag his spurs toward the rear door. "Watch out for trouble," he added softly. "If one of those hyenas out there bats an eye, don't argue—put a quick window in his skull."

"You're hellbent on pilin' up a lot to answer for, Bill Dorne," Borst said, and his thick lips tightened ominously. "An' you'll answer for it, too! You're cock of the walk right now, but how long will it last? A man's luck, Bill, is a fickle thing. You better take it easy. What do you think you're figurin' to do with that axe?"

"The answer to that," Bill grinned, "is goin' to cost you money, Borst. Good money. An' a lot of it."

Borst sneered, "Bah! Pride goes before a fall—an' you've sure got pride by the horns."

"If you feel lucky, fill yore hand."

"I'll wait," Borst muttered, and his high blood laid a definite flush across his beefy cheeks. A wicked restlessness seemed to be tugging at his lips, and it narrowed down his sleepy lids, hooding his eyes like a mask. But the hand that removed a cigar from his coat pocket and put it between his teeth was steady, and so was the hand with which he lit it. "I'll wait," he repeated, and filled his lungs with expensive smoke.

"You always was a good waiter," Bill jeered heavily.

"Yeah. An' I'll still be waitin' round this one-hawss town long after you been planted."

"Waitin' for more suckers like that dude, I guess."

"That's it."

Tranter came in with the axe and looked enquiringly at Dorne. So did Borst turn his regard that way. But it wasn't enquiring; it was expressionless as the unblinking eyes of a snake.

Bill said, "Wreck that bar."—Like that.

Borst let out an oath, and there was a wicked viciousness in his tone. "By Gawd, you can't cut it, Bill—!"

"Watch me. Go on, Buck—I wanta see some kindlin'. Quick."

TWELVE
"CARRIED OUT FEET FIRST"

THERE WAS one long instant of total silence inside that room; a hush peopled with unuttered thoughts. A stillness that brought lines of strain upon the faces of those gaping watchers who stood peering in from beyond the windows. Then Tranter, gripping his rusty axe with grim right hand, started for the bar.

Even now Borst did not let his temper rush him; did not let it push him into a situation from which he might have found it necessary to retreat. It was worth something to Dorne to see him standing there, face bloated and purple from the spur of rage, yet raising not a finger as Tranter brought his axe up in an easy lift.

Borst's desire to come to physical grips with Dorne showed in his tautened cheeks like letters of fire. But he held his rage with an iron hand. This, his actions said, was not the time to stage reprisals—but the time would come! The look he drove at Dorne said that nothing could hold Pecos Borst back; that nothing ever had and nothing ever would!

And all this time Tranter was working with a will, a

wide tight grin framing his yellowed teeth. The muscles bulged beneath his shirt each time he brought his rusty weapon down. He was wasting neither time nor strokes. Every downward swing was being made to count.

Dorne watched Borst with a steel-cold attention, yet he stood in an easy hipshot slouch that robbed his pose of menace—or added to that menace, according to the angle a man was viewing it from. Menacing or not, it kept Borst's hands away from his hips; kept them out of his pockets, too, and away from his sweaty armpits.

Yet maybe it wasn't Dorne's pose that kept Borst's position static. Perhaps it was something the big saloonman read in Dorne's blue glance. Or the cold grin that curled Dorne's saturnine lips.

Dorne said wickedly, "Like a picture from Carry Nation."

"It's a picture," Borst gritted, "I'm goin' to be a long time forgettin'."

"I'd bet on that," Dorne grinned back. Then to Tranter, "That'll be enough, now, Buck. Don't want you to wear yorese'f down to a shadow. Hold off awhile; there's other things to be done."

He flashed another look at Borst. "Got everyone outa here? Upstairs? Back rooms?" And, at Borst's sullen nod, "Well, if you ain't it's just their hard luck an' I ain't goin' to shed no tears about no cremated trash like the kind what runs in yore pack."

Borst's face showed a tinge of grey as some of its lively red washed out. "What's that?" The words come from him hoarse, gruff. "*Cremate?*"

"That's what I said. Ain't nothin' wrong with yore hearin', is there?" Dorne's mocking laugh cut across the stillness. "Ain't you grabbed holt of the idee yet? I'm goin' to burn this damn joint down."

Borst whispered, "You—you—"

"*Outside!*" Dorne snapped, and drew his gun from its holster.

For an instant then, it seemed that Borst would grab for his pistol anyway. The man looked on the ragged edge of murder, and his frame was shaking as though with ague. His mouth hung slack, and it seemed as though his eyes would burst from his apoplectic face.

"Look out," Tranter jeered, "yuh'll git a stroke."

Dorne motioned with his pistol toward the door. And Borst moved toward it as if filled with Jamaica rum, his gait almost a wooden stagger. He paused once and slowly turned his head toward Bill. A streak of rashness threw a fleeting shadow across his drawn and paling cheeks. Then it was gone and, with a tightening of his jaw, he strode outside.

* * *

"BILL," said Tranter, when once again they were comfortably ensconced in the Sheriff's Office in Spavined Nag, and the sun was drifting down behind the mountains to the west, "you've got more durned nerve'n a brass monkey!"

Dorne's lips streaked a smile as he rolled a cigarette.

"More nerve than sense," continued Tranter, warming up to his subject like a cat beneath a stove. "By Cripes, I dang near bust when yuh tol' Borst yuh was sorry the rest of his powder-an-ball men weren't round so's they could enjoy the moral o' what yuh was doin' as much as he was enjoyin' it! When he seen his place goin' up in smoke he was mad enough tuh chaw railroad spikes! Just what would yuh 'a' done if he'd called yore bluff? That's what I'd admire tuh know."

"I wasn't bluffin'," Dorne said shortly.

"Yeah—an' he wa'n't callin' none, neither! But you ain't kiddin' no ranny what's been around like I hev. If he *had* 'a' called yore bluff—"

Dorne said, "He didn't. Best let it go like that. Sufficient the time to the evil thereof. That's one of my mottoes. Another is, never trouble trouble till trouble troubles you. Abide by the Golden Rule, Buck, an' give all men a even break. Live in peace an' love yore neighbors an'—"

"I can see," Tranter snorted, fishing a battered and evil-smelling pipe from his trousers pocket, "that you've done got religion. You been listenin' tuh that sky-pilot till yuh're gettin' tuh palaver jest like 'im. You know dang well yuh can't live in peace an' amity with Brother Borst—not after what yuh done tuh him this afternoon. Cripes, he was plumb frothin' at the mouth when we cleared outa there. An' he'll keep right on a-frothin' till he evens up the score!"

"What a little ray of sunshine you turned out to be."

"Sunshine, hell!" Tranter snorted. "I believe in lookin' facts square in the eye!"

An apparently unbreakable serenity was observable now in Bill's blue glance. It made Tranter fidgety. It appeared to him that Dorne was all puffed up with his success. He didn't feel so optimistic himself. "Listen," he said. "That Borst hellion ain't gonna git no kind of rest till he's put his heel on yore neck. Depend upon it. That fella means bizness—I seen blood in his eye when he looked at you."

Spur chains jingled to the clump of booted feet without. A moment later a tall lean shadow darkened the doorway and Parson Jones followed it into the room. "Brother," he said solemnly, fixing Bill with a serious glance, "constant exposure to dangers lendeth contempt for them."

Dorne grinned. "I got an answer for that one. It's a heck of a lot healthier to meet danger than to wait for it. One of my mottoes," he added modestly.

"There's no fool like a young 'un," Tranter said, and lit his pipe. "I been tryin' tuh tell him, but he knows it all. They ain't no use in arguin' with 'im, Parson. His head's got so big now he'll hev tuh git a new hat."

"What's the matter with you rannies?" Dorne asked, grinning. "I don't need no nurses."

"Not yet, mebbe," Tranter muttered testily.

"Borst ain't goin' to take that sittin' down, son," Parson Jones opined. "You better not hang around lighted places after dark. Nor ride along high ridges when you take yore horse for an' airin'."

"Is that," Dorne asked, "general advice, or somethin' special?"

Jones said, "I ain't a fella to talk just to hear my teeth rattle."

"An' a wink's as good as a nod to a blind mule," Tranter added, disgustedly. "Parson, yuh're wastin' yore breath."

"What is this anyway? A wake?"

"There's talk goin' round this town," Jones said darkly.

"What kinda talk?"

"Just talk, son," the sky-pilot answered cautiously. "Things are bein' said, an' a number of hard cases has got their heads together. They seen that fire in town here. An' yore movements are the subject of considerable int'rest.

Dorne said, "Such popularity must be deserved," and his rash grin played across his lips.

"Listen," Jones said grimly. "Did you tell Borst to head for the tall tules?"

"I told him to hunt a hole, crawl in an' pull it in after him," Dorne answered. "I told him if I caught him runnin' another dive in this county, it would be the last one he ever ran anyplace."

"An' I expect quite a passel of hombres heard you?"

"They sure did if they was list'nin'."

"Don't you know that puts it up to Borst to make good? If he don't plant you now, he'll be laffed clean outa the county," Jones told him seriously.

"I want him out of the county," Dorne announced flatly. "I told him three days ago right here in town. An' he'll go under his own motion or he'll be carried out feet first. I aim to make this county, *an' this town,* fit places for people to live in."

"Well," Jones admitted, looking from Dorne to Tranter and back again, "a polecat like Pecos Borst *does* contaminate God's good scenery. But—I'm allowin' you've bit off more than you can chew, son. You ain't goin' to be able to enlist much help in a fight against Borst's crowd. They're too powerful. Leastways, for the married gents to buck. And the single fellows . . . Well, the unmarried boys are too hell-bent on havin' a good time to want to see you close things down. I admire yore spirit, but—"

"Fine, Parson," Dorne grinned. "I'm sure glad to hear you say it. Let's all go get a drink."

* * *

THEY WENT to Venta's place, the Broken Harp. Dorne vetoed Tranter's suggestion that they go to Ortega's Black Bottle Bar. He was still thinking about the desert rat killed by Mendota there, and how Ortega had sworn the sagebrusher was first to yank a gun.

Venta was behind the bar when they entered. He greeted them with an oily smile. "Name yore poison, gents. The treat is on the house."

The three gave their orders and, when filled glasses were slid before them, Tranter said, "To the rubbin' out of Pecos Borst. Drink hearty, gents—an' you, too, Venta."

The drinks were downed. Venta beamed and his oily smirk reached nearly from ear to ear. "That Borst ain't helpin' my business any," he growled loudly. "I'll be glad to see the last of 'im."

"You have," Dorne told him calmly. "He's plumb washed up in this county. He'll be clearin' out, I reckon, soon's he can sell his spread."

Dorne bought a bottle then and the three of them adjourned to a table in the rear. Staring down into his drink with a morose eye, Parson Jones reflected, "Somethin' tells me this thing ain't over yet. Borst's takin' this too calm. Dorne, there's blood on the moon these days. I hate to say it, but I've got a hunch there's goin' to be some more killin' round here before we git a ordinance perhibitin' the carryin' of lethal weapons. They're still goin' strapped to every man's hip, an' when a man's got a thing, he usually likes to use it."

"Wonder if Borst got that dude's roll?" Tranter said.

Bill suggested that if he hadn't got it before killing

him, he most certainly had got it afterward. Wasn't that what they'd killed him for?

Here Jones interrupted with an unexpected revelation. "No," he said, "I don't reckon it was. That dude was a Cattlemen's Association man. An' it's my guess Borst knew it."

Here, Dorne mused, was food for thought, and put his notion to the test.

If the dude, as Jones said, really was an agent of the Cattlemen's Association, it meant that the Association kind of thought that Borst might be mixed up in the wholesale rustling activities going on in the locality. Spavined Nag and the surrounding range was putting on its war paint for rustlers, looked like. Honest ranchers would soon be coming into town with blood in their eyes and guns on their legs, they would be only to glad of an excuse to use.

And he was Sheriff of the county!

He smothered an oath beneath his breath, and resolved to get busy pronto on the rustling angle. He said, "Buck, I reckon we'll just stick Tumbleweed onto that job. He's the logical candidate for it anyhow, 'cause he's already got a foothold in Borst's camp. Right now, I'm countin' heavy on him to get us news if Borst tries to pull anythin' slick. He—"

"This here Tumbleweed gent," Tranter observed sourly, "ain't my idea of a up-an'-comin' law officer. He looks more tuh me like Billy the Kid's second cousin', or mebbe Butch Cassidy's twin brother."

"Do I know the gentleman?" Jones asked, interested.

"Nope," Tranter growled, "but he's a brand fer the

burnin', an' it mightn't do no harm if yuh looked 'im up."

"If you *do* see him," Bill cautioned, "don't let anythin' drop about him bein' one of my deputies. There ain't nothin' wrong with him," he added, "except his feet ain't twins an' Nature sold him short when it come to passelin' out the looks. But I reckon he's honest."

"Yeah—yuh oughta be a parson yoreself," Tranter jeered, "yuh're that optimistic!"

"It is man's duty to give his fellows the benefit of any doubt," Jones reminded gently.

"Tuh my way o' thinkin'," said Tranter sourly, getting to his feet, "yuh c'd give that pilgrim the benefit o' *all* the doubts an' he *still* would stink! But you'll learn —by the time they're shov'lin dirt in yore face. Wisht I c'd recollect where I seen that skinny wart before ..." He jingled thoughtfully toward the swinging doors. "Well, anyhow, yuh mark my words, Bill—that jasper an' Pecos Borst is thicker'n splatter. He'll be hookin' the linin' plumb off'n yore silver cloud, less'n yuh cut loose of him pronto."

THIRTEEN
BORST STRIKES BACK

DORNE GRINNED at Gospel Jones as Tranter passed through the Broken Harp's batwing doors. "Buck," he chuckled, "is about as happy as a bloodhound's eye. Never see such a fella for throwin' cold water an' hangin' crepe. His food mustn't sit real well. Always preachin' calamity—"

"An' he can dish it out, too," Jones cut in grimly. "You don't want to underrate Tranter, Bill. He's dauncy, all right," he admitted, rasping a calloused hand across his beard-stubbled chin reminiscently, "but he's seen a lot of the seamy side of life. He's done most of his travelin' as you might say, among the Philistines—an' Buck's a man who believes the old sayin' about Rome. He's been around, Bill. His name's been carved on more'n one Boothill epitaph."

Dorne looked at the rangeland parson curiously. "Yeah?"

"Uh-huh. Such epitaphs as this: 'Ed Lock was buried here. Ed was rated pronto quick till Brimstone Tranter slowed him down.' I can remember Ed pretty well. Reckon I ought to; he was a holy terror to Bible-packers down in Texas. Yes, Bill, Tranter's been around. I've heard of him over in New Mexico, too, one place an' another. He's left his mark on this Western country. I've heard he come from Missouri when he wasn't knee-high to a jackrabbit. But he got his early rearin' down Tombstone way. His father was a frontier marshal. A close friend, they say, of Doc Holliday an' Wyatt Earp. Buck always had a wild streak in him, though. Restless, he was, an' always wantin' to be up an' doin'. When things was quiet he'd sort of drift away to turn up five-six months later, clear across the state—or outside of it. Between you an' me, I don't reckon he's always kep' his feet on the straight an' narrow."

Dorne nodded thoughtfully. "It don't make no never-mind to me, though," he offered. "What a man's been is his own business, the way I look at it. I usu'lly judge a man by what he is an' what he does when I know him."

Gospel Jones said, "You're right, too. What a man has been in the past is between him and his God. It's the present that counts the most. No man is perfect. The Lord don't expect it. Let a man repent, make resti-tution in so far as he is able, and—"

Jones broke off as a short, squatty puncher with squinty eyes and bulbous nose pushed through the crowd and paused before their table. "One of you gents the Sheriff?" he muttered.

"I am," Dorne answered, looking the man over closely. "You lookin' for me?"

"I'm not, but there's a fella over in yore office what is. Fella named Krayson. Used tuh work for the Wine glass—"

Bill shoved back from the table and got to his feet. "See you later," he said to Jones, and hurried toward the entrance. Shoving through the batwings, he reached the porch and paused, dropping to its warped planking as a burst of lurid flame beat outward from the horse-packed hitch rail fronting the resort.

When Dorne's body struck the porch flooring he rolled for the steps and down them, getting out his pistol as he did so. When he came to a stop on the plank walk he surged to his feet, the gun weaving in his hand as startled pedestrians scuttled for shelter. Bill had not been hit, but a slug had pierced the crown of his Stetson and another had ripped through the fluttering ends of his lavender neckerchief. And he was mad —plenty mad!

But the fellow had got clear away before he'd come to his feet. He could have heard the fellow's pounding boots, he felt, had not so many other gents been running at the time, in an effort to get out of any possible line of fire. As it was, the would-be assassin had made good his escape.

With a smothered oath, Bill strode back inside, shoving men off his elbows as they crowded round the door with expectant eyes. "Nobody hurt," he growled. "Don't block this entrance—there might be *another* fire."

Ortega was standing at Venta's side not five feet from the door and in direct line with a window overlooking the porch. Venta's swarthy features paled as he found Bill's glance upon him and the meaning in Bill's words grew clear. Bill's cold grin fired up his face and made it reckless. "You better have more luck next time, 'cause it'll be the last chance you'll get," he drawled, and left Venta and his friend to digest this at their leisure.

He strode straight to the Sheriff's Office and found the place dark. He approached it cautiously. No telling what might happen next. It struck him suddenly that the whole thing was bait to get him into the light from the flaring torches affixed to the front of the Broken Harp, where that dry-gulching killer could have a chance to earn his money. It was dollars to doughnuts, he told himself bitterly, that Krayson hadn't been within a block of this office.

He'd swallowed the line, sinker and all. Only Providence, or the bushwhacker's hurried aim, had saved him. He'd acted like a damnfool kid. Small wonder folks called him wild!

He paused at one side of the open office door and listened for a full five minutes before, satisfied that the place was empty, he entered with a snort of disgust. Moving toward the wall beside his desk, he reached up and found the lamp bracketed to the wall. He removed its chimney and struck a match. When the wick flared up he replaced the chimney and—

Wham!

The echoes of the shot drowned the tinkle of shattered glass. In total darkness Dorne crouched where he had whirled, facing the open door. Then, at the sound of running feet, he made for the door with angry strides. Twice was too many times to be made a target of in the same half-hour! Somebody was going to be shown it did not pay to monkey with the Sheriff of Spavined Nag!

He reached the doorway and was through it in three swift steps. Too bad there wasn't more light on this side of the street. Some drunken fool must have shot up the lantern that was customarily lit above the doorway of the express office two doors to the right. He paused abruptly to try and catch the direction of those running feet.

It was all that saved him, that pause!

There was a *thwunk!* He flicked a glance across his shoulder and in the reflected light from the honkytonks across the street he saw the vibrating gleam of steel. A knife—imbedded in the wall at his side, on a level with his chest!

He knew where that had come from! The blade had been thrown from the mouth of the alley running between the express office and the building in between. A saddle shop; closed.

Dorne wasted scant time in thought. Even as these things blurred through his mind, he was reaching down with his left hand and removing the spurs and danglers from his high-heeled boots. Then, weaving forward with cat-footed stride, he rounded the far corner of the Sheriff's Office and found things black as the inside of a dead cow's stomach. This was not so good, but he consoled himself with the thought that what he couldn't see, that ornery knife-thrower could not see, either.

Realizing the need for caution here, unless he wished the feel of a slithering blade between his ribs, Dorne advanced slowly down the alley between the office and the jail, making toward where the alley used by the knife-wielder opened upon it.

Every few steps he stopped to listen. Once he imagined he heard a pebble crunch beneath a booted foot, but he could not be sure. From afar came the muted sound of off-key music from one of the resorts, and the sing-song drone of the prompter. But in this alley it was still as death.

In the swirling gloom, Dorne's jaws were clenched and his wide lips thinned and determined. Three attempts in one night on the same man's life was carrying things too far! Before he got through, he allowed he was going to make some durn jasper realize it wasn't safe to play such pranks with Wild Bill Dorne.

Where in hell *was* that squirt? Standing motionless with bated breath, Dorne could hear no slightest sound of stealthy bootstep. Nor could he hear the subdued breathing of the unseen skulker. Had the fellow, like his predecessors, got away?

And just then, through the blanketing darkness, an outstretched hand with a knife in it came up against Dorne's cheek softly.

Dorne's reaction was instantaneous and even swifter than was that of the hand's owner. Up came Bill's gun-weighted right in a smashing arc that crunched soddenly against flesh and bone—but it was only the assassin's shoulder. And the left shoulder, at that. As Dorne realized a second later when the knife's dull glint bit a sweeping circle a scant inch short of his chin.

Shouts and the pound of running feet in front of the Sheriff's Office told Dorne now that men had been attracted by the shot that had smashed the lamp. But he gave them no portion of his attention. He was engaged in an encounter with an unknown adversary whom he felt sure would like nothing better than to plant his naked steel in some vital part of the Sheriff's anatomy.

This intuition fanned the flame of Dorne's fierce temper and made him suddenly reckless. Throwing back his right clenched first, he reached forward in a circular motion with his left. But it did not touch the unseen knifeman. *Where had the fellow gone?*

Bill knew the next moment when the fellow's steel ripped his sleeve from wrist to elbow! With a smothered oath, Bill let drive with his right, gun-weighted fist. It struck the would-be assassin a punishing blow, drove him staggering back. Bill could hear his labored panting as he sought to keep his feet. But even as the man went lurching backward, he must have flung his blade. For Dorne heard its whistle and felt its breath as it passed between his extended arm and his right side. He heard it *chunk!* against the building two feet away, and vibrate wickedly.

Sure that he had the fellow now, Bill went plunging forward. And his chin plowed through the dust as he tripped over the marauder's low-crouched form. And the breath was for a moment knocked completely out of him. It was his antagonist's chance, and the fellow took it. Though not as Bill had expected—his bootheels thumped out a swift retreat.

As Bill picked himself out of the dust a moment later, he realized why. The light of an up-held lantern came round the opposite corner of the building, and behind it came a shadowy group of men with determined faces. There were two or three swiftly indrawn breaths and a couple of muted oaths as these citizens caught sight of Dorne.

"Suff'rin' sidewinders!" Tranter snapped, and lowered his lantern. "We thought they'd got yuh that time! What the heck's been happenin' round here?"

Bill told them tersely. The men, solid citizens, shook their heads. "We heered that shot," Tranter told him.

"Heered about that trouble yuh had in front of the Broken Harp, too. I didn't figure Borst would crawl off with his tail 'tween his laigs—an' he ain't. This is some of his doin's; yuh kin bank on it! Them hellions won't rest till yo're planted—"

"An' I ain't figurin' to rest," Dorne said, "till I've run them rannyhans clear outa the country! So you can look forward to a right uproarious time!"

FOURTEEN
WET-BLANKETED CATTLE

BACK INSIDE THE OFFICE, and with the shades drawn down to the sills and the front door closed as an added precaution, Buck Tranter said to Dorne.

"I been talkin' a mite with the Gospel-slinger. That fella kin use his eyes; he give me a chin-picture of this hombre what told yuh Krayson was waitin' in yore office that was dang near good as them what these jaspers with a black box an' a tripod takes. That mealy-mouthed liar was that sawed-off squirt of a Dode Harniss—the guy which owned the knife Fisk was packin' in his pocket."

"I'd begun," Bill said, "to figure as much myself."

Tranter nodded, and getting out his battered pipe, said: "It was. You got any spare tobacco, Bill? I'm fresh out an' this yere hod needs exercise."

Dorne eyed the pipe distastefully, but passed over his sack of Durham. "You got any idea what Harniss passed me that word for?"

Tranter, packing his pipe, grinned. "It's as clear as the nose on yore map, Bill. He was figurin' to git yuh outside where Krayson, hidin' 'mongst them hawsses by the hitch rack, could snuff yore light with a minymum of danger."

"Sure—but *why?*'''

"Don't ast me questions like that. I ain't good at riddles. Lemme ast you one. If a hawss is sixteen hands high, got a mean eye an' a long Roman nose, an' weighs round 'leven hundred pounds, how old's his rider?"

Bill snorted. "I'll ask the questions," he growled. "I can answer 'em, too," he added grimly. "Harniss an' Krayson joined them rustlers of their own accord—if they wasn't already hooked up with 'em! Otherwise, they wouldn't be walkin' round this place leadin' solid citizens into trouble; they'd be dead or prisoners."

"Sounds reasonable," Tranter admitted, puffing out a thick blue cloud of aromatic smoke through which he eyed Bill sharply. "I kin add tuh that. Harniss has been a two-bit rustler ever since I've knowed him."

"Why didn't you tell me that right off?" Bill growled.

"A wise man," Tranter grinned, "keeps his lip buttoned an' don't do no oratin' outa turn. I recollect a fella once what talked himself into a decoration fer a cottonwood branch."

Bill snorted. "You go over to the printer's—he sleeps out back of his place—an' get him to run you off two-three hundred flyers offerin' a hundred-an'-fifty bucks reward for information leadin' to the arrest an' conviction of Dode Harniss an' Ed Krayson, ex-Wineglass punchers, wanted for participatin' in the wholesale rustlin' of Wineglass cattle. When he runs 'em off, I want to see that they get tacked up in prominent places —*quick*. Get at it."

"Jest a second," Tranter grunted, getting to his feet and knocking out his pipe. "You got any idee who that knifeman was?"

"I got a sneakin' notion," Bill said, "that it was Pedro Mendota. I'm figurin' to look him up right now. "An'," he added ominously, "if he can't give a damn good account of his movements for the last coupla hours, somethin' unpleasant is goin' to happen."

Bill went over Spavined Nag with the proverbial fine-toothed comb, but he did not find the wily Mendota, nor anyone who would admit they'd seen him all evening. It was mighty irritating. If he could only have laid hands on the fellow, Bill believed he would have got a considerable distance toward the solution of his troubles. If Mendota himself had not been mixed up with the rustling operations being carried on in the vicinity, Bill believed the Mexican could have given him the names of a number of gents who were. But now that the swarthy gun fighter had vanished, he could not put this notion to the test.

He did, however, visit the Broken Harp and Ortega's Black Bottle Bar—the town's two largest resorts, now that he had put the Golden Stack into the limbo of forgotten joints. In these two dives Bill read the riot act. If, he drawled, another shooting, knifing, or other form of fracas took place in either, he would serve them the same potent dose he'd given Borst's Golden Stack! And it was plain that he meant exactly what he said.

* * *

THREE DAYS SLID BY, and then, early on the morning of the fourth, a white-faced rider swept into town on a winded, lathered bronc. Hitting dirt on skidding boot-heels, this panting buckaroo banged his boots across the boardwalk, pelted up the steps and came jingling into the Sheriff's Office, where he jarred to a sudden stop. There was a wild look in his eyes, and breath was coming in panted gasps that shook his wiry body.

"Take it easy," Bill advised. "I'll still be here when you get yore wind."

"Heck, yes," Tranter added. "Rome wa'n't built in no day, an' it's too dang hot in this country tuh rush yuh're life away. Jest take it easy pilgrim—we'll bear with yuh."

"Listen!" the puncher gasped. "Listen—Borst's raised hell right, an' shoved a chunk under it! He's gone mad as a hatter!"

Dorne looked from the rider's trail-grimed countenance to Tranter. And back again. Then he got up and took a pace or two about the room, his hands deep-thrust in the leather pockets of his chaps.

He said, "S'pose you chew it finer, pardner. An' remember that jestin' lies usually bring serious sorrows."

"Ain't it the truth?" Tranter butted in. "I recollect the time—"

"Recollect this ain't the time to tell it then," Dorne growled, and looked at the rider again. "Well?"

"It's like I said. Borst's gone clean off his button. Some folks has alius suspicioned that he's had a hand in this wholesale rustlin' that's been goin' on, but nobody ever hoped tuh prove it. Ain't no need of provin' it, now! His spread's plumb lousy with rustled steers! I was comin' through there—through his south-west range— late yestiday afternoon, an' I shore seen plenty! Blotched brands all over the hills!"

"What brand of likker do yuh drink?" Tranter cut in, when the buckaroo paused for breath.

"O1' Crow—why?"

"By cripes, I'm gonna order me a barrel. Bill, that's the kinda stuff we oughta equip this yere office with. Must be marv'lous!

"Say!" the rider snarled, "yuh don't think I'm lyin', do yuh?"

Bill said, "Well, I don't know you well enough for that. But it wouldn't surprise me none if this was yore idea of humor."

"*Humor!*" the fellow snorted, and ripped out a couple of choice oaths. "Humor—hell! I'm tellin' you there's rustled critters on the Hashknife range. I seen 'em with my own eyes. An' by cripes I guess I know what I'm seein' when I see it!"

"Shucks," Tranter drawled. "Fer all we know, yuh couldn't tell a hawk from a handsaw. What spread you ridin' for?"

"Them that sows brambles better not be goin' round barefoot!" the fellow growled, a resentful glint in his eye. "You dang stringbean! Fer two cents I'd work you over! What spread am I ridin' for? I *own* my brand; the Bar B 4—my steers is thicker'n cloves on a Christmas ham! Where in hell did you come from?"

Bill said quickly, before Tranter had a chance to answer:

"Where do *you* come from?"

"Sunset County—an' thank Gawd the lawmen over there ain't dumb as you two yaps!"

"Yaps, is it?" Tranter started rolling up his sleeves.

But Bill pushed him back in his chair. Bill said, "Sunset County, eh? Well, would you mind oratin' how-come yo're tellin' me about yore troubles? If yore star-packers is so all-fired up-an'-comin', seems like you'd do well to pack this grief to them."

The owner of the Bar 4 threw his hat down and jumped on it. "By George, I didn't know *any* county— even Spavined Nag—paid good hard cash for such poor excuses of peace-officers as you birds!" He divided a scathing glance between them, adding, *"Borst's ranch is in yore county, ain't it?"*

Bill swallowed his resentment at the other's abuse abruptly. Borst's spread *was* in Spavined Nag territory, at that—unfortunately. Before he could answer, however, Tranter said from his position by the window:

"Another jasper bulgin' down the road! Cripes, this place is gettin' busier than a flea with pups!"

Bill whirled to the window, took one look and said, "Ol' Man Globe!"

"The Mayor?" the stranger growled.

"Yeah."

"Mebbe I'll git some action, then—unless he's petrified, too!"

"Brother, I'd admire tuh know yore handle," Tranter purred softly. "Some day when I ain't so busy— and the climate's cooled off a bit—I'm allowin' tuh look you up."

"Bar B Smith, that's me. An' yuh can look any damned time yuh want to," the man who drank Old Crow snapped belligerently. "Any time you're a-figgerin' tuh pack a quarrel my way, jest fork yore bronc an' come a-foggin'."

Globe slid from his skidding horse outside the door

and came clumping in on the double-quick. "Bill," he panted, "Borst's come into the open. I seen sixteen head of rustled critters on his no'theast range!"

Dorne swore. "What is this, anyway? I'm as anxious to smash Pecos Borst as you gents are to have me, but—"

Tranter said in reply to Globe's surprised look, "That bow-legged jigger claims *he* saw smears of rustled steers on Hashknife's south-west range." And, strangely, he grinned a bit as he said it, as though pleased at some secret joke.

"That clinches it," Globe muttered. "Borst's come into the open. Must think he's so big we don't dare tackle him—but he'll find out diff'rent. Get a posse, Bill! We'll go right—"

"Hold on a second," Bill said flatly. "I'm still sheriffin' this county. Let me get this straight, now. How many rustled steers did you see?" he looked at Globe. "An' just where? An' how you know they're rustled?"

The Mayor gulped, and glared. "Listen," he spluttered, "when I say I seen rustled cattle, you can bet yore damn boots I seen 'em!"

"All right," Bill said. "Where?"

"Near the mouth of Hard's Pass Draw! Sixteen of 'em—hand-counted an' hand-runnin'!"

Bill nodded. "How'd you know they was rustled?"

"How do I know I got my own hat on!" Mayor Globe snorted. "A fine son-in-law you'll make! Don't you s'pose I know my own steers? S'pose I can't tell a blotched brand when I see one? *Hell!*"

"Yeah," snarled Bar B Smith. "That's what *I* say!" He glared at Bill vindictively, and snapped at Globe, "How'd yuh ever come tuh make a sheriff outa such poor material?"

Bill grunted to Tranter, "C'mon—let's go!" and started for the door.

Tranter followed, a saturnine twinkle in his faded eyes. Behind him stamped Bar B Smith and the Mayor of Spavined Nag.

Bill wasn't as slow on the pick-up as he had let on— not by a darned sight. But, unable to believe his ears at such good luck as a slip like this on the part of the slick and crooked Borst, he had wanted to make absolutely sure.

If he went out there half-cocked, Borst would make him the laughing-stock of the whole blamed country.

But, now that it seemed Borst actually had made such a bull, he intended letting no grass grow under his boots. Although he was still a mite skeptical. Globe and Smith, he felt, might actually have seen what they claimed they saw. But the chances of those rustled cattle being on the premises when they got there, was something else again!

Nevertheless, hardly ten minutes later, he, Tranter, Globe, Smith and three other fight-loving possemen headed out of town on fresh broncs along the trail that led to Pecos Borst's Hashknife outfit, some thirty miles away.

In the book and print-lined office of his ranch house on the Hashknife range, Pecos Borst strode nervously up and down the room, an unlighted cigar gripped savagely in one corner of his thick-lipped mouth, a smoky light in the depths of his frowning eyes.

Pecos Borst was feeling ringey as a sore-pawed wolf.

And with good cause, he thought malignantly. Every stride was packed with venom and an ominous threat might be read in the forward throw of his massive shoulders. Indeed, it was read there by the silent watcher across the room.

Phoenix John Muroc, Borst's chief gambler, sat over there in a cowhide chair, the consumptive pallor of his bony features emphasized by the glow from the yellow lamp. For over an hour Muroc had been sitting there, content to hold his silence while he watched the big man pacing back and forth.

Nor did he speak now until Borst growled:

"How long you figger Mendota's been gone, Phoenix?"

"'Bout two hours, I'd allow."

"Then he's had time to learn the straight of it. Oughta be back here any minute. An' he better," he added ominously. "I tell you, I don't get this! Pete swears he ain't put no critters on that part of the range. If Pete ain't lyin', who the hell put 'em there?"

"Couldn't say, " Muroc answered. "But I don't reckon Mendota's stretchin' things when he claims he ain't drove no steers onto the north-east nor south-west fodder. He'd know better'n to pull a cropper like that. You can bet he tucked them steers away in some hidden box canyon or gulch back in the hills."

"Then what in blazes are they doin' on my range where some damn fool can see 'em an' hotfoot the information to that damn Dorne?"

Phoenix John saw no use in answering that. *He* didn't know.

For some minutes longer Borst continued his savage pacing of the floor, so many steps this way, so many steps that. At last he paused to wheel toward the lamp on the table in the corner, pulling a crumpled envelope from his coat pocket as he did so. From this he pulled a soiled bit of cheap notepaper on which several lines had been scrawled with a blunt pencil. For the twentieth time he read them:

Deer Pecos:

If you got any regard fer yore skin, you'll move them blotched critters what's feedin in large numbers on yore north-east an south-west range.

A FRIEND.

For the twentieth time Borst's beefy face flamed with rage. "By Gawd, if there is rustled cattle on my spread, I'm gonna make mince-meat outa the guy what put 'em there! I'm gonna—"

Out of the side of his bitter mouth Muroc said, "Rider comin'."

"What—?" Borst thrust the letter into his pocket and wheeled to watch the door, one hand at his side within fast reaching distance of the heavy Colt that swung in the holster against his hip. "Must be Pete."

It was. The door swung open abruptly and Pedro Mendota stepped swiftly into the room, the glint of anger in his snapping glance. "Señor Borst, it ees the trut' what that note say! The range, she ees covaired weeth them cattle we wet-blanketed!"

FIFTEEN
BORST RECEIVES A VISIT

FOR A LONG SECOND there was silence, a thick and dangerous stillness through which Borst eyed his Mexican lieutenant with a glance that would have curled up many another hardy soul like a dead leaf. But not the dust-stained Mendota, whose swarthy face abruptly creased in a laugh that was smooth and easy, the while he shrugged his graceful shoulders. "But the luck, Señor, she ees due for change. No man can have soch bad luck forevair."

Borst scowled the attempted consolation aside with an oath that crackled.

He snarled, "Did you have sense enough to get hold of your men an' start 'em hazing that rustled stock off somewheres where it wouldn't be seen?"

"But yes, Señor—*seguro* si." Mendota put his panther-lean hips against the wall and crossed his chap-clad legs. He rolled a cigarette with a swift left-handed nonchalance. Snapped a match to flame with his right thumbnail and held an end of his brown-paper smoke above it; when it caught and was going, he put its other end in his mouth. He watched Borst through its upward-drifting smoke.

When it became apparent that Borst was waiting for further and more detailed information, Pedro Mendota supplied it with an easy assurance. "I have left Gleed, Krayson, Harniss an' that Tumbleweed to drive them dogies off."

"That Tumbleweed," the pale-faced Phoenix John cut in, "is an odd stick—uncommon odd. Talks too damn much without sayin' nothin'. Who the hell is he? Where'd he come from? How do you know he ain't a spy from the Cattlemen's Association? Or a pussy-footin' keyholer from the Sheriff's Office?"

Borst smiled thinly. "You don't need to worry about him." He turned his big shoulders back toward the Mexican, and his smoky eyes regarded him unblinkingly from beneath his sleepy lids. "Then you think we needn't worry none about this business, eh?"

Mendota grinned "Why should we? We have nevair worried before."

The flame of some inner heat lay a line of color across Borst's heavy jowls. "If I ever locate the skunk that hazed them critters into the open," he said, "I'll cut strips from his gizzard an' ram 'em down his throat!"

Mendota shrugged, and his teeth showed whitely against the swarthy copper of his face. "*Por Dios,* I shall help you," he smiled, and his dark little eyes were alive with flashing sparkles.

"If he'd nine lives," growled Phoenix John, "I'd snuff each one with a slow pleasure an' then feel sorry he hadn't more! D'you suppose it's Wild Bill Dorne?"

Borst shook his head contemptuously, as though

such an idea was unworthy of sober thought. "How could that profit him? He—"

Phoenix John broke in:

"It would give him a swell chance to railroad you!"

Borst's expression showed that he was giving the idea attention. Then, "Where's Lola?" he demanded suddenly.

Mendota shrugged. Muroc said, "I ain't got no idea."

Borst stuck his head out the door, shouted something into the thickening dusk. A man came running up from the bunkhouse. Borst said: "Hunt up Lola, an' when you find 'er, send 'er in here." The fellow departed, and Borst withdrew his head and shut the door. "I don't like the way that skirt's been actin' lately. I got half a notion she's fallin' for that damned Bill Dorne. A fella oughtn't use women in this game; they're a heap too blamed uncertain. You was suggestin', John . . . ?"

"I was sayin' that if Dorne happened to think of it, an' knew where we was holdin' them cattle, he mighta been the one to shove 'em onto our open range. It would give him a chance to 'discover' 'em. *That* would give him what he's been lookin' for all long—the chance to railroad you to the pen!"

"It would, yeah," Borst answered slowly. "If he could cut it. But I don't think Dorne did it; it ain't his style. He's the kinda fool who plays straight out from the shoulder. No," he shook his head, "I don't reckon Bill done it. An' if nobody's seen 'em an' forked a bronc into town to spread the news, it's a heap likely he don't know about 'em yet."

"Well, I wouldn't count on it, was I you," Muroc growled sourly.

Before Borst could reply, had he been of a mind to, the jingling clump of spurred and booted feet announced the approach of someone. Came a knock on the door and, at Borst's soft "Come in," one of the Hashknife punchers— a burly ruffian—came into the room. Before he spoke he shot a cold glance about the room, which seemed to rest longest and with an open disapproval upon the Mexican gun fighter, Mendota.

Then, as his glance swung round to Borst, he said, "That skirt ain't on the place."

The quickening of Borst's high blood laid a pronounced flush across his cheeks. His long, smoke-colored eyes grew cloudy, muddy as the darkening thoughts churned round in that wide, high, florid fore-head. His big, rocklike figure seemed to tense, to expand. Then, unexpectedly, he chuckled deep down in his bull throat. And it was not a pleasant sound.

"So!" he purred. "So that's her game, is it. By Gawd, I'll bloody well wring that ivory neck of hers if she don't kick clean." And his lips made a sinister curve against the tautness of his face.

Without quite knowing why, the puncher shivered. Borst's gaze was on him squarely. Borst said, "Are you sure?"

"You can have some other hairpin take a look if you don't think so," the puncher blustered, to cover the embarrassment he felt at his momentary exhibition of weakness by shivering under Borst's regard.

The boss of Spavined Nag said, "I ain't in the habit of havin' a second gent check the work I set another bird to do."

"That's all right with me," the puncher growled. "I looked an' she ain't here. Anyways I'm gettin' plumb fed up with workin' fer promises. That," and he swung a truculent stare toward Mendota, "blasted breed ain't paid—"

But he got no further, for at that precise moment Mendota's right hand dropped to the brass-studded holster that sagged his gunbelt at the center. There was a spit of flame, a loud report and the puncher abruptly doubled up and pitched face downward across the floor.

Mendota said nothing, but his eyes were on Borst closely as, with an appearance of nonchalance, he blew the smoke from his gun and replaced the spent cartridge with a fresh one from his belt. Whether by accident or design he seemed to forget to put the gun away, and its muzzle remained slightly tilted in the direction of Pecos Borst.

Phoenix John Muroc licked dry lips with an edge of his pink tongue. But Borst's grin licked a thin line across his mouth and he said "Fast work," with a peculiar husky softness to his tones. And—

"You were right, Pete; we can't have insubordination in the ranks."

"No sabe that word, *señor*" Mendota smiled. "But if you mean we cannot pay the fools who work for us, *por Dios,* that ees all right weeth me. But don' forget, *señor,* there ees a pleasure which ees born of pain. Do not try to double-cross weeth Pedro Mendota—he expects for to get the pay." And that grin on his lips curled wickedly as he stared at Pecos Borst.

Borst shrugged. "You'll get paid," he said easily. "Stick with me a spell longer, Pete, an' we'll show a few wise guys a couple of things. I ain't done in this country by one hell of a long ways." His smoky eyes played over the Mexican's panther-lithe figure. He said with a casualness that did not deceive anyone.

"By the way, Pete; how-come you shot that sagebrusher at the Black Bottle the other day?"

"Gov'ment agent," Mendota said laconically.

Borst's eyes showed interest. "A Federal man? How'd you get onto him?"

"He was sneak around two-three times where I been. I watch heem. See heem talk with many hombres in the low voice. I put two an' two togethair. She spell gov'ment man to me."

Borst nodded thoughtfully, his glance on the raftered ceiling as though in speculation. Outside the night was thickening, cooling off, taking on mystery and enchantment in the light of the rising moon.

From afar came the faint, dim flutter of many hoofs; sometimes they swelled a little in volume, as though their owners had carried them up out of some distant valley. Then they would dim again. But always, as they swelled, their volume perceptibly heightened as though the unseen mounts were nearing.

The three men exchanged silent glances, and unuttered thoughts shone from the eyes of each.

Borst said abruptly, "If that's Dorne, you birds take yore cues from me. This ain't no time for slip-ups. Don't either of you crack a smile unless I give the sign."

With a springy step he moved to the window overlooking the yard. "Douse that light, " he growled.

It was in darkness then—darkness save for what pale light the moon shed down—that Borst and his two companions watched the arrival of a group of shadowy horsemen who slid their broncs to a halt just short of the veranda steps, and hit dirt with the creak of released saddle leather and clink of jingling spurs.

From out of this blurred huddle rose a voice "D'yuh reckon anybody's home?"

And another voice called, "Hallo the house! You home, Borst?"

"It's him," Borst growled, and swore.

"FETCH A LAMP," Borst said, and said it softly. When Muroc brought him one, Mendota not stirring so much as a finger, Borst snapped a match to flame and lit it. "Stay in here till I give the word an' have yore guns where you can get at 'em handy." With the lamp in hand he started for the door, reached and opened it, and strode blinking out upon the veranda.

"Howdy, gents," he said then, easily. "What's all the excitement? Dorne eloped with that yellow-haired Lola-girl?"

Came a muttered imprecation, and then Dorne's own voice:

"Not this time, Pecos. I'm here on business. An' it's connected with you. Comes plumb close to you, it does, an' I'm allowin' you better be right careful what yuh do an' what yuh say."

"You sure can paint 'er creepy."

"It's a creepy subject," Dorne said flatly. "Borst, the sand in yore clock of time's about run out. How many more minutes you got left is likely to be determined by yore ability to talk." He paused to let this sink in and then, as Borst said nothing, added: "First thing I crave to know is how'd yore brand get on so many rustled cattle?"

By the light of the lamp in his hand, Borst's features registered surprise. "What rustled cattle you talkin' about, Bill?"

Dorne gave him a hard glance, and Dorne's glance was emulated by a number of others directed at Borst. Borst saw them all and felt a vague uneasiness that was not as vague as he could and would have wished. "Has somebody been stealin' cattle?"

"You know damn well," Dorne snapped, "somebody has. An' if I ain't gone plumb stark an' ravin' crazy, you know durned well who the somebody is!"

"Where are these critters?"

"On yore south-west an' north-east ranges—or at least they was. Right now, I reckon they're sorta driftin' loose-like clean across this patch o' prairie. Back where they come from, I shouldn't wonder. I come across some of yore friends actually tryin' to tool 'em outa sight. But they was a little slow, an' the cattle was tired. I seen 'em, all right, so there ain't no use you trying to lie out of it; they was somebody else's steers, an' they had yore brand slapped over their rightful marks. Do you plead guilty or—

"You been elected judge an' jury for this county as well as Sheriff?" Borst asked with a sour dryness.

"Where I come from," cut in a voice Borst recognized as belonging to the ragged deputy, Tranter, "we don't waste no time with cattle thiefs. We string 'em up to the nearest branch!"

"Slow down, Buck," Dorne said. "This kinda business has to be done all smooth an' legal-like. The law says cattle rustlers shall be given fair trial, same as any other kind of snake. Borst, you got anythin' to say for yoreself?"

"Sure I have," Borst came back, shoving his jaw out belligerently. "I got a lot to say, Mister. Such raw stuff as this can't be pulled an' got away with. You know well as I do that I never stole them steers—if any's *been* stole!" he added nastily. "I been right here in the house ever since you ordered me away from town, an' before that you know damn well I never had no chance to go gallopin' round the range slappin' my mark on other folks' cattle."

"Sure, I know you didn't do it personal, Pecos. But if you hadn't been standin' back of the ornery bunch of whippoorwills what done it, they wouldn't of had the nerve. You're guilty as they are, Borst—guilty as hell."

"An'," Tranter threw in, "yuh're goin' ter make what the story-books calls the 'supreem sacryfice'!"

"Right!" snapped Mayor Globe. "Unloosen his collar, Buck."

"I wouldn't advise any of you gents to make a false move—any kind of a move, in fact. There's two of my men in the house with guns trained right on you birds. That's what I got this light for—to make good targets out of you. Hell, if you'd had a gram of sense," Borst sneered, "you'd have known you couldn't run no blazer like this on Pecos Borst!"

"Listen at the coyote," Tranter jeered. "Do yuh think we're scared of yore damn gunmen? Let 'em shoot! Tuh hell with 'em!" And with the words Tranter started forward, hand extended for Borst's collar.

But it didn't get there—not just then. One of the

punchers beside Tranter was moving forward, too. And he was between Tranter and the house. From a flanking window a gun went off abruptly, smashing its echoes across the night stillness, blasting the puncher beside the ragged deputy off his feet and down on his face in a gurgling sob.

Tranter swore and his right hand went streaking down as both Borst's hands went up above his head in a sign of peace. Flame licked out from Tranter's hip, chunked viciously into something inside and beyond the window. But it wasn't a man his lead had targeted, for all could hear the hurried pound of booted feet that heralded swift evacuation by Borst's allies.

Snapping out his orders into the milling huddle of his posse, Dorne sprang up the steps and through the door, two possemen at his heels. Borst felt something hard dig into the folds of his paunchy stomach and, looking down, saw that it was Tranter's gun. Saw, too, the wicked smirk on Tranter's lips. "One hurried breath," Tranter said, "an' yore light goes out—an' I ain't referrin' to the light in that there lamp!"

"You ain't heard the last of this," Borst purred. "I wouldn't be surprised to learn that you're mixed up in these rustled cattle somehow—"

"You ain't far from right, at that," Tranter said, and chuckled. "But I ain't the gent what slapped them crooked brands on. An' I don't need tuh hire no Kraysons nor Harnisses tuh do my dirty work—nor no damn back-shootin', bush-whackin' Pedro Mendotas. That's one of the differences between you an' me."

Borst turned his attention to the possemen searching the surrounding brush, to the possemen herding the Hashknife crew from the bunkhouse—such of the crew as occupied it, anyway. And Borst's lips curled as he watched and listened. And that which he listened for he wasn't long in hearing—the swift rata-plan of hard-hammering hoofs as Mendota and Phoenix John lay low along their hoses' necks in a dash to elude the shouting, swearing possemen who now came running for their broncs.

With a sudden twist of his heavy body Borst shook free of the pistol in Tranter's hand, threw himself back-ward and sent his lamp hurtling straight into the huddled group of snorting posse horses. The startled broncs yanked their reins from the grip of the men dele-gated to hold them and went scattering away in half a dozen different directions. That was the last thing Borst saw for a number of minutes, for just then Tranter brought the barrel of his gun down squarely on Borst's wide forehead and everything went black. Yet, even as he fell, Borst laughed.

Borst came back to reality with the knowledge that rough hands were jerking him to his feet, and that a rougher hand was slapping him across the face in a way that stung. He opened his eyes with a mounting rage and found Bill Dorne's face squarely in his vision. And Bill Dorne's face reflected an anger at least as great as his own. Recollection came then, and Borst laughed.

Dorne's blue eyes went cold and bleak. "That trick, Mister, is goin' to cost you something."

"Yeah?"

"You'll know it!" By light of the lantern held in Tranter's hand Borst could see that the sweat of some recent exertion had dried across Bill Dorne's rugged cheeks, gluing to them the powdery grit of alkali. And alkali grit was likewise plain along the edge of Dorne's red hair, where it showed beneath his shoved-back hat. Dorne's mouth was a straight white line.

"I don't have to be told who fired that shot, Pecos," Dorne said. "It was Mendota or the gent with him. I saw Mendota plain as he forked his nag. The other bird kep' his mug outa sight, but I'm bettin' strong it's Phoenix John. I'm tellin' you right now I'm gettin' out rewards for them two pronto; chargin' 'em with murder. An' as for you— "

"You ain't got a thing on me," Borst jeered.

"I got enough on you," Dorne came back, "to send you away to a place where you'll have plenty of time to think over the evil of yore ways."

"Wind!" scoffed Borst. "Bluster an' hot air, Bill. You ain't scarin' me worth a damn." And turning his shoulders toward where Tranter stood with the lantern, Borst added, "As for you, fella, you better hunt yoreself a hole an' pull it in after you. 'Cause any gent that swipes Pecos Borst over the head with a pistol is goin' to be made mighty hard to find."'

Tranter grinned. "What was that yuh said about hot air?"

Borst was standing on the veranda and he placed his back now against one of its roofs supporting columns. He had discerned several moments before that his holster was empty, so there was scant use in leaving his arms hang down or placing them akimbo— such a pose without a gun to back it up might be apt to seem ludicrous. Borst crossed his arms upon his chest and, though his heavy lids hid the expression of his eyes, they did nothing to lessen the steel-cold attention with which he eyed Bill Dorne and his ragged deputy. Apparently the rest of the posse had taken after

Mendota and Muroc as soon as they'd recovered their ponies. To test this theory, Borst observed:

"I suppose Mendota and Phoenix John made a clean getaway."

"You better quit supposin'," Dorne growled back; "it's gonna be bad for yore health—less'n you loosen up an' admit you been engineerin' this rustling."

Borst stood with his face turned toward the wastelands off beyond Buck Tranter. Out there all the desert seemed to run together in one pale sea of sand that was wonderfully softened by the argent glow of a horned moon. In the daytime, Borst was thinking, that land out there would be a veritable inferno of baking heat. But it offered refuge. . . .

He looked at Dorne. There was nothing, he reflected, that would please him better than the feel of his own big knuckles smashing against Bill Dorne's rugged chin. Unless it was Bill Dorne's vulturine nose crunching beneath those same knuckles. The desire ran through his mind like a white-hot iron.

But Borst fought it off. Though his eagerness to avenge himself on Dorne was tumultuous, he was determined to see his enterprises, his plans and hopes in, for and about this country crowned with success. Only by holding his temper, he knew, could he hope to see that happen. Bill Dorne might be kind of dumb, he mused, but Bill Dorne was an antagonist to whom no advantage whatever could be afforded. Caution, strategy and craft must be his watchwords. He had always boasted that he was a good waiter; this fight with Dorne should prove it.

Nothing could ever hold Borst back; nothing ever had and nothing ever would!

"Oh, I don't know," he said easily. "Knowing yore

cravin' for passing old saws, I expect you know the hairy one about there bein' many a slip . . . ? Might be applicable here. Worth a bit of thought, Bill. I ain't through in this country, yet. I'm still a big factor. How far do you think you'd get if you was to take me in, charged with rustlin' my neighbors' cattle?" And he smiled squarely into Dorne's flushing face.

"Not very far, mebbe," Dorne admitted with a scowl. "It's got so you just about own the courts, body an' soul. An' any jury a man'd be apt to pick, I reckon you'd have packed to the guards. Yeah, Pecos, I reckon you'd get off scot free. But I've got a sort of hankerin' to find out."

"You're wastin' yore time, Bill."

"I ain't convinced of that. I've swore to run you out or plant you, Pecos. An' I'm still aimin' to do one or the other. Like I suspected, this rustlin' business is a heap apt to miss fire if I try to ring you in as top screw. But, like I said, it's a matter open to argument, an' I reckon I'll give the thing a whirl."

Borst saw, as Dorne paused, the Sheriff's eyes upon him closely.

Dorne said across a tightening silence, "You've been this country's dawg with the brass collar long enough. There ain't been nothin' too ornery for you to touch, long as you could see a profit in it. Now, take this rustling business . . . I'm morally certain you're a rustler, Pecos. If not the king-pin, at least an egger-on and sharer-in-the-profits.

"Fact is, Pecos, I'm puttin' yore gun back in yore holster an' I'm callin' you a rustler to yore face. I'm callin' you a crawlin' Gila Monster—a thing what's lower than a snake's belly! *Now draw—if you got the guts!*"

Borst's fierce hate and rage flamed up like tow and sent the heated blood across his cheeks in a flood of color. The smoldering eyes below his high wide forehead filled with scintillating sparks, and the knuckles of his clenched fists gleamed white as snow.

But he did not draw. Nor did either hand make the fraction of a motion toward the holster beneath his open coat where Dorne had just deposited his gun. He could feel the weight of it against his hip, but he felt no inclination to reach for it. He hated Dorne with all the power of his warped soul, but he could not bring himself to match his draw with this cold-eyed reckless sheriff.

The silence lay across the veranda like a visible thing. It was filled with unuttered thoughts, one or two of which were contemptuously framed in words:

"Hell," sneered Tranter, "there ain't a grain of sand in the baboon's craw!"

Dorne said, "Borst, you're yaller as a mongrel pup!"

"Even a *rat*," Tranter added, "will put up a scrap when cornered."

"But Borst," Bill threw in, "ain't even got the gumption of a gnat."

Borst paled. But his resentful rage, like his hatred, was a thing that could be kept and added to. It was a thing equipped with an escape-valve of caution—and that caution was shrieking now in Borst's ears like the cry of a locomotive. He *knew* that if his hand touched the pistol in his holster now, the act would be his last.

"I can wait," he muttered thickly. "I can wait."

"Then here's somethin' for you to be thinkin' over

while you're doin' it," Dorne drawled. "This place is goin' to be confiscated by the law and auctioned off at Sheriff's sale. This an' every stick, stone an' steer carryin' yore brand. It's goin' to be auctioned off to pay back the people you've been robbin'. Savvy?"

Borst said nothing, but his glittering eyes were wild with venom.

"If that won't make you fight," Bill said, coldly contemptuous, "then nothin' will. We're goin' to town an' put you in a nice warm cell. Git movin'."

SEVENTEEN
THE WOMAN SCORNED

WHEN WILD BILL DORNE climbed out of the saddle by the pole corral out back of the express office, both his bronc and the horse Tranter was forking were lathered with sweat and beginning to blow. Both stood there on widely braced legs, heads down, while Bill and Tranter stripped their gear off and hung it on the corral's top pole.

"It sure is hell," Tranter observed, wiping the sweat from his forehead, "but yuh'd ort to have been more careful, Bill."

"Careful!" Dorne snorted. "I'd like to know how any gent coulda been any more careful than I was. I admit I was taken in by that sidewinder's meek an' humble actions. But I was watchin' him every minute."

"Almost," Tranter corrected with a grin. "You wa'n't watchin' him any more'n I was when he run that sandy on us. We gotta keep this dark—"

"We sure have," Dorne grunted. "The reputation of this office is at stake, Buck. Why, we'd be the laughin'-stock of the whole country if it ever got out Borst slid out right under our noses. We'll give out that I warned him outa the country an' he took the advice to heart an' left."

Tranter nodded dubiously. "Be all right if he really leaves, I reckon. But, yuh know, somehow I got the feelin' that vinegaroon ain't a-goin' to leave. Leastaways, not till be evens up the score fer all the hell you done raised. Cripes, you've knocked the props clean out from under his Number 12's—most of 'em, anyways. Nope, I wouldn't bank too high he's pulled his freight, Bill, was I you."

"I got that same damn feelin'," Bill admitted, with a sheepish grin. "Buck, that Borst pelican is a slippery customer."

"Slipp'rier'n calf slobbers," Tranter solemnly agreed. "An' plumb obstreperous. His craw-fishin' wa'n't foolin' me a mite."

"Me neither," Dorne said, and they both laughed. Dorne sobered quickly. "You go over to the printer's an' get him to run you off a bunch of fliers offerin' one thousan' bucks apiece for the apprehension of Pedro Mendota an' Phoenix John Muroc for the killin' of a deputy sheriff while in performance of his duty. Get their description on them han' bills, too. An' the word DANGEROUS in capital letters. Get him to put the reward in red, so's it'll show up an' attract attention. I want them two hellions bad. When you get through, you can hit the hay. . . . Oh, wait a sec! Better have him run off a handful of bills advertisin' a Sheriff sale of the Hashknife ranch property. Set the sale for . . . Let's see, today's Friday. Set the sale for Monday afternoon at 3 p.m."

Tranter nodded abstractedly. "Yore big mistake," he

said, swinging back to the late prisoner's escape, "was in givin' Borst back his hawg-laig. If he hadn't had that gun, he wouldn't 'a' had the nerve to make a break. I only hope he's got sense enough tuh clear out fer good—but I ain't believin' it," he added pessimistically.

Dorne, with an irritable grunt, headed for the office and Tranter, thus left alone, turned the horses into the corral, rubbed them down, and clumped off toward the printer's shop.

* * *

BILL DORNE STEPPED into the Sheriff's Office and stopped short. He had noticed when they'd ridden into town that the light was on, but hadn't given the fact much thought. He gave it some thought now. Lola was sitting on his desk, dangling her silk-clad legs and showing them to such good effect that he caught a blushing glance of her dimpled knees.

"I thought you were never going to come," she greeted him. "Where have you been all night?"

Dorne glanced at the battered clock on the top of the safe. Three-thirty. "You hadn't ought to have hung around here all this time," he said irritably. "Folks'll be gettin' ideas."

"What do you care. After we're married—"

"Married?" Dorne cut in. "Who said anything about gettin' married?"

"Why, I thought, after the other night . . ." She let the sentence trail off and held his glance while through the silence the ticking of the clock seemed uncommonly loud. In the deep green pools of her eyes he seemed to read a vibrant, slumbering passion that was reaching out for him, that was spreading to enmesh him. As always, he sensed about her a strange magnetism. It stirred him, but he did not lose his head. He did not love this girl, and knew it. And he had no intention of letting her get away with a fast one like this.

"What you thought," he told her, "ain't the point. I never said I was going to marry you, Lola. You knew the other night that I was engaged to Marcia. What are you tryin' to do, anyway?"

"Well, I'm not trying to high-pressure you, if that's what you mean," she said scornfully. "I don't have to ask any man to marry me! I wouldn't ask the best of them. I wouldn't need to," she added fiercely. "But after the way you acted the other night, and the way you talked, I naturally supposed—"

"Well, you supposed wrong," Bill told her flatly. "I'm goin' to marry Marcia Globe."

She came to him swiftly, stood before him looking up into his face. "There's something about you that changes people, Bill." Her red lips made a long wistful curve against the alabaster pallor of her face. "I've reformed; no more cards for me. No more dance halls and honky-tonks. I've quit Borst flat. An' all because of you.

"Oh, I know you never asked me to," she rushed on before he could interrupt. "I give you credit for that. You never *said* much of anything. It was just the way you said the few pleasantries you threw me, like some people throw a useless bone to a dog. It was just what I thought I read in your eyes when you looked down into mine. The way you held my hand; the tingles that went up and down me when you touched me. Just the nearness of you in the same room used to make me feel different—like I was being uplifted out of the muck of my profession. Like . . . Well, skip it Bill." The long yellow lashes fell across her lovely eyes and she stared at the floor while her head drooped a little forward as though she scanned the hopelessness of her position. Then her head lifted and she faced him bravely.

"It's all right, Bill," she said it softly, feelingly. "I understand. You've treated me swell. Like a lady. I wish to God I'd known you years ago. I—I might have been different."

Bill saw the moisture in her eyes. They were big and wide and dark. He started toward her with some vague impulse of comforting her.

But she waved him off. "I don't want any consolations, Bill. I—I couldn't stand it. Not after—not after the other night. Just let me keep my memories of that, Bill."

She turned at the door and faced him through her tears, one arm extended as though to ward him off. "Please don't, Bill. I'll—I'll be all right. Congratulations to—to you and Marcia. I don't know if it's acceptable from me, but I'm—I'm wishing you both all the luck. Good-bye, Bill."

* * *

FOR A LONG TIME after Lola had gone Bill stood there by the desk, his troubled glance vindictively upon the floor. What had he done? What had he said the other night to have made her feel like that? How could he have been such a fool as to have raised her hopes that way? How . . .?

Carefully, step by step as well as he could, he

retraced in his mind the events of that fateful night when he had walked with her beyond the edge of town.

He'd met her that night while making a round of the resorts with Tranter. She had come walking along the street through the crowds of hell-raising merry-makers. He'd suggested they take in the sights. She had seemed a bit reluctant, but had let him hold her hand. He couldn't see now why he had even wanted to hold her hand; he must have been kind of daffy in the head that night. Moon-struck, maybe. They had walked along in silence for a spell, not heading in any special direction, but sort of gravi-tating toward the edge of town. Bill couldn't remember now whether it had been he or she who had pointed their steps in that direction, but if it had been he, he decided grimly, he had ought to have been shot! After all, he was in love with Marcia Globe. Why in the devil had he ever suggested going for a walk with Lola? "It just goes to show," he muttered, "the crazy things a gent'll sometimes do when his mind's on somethin' else. If Marcia ever hears of this, she'll prob'ly nail my hide to the fence an' fill it full o' buck-shot! Don't know's I'd blame her much, at that."

It didn't seem noways possible that a grown man could be so foolish—yet there it was. He sure had been! It looked like some gents just had the Devil's own luck at getting into scrapes—out of one and into another!

Lola, after leaving Bill, quickly dried her tears, and the glint of a heady anger drove considerable of the loveliness from her jade-green eyes. She struck out across the road with a vicious swing of the hips, her determined stride swiftly eating up the interval between the Sheriff's Office and the Broken Harp saloon of Emanuel Venta.

There were not many patrons still inside when she pushed through the swinging doors. But Venta was there, as usual, behind the bar, and he greeted her with an unctuous smirk.

With a beckoning jerk of the head, that shook her golden curls, Lola headed straight for Venta's rear room and living quarters. It was a squalid, depressing place, but Lola was in neither the mood nor the interest to lavish attention upon unimportant trifles. Grabbing a dirty pillow off the rumpled bed, she mopped it across a chair and threw it aside. Sitting down she looked at the still-grinning Venta closely.

Her lips curled with contempt and loathing. "What in hell strikes you as being so funny?" she demanded coldly.

Venta's wiry form drew back a pace before the look that was in her eyes. But he did not lose his oily grin. "Yore man, he ees on the run," he chuckled. "Thees fella Dorne, she's pin the deadwood on heem."

"What are you talking about? Talk English, won't you? Who are you callin' 'my man'?"

"Pecos Borst," said Venta, and showed surprise. "Is eet not so?"

"Borst's a fool," she snapped. "I've broken with him. I'm on my own, now. An' I've got money," she added with soft suggestiveness. "Plenty dinero." She watched the glitter come into his little eyes and her red lips curled again.

"I've got a throat that's needing cutting. Are you up to it?"

"*Carramba!*" Venta muttered. "Whose throat is thees you are talk about, eh? Borst's? For all the dinero

in thees lousy town I would not fool weeth that one."
And he made fervent haste to cross himself.

"Pah!" Lola sneered, lighting a tailor-made cigarette
and inhaling deeply. "I thought you said Borst was
through."

"Well . . ." Venta shrugged. "It ees possible I am
make the mistake, señorita. Señor Borst, he has the w'at-
you-call' long arm.'"

"You can forget him. It isn't his throat I'm talking
about," she said shortly. "Do you know, or did you ever
hear of a fellow who calls himself Tumbleweed?"

Venta shook his head dubiously.

"It makes no difference. He's the one I'm talking
about. He fancies he's in love with me. In fact, it's his
notion that I've fallen for him. Well, I ain't. He's apt to
gum things up—I've got a deal on that's goin' to be prof-
itable if it's worked right. And I mean to see that it is."
She studied Venta appraisingly. "Now look," she said
confidentially. "You stop this Tumbleweed hombre's
clock an' I'll sweeten your pocket to the extent of five
hundred dollars—"

"One moment, señorita," Venta held up a hand.
"Who ees thees guy, Bumblesneed?".

"Tumbleweed," Lola corrected. "He fancies himself
something of a gun thrower. But you needn't worry
about him. I saw him shoot. He aimed at a fellow not
twenty feet away—and dropped the gent beside him!
He couldn't hit the broad side of a barn door. And,
anyway, if you're scared, there's nothin' to stop you
from bushwhacking him, is there?"

"Seex hondred dollars."

"What do you take me for? Do I look like a walkin'
gold mine?"

"You said you got dinero," Venta reminded. "Thees job, she's wort' seex hondred. Take eet or leave eet."

Lola counted out the money. "He'll probably be in town tonight. He's puttin' up a show of workin' for the Sheriff. He'll be in by daylight, sure. Your job's to see that he don't get out again. And," she finished grimly, "I'll be back after the balance of this money if you don't stop him permanent."

He watched the swing of her lithe figure as she moved to the door. But at the door she turned, "What," she asked casually, "would you say would be the proper time to call upon a lady?"

Venta blinked and stared at her curiously. "You goin' to keel a lady, too?"

"Don't be a fool! There's other ways of skinnin' a cat. What time?"

Venta scratched the black bristle that covered his head. "Mebbeso one hour after siesta, I'm think."

With a swish of her short silk skirt Lola wheeled and took her departure.

EIGHTEEN
STARTLING DISCLOSURES

BILL WAS STILL THERE, dozing at his desk, when Buck Tranter—refreshed with a shave and a good breakfast— arrived at seven o'clock with the bright sunshine pushing the long blue shadows across the warming range.

"Top o' the mornin'," Tranter grinned, getting out his evil-smelling pipe and packing it with tobacco from the sack he had dexterously lifted from Dorne's shirt pocket. "Got the troubles of Spavined Nag all ironed out?"

"Gents with beamin' faces don't agree with me before breakfast," Dorne growled, sitting up to yawn and stretch. "Cripes—who'd want to be a sheriff? I wish to hell I'd stuck to ranchin' like a civilized gent had ought to! This hazin' of other folks' problems is no sinecure. By gosh, I got troubles enough of my own."

"You shore look it," Tranter said, with a vast disregard of tact. "What did that Lola skirt want around here las' night? I seen her leavin'."

"She wanted," Bill said, scowling, "to warn me against hirin' nosey squirts like you."

"I wouldn't be surprised," said Tranter, puffing complacently. "She knows I got her number. It's a funny thing, Bill, but human naichure's like that—if a fella does somebody a meanness what somebody else knows about, he shore takes on a hate for the second somebody which, if it could be harnessed like a water-fall, would run all the dang mills in this yere country."

Bill stared at him grimly. Then, wheeling, he snapped, "Quit blowin' that dang smoke at me! Makes me smell like a ol' rotten cabbage!"

"Wal," Tranter grunted, "if yuh'd sit down fer a spell, 'stead o' waltzin' round like a hen on a hot griddle, this yere smoke would be able tuh git out the door."

"Aw—make a noise like a hoop an' roll away!"

Tranter looked him over curiously. "Seems like you're cloudin' up fer a squall. I'm allowin' you'll rare plumb outen yore trousers when yuh hear the latest."

Bill whirled. "What's happened now?"

"Bill, a fella was killed las' night—early this mornin', rather. There was a knife stuffed dang near out o' sight in his gullet!"

"Who?" There was impatience as well as irritation in Bill's single word.

"Guy that used tuh run the Broken Harp—Venta."

"Venta!" Bill snarled. "Who'd wanta knife that fool?"

"I don't know who'd wanta—but some gent sure did. Or," Tranter added thoughtfully, "mebbe it was a female. I seen that Lola dame tramp into Venta's place this mawnin'. It was right after she left here." And there was speculation in the glance he flipped at Dorne.

"Don't act no dumber than Nature made you. Why should Lola want Venta out of the way?"

"Couldn't say," Tranter shrugged. "That's yore problem—if yuh're int'rested." He smoked a moment in silence, then added, "She sure as hell went into the Broken Harp when she left you. Why should she go there, anyhow, since we're askin' questions?"

Bill had no answer for that. He would like to know himself.

"That skirt," Tranter offered, "is pow'ful easy on the eyes. But them's the kind that gits a gent in trouble. I've sweated round cowhands long enough tuh know that yuh can't never tell what fool thing'll appeal to a puncher as bein' a reasonable thing tuh do."

"Why," Bill growled, "don't you stick to one subject?"

"I am. The Lola dame."

"She didn't have nothin' to do with Venta's gettin' knifed, so get it out of yore thick head."

"Did she have anythin' tuh do with yore takin' a walk out past the aidge of town the other night?"

Bill swore, glared for a moment and went stamping out of the office. He was so mad and resentful and irritated with Tranter and everything else in general that he almost walked smack into a man heading for the office. He looked up with a muttered apology and saw that the man was Tumbleweed.

"Got some news fer yer," the scar-faced deputy said from the corner of his mouth. "In a hurry?"

"No," Bill grunted and, swinging into step beside him, headed back toward the office.

"Borst," Tumbleweed confided, "didn't know nothin' about them rustled cattle bein' on his range.

He was madder'n a hatter when one of the boys brought him word. Swore someone was out ter frame 'im."

Dorne stopped. He looked at Tumbleweed closely. "You sure of that?"

"Wal, I was there when the puncher brung the word."

Tumbleweed's seamed and sun-darkened countenance looked serious and candid. Dorne could not doubt that the man spoke the truth. This was putting things in a muddle, right, he thought. Surely no one else in this country would be loco enough to slap that Hashknife brand on other folk's cattle. And yet, if Tumbleweed had been on hand when the news had been brought Borst—

Shucks, he reflected. Tumbleweed might be speaking in good faith, and yet be mistaken. He said, "Well, that certainly puts a different complexion on a couple of things."

"I figgered it would; thought yer'd be wantin' ter know," Tumbleweed nodded. "An' by the way, a fella was stabbed here in town this mornin'. That guy what runs the Broken Harp. He—"

"I know about that," Bill growled. "I gotta go see about a inquest on him."

"Inquest?" Tumbleweed's voice had not raised much, but it had raised. "I didn't know the law held a inquest on a gent unless he was daid."

Dorne looked at him curiously as they resumed their way toward the office. When they reached the steps, Bill said, "It don't."

"But," muttered Tumbleweed as they stepped inside, "that fella ain't daid."

"Wal, he never admitted it, mebbe," Tranter grunted, "but we planted 'im jest the same."

Dorne looked from Tumbleweed to Tranter and back again. There was a startled expression on Tumbleweed's face. A sardonic leer curled Tranter's saturnine lips.

Tumbleweed snarled "Well, he wasn't—" and closed his mouth tightly on the rest.

"Says which?" Tranter grinned. "Don't be modest, now. Let's hear the rest o' that thought yuh was fittin' wings to."

But Tumbleweed stood there, morose and silent—alert.

Dorne said, "Tranter, what the hell did you want to bury that bird for before we held an inquest? Now he'll have to be dug up again!"

"What for? He was killed by a knife-wound, wa'n't he? What more do yuh hev tuh know?"

"We have to find out who killed him, of course. We—"

"Well, no inquest is gonna tell yuh that!"

Dorne smothered an oath. "Tumble tells me that Borst didn't know there was rustled cattle on his range—"

"Tumble tells a heap o' things besides his beads," Tranter snorted, and eyed his brother deputy with open contempt.

"Listen, you!" Tumbleweed growled. "Don't ride me too far less'n yer anxious ter step inter smoke!"

"Hell, you couldn't fog a winder pane in a thirty-below freeze!"

Dorne said, "Cut the wranglin' or I'll knock yore

heads together. This is a sheriff's office an' what we're discussin' is serious business."

"Then you better git some other hombre in place of this polecat Tranter," Tumbleweed said wickedly. "He's the bird that drove them stolen beeves onto Borst's range! I lay out on the rimrock an' watched him do it!"

Dorne whirled on Tranter with an oath.

"The skinny wart is right," Tranter chuckled, looking Bill squarely in the eye. "Fer onct he told the truth."

"You drove that rustled stock on Borst's range!" Dorne blazed. "What in hell did you think you was doin'? By cripes, I got a notion—"

"Save it then," Tranter sneered. "I drove them beeves onto Borst's range because they had Borst's brand on 'em —fresh over their original marks. Borst had 'em cached in a box-canyon what had a pole fence built across the open end. They was goin' onto his range, anyhow, eventually. What do yuh s'pose he had his waddies out there rebrandin' 'em for? I jest hazed 'em into the open a mite arly, is all, workin' on the theory 'eventually-why-not-now.' An' if this little sidewinder saw me do it, he must be in with Borst, 'cause that canyon was plumb concealed to the average eye an' the chances of him stumblin' acrost it by accident is plumb remote."

"You found it!" Tumbleweed snarled.

"Sure I found it. I was lookin' fer it, an' I'm a gent what knows his way around. I guess you was lookin' fer it, too!"

"Yeah. *AN' I WAS LOOKIN' WHEN YOU WAS HEATIN' UP YER BRANDIN' IRON!*"

"Why, yuh lousy, lyin' sidewinder!" Tranter's gun

was in his hand and the hammer was nearly full back when Dorne grabbed his wrist and forced the gun's muzzle toward the floor. Tranter abruptly yielded to superior opinion and relinquished the weapon. Bill put it on the desk out of reach.

"I don't know which of you birds to believe," he growled. "But one of you's lyin' sure. Question is, which?" And his cold stare went from one to the other angrily.

"Better can us both," Tranter suggested. "Then you'll have the double-crosser where he can't get into mischief fer a while."

Tumbleweed just glowered.

Bill said, "Tumble, you go on back to the Hashknife an' keep yore eyes peeled for a chance to rejoin Borst, if he's still in the country an' comes back to his spread for anythin'. I'll see you out there Monday afternoon. We're confiscatin' that property an' are goin' to auction it off at a sheriffs sale. If Borst comes back, you stick with him till you find a chance to get me word of his whereabouts without him gettin' suspicious. Get goin' before you an' Tranter get to throwin' lead."

And, as Tumbleweed started for the door, Bill said to Tranter, "You come along with me. I'm goin' to look into this Venta killin'. An' I better not find you did it because he had it comin' to him and would have got it anyway sooner or later!"

Tranter's scowl dissolved into a sheepish grin. "I thought that was a cute trick I played on Borst. After all, the big lobo was havin' his men rebrand 'em. They was stolen critters. They—"

"Skip it," Bill said curtly. "I heard enough about them steers."

* * *

FROM THE CORONER, Bill learned that what Tranter had told him about Venta's stabbing was true. There was one knife thrust, or rather, wound, in Venta's body, the coroner said. No other marks of violence. And the knife had been in the wound when he and Tranter, summoned by one of the Broken Harp bartenders, had first examined him.

Bill thanked him and, followed by Tranter, turned his steps toward the Broken Harp. At this time in the morning no one was in the place save a sleepy-eyed barman and a slow-motion swamper.

Bill eyed the bartender coldly. "You the bird that found Venta?"

The barman nodded, surly.

"What time?"

"'Bout 4 o'clock this mornin'."

"Where?"

"In the back room."

"Elucidate," Bill snapped. "Where was he layin'? Or wasn't he?"

"He was layin' on his back with a knife stickin' out of his chest an' blood all over," the bartender said uneasily, his shifty glance traveling from Bill to Tranter and back again. "Yuh needn't look at me like that," he blurted. "I didn't kill 'im!"

"Nobody's accusin' you of killin' him. Who was in the room with him?"

"A skinny gent with a knife-scar along the left side of his face from chin to ear. I seen him around before, once or twicet. But I don't know who he is. Some stranger. He's got a mean look an' a pair of pale eyes that are enough to give a gent the creeps."

"Tumbleweed—sure as I been weaned a week!" Tranter ejaculated joyously. "I tol yuh that scorpion was a wrong 'un! I can spot 'em every time! Wisht tuh heck I could recollect where I seen his mug before."

Bill Dorne's face was a study. It was hard for him to believe that Tumbleweed could have stabbed Venta. Yet the implication was plain as the nose on Tranter's face.

"But Tumble's a trigger man," Bill muttered weakly.

"He's a guy which uses whatever's handiest at the time he wants tuh use it," Tranter said emphatically. "You slipped, Bill, when yuh made that bird a depity. Why don'tcha admit it? The guy's crooked as a dawg's hind laig!"

But Bill was loyal. "I gotta see it proved," he declared. "I'm bettin' Tumble will have a explanation—"

"Sure he will! He'd be a fool if he didn't," Tranter scoffed. "An' whatever else he is he ain't no fool. Why don't yuh look up his references? Why don't yuh drop a line tuh them places where he says he's worked? Find out what they know about him. Cripes, fer all you know, he mebbe murdered the las' guy he worked for an'—"

"Why don't you give that imagination of yores a rest?" Bill growled irritably. "You'll be wearin' the damn' thing out!" He swung his fighter's broad tapering shoulders toward the bartender squarely. "How long was this fella back there with Venta? You remember?"

"'Bout ten minutes—mebbe less."

"How do you place the time so close?"

"Well," the fellow rasped his chin, looked at Bill

uncertainly, blinked and shifted his feet uneasily. His mouth was partly open, but he didn't look as though he contemplated saying any more.

Bill's narrowed eyes took on a steely glint. He took a forward step with a grimness that drove the other back. "You talk, by gosh, or I'll scatter yore dad-blamed teeth all over this place!"

"But—but," the man stammered, "if I say what I got in my mind you'll be apt to put the wrong interp—"

"You say it an' let me be the judge of the way to take it," Bill grunted coldly. "How did you fix that time so accurate?"

"You're askin' fer it," the bartender said. "I know this hombre was in the back room with Venta because jest after they went back there a dame come in here lookin' for Venta, an'—"

"*What dame?*"

"Lola—the gal that used to work for Borst."

NINETEEN
VILLAINY AFOOT

BILL DORNE'S pugnacious underlip thrust grimly forward in the drive of his rising passion. The gathering violence in him could be seen definitely in the bulging muscles along his jaw and the tautness of the cords in his flushing neck.

The bartender gave back a few uncertain steps, paling visibly, one hand lifted before him as though to ward off an expected blow.

And, indeed, Bill's expression gave cause for such alarm. Bill snarled, "I got no special interest in Lola; get that straight. *But*—I don't never stand by an' twiddle my fingers when a good woman's name is slandered, be she a dance hall girl, a waitress or the President's wife! *Get me?*" "Nobody's slanderin' her," the barman said with shaking lips. "An' if it sounded like a slur to you, I'm apologizin'. No slur was meant."

Most of the anger washed from Bill's cheeks and a cold contempt replaced it. "You sure crawfish graceful," he drawled scathingly.

"You didn't give me time to finish what I was tellin'

yuh when you jumped me," the barman protested. "Hell, Sheriff, I wasn't figurin' to slander Lola. Nor any other girl. I was tellin' you about Venta—"

"Well, get on with it," Bill growled coldly.

"I fixed the time," the man resumed with a faint tinge of resentment coloring the pallor of his face, "on account of Lola comin' in right after him an' likewise wantin' to habla with Venta. She seemed some impatient. Kept pacin' the floor like she had somethin' on her mind. An' I reckon she did have. 'Cause after eight or ten minutes, she mutters somethin' under her breath an' starts fer the door of that there back room," and he flung his arm out toward it in a dramatic gesture that would have done credit to a first-rate Shakespearean.

Bill and Tranter looking duly impressed, he went on:

"I says, 'Yuh better not go in there till that other gent comes out. Venta give me orders he wasn't to be interrupted.' But she gives me a sour look an' keeps right on waltzin' towards the back room. 'My business,' she says, 'is jest as important as anybody's. I want to see Venta pronto—an' I'm goin' to.'

"She grabs the handle an' yanks the door open real determined, an' goes on inside—"

Bill growled, "How many people was in here when she done all this?"

"Nobody," the barman said, "'ceptin' me an' her. Venta had thrown the last drunk out half an hour before. He was closin' up for the night."

"I told him to close this joint at two," Bill drawled. "If he'd 'a' done it he'd be alive this minute instead of bein' six feet under the sod."

The barman nodded. "I reckon there ain't no doubt

about that. It goes to show that it's a heap healthier to obey the law," he said, and scowled at Tranter's sardonic grin. "Well, to git on with the story—Lola opens the door to Venta's private room an' goes on in. Seems like I heard a start, but I couldn't swear to it. Anyhow, a coupla moments later she lets out a squawk an' comes outa there like she'd seen a ghost. Cripes, her face was whiter'n a frog's belly!"

He paused to be sure his audience was getting the full measure of appreciation from his oratory. Then he said in an awful whisper, "She tells me Venta's sprawled on his back inside there with a knife buried in his guts!"

"It was in his chest," Tranter said.

The barman scowled. "Who's tellin' this story? You, or me? . . . Well, then, let me tell it. *She said* it was buried in his guts!"

"What did you do?" Bill asked.

"I took a look an' sure enough it was like she said, only the knife was in his chest," he shot a scowl at Tranter. "Soon's I saw what was up, I dashed out into the street, figgerin' to rush for yore office. But there was Tranter goin' by, so I yells at him an' he sent me to get the coroner."

Bill looked at Tranter. "Where's the knife?"

"Coroner's got it," Tranter grunted, and getting out his battered pipe, lifted the barman's sack of Durham and filled the blackened bowl.

The barman kept his mouth shut, but his looks were plenty significant. They became more so when Tranter put the sack in his pants pocket and, lighting his pipe, went strolling toward the bat-wing doors.

"Thanks," Bill muttered, and followed Tranter out.

On their way back toward the Sheriff's Office, Bill said, "This sure is a mess."

"A helluva situation an' no mistake," Tranter agreed equably. "You goin' to write them letters?"

"What letters?"

"Them letters to the Box o B an' Deer Lodge—where Tumbleweed, the damn' liar, says he used to work."

"Well, it's an idea," Bill admitted. "Mebbe I better wire them places. If Tumble's crooked, like you think, the sooner we find it out the better for all concerned."

"Yeah—the better fer us, anyhow. Let's go wire 'em now."

The wires sent, with a request for speedy answers, Bill said to Tranter,

"Tell you what, Buck. This is a durn good time to hunt up them Wineglass two-year-olds that was rustled three-four days ago. Let's get our hawsses."

"Where you figgerin' tuh hunt?"

"Thought we might cull through some of that rustled stock you drove onto Borst's range the night before last.

That was a dumb stunt you pulled. If you'd left the critters where you found 'em an' come in an' told me, we could have nailed his hide—"

"We could of et beans, too," Tranter scoffed. "D'you think with that scurvy Tumbleweed atop the rimrock, they'd have been there when we got back?"

"But you didn't know he was up there."

"The hell I didn't! I didn't know it was *him*—but I knew someone was there. I seen the glint of his rifle. I was expectin' the bite of its lead, too, I can tell you. I had a bad few minutes gettin' them critters outen that dang box-canyon. An' a lot of thanks I got fer doin' it!"

"Did you expect me to kiss you?" Dorne snorted.

"Well, I've been kissed by better lookin' speciments than you! C'mon, le's get the nags an' be on our way before I git mad an' tell yuh where tuh stuff this job."

* * *

"HOOT OWL" Polsky, Globe's Wineglass foreman, dismounted in a shallow draw shaded by cottonwoods and, leaving his mount on trailing reins where it was concealed by the dusty foliage, placed his back against a cottonwood's bole and rolled himself a brown-paper cigarette.

The golden ball of Apollo had long since dipped behind the serrated crests of the purple western mountains when at last Polsky, looking across the miles of yellow earth, beheld a horseman cantering out upon the trail from the distant pass.

Polsky heaved a sigh, pinched out his cigarette and stowed the butt carefully in his pocket. Then he got to his feet and stretched. He would soon be getting back to the outfit. The cook would likely do a tolerable amount of grumbling, but would eventually produce a tardy supper for him. Polsky heaved another sigh and smacked his lips in anticipation. Riding the Spavined Nag Range was one sure way of working up an appetite, he reflected.

He could hear the distant horse's hoofs now, faintly. In a few minutes the rider would enter this draw. Polsky loosened his gunbelt a notch so that it would sag his holster at a handier angle. He examined his gun to make sure the mechanism was free of grit. When he shoved the weapon back in its sheath, his features looked as smoothly inscrutable as those of a Chinese gambler.

Five minutes later Tumbleweed dismounted in the cottonwood grove and nodded to Polsky curtly. There was no sign of his usual slurred dialect when he spoke; his words were clipped and terse:

"What did you find out?"

"The bulk of the Wineglass' marketable beef will be held tonight at Keystone Canyon and a heavy guard set over 'em to make sure they ain't got away with by Borst's rustlers," Polsky said, and watched the other alertly.

"Have you contacted Krayson or Harniss?"

"No. I couldn't get at 'em. They've definitely swung to Borst."

Tumbleweed scowled, then shrugged. "All right. Let 'em go. Where's Globe?"

Polsky eyed Tumbleweed curiously; but nothing was to be read from that ugly, sneering countenance. Nothing ever had, Polsky reflected bitterly. It was no cinch, he thought, working for a man who kept a fellow as much in the dark as Tumbleweed kept him. Who was this Tumbleweed hombre? It was a thing he'd often wondered in the last eight months since Tumbleweed had contacted him and offered to get him a job as foreman on the Wineglass outfit, in exchange for a little information occasionally. It struck Polsky now as he looked at his companion, that he would not have to go far to put his hand on the brains of Borst's rustling gang.

He was wrong, but he never found it out.

"Where's Globe?" Tumbleweed repeated.

"In town—but he sent out word he'd be at the ranch tonight." Polksy ran his tongue across his lips, squared his shoulders in such a way that his hand, hooked in his gunbelt, was close to his holstered weapon. Then he said suggestively, "Be interestin' to know what you've got on Globe. Or against him."

"Do you think so?" Tumbleweed's voice was soft, and the knife-scar that ran from chin to ear along the left side of his face began to glow.

But Polsky had figured his chances and was determined to carry his plan through. He had never seen Tumbleweed draw, but he had a pretty good notion that Tumbleweed was two-thirds bluff and the other third hard looks. But he wasn't taking any chances; his hand was so close to his gun that he could flip it free of leather with a single flick of the wrist. And he aimed to do so if Tumbleweed gave indication that he was going to act up.

"Think so?" he jeered. "Hell—I *know* so! In fact, fella, I know enough about yore game to know I'm bein' damn well took advantage of. I want more money. In the future an' for the past. An' I'm wantin' my back pay right damn now!"

"Shucks," Tumbleweed murmured easily. "You don't need no money."

"You think not?"

"No," Tumbleweed grinned: "They don't use money where you're goin'," and shot him through the heart.

There was a hunted, haunted light in Lola's jade-green eyes as she walked toward Globe's town residence through the blazing heat of the midday sun. The air was scorching, breathless, yet she did not seem to notice. Nor did she feel the blistering heat of the sand as she crossed the road to avoid a group of freighters who were unloading barrels of whisky before the Black Bottle Bar. Her mind was absorbed with a scene she could not thrust from her memory—the picture of Venta writhing and groaning on the floor, and of herself bending over him and thrusting home that knife protruding from his chest, and of the spurting blood and the awful terror in his eyes. But the eyes and the blood were far the worst; she could see the bulging whites of them now—they had followed her all morning, no matter where she went or what she did. Not for an instant had they vanished, and their curse was just as potent now as when she'd driven home that blade. And the blood—Gawd! she could feel it on her fingers now!

Why had she ever touched that blade? Why had she ever let herself kill that murdering bravo? Why—

But she knew. She had seen him lying there and the thought had flashed through her instantly that he' had failed in the task she set for him. He had been alive, though—conscious! If he hadn't talked already, he would as soon as he got . . . And then some tiny inner voice had whispered— *"Kill him, you fool! Dead men do not talk! Tumbleweed can wring no confession from a stiff!"* And she stooped and thrust the knife in deep and turned it. *Ugh!* That blood! And the curse in those bulging, dying eyes!

She hurried her steps unconsciously, keeping pace with her turbulent thoughts. Her fear of Venta talking had been born of panic. She realized it now. If Venta had intended talking he must have talked before she'd found him. He'd been dying then. She'd been a fool to put her hand to steel already buried!

And even if he'd lasted long enough to tell the law how he'd come to such an untimely end, who would have believed him? Not Dorne, surely! Dorne was not even aware she was acquainted with Tumbleweed. Dorne could have found no motive, no incentive for her to have hired a man to do away with Tumbleweed.

"Damn Tumbleweed!" she muttered, and cursed the night their paths had crossed.

She could not think how Tumbleweed had conceived of Venta's intention in time to turn the tables as he had done so neatly. Venta must have blundered.

She looked up to see the Globe gate in front of her. By sheer willpower she composed her features, unlatched the gate and walked to the veranda, went up the steps and knocked with a steady hand upon the door. The same hand from which this morning she had scrubbed the sticky blood. It had been pure luck, she thought, that the pale-faced bartender had not noticed that reddened hand.

From the interior of the house she could hear light footsteps coming toward the door. And then Marcia stood there before her. The delicate, pretty features of the Mayor's daughter reflected wonder and curiosity as she realized her visitor's identity.

"Could I come in a moment?" Lola asked in a husky voice that seemed to catch deep down in rounded ivory throat. "I—it's—it's about the Sheriff. About Bill Dorne. I—I just had to see you. I—I knew you'd understand."

Wonderingly, a trifle frightened, too, Marcia held open the door.

"ON THE ORDERS OF PECOS BORST!"

"WELL," said Tranter, as he and Dorne turned their horses' heads toward town, "that's shore that."

"It sure is," Dorne said, turning up his collar against the chill wind sweeping up off the range now that the sun was down. "It most usually is, in fact. We've got Pecos Borst dead to rights. There's only one thing, now we've found Globe's missin' two-year-olds with the Hashknife brand blotched over the Wineglass, that could be a bigger card to our hand. An' that's for you or me to see Friend Pecos with a runnin' iron in hand kneelin' over a tied-up dogie."

"Some gents," said Tranter drily, "wouldn't be satisfied with a castle, less'n they had a picket fence built roun' it—an' then they'd prob'ly yowl about the color of the paint!"

Bill snorted.

"What kinda knife was that blade that was used to boost Venta into the Happy Hunting Grounds?"

"Jest a ord'nary bone-handled bowie. Won't do yuh no good tuh look at it. Looks jest the same as forty thousan' others. Every sheep herder an' his brother totes one of 'em. Some Mexicans I've met, packs two. Down in Arkansaw they make 'em out of ol' rasps. They're wicked weapons, all right, but dang few of' em has distinguishin' marks. This one shore ain't anyhow."

"Gettin' back to the matter of Venta's death," Dorne cut in, "why do you reckon the fella used a Arkansas toothpick on him? Reckon he had some special reason?"

"I opine he figgered to use the first thin' he clapped hand to," Tranter said. "Or else he heard the ol' saw 'bout silence bein' golden an'—" He broke off to eye Bill searchingly. "Yuh know, the more I think about it, the more I'm inclined tuh place my bets on either that skinny Tumbleweed jasper or that Lola skirt as bein' the most likely candidate for—"

"Leave the girl out of it," Bill growled brusquely. "She couldn't have no motive. And as for Tumble—"

"*Say!*" Tranter broke in wide-eyed. "I jest recollected where I seen that skinny gopher before! I was pawin' through that drawer of ol' reward notices in yore desk the other day. There's a picture in there what fits that pelican like a glove! Cripes, you wait an' see! Them places yuh wired won't know a thing about him!"

Tranter was wrong—but not very.

Lola, from her seat in Mayor Frank Globe's most comfortable rocker, eyed Marcia where she stood beside the center table with one hand caught to her breast and the other holding to the edge of the table as though for support. Why, Lola wondered contemptuously, should Bill Dorne prefer this girl instead of herself? What had Marcia Globe to offer a man like Bill that she had not?

Looks? To be sure, Marcia was pretty in a dark, brunette way, Lola admitted grudgingly. She seemed very feminine with her dark black hair tied in a loose knot back of her neck, and her gingham dress and her eyes— deep brown pools these latter were. But her nose! Lola's red lips curled. What man would be fool enough to prefer a snub nose, with freckles marching across its bridge, to a straight and slender patrician affair like her own? No, she decided, it couldn't be looks, for she knew —her glass had told her many times—that she was far the better looking of the two.

What was it then? Was it because Marcia was the Mayor's daughter while she was the ex-faro dealer of Borst's late Golden Stack? Could *that* be it? Little fires sprang up in the depths of her jade-green eyes. But she quickly veiled them with her lashes. This little fool might have a bit more perception than one would think. It was best to take no chances.

Lola hid her hate behind a mask of sadness, a mask displaying shame and humiliation and other things less easily definable, as well. Her voice came huskily when she spoke and there was a moist brightness to her eyes that surely, she thought, the little fool could see.

Marcia did see. "Why you're crying!" she said, drawing closer with a ready sympathy. She knew the sort of woman Lola was—one could hardly help it in a town of this size. But she stifled her natural repugnance in the fullness of her generosity. Lola was a girl in trouble; she had come to her for help, perhaps advice. She must be looking on Marcia as a possible Good Samaritan—or a beacon light shining whitely through this wilderness of sin.

Marcia's thoughts were growing complex. She shook free of them. This woman was here for help or guidance. And she should have it, if it lay within Marcia's power to help.

Her arms went round Lola comfortingly, reassuringly, protectingly, as she knelt beside her on the carpeted floor. "You poor girl," Marcia's words were soft with sympathy. "You poor, poor girl. Will it make things easier for you if you tell me about it? Maybe I can help. Maybe—"

"Oh, you don't know, Miss!" Lola said burying her face against Marcia's shoulder, and allowing her own shoulders to shake convulsively. She was a good actress and she knew her part and lines. She proved it when she raised a tear-stained face to Marcia's and moaned. "You think I'm a bad woman—Oh, I know you do! You think I live in sin and—Oh, you'll never believe me when I say I've always been good, even if I never had a decent chance in life. You won't believe me when I tell you that I never let a—that I never did a—that—that—" she floundered hopelessly, gulped, and bravely finished, "That I'm going to have a baby and it's not my fault." And she looked at Marcia piteously, with her lovely eyes all blurred and red.

Marcia looked a little shocked, but she was all compassion, sympathy. She hugged Lola to her closely and sort of rocked her as a mother might a sick or frightened child. She spoke soft soothing words until the paroxysms and the sobs that came from Lola ceased.

She patted Lola's shoulder and cried a bit herself.

But presently Lola wailed, albeit softly, "Oh, what shall I do? What *can* I do? How will I ever hold up my head again?"

"Now," whispered Marcia soothingly, "everything

will come out all right. All things happen for the best; believe it. God is just—"

"No he isn't!" Lola panted fiercely, between her tears. "What did I ever do to deserve this? *I*, who always lived by the Golden Rule and never harmed anybody? Why, do you know—that lousy Borst flung me out of his place before Bill—before Sheriff Dorne burned it down because I wouldn't use marked cards to cheat people out of their hard-earned money! Threw me out like an old shoe! And knowing I couldn't get a job and was going to have a—"

"Did—is—is the baby his?" Marcia stammered hastily, her cheeks scarlet.

"No," Lola said emphatically. Then huskily, "But I'll never tell who its father is—I never will! If Bill don't want—Oh!" she caught a hand to her lips and looked at Marcia wildly.

She had not needed to worry about Marcia's perceptions. She knew it now when she felt Marcia's form grow stiff and saw the startled pallor that washed the color from Marcia's cheeks and widened her eyes incredulously. She felt Marcia's fingers digging into her arms cruelly. "Did—you say 'Bill'?"

"I won't tell!" Lola sobbed. "I won't! I won't! You've got no right to ask me things like that!"

"If you're talking about—" Marcia bit the disloyal words off swiftly. But there was a light of determination in the brown glance she sent to Lola's face. "You'll have to tell me who this man is," she said quietly, insistently. "I've got to know. I've got a special reason for wanting to know. I—"

"Well, I ain't going to tell you!" Lola flashed. "Don't

you think I've got some pride? Just because I've worked in a gambling dive, you needn't think I—"

"Tell me!" Marcia was firm. "I'll help you all I can, but you've got to tell me this Bill's full name. Can't you see you've got to? How can I help you unless you tell me—"

"I ain't going to!" Lola said doggedly. "I—I guess I came to the wrong place after all. I might have known —" she let the sentence trail off and made as though to rise. But Marcia was too quick for her, as Lola hoped she'd be.

"No," Marcia said. "You're not going until you tell me that man's last name. Bill what?"

"Bill Dorne—if you've got to know!" Lola flared with curling lips. "I hate him!" I don't know why I should protect his good name; he didn't give a damn about mine! Bill Dorne—that's who he is!"

Marcia slowly, automatically, straightened to her feet. Her cheeks had gone deathly pale and all the light and laughter that had been in her when she had answered the door to Lola's knock was gone from her. There was a dead, vacant look to her eyes and she shivered slightly as she stood there with her hands at her breast.

"Bill Dorne," she whispered huskily. "My Bill!"

She was looking at Lola, but she did not seem to see her. She seemed to be seeing something crumble and wither inside her soul.

Looking at her, Lola felt a moment of remorse But she stifled it instantly at the thought of Bill. Bill was her man; she wanted him and she was going to have him—cost what it might to others!

She got to her feet, remembering that she must not

forget her role. She looked at Marcia as though uncertainly. "What did you say, Miss?"

"Nothing," Marcia answered dully; "nothing that matters, now. I guess perhaps you were right. You'd better go."

And as Lola tiptoed from the room she heard Marcia sink heavily to a chair and her lips curled contemptuously. "Serves her right, the stuck-up hussy!" she said viciously beneath her breath.

* * *

"WHERE DO YUH RECKON MENDOTA AN' that gamblin' Phoenix John lit out to?" Tranter asked, as he and Dorne came jogging into town. The dusty road was dappled with bars of light from the open doors and windows, and sounds of Spavined Nag's eternal night life blared from the saloons and honkytonks they passed. "Yuh reckon they've left the country?"

"I hope so," Bill said wearily, "but I doubt it. No such luck. I allow this business will have to be fought out to a finish, Buck. I reckon you was right when you said Borst wasn't the quittin' kind. I've sorta got a hunch we're goin' to be hearin' from him again. I only hope I can get my hands on him before he—"

"Shucks," Tranter cut in, "I allow yuh'll get yore hands on him—eventshully. Course he might stick up the bank again an' two-three other meannesses, but— Say! Ain't that the coroner coming'?"

Tranter's eyes were good, keened no doubt by many a midnight ride along the owl-hoot trail. The coroner was coming toward them out of the shadowy lane that led to his establishment some distance back from the street. There was another man with him, who looked to Bill like Gospel Jones. And so it proved to be.

The coroner and the parson came up to where Dorne and Tranter sat their dusty broncs. The coroner flourished a paper; thrust it triumphantly at Dorne. "I've pegged yore bank-robbers, Bill," he panted. "Got a signed confession—read it!"

"It'll keep," Bill said, and thrust the paper in his pocket. "Who are they?"

"An' how'd yuh git the confeshun?" Tranter echoed.

Gospel Jones cleared his throat. "Well," he said apologetically, "we maybe overstepped our authority a bit, but we led Joe Fuddabaugh to believe his condition had taken a turn for the worse. Fact is, I hinted he was dyin' an' had better make his peace before 'twas too late. He got some scared, what with that brimstone sermon I up an' preached him, an' the coroner here took down his statement."

"Yeah," Dorne growled impatiently, "but who robbed the bank?"

"Him," the coroner squeaked. "Him an' his pardner, Smoky Leupp, on the orders of Pecos Borst, an' aided an' abetted by Banker Fisk!"

TWENTY-ONE
ACTION!

WELL, Bill reflected sardonically, now he knew. But like most knowledge, when one has it, it didn't do him any considerable amount of good. Joe Fuddabaugh would not busy himself in robbing any more banks for quite some while, for in that gun battle before the burning of the Golden Stack Joe had absorbed a tolerable amount of lead, and Smoky Leupp had quit the business for good.

Giving orders that Joe should be removed to the jail as soon as he had convalesced past the danger point, Bill grunted a "Come on," at Tranter and, kicking his horse in the ribs, moved on down the street in the direction of the telegraph office, an installation of the express company and uncommon handy in these days of turbulence.

"Ain't but one woeful wire come in for the Sheriff's Office," the telegraph operator grinned, when he saw his visitors. "Here y'are Mr. Dorne," he added, and passed Bill a yellow envelope which Bill ripped open pronto, and from which he swiftly extracted a folded yellow paper. Spreading it out, he saw it was the answer to his wire to the Box o B at Salty Crick, Nevada.

NO TUMBLEWEEDS EVER COME ROLLING ONTO THIS SPREAD STOP NOR ANY GENTS ANSWERING YOUR DESCRIPTION STOP RECKON YOU MUST HAVE THE WRONG OUTFIT OR WRONG SALTY CRICK STOP TRAVIS

Bill read and swore disgustedly. And Tranter, reading over Bill's shoulder, chuckled openly and with apparent gusto. "What'd I tell yuh? I knowed that jasper was crooked soon's I set eyes on 'im!"

The telegraph operator cut Dorne's disgusted snort in two by saying brightly:

"By the way, Sheriff; that wire was sent collect. You owe this office—"

"Never mind," Bill grunted. "You charge it to the county. Bills payable at the end of the month." He broke off as the operator listened to the clacking of his instrument and scrawled hurriedly on a sheet of yellow paper with his left hand. When the instrument quit clicking, he shoved the paper toward Dorne.

"This 'un's paid for. It's from the penitentiary at Deer Lodge."

Bill stared at the note the operator had so hurriedly scribbled; stared again and scowled. "Hell!" he growled, and passed the form to Tranter. Tranter read:

SHERIFFS OFFICE
SPAVINED NAG ARIZONA:

RE YOUR QUERY STOP DESCRIPTION FITS
NO 875649 TEN SPOT TRULL SENTENCED
TO TWENTY YEARS IMPRISONMENT
SECOND DEGREE MURDER WIFE STOP
TERM STILL HAD FOUR YEARS TO GO
WHEN TRULL BROKE JAIL MARCH 16
STOP TRULL STILL AT LARGE STOP
CHECK DESCRIPTION REWARD NOTICE
OF THAT DATE STOP S2500 REWARD

    ED LATHAM,
    WARDEN: DEER LODGE.

"You rush over to the printer's right away," Bill growled. "Get him to run you off a smear of handbills offerin' 2,500 bucks for capture of Tumbleweed, alias Ten Spot Trull, gambler and gunman, DEAD OR ALIVE! Give 'im Tumble's description an' see that he gits it on in big letters. See that he gets 'em distributed right away an'—"

"Cripes," Tranter interrupted. "He won't distribute 'em or do a dang thing with 'em once he runs 'em off! I can tell yuh that—"

"Don't tell me a thing," Dorne snapped curtly. "*I'm* telling *you!* You tell him I got somethin' more important for you to do an' that I'll make it right with him on payday. Also, while you're over there, see that he gets out some notices on Fisk an' Borst, connectin' 'em with that damn bank robbery! *Now git!*"

"What am I supposed to do after that?"

"You come to the Sheriff's Office an' find out!" Bill growled, and headed for that place himself with long ground-eating strides. Over his shoulder he added, "An' take my horse with you. Leave it at the livery with yore own, an' get us a coupla fresh broncs."

"Don't tell me we're goin' tuh do some more damn ridin' at this late hour!" Tranter bellowed.

Dorne strode off without bothering to answer. When a gent worked for the Sheriff's Office, as he himself was finding out, he worked *all* the time! There were no *ifs* or *buts* about it!

Dorne was anxious to take a look at that reward notice mentioned by Tranter as being among that faded pile in his desk drawer. He wondered if it was the same referred to by the Deer Lodge Warden. In an effort to save time, Dorne cut down a dark lane and angled toward a darker alley—the latter running between the Black Bottle Bar and the Cherokee House next door. This alley would lead him to the dusty main street directly across from his office.

His mind was not idle as he strode savagely through the thick murk.

"'Workin' for the government!'" he snorted, recalling Tumbleweed's statement in connection with Deer Lodge. "I'll say he was—makin' little ones outa big ones, I allow! The dang skunk! An' he used to be a gambler—must've been, with a monicker like that. Murdered his wife, did he? Tranter sure was right in callin' him a scorpion an' all them other choice adjectives. I could add a few myself!"

Dorne was as much resentful at the manner in which he'd been taken in on his own snap judgement of Tumbleweed as he was at the fact that the fellow was an escaped convict who had murdered his wife. In fact, he was more resentful about the former, being that his code said that a man's personal affairs were his own and the concern of nobody else.

Had he been in a normal state of mind instead of a seething chaos of disconnected thoughts and conjectures, he never would have entered that murky alleyway that ran alongside of Ortega's Black Bottle Bar, knowing as he did the fellow was a minor ally of Borst, and hated the Sheriff on his own account because of Dorne's enforcement of the early closing hour ordinance. But he was too busy with his thoughts just now to give a damn where he was going, just so it got him to the office in the least possible time. There was plenty of work to be done tonight, and now that he had a few leads to follow he was in a high sweat to accomplish a few things.

His mind *did* swing to Marcia Globe for a moment, and he resolved to go and see her at the earliest opportunity. He sure had been neglecting her the last couple of days. "Heck of a way for a prospective bridegroom to be actin'!" he grunted. And just then there was a sibilant *swish!*

Dorne's reflexes were set on a hair-trigger. He ducked instantly, throwing himself sideways toward the window from which that *swish* had come, and the rope's loop that had been meant for his neck' slid harmlessly past his drooping shoulders.

He could not see a thing in the black opening of that window, but he reached right in just the same—with both hands. And got himself a grip on something soft and yielding. He grabbed hard, twisted and yanked. He knew he had the wielder of the rope and as he yanked a snarled oath confirmed his knowledge. The next moment he had the sly roper out in the alley. His flailing fists gave the roper no time to reach for a gun, but slammed out hard and fast. Dust rose in ballooning clouds. Grunts and panted oaths from his adversary, who didn't seem to be landing many hard ones, filled the air. But Bill went right on with his work. What he did might best be described as the swiftest, slickest, and most effective and thorough ladling out of justice that Spavined Nag had ever seen ladled! It was a pity, Bill reflected between punches, that a few of the town's tough citizens weren't at hand. But he didn't let that cramp his style. When the fellow sagged, Bill straightened him; when the fellow dropped, Bill picked him up and knocked him down again. When he was through, and he only quit for lack of breath, he got a grip on the fellow's collar and dragged him out of the alley and into the street where the lights from the roaring honkytonks showed that the roper was Señor Ortega himself. Though even his mother would probably have been hard put to have recognized him now.

Bill dragged him to a watering trough and doused his head in three or four times. Ortega eventually came up spluttering. Blood was drooling down his chin, mingling with the water which had brought him to. When he swore Bill saw that he had lost most of his front teeth and that one of his eyes was swollen shut.

"You're a helluva lookin' specimen!" Bill jeered. "I wish to heck I had the chance to put a few more of the hard cases round this burg in the same category! You're goin' to jail—git movin' pronto!"

Ortega was inclined to argue, but a second glance at Bill's cold eyes sent him shuffling along ahead of Bill toward the one place he had never thought to find himself. "By the time you get out," Bill told him, "you'll know better'n to make a pass at another peace officer."

"Peace—hell!" Ortega swore. "Gimme a cyclone any damn time!"

With Ortega safely deposited in the jail, Dorne strode into his office, sat down in the chair behind his desk with a heavy sigh, and pulled open the drawer in which excess reward notices had been dumped by his predecessor. Taking these dusty fliers out he pawed through them swiftly till he found what he wanted.

"Cripes," he grunted, studying the picture below the monetary notice, "that's Tumble, all right. But he sure has changed since he busted outa Deer Lodge! An' he'll change more, when I get my hands on him. What I done to Ortega won't be a patch to what I'll do to that double-crosser! I betcha he was workin' for Borst all the time, damn him!"

The jingle of spur chains, together with the clump of run-down bootheels, announced Tranter's arrival. "Did you get them dodgers?"

Tranter grinned. "Printer's still workin' on 'em. That promise of a little graft on payday sure worked wonders with that fella! He's promised to plaster 'em clear 'crosst the county by mornin'. I dunno how—but he says he'll do it if he has tuh tack 'em up hisself. I got the fresh nags. They're draped tuh the hitch pole outside. Got any more l'l orders yuh wanta git off'n yore chest?"

"Yeah," Bill growled, still studying the picture of Tumbleweed, alias Ten Spot Trull. "Go out an' comb this town for some respectable hellions that're agreeable to posse duty on double pay. Pick a stem-winder to boss 'em, swear 'em in an' send 'em out to get those Wineglass cattle. Then come back here an' I'll have more chores for you.

Tranter clumped out, muttering under his breath.

Bill turned his attention to the small lines of print under Tumbleweed's description. He found that Trull had been convicted of an unpremeditated murderous assault upon his wife when he found she'd been philandering with some neighboring rancher. It had all happened over in Texas quite a few years ago.

Something clicked in his mind as he digested this information. "Marcia told me once," he muttered, "that she and her stepfather came from Texas. I'd dang near forgotten Ol' Globe wasn't her real father. Now I wonder ..."

When Tranter returned, Dorne said, "Buck, I got a hunch. Sounds far-fetched as hell, I admit. But I always act on my hunches. This 'un might be like the one I had on Tumbleweed, but I got a notion it ain't."

"What's the hunch?" Tranter asked resignedly. "Somethin' about the location of some more chores fer me?"

"Listen," Bill said. "Listen—Globe came from Texas. Tumbleweed came from Texas. Tumbleweed murdered his wife in a blind rage because he caught her philanderin' with another man. Tumble's wife had a kid girl who vanished about the time Tumble went to the pen. This notice don't say nothin' about the gent Tumble's wife was messin' with, so we can take it for granted that Tumble didn't get a chance to even the score with him."

"So what?"

"Get this," Bill grunted earnestly. "Globe ain't Marcia's real father; he's her stepfather. Buck, I'm bettin' heavy that Globe is the fella that Tumbleweed's wife was sweet on!"

Tranter's eyes bulged as the significance of this sank home. "Cripes!" he muttered. And, "Prancin' prairie chickens!"

"Exactly!" Dorne snapped, surging toward the door. "We gotta warn Globe quick—if it ain't too late already!"

TWENTY-TWO
HELL ALL AROUND

AT THE RANCH headquarters of the Wineglass outfit, lights were burning in both the main house and the bunkhouse. The man who stood in the deep shadows of an alder clump on the low ridge above the buildings could see this clearly. That meant, he decided, that Globe was here, and a faint malignant grin twitched the corners of his mouth. "It's been a long time," he muttered hoarsely, "but by Gawd, we'll clean the slate to-night! That pussy-footin' Lothario's forgotten Teresa's gamblin' husband long ago, I shouldn't wonder. But his memory's due to get a jog when he sees me come walkin' in!" And he glanced downward in the dim light at the black funereal garb of the professional gambler in which he had togged himself for this occasion.

With ugly knife-scarred face alert, muscles taut as coiled spring-steel, the unseen watcher moved stealthily forward, flitting from one patch of shadow to another. The moon was often obscured by scudding clouds, but the man stalking the Wineglass was taking no chances. Too long had he waited for this moment to risk spoiling all by a premature discovery. The man who had waited sixteen years could afford a few extra minutes now, more or less, and was entirely willing to afford them should they make his vengeance the more certain.

Unaware of the menace stalking constantly closer, creeping forward foot by cautious foot, Mayor Frank Globe sat in his ranch house office going over accounts with his manager. "Funny," he said for the tenth time. "where Polsky is."

The manager looked up with a frown. "I can't think what's keeping him," he answered. "He went out on his customary round of inspection this afternoon. He ought to have been back hours ago. Yuh know, Frank, somehow I don't cotton to that jasper. There's too much of the fox about him with his little pointed ears an' his sly, black-button eyes. Frankly, I got a hunch that fella's crooked."

Globe looked at him shrewdly. "I've never seen him, but he came well recommended. He had letters from two big ranchers I used to know in Texas. Both these fellows described him as a hard worker an' a man who knew cows."

"That may be—but it don't prove he ain't a crook. *He* was the one that hired Harniss an' Krayson. An' they sure turned out crookeder than corkscrews."

"What's on your mind?" Globe asked bluntly.

"This. I got a hunch he's in with these rustlers hand-in-glove."

"You think he's on Borst's payroll?"

"If Borst is backin' the rustlers, yes."

"Well—" Globe said, and stopped, his face going the color of chalk as he lurched mechanically to his feet.

The manager growled, "What the hell?" and turned to follow the direction of Globe's bulging eyes.

* * *

TRANTER AND BILL DORNE reached the door simultaneously, squeezed through and bulged out onto the plank sidewalk and thence into the dust of Spavined Nag's main street. Simultaneously, both men's right hands went to the reins while their lefts grasped the horns of their saddles and their left legs started from the ground for the stirrups. In this position they abruptly froze to the hammering reverberations of pounding hoofs, heard even above the raucous sounds of revelry dinning from the honkytonks which, at this hour, were in full swing.

Across Buck Tranter's tense back Dorne said, "Somebody comin' hellity-larrup!"

"Gonna wait?"

"Yeah, we better. No tellin' what's up," Dorne answered and, releasing his grip on the horn, lowered his left foot and straightened, keeping in the shadow of his horse. His hand had dropped automatically to his gun and his cold eyes were hard and alert.

"Shore must be important," Tranter growled. "Look at 'im swing that quirt!"

Dorne, as he watched the oncoming rider, felt a vague prickling along his scalp. It was a feeling his system had reserved for times of danger and unusual stress. It told him this man would be the bearer of disquieting news at best.

As the buckaroo drew ever nearer, Dorne could see that he was stretched low above his horse's neck, where he could and was with quirt and spur exacting the best his wiry mustang could give. The fellow's hat, by the wind of his passage, was plastered back against his head; only its chin strap held it on at that breakneck pace. The horse's nostrils were wide and blowing, and of a sudden there was a perceptible falter in its stride.

"That's a—Hell!" Dorne swore, stepping into view of the coming horseman, "that's one of the boys from the ranch! Now what? Ain't there no dang end to the trouble that jumps a sheriff's way?"

"Cripes, no!" Tranter muttered. "Sheriffs an' their depities is jest nacherly targets fer trouble an' ringtailed rannyhan's pistols!" And he snorted, adding: "It's a livin' wonder to me we ain't been blowed plumb off'n the map a'ready!"

"Before you got so ancient a prune looked young beside yuh," Dorne growled, "I bet yore Maw called yuh Sunshine!"

"You know it! I was the sunniest jasper—"

The rest of Tranter's brag was lost in the crash of the oncoming horse. The rider shot forward over its head and lit on braking bootheels; came to a sudden slithering stop before the officers. Dust, ballooning up from around the threshing horse, almost obscured them. Through it, the rider barked:

"Listen Bill! There's sheep all over our range! Thousands of the blattin' stinkers! Range boss said tuh git the word to yuh quick if I had tuh bust a gut tuh do it!"

"Sheep!" Tranter snarled. "Sheep in a cowman's country?"

"A whole damn lan'scape filled with 'em!" the puncher croaked. "Bah-h-h! Bah-h-h! Cripes, it's enough tuh makes the ghosts o' cowmen turn plumb over in their graves!"

Up to this point Dorne had said nothing; he did not say very much now, but it was potent: "Borst!" The single word connoted many possibilities. This, that word told Tranter, was Borst's revenge!

He opened his mouth to speak, but Dorne beat him to it. "Who'd you put in charge of that round-up posse? An' have they left?"

"They've left!" Tranter said emphatically. "Half an' hour ago. An' that Bar B Smith from Sunset County's got charge of the posse. I figgered he'd make 'em look harder, bein' some of his own critters was mixed in, too."

Dorne nodded, and the tiny move saved his life so close had the shot whose echoes now beat back and forth between the buildings missed him. So quick were his reflexes that his own gun was out and spitting lead toward the window across the street, where a flash had marked the sniper, almost as the lead whistled past his ear.

"Round up another posse an' hold 'em here! I'm goin' to get that lousy son—but I'll be right back!" Dorne snapped, and went plunging through the hock deep dust toward the Black Bottle Bar, from one of whose front windows the bushwhacker had let loose his murderous slug.

Even as Dorne went crouching forward in a zig-zag run, the fellow fired again. But his nerves were jittery now, evidently, for the shot went wild, and through its dimming echoes Dorne could hear the pound of scuttling hoofs.

He reached the steps of Ortega's joint and cleared

them in one bound that carried him smashing through the batwing doors in time to see Fisk darting through the gasping crowd toward the door of a back room.

As men jumped right and left to get out of danger Dorne drove three swift shots into the door Fisk's outstretched hand was reaching for. Fisk froze with blanching cheeks and shoved shaking hands above his head, one of which still held the smoking pistol with which he'd tried to snuff Bill's life.

"You damn shoot-an'-run killer!" Dorne's voice snapped savagely across the stunned silence. "I'd ought to gut-shoot you as a moral lesson to the rest of yore yeller breed! Drop that gun."

Fisk dropped it without parley. His twitching lips and shaking hands told the terror he was in. He was trying to stammer out some framed-up explanation but the words did not make sense.

Bill crossed the floor in swift strides. He got one hand in the collar of Fisk's shirt and shook him like a terrier. Fisk's eyes seemed popping from his head when Bill desisted and snarled, "Where's the money Fuddabaugh an' Smoky Leupp took outa the Stockman's Bank, you dirty crook?"

"It's—it's—it's still in there," Fisk stuttered, trying to get his breath. "They never took it out—I just transferred it to my own private safe. But I was forced into it," he pleaded. "Borst made me a party to that—"

"Made hell!" Bill swore. "If you had a backbone 'stead of a wishbone, you'd'a' had the guts to tell Borst where to go! *You're goin* to jail—*c'mon!*"

They reached the street without untoward incident; in fact, without any demonstration of any sort on the part of the crowd in Ortega's dive.

There was a brightness to Bill Dorne's eyes that warned them he meant business, and his savage stride said plain as words that he had his war paint on and was ready to take on all comers!

"How'd Harniss' knife come to be in yore vault?" Bill asked, as he shoved Fisk into a cell beside Ortega. "Thought Harniss was workin' with you an Borst?"

"I told you before I ain't got no connection with Borst," Fisk said desperately. "He forced me into this deal. Said he'd have the bank looted anyhow, an' that I might's well help him out an' take a cut. If I wouldn't agree, he was goin' to have them gunmen rob it anyway, an' shoot me so's I couldn't talk!"

"Oh, yeah?" Bill said skeptically. "Well, what about Harniss' knife?"

"That was Borst's idea of a joke. He had Mendota borrow it an' then gave it to me to plant."

"Nice playful fella, that Borst," Bill commented. "But I gotta kinda hunch his playin' days is about wound up. You're goin' to be in here now anywhere from ten days till a month before yore trial comes up. You'll have time to ponder on the error in yore ways. I'll have Gospel Jones lend you a Bible so's you can see what the Lord thinks of yore kind of skunk."

Slamming the door on the now-spluttering Fisk, Bill sprinted for the front of the Sheriff's Office where he found that Tranter had raked up a second posse in record time. Six men, counting the ragged deputy, sat their saddles with Savage repeaters across their knees; six men with stern, determined faces—solid citizens who were tired of the sporting element's lawless rule. Bill sized them up at a single glance, and knew they were men to ride the river with, sturdy warriors who could be relied on.

He outlined the situation relative to the sheep he suspected Borst of bringing into the country, and did so in a few choice words. Then, climbing into the saddle, he said:

"Do yore shootin' first an' yore talkin' afterwards. Let's go!"

* * *

GLOBE'S frantic eyes were fixed upon the open door. Whirling in his chair, the Wineglass manager saw that a man was framed there against the starry night. A man in the black frock coat, rusty string tie and flat-crowned hat of a gambler—a man with blazing killer eyes above a jeering twisted mouth that drawled with wicked softness:

"Fella—keep yore seat. My business is with that yaller-striped polecat, Globe."

Globe's face was ghastly. His lips were working, but no words came forth.

Tumbleweed laughed across the tightened silence. "Been quite a spell since we seen each other" across a room, eh Frank?"

Globe whispered, "Trull! My Gawd—*Trull!*"

"Guess you been figurin' I was goin' to stay in that damn jail for life, eh, Frank? Guess you didn't hear I'd busted out. Well, I did an' here I am. Been a long wait, Frank, but this is sure worth it," and he laughed again, a chilling, mirthless cluck of sound that sent a shiver over Globe and caused him to take a few uncertain, backward steps.

"No, Frank," Tumbleweed went on in that same soft wicked drawl, "I ain't in the pen now, an' I ain't dead, though that last is what you're goin' to be right sudden. You've taken a look at yore cards an' we're ready for the draw. Frank," he grinned, "I'm goin' to put you under the daisy roots—down there with the rest of the worms where you belong!"

And even as he finished speaking a jet of flame licked out from his hip.

Globe was reaching for his gun when Tumbleweed's lead struck him, whirled him half around and crashed him sideways where he struggled desperately to maintain his feet. But failed.

He was done and Tumbleweed's pistol had not even cleared leather. Nor did it clear leather now as he backed slowly away from the door into the night from which he came. But his pistol's snout stared wickedly at the Wineglass manager from the open toe of its holster. And the ranch manager made no move for he rightly read the look in Tumbleweed's shallow eyes.

Marcia Globe sat motionless in the chair where the departing Lola had left her. No tears coursed down her cheeks from which all color had fled. And her deep brown eyes were dull with pain and in her lap her hands twisted nervously at a fold in her gingham dress. How long she had been sitting there she did not know. But suddenly a step on the porch roused her, and the slow glance she sent in that direction told her that it was dark and that the stars winked coldly against the distant skyline. The figure of a man was outlined against it too, a darker shadow in the darkness of the open doorway.

She did not know who he was and could not make out his features, but the unmoving, unspeaking presence of a man staring at her as he must be staring made her catch her breath. And a faint tinge of fear came into her as she realized that this house was at the edge of town and that she was alone with this unknown watcher.

Softly, slowly, that he might not observe her movement—or if he did, might not guess its significance—she reached for the matches in the little tray beside the lamp on the nearby table. When she found them, she turned sidewise in her chair and with her left hand raised the lamp's chimney as her right hand struck a match and ignited the wick. Nothing happened as she replaced the chimney and turned the wick to the proper angle. Swiftly, then, she flashed a look toward the door.

The man still stood there—a Mexican in range clothes, and he was smiling with a gleam of teeth.

"'Allo, Keed," he said, and widened his grin for her approval. One arm was extended across the doorway, its hand resting on the opposite side of the frame from which his pantherish body leaned. With the other hand he was caressing a tiny black moustache. "Feelin' lonesome?"

"What do you want here?" Marcia said and got to her feet.

"You, señorita; you," Mendota said with a leer that drove her backward behind the doubtful safety of the table. "I'm theenk thees is w'at you call the beeg night for Pedro Mendota, no? The whole damn town, she seem to be away on vacation, only the sporting crowd here. An' they," he added suggestively as he advanced into the room with a catlike grace of movement, "weel not care what happens weeth you."

* * *

DORNE AND HIS HARD-RIDING POSSEMEN, attracted by the swift flashes of gunfire and the sharp flat reports of rifles, veered southward once they struck Bill's Picketwire spread, and headed for that part of his range adjoining Globe's. A battle was in progress over there and they were anxious to get into it and wind things up in a hurry, so as to leave them free to drive off or exterminate the hated sheep.

"Supposin' it ain't Borst that's back of this sheep business?" one of the posse called.

"It is," Bill growled. "It's got all the earmarks of his kind of deal."

"That's right," put in another man. "There ain't nothin' too raw for Pecos Borst. An' he's been layin' fer you, Bill! He ain't aimin' to lose his Hashknife spread if he can rely on it. An' rubbin' you out or crowdin' a passel of woollies onto yore range may give him a chance to dig in an' get set to grab his ol' place back again."

"Sure," Tranter put in. "With Bill outa the way there wouldn't be no Sheriff's sale of the Hashknife property. He knows that well as we do. There ain't no one else in this country got the guts to face Borst down the way Bill's been doin'."

"Looks like my boys have got them fellas holed up in that pile of rocks over by Big Toe Butte," Bill grunted to Tranter. "D'you suppose Borst's with these sheep? Don't hardly look like he would be."

"Naw," Tranter snorted. "He'll be in town, knowin' you'll be out here fightin' off them dang blattin' ba-ba's he wished on you."

"Gosh!" Bill ejaculated suddenly. "We plumb forgot about Tumbleweed an' Globe. Buck, you take charge of this posse—I'm goin' to the Wineglass, pronto!"

Lather was coming out along the edges of Bill's saddle blanket like shaving soap when he slid off his heaving bronc before the Wineglass ranch house door. That something was wrong he'd known as soon as he'd topped the ridge, for Globe was not in the habit of having lamps lit in every room—not all at the same time, leastways. So now he was out of the saddle and across the porch before his winded horse had slithered to a stiff legged stop. The next instant he was hammering on the door.

"Hetton!" he called to the manager. "Open up! It's me, Bill Dorne!" And—"Where's Globe?" he asked when Hetton, pale of countenance, stood in the abruptly opened door. "Anything wrong?" he added mechanically, although he knew darned well something was off color besides the manager's complexion.

"Globe," Hetton said in a hushed and solemn voice, "is dead, Bill—murdered in cold blood not half an hour ago." Briefly, then, he gave Dorne the story. Dorne took it hard.

"I had a hunch somethin' like this was goin' to happen. I was headin' out here to warn Frank, when one of my punchers came larrupin' into town with news that some damn skunk has driven a flock of woollies onto my best range. If I'd only come on here directly—"

"You'd have been too late then just the same," Hetton said. "I blame myself for not doin' somethin'. Hell, I was sittin' right there when the whole thing happened." He flushed. "I can't understand why I didn't try to stop that son—but if you'd 'a' seen his damn eyes—"

"I've seen 'em before," Bill growled, "an' I'm hopin' to see 'em again right soon! I'll see you later," he muttered, and swung toward his horse.

"Hell, you can't ride that nag any place—not for some while, anyhow," Hetton protested. "Wait a sec. I'll have one of the boys rope you out a fresh one."

While this was being done, the Wineglass manager said, "What was that you was oratin' about sheep?"

"There's sheep on my range, driven there, I don't doubt, by Borst," Bill answered. "An' they're driftin' towards Wineglass territory now. My boys an' a posse I brought from town are out there foggin' up the birds that brung 'em. I figure Borst is prob'ly in town now, fixin' some trap for me or somethin'. What's more, I'm goin' to give him a chance to spring it. I'm headin' for town right now. I got a hunch that most of his crew—what ain't with the sheep—are in town with him. Tumbleweed's likely headed there, too. Probably Borst's figurin' to take the town over again an' get set while I'm tendin' to those sheep."

"Hell," protested Hetton, "you can't fight Borst an' the sportin' element by yourself, man! They'll—"

"Well," Dorne answered grimly, as the Wineglass puncher came up with a fresh mount, "I'm figurin' to."

And while the Wineglass manager was still protesting about the foolhardiness of such a course, Wild Bill Dorne swung one hand to the horn and slapped his left foot into the stirrup. The borrowed bronc was moving at a hard run when Bill settled into the saddle.

TWENTY-THREE
"HUNT UP GOSPEL JONES"

AS MENDOTA ADVANCED upon the table, Marcia had to summon all her will-power to resist the urge to back away. But some inner voice told her if she left the doubtful sanctuary of this insensate bit of wood, all would be swiftly irrevocably lost. She was not sure of what it was she was afraid, but there was a tiger gleam in Mendota's dark little eyes she found distinctly sinister.

Mendota chuckled, catlike, a little purr of sound that roughed up gooseflesh along the girl's spine. But she would not give way to hysteria, she told herself. She would be brave and courageous and face this thing out. She came of pioneering ancestors, hardy stock whose courage in the face of adversity and threatened danger was beyond question—like Caesar's wife, as Tranter would have said. But Tranter was not here now to help her, and Bill—No, she mustn't think of Bill in this hour of need. For Bill had failed her shamefully. Outwardly Bill was all fire and fine-tempered steel, but inwardly he was like the spongy core of a rotten apple; a philanderer, a despicable Lothario who preyed on young and innocent girls, and led astray even wiser ones like Lola. No, Bill was out; she would not see him again. Or if see him she must, it should be a brief and icily courteous meeting wherein her only words must be negative.

It was strange, she told herself, that she could think these things at a time like this, while that Mexican was slowly closing the scant interval between them. It was as though she were detached and aloof from herself, as though this tableau was being enacted by other people and she was observing it from a safe distance. But she wasn't, it was she this swarthy renegade was stalking.

For a moment, as some tipsy reveler's footsteps went past outside, his striking profile was toward her as he listened. Then with a shrug he swung his shoulders toward her and there was a bold intentness in his eyes and a cynical salacious curve to his thin, cruel lips.

She caught her breath as he reached out and grasped the table's edge in one strong brown hand. Fascinated, she watched the swelling of the muscles of his bare arms and the cord-like strain observable in his long fingers. It came to her that he was about to hurl this fragile shelter aside and leave her without protection from this thing he had in mind. She tried to scream, but no sound left the parchedness of her mouth.

* * *

THROUGH THE WIND-WHIPPED NIGHT, Bill Dorne rode low along his mustang's neck with the hard-running animal's mane slapping his face, and his cold hard eyes keenly alert for any sign of ambush. He rode well away from brush and chaparral wherever possible, for he knew how tempting were such shadowy spots to killers of the type employed by Pecos Borst.

His fury against Borst and Ten Spot Trull burned like a white flame in his mind, excluding all other thoughts; excluding even thoughts of Marcia Globe, save as he was vaguely aware of the hurt and loss which must be hers when news should reach her of her father's murder. Her foster-father's murder, that was—for Tumbleweed, alias Ten Spot Trull, was her real father. It was a fact he did not intend allowing her to ever learn. For such knowledge could bring her no happiness. No, the past's secrets were better buried in the past.

His antagonism toward Borst was like a mighty river, an accumulation of minor angers and resentments, commingled with the bitterness of public wrongs and personal prides. Even before election to the shrieval chair, Dorne had not cottoned to the big boss of Spavined Nag; and since election he was determined to rid the town of its incubus. Straight from the shoulder he had made this plain to Borst, and Borst's doings and schemings since that date had been his manner of defiance. But this foisting of sheep on a cowman's paradise had been Borst's crowning insult—Borst's final throw.

Dorne was sure he'd find the man in town, and he was likewise certain that most of Borst's big-guns would be there with him, awaiting Dorne's arrival for the final scene. That Borst would have the cards all stacked was a lead-pipe cinch. But true to his name, Wild Bill Dorne cared not a damn. He would smash Pecos Borst though all hell, hot lead and high water stood in his way.

For these last few miles Bill had been riding with a loose rein, letting his gallant mount pick its own way pretty much. But now, nearing town—indeed, seeing the twinkle of its distant lamps—Dorne crouched low in the saddle and applied both quirt and spur. If the fates decreed that by some foul chance Borst should go free, Bill Dorne would go down fighting after the manner of his kind.

* * *

PEDRO MENDOTA'S lithe brown arms were around Marcia fiercely, and his hot labored breath was against her face. One shoulder of her gingham dress was ripped and fallen to expose the white creamy flesh beneath, and Mendota's lewd and avid gaze was on this intently as they struggled back and forth above the wreck of the broken table. Marcia's silent battle for her virtue and perhaps her very life was no more silent than was Mendota's struggle to overcome her resistance—to "gentle her" he would have said—for when it came to a thing he coveted, Pedro Mendota was a man of few words.

Only the labored panting of their breathing, and the stamp of their shifting feet, made sound in the narrow room. And to them, had they been less intent on their own hopes and fears, the tinpan music and oaths and laughter of Spavined Nag at play would have come faintly through the open door and windows. But they heard nothing, not even the soft clump of spurless boots, until—

"A bear with the women, ain't you?" a rough voice drawled with wicked softness.

Over his shoulder as Mendota tensed Marcia saw the ugly, seamed and jeering leathery countenance of the man leaning indolently in the doorway, even as Mendota himself had leaned not so many minutes before. There was a long and livid knife-scar on that countenance, that running from chin to ear along the left side. And the eyes below the stranger's hatbrim were pale, intent and sinister.

Mendota flung loose of Marcia's form and whirled on squeaking bootheels, handicapped by the lust and blind red rage that gripped him, and by surprise at this interruption to his desires. Yet even so, his spinning leap was like that of some startled cat, and just as fast and sudden.

Marcia, standing paralyzed with fear three feet away, heard the rip of steel on leather as Mendota's racing palm smacked gun-butt; caught his snarled *"You damn' peestol-tipper!"* Then the room was shaken by a rocking, roaring world of jarring sound, and it seemed as though her ear-drums must surely be shattered.

She saw that flame appeared to burst from the region of both men's thighs simultaneously. Yet it was Mendota's wiry form that seemed to suddenly lean as though to meet the spurt of flame that belched from the ugly stranger's bottomless holster. Then the hinges of Mendota's knees were letting go and he was crumpling, sagging forward on the old worn carpet.

And when she looked at the doorway the man with the ugly scar was gone, fading into the black night as silently as he appeared. And then she knew no more until she opened her eyes to find her head pillowed in the lap of the faro-dealer, Lola, and heard Lola's husky voice making soothing sounds.

"I lied, *querida*," Lola was whispering softly. "Oh, God, can you forgive me for such lies? I lied when I said those things to you about myself and Wild Bill Dorne ... I said those things because I knew it was you that Bill was crazy about an' was going to marry. And I wanted him myself—you'll never know how much I want him, need him! I loved him the first time he came into Pecos Borst's Golden Stack Saloon. There has been a terrible hunger in my heart for a man like Bill; I've always dreamed of being loved by such a man and when I saw Bill I wanted him, and I made up my mind I was going to have him. But I can't go through with it, Marcia Globe—I can't! I thought I could, and I've schemed and killed and lied to get Bill Dorne. But he won't have me —it's you he wants, so I'm telling you those things I said were lies."

Marcia was gazing at her with new life in the brightness of her deep brown eyes; new life and hope— incredulous hope.

Somehow they found themselves upon their feet, facing each other, and Lola was backing toward the door. For the first time she saw Mendota's huddled body, and she screamed and thrust one hand across her mouth.

"My Gawd! What's happened here?" she cried, her eyes growing green and narrow like a startled cat's. "Who killed that breed?"

And Marcia described mechanically the things she'd noticed about the ugly stranger, and Lola gasped, "*Tumbleweed!*" and ran for the door.

* * *

IN THE BLACK Bottle Bar Lola found Pecos Borst, and a flame flared up in his smoke-grey eyes when he saw her and a low chuckle boomed in his bull-thick throat. "The prodigal returns to the fold," he sneered, and started toward her.

But she seemed not to notice the rash grin that tightened the bold line of Borst's thick lips. "That Tumbleweed killer of yours has run amuck!" she cried insistently. "Mendota's layin' dead on the Mayor's carpet—"

"Yeah," Borst purred, "and what were you doin' at the Mayor's house?".

"I was—" Lola began, and checked herself, and the creamy whiteness of her unrouged cheeks went a pasty grey as she realized she could not admit to Borst that she'd been angling to get Bill Dorne. And yet, the thought struck her suddenly, she might do worse than tell a part truth which could be twisted to her advantage. "I was over there laying pipe to trap Bill Dorne—"

But Borst cut her off with a savage laugh and caught her by the shoulders in his big rough hands. "You damn little liar!" he snarled, his florid face going livid as he thought that here again Bill Dorne had beaten him, stealing from him this girl's love without even visible effort. "You've been layin' pipe to add Bill Dorne to yore conquests, you little slut!"

She tried to raise her arms to slide them around Borst's neck but he held her paralyzed by his rough grip, and she saw the passion and resentment in him mounting like a wall of water. Abruptly he released her with an oath, a shove from one ham-like hand sending her crashing back against the bar, and she saw the grins on the faces of his watching men. Something seemed to snap within her and her right hand sought the neckline of her low-cut gown.

But it never touched the tiny pistol nestled between her breasts. Borst knew of the gun she kept there and he guessed what she was about to do. Flame darted from his hip and smashed her back against the bar; again and again he fired as though to ease his mighty spleen, and when his gun was empty, she lay in a silent, huddled heap across the rail.

* * *

BILL DORNE SLID from his lathered bronc before the hitch rail fronting Ortega's resort with the crash of gunfire in his ears. He did not pause but, yanking his gun, ducked under the tie-pole and took the dive's board steps three at a time and burst his sudden way through the swinging doors.

He saw the lifeless body of Lola lying there across the brass footrail of the bar. And he saw Borst with the smoking pistol still in hand, and the, wooden-faced gunslammers that ringed him, clawed hands poised above their holsters. Phoenix John, Dode Harniss, Krayson, Gleed. And he saw Borst's narrowed eyes whip toward him and slowly widen, proving Borst had not been expecting him so soon.

"Woman-killin' added to yore line now, eh?" Dorne said bitterly. "You damned low-down rotter, Borst—you'd oughta be boiled in lard. Yes, an' by cripes, I'd admire the job of stirrin' you round in the kettle!"

"Always the blusterin' big bad bull in the china-shop, ain't you, Dorne?" Borst sneered, transferring his gun to the left hand, thereby telling the watching sheriff that it was empty. "Hell, I don't need to use a gun on yore kind of four-flusher," Borst added, with a sneer, and threw the weapon across the room—drawing another from beneath his coat as, momentarily, Dorne's eyes instinctively followed the thrown gun's parabolas.

But Dorne saw Borst's second movement out of the corners of his eyes; saw too the reaching hands of Borst's gunslammers darting thighward, and his own pistol came up in a burst of flame as the room appeared to sway and buckle with the monstrous detonations. Then, through the powder smoke, he saw Borst doubling up, clutching wildly at his middle, lurching backward. And he saw Dode Harniss fall slantways across a poker table, and Gleed scuttling for a window. Lead was tugging at Dorne's neckerchief, at his vest; he felt the jar of impact as a slug tore the heel from his right boot. But still he crouched there, wreathed in a fog of gun smoke, his forty-five jetting streaks of flame as he drove hot slugs across the ten-foot interval.

And then suddenly it was over, and the crash of guns but dimming echoes. Krayson was backed against a wall with his hands stretched high and empty above his head, his bronzed features gone a pasty, mottled white. Harniss was an outstretched motionless entity near the far end of the bar, and across Lola's motionless legs Pecos Borst lay sprawled, and something about his posture told Bill Dorne that the boss of Spavined Nag was boss no more— would never rise again.

Half an hour later, having locked Krayson in a cell alongside Ortega and Banker Fisk to await a trial that seemed assured of being marked by the stamp of Justice, Bill Dorne went into the Sheriff's Office and slumped heavily in his chair. He was sick of fighting, weary of the sight of blood and crooks and violence. He wanted peace and Marcia Globe and—but he had to wait for the reports of his two posses. He got them, too, several hours later, when close to dawn one of the men who had gone with Bar B Smith to recover the stolen cattle, rode in to report that his own and Smith's and Globe's had been located and were being driven to their respective ranges by the posse.

Ten minutes later, Tranter rode in and dismounted stiffly before the hitch rail. He stamped grumbling into the office and growled at Bill:

"Some night! But by cripes, we drove them lousy woolies to hell-an'-gone back onto Borst's spread an' into his fenced north section. Shot up four-five of the herders that was with 'em. An' say! Yuh know that bouncer, Gleed, what used tuh work fer Borst? Well, I come acrosst him ridin' his bronc like mad. Looked like he was headin' fer the Mex border. I hailed 'im but he kept goin' like Lucifer was headin' him with a pitchfork! I reckon he's goin' yet—if his nag ain't give plumb out!"

Bill told him tersely of the fight in town.

"Well, I'm shore pow'ful sorry I wa'n't around tuh lend a hand," Tranter said dolefully. "I guess this about cleans up this hell-roarin' range. Reckon bad men'll beat a premium after the county pays off fer the ones that's been snuffed in the las' few hours. Hey!" he added hastily as Bill got up and started for the door. "Where'n heck are you goin' *now*?"

"I'm goin'," Bill said grimly, "to hunt up Gospel Jones before any more trouble pokes its head over the horizon to delay again my already postponed noopshals. I'm goin' to get married—that's where I'm goin'! Marcia's waited long enough, an' she's goin' to need a man's sympathy when she learns that her ol' man was murdered out to the ranch last night. I'm figgerin' on gettin' hitched up soon's I can locate that psalm-singin' sky-pilot. *Got any objections?*"

"Hell, no!" Tranter said, grinning. "Them's the best words I've heard yuh say since I come tuh Spavined Nag!"

IF YOU LIKED THIS, YOU MAY ENJOY: THE COMPLETE DAVE HUNTER AND ASH MAWSON SERIES

BY GORDON D. SHIRREFFS

Take a journey with Dave Hunter and Ash Mawson in this four-book western collection by Gordon D. Shirreffs. If the terrain doesn't kill them, the bullets certainly would...

In *Hell's Forty Acres*, Bounty Hunter Dave "Treasure" Hunter enters the Colorado River area searching for a lost silver mine, but finds a woman with a mysterious past, hostile Paiutes, and betrayal. It was rich with the promise of silver—and sudden death. In *Maximilian's Gold*, Hunter teams up with his buddy Ash Mawson to find the Mexican Emperor Maximilian's gold, stashed somewhere on the treacherous Chihuahua Trail. Gold can make a man as rich as a king. If it doesn't kill him first.

In *The Walking Sands*, South of the Arizona border is the Gran Desierto, a vast area of shifting sand hills. It is there that a church was buried beneath the sands, never to be found again. Hunter believes the Jesuits' treasure is there for the taking—but so do some other very dangerous people. And in *The Devil's Dance Floor*, Hunter returns, this time doing fancy footwork for a religious figurine. His search for the Virgin Mary figurine means crossing the Sonora Desert—the Devil's Dance.

The Complete Dave Hunter/Ash Mawson Series includes: *Hell's Forty Acres, Maximilian's Gold, The Walking Sands,* and *The Devil's Dance Floor*.

AVAILABLE NOW

ABOUT THE AUTHOR

Nelson C. Nye (1907–1997) was an American author, editor, and reviewer of Western fiction, and wrote non-fiction books on quarter horses. He also wrote fiction using the pseudonyms Clem Colt and Drake C. Denver. Nye wrote over 125 books, won two Spur Awards: one for best Western reviewer and critic, and one for his novel *Long Run*, and in 1968 won the Saddleman Award for ""Outstanding Contributions to the American West."

Nelson Nye was born in Chicago, Illinois. Before becoming a ranch hand in 1935, he wrote publicity releases and book reviews for the Cincinnati Times-Star and the Buffalo Evening News. He published his first novel in 1936 and continued writing for 60 years. He served with the U.S. Army field artillery during World War II. He worked as the horse editor for Texas Livestock Journal from 1949–1952.

In 1953 Nye co-founded the Western Writers of America and served as its first president during 1953–1954. He was also the first editor of *ROUNDUP*, the WWA periodical that is still published today.